WARRIORS OF LIGHT

WARRIORS OF LIGHT

Gloria Johnson

"The sons of god saw the daughters of men that they were fair and they took them wives of all which they choose."

Genesis six chapter second verse

Please note: This is a work of fiction and no religious statements are intended as facts.

Order this book online at www.trafford.com
or email orders@trafford.com

Most Trafford titles are also available at major online book retailers.

Printed in the United States of America.

ISBN: 978-1-4269-9539-2 (sc)
ISBN: 978-1-4269-9540-8 (e)

Trafford rev. 10/25/2011

www.trafford.com

North America & international
toll-free: 1 888 232 4444 (USA & Canada)
phone: 250 383 6864 • fax: 812 355 4082

DEDICATION

This book is dedicated to the two people who have had the most profound impact on the direction and growth in and on my life.

To Arbra my childhood friend, who taught me how to face my fears by laughing at the darkness! This lesson has helped me through out my life; in more ways and situations than I can express.

To the man I will refer to as James (for personal reasons I will not use his real name) who taught me the enchantment and beauty of love, as well as, love's loss and pain. All of which showed me aspects of myself that, up until that point, I did not know existed . . . aspects that have contributed greatly to the growth and development of the woman I am!

I thank you both and wish each of you health, happiness and love.

PROLOGUE

Justin was in full battle mode, he was fighting with a mid-level demon. A demon that was old enough to know who he was, but young enough not to listen to the voice of reason especially when his judgment was clouded with anger. That voice of reason, would have informed the demon of some vital knowledge. Knowledge that may have caused the demon to make different choices and decision, knowledge that was all but lost to him now.

Justin fed the demon's anger, Justin knew that the calmer he was the angrier the demon would get and Justin was extremely calm. This was not the reaction that most humans exhibited, when faced with a demon. Justin looked the demon straight in the eyes, this was another clue that the demon should have picked up on. Demons have a hypnotic stare which causes most humans to react like a baby bird looking into the eyes of a snake. Yet nothing in Justin's movements or stance gave any indication that the demon's hypnotic stare was working on him. All of these things and more, the demons should have noticed, would have noticed, if intense anger was not clouding his judgment.

Justin was monitoring the demon's frustration levels through the amount of wild gestures the demon was employing, gesture which were in stark contrast to Justin's economy of movements. Justin also noticed an increase of flames in the demon's eyes, just before he launched another attack (younger demons, to a greater degree and mid-level demons to a lesser degree, usually gave away there intentions with some gesture or habit which indicated the change from thought to action). Only an older demon hid any indication of his intentions, like any good poker player.

Of even more importance, Justin was monitoring the demon's energy levels. Justin knew that the demon's attacks would correspond directly with his energy reserve. At a forty percent energy capacity, younger to mid-level demons moved into desperation mode. This meant that the demon would make one strategic attack, using twenty percent of his remaining energy reserve.

If the strategic attack did not work, the demon would use his remaining twenty percent of energy to cut his losses and to get away from the battle as soon as possible. Justin judged that his demon was at about fifty percent energy capacity. This meant that the demon would continue fighting in general, while he formulated his strategic attack. Ten minutes later, Justin noticed the flames leap in the demon's eyes just at the point when his energy reserve dropped to forty percent.

The demon faked to the left then whirled around to attack from the right. The demon used an attack strategy that worked extremely well, ninety-five percent of the time on humans. The attack consisted of an emotional attack first; the demon sent out waves of thoughts of overwhelming fear and loss to the human. Then the demon sent the sincere belief that if the human would stop defending himself and begged for mercy, the demon would spare him. The final thought the demon sent out was that the human's only chance to survive was to following the action he had outlined.

Most humans receiving the above message would be momentarily unsure which would cause them to pause or hesitate and in that moment of uncertainty the demon would strike, following up the emotional blow with a physical one. The problem for this particular demon was that Justin was not human! As the demon sent out the negative emotional thought attack, Justin's shields flashed as they deflected the negative thoughts back to the demon.

It was only then that the demon, was taken momentarily off guard, as he noticed Justin's shields (for the first time) right before the mental attack was sent back to him. As the demon tried to adjust to this unexpected turn of events and before he could, the situation had created an opening and Justin struck swift and clean.

Justin snatched out the demon's vocal cords first, for two reasons: one, the sound of demon screams hurt his ears and two, to prevent the demon from calling for reinforcements. The next blow went right between the demon's eyes. This blow stunned the demon and disoriented his memory. This prevented the demon from remembering that he did not need vocal cords to call for help, he could do it with his thoughts, assuming that he could still think. The two blows were so rapid and each blow flowed so smoothly into the next one, they almost looked like one action.

Next Justin pulled out his sword and cut the demon's head off. Justin watched as lines began to appear on the demon's body. The demon's own energy was acting like a laser knife following the lines of the pattern which just appeared on the demon's body. The demon's body began slowly to break apart into pieces. Pieces that would be transported back to hell where hungry shades, shades that were not permitted to hunt for food, would fight over the much needed food the demon's body would provide. They would grab the pieces from the sky before they hit the ground and eat them. Justin knew that the demon, a few feet away from him, would feel each and every bite as well as the long slow digestive period inside the shades that consumed him . . . for a very long time to come.

Justin also knew that this extremely slow digestion period, was a cycle of punishment that the demon would be forced to endure for decades, until every last piece of him was eliminated from the shades that consumed him. After his body broke up into pieces, the demon would re-assemble as a shade and be permitted to forge on the streets of hell, waiting for the next demon to fail to capture his prey.

Until then the ex-demon/new shades hunger would eat at him growing stronger each and every day. The only hope of ease would come when another demon failed and their flesh provided nourishment for any starving shades strong enough and lucky enough to get a piece and eat it before another demon tried to take it away. After all, one never knew when or where food would fall to from the sky.

Failure was not an option in hell and the punishment for failure was severe. Once a shade was given hunting rights and demon status again, few demons ever failed twice. Justin watched as the energy flowed from the demon and pieces of him began to break away from him body as pain radiated through out the demon's body.

Justin heard a faint voice that said,"What are you?" Justin dropped his illusion and showed his true self to the demon, knowing that a few seconds after the demon saw him he would not believe or remember what he saw. The demon screamed,"this is not fair!" Justin replied,"few things in hell are." The demon's last thoughts, as his body completed the separation process and the broken pieces began to rain down in to different sections of hell was "this is impossible . . . you do not exist!" The demon let out one final frustrated scream, which quickly turned to a scream of pain as the last pieces of his flesh fell off his body and he felt the first bite, as a dammed shade began to consume his flesh!

Chapter One

It seemed that Katelyn had always been alone. At age twenty-seven, Katelyn was a beautiful woman who hardly ever smiled. On rare occasions she could remember that her world had once had a different feel. She was little; maybe three or four and she could feel the love of her parents wash over her. There were times when her mother seemed to glow with warmth and sweetness. Katelyn's father reminded her of the earth, full of strength and comfort. This was before the accident that had killed them both when they went away for, a long deserved treat, a romantic weekend alone.

Katelyn had always held on to those few precious memories. During the times (when she was growing up alone with in one foster placement after another one) that she felt the most despondent and miserable. Katelyn would retreat into them and remember that she had been really and truly loved once; her parents had not chosen to leave her.

Some how when she needed them the most, she could retreat and bring up one of those treasured memories and concentrate on every aspect of it until it seemed as if she had stepped back in time, into the past and she could feel, actually feel their love surround and flow through her. That love warmed her very soul and gave her the strength to keep going, especially when she could find no warmth, love or peace in any other area of her life.

Katelyn had lived in several foster placements after her parents died in the accident. The last people that she lived with did not treat her badly but they simply did not love her. Katelyn was a means of receiving an additional income in hard times. They were not intentionally cruel to her, they simply possessed a limited ability to love and all of the love they did have, went to there own child. If she was considered at all, she was simply as after thought. After a while Katelyn did not mind being alone and on some very deep instinctual level, (one that Katelyn could not name or truly understand) she tried not to judge them too harshly or even be upset. Simply to accept the little that they offered her, because this was all that they had the ability to give. Once Katelyn accepted and worked from this instinctual information, she began to look at her foster parents differently. She told her self that, all things considered, it could have been worse.

When Katelyn graduated from high school, she took advantage of the grants that her foster-child status afforded her and applied for college at an out of state schools. Katelyn had always preferred the elegant simplicity of math and computers. Two plus two always equaled four, unless a glitch was in the system on some level where two plus two equaled five. Then you simply backtracked until you found the five and changed it into a four; then the system ran smoothly again. That is, until you ran into another glitch. Then you simply did the same thing all over again until the program ran with smooth perfection.

Katelyn loved the logic of computers because they had no hidden agenda. In fact, she loved everything about them. Katelyn had a rare discernment about how they worked and a genuine understanding into there unique language. Katelyn even had a perceptive knowledge of the strengths and limitations of computers, which afforded her the unique ability to develop programs that others did not believe the computer was capable of achieving. Katelyn graduated at the top of her class, job offers poured in and she was able to pick her choice from them.

Katelyn's first job was that of a program manager, what she lacked in experience she made up for in knowledge and pure talent. The field where Katelyn was truly limited in was in the area of relationships. Katelyn had many opportunities for establishing relationships; the problem was that after a few dates she seemed to "know" exactly what they wanted from her.

Katelyn had learned through harsh repercussions growing up, that she needed to listen to her instincts and be truthful with herself. Katelyn was by nature a truthful person, but on a few occasions, she broke her own rule. The backlash from this action was, at its mildest, extremely painful and at its worse devastating. She had only broke this rule on a few occasions (occasions when she was trying to meet the needs of others, needs that overwhelmed her good sense) and each time, she was like a drunk on the morning after, swearing that she would never touch another drop of alcohol again. Now she got it, under no circumstances could she be anything other than who she was.

Initially, when she began college, all of her dates wanted sex and help with their computer programs. After several dating experiences, some instinct seemed to "know" after the first conversation, what they really wanted from her. This instinct seemed to know every level of usage or need that they intended her to forfill for them. Soon, especially when her instincts seemed to be accurate in every situation, she hardly dated at all.

When she met the representative from her first job, she knew he wanted to recruit her because it would have been a real plus for him (Katelyn graduated as the valedictorian of a truly prestige's university). Katelyn also knew that he was attracted to her and since she was equally attracted to him she decided that "just this once" she would not listen to her instincts, she thought "why not take the job and see where it goes." Shortly after she took the job, her instincts again proved to be correct in that she was simply a means to an end for him, in more ways than one. Steve was only interested in furthering his career and receiving casual sex.

Soon, Steve was promoted and informed her that he was not looking for a long term commitment. This hurt, mainly because Katelyn knew that what he said was not true. Steve was looking for a wife but one that could advance his career. Currently, Katelyn had little more to offer him in this area.

Katelyn had served her purpose by being the catalysis for his promotion. This was one of the few times in the past, when she tried to quiet her personal truth and tried not to see the man she was dating, this action turned out to have devastating results. She almost did not make it through the level of pain that his actions caused her. What helped her to accept or come to terms with the situation was the fact that she knew with clarity that she did not love him and that knowledge alone helped her work herself out of this pain of rejection. Then her fear would hit her with this thought . . . "what would have happened to me if I had loved him."

The whole experience hurt because she had lied to her self, as Katelyn examined the pain she realized that Steve had never made any promises and it was her hopes which were hurt, not her heart. Katelyn wanted to belong to someone and some where but after thinking about the situation long and hard, she understood that with out love there relationship would only have been an illusion; one which would have caused her more pain in the end.

Katelyn thought, "it must be something seriously wrong with me because the one thing I want more than anything in life was to love and be loved by a good man or the right man." However, this was the one thing that she no longer dared to look for because if she was wrong and loved a man who could not or chose not to love her in return (she did a quiet shutter at the thought) . . . this would equal a level of devastation that she knew (with a certainty that she could not explain) could break something inside of her so deep, that she might not ever be able to fix it. So Katelyn though it was simply best that she genuinely tried to let this need go. She thought, I do not need to risk something (my soul), looking for a relationship that may ask more of me than I can afford to loose.

Usually Katelyn never lied to her self; so she stopped feeling sorry for her self and re-assessed her overall situation. She was with a good company and she liked her job and she was earning a good salary and gaining the experience she needed. Therefore, Katelyn decided to stay with the company until she had a little more experience to add to her training and ability, Katelyn stayed for three more years.

Four years had passed since the day that Katelyn had swore off men. Yet here she was again, trying to talk her self into believing that men were an unnecessary complication in her busy life. To reinforce this idea she thought, look at the hurt I could have avoided if I had simply, listen to my instincts four years ago. The problem with this concept was that the one thing that Katelyn wanted more than anything was to have the right man in her life. However, Katelyn thought, "I must have some seriously messed up karma because everyone I have tried to love and or extend friendship too or simply tried to help turned out to either harbor feelings dislike or feelings of hatred toward me." They either tried to use her or strived to manipulate her in some way. The one and only exception to this rule was her parents. Strangely, her memory of them had not dimmed through the years and when she needed them she could still feel them.

Sometimes at night when her mind was floating just before sleep this need, to love and be loved, would rise up from the hidden level of her soul so strong that the next morning she would wake up with a feeling of sadness so profoundly deep that it actually felt like a physical ache. An ache she had to fight to push back down, deep inside of her . . . she was actually wrestling back control of her life from her emotions.

It was in mornings like that that she felt a low hum of sadness which ate at her through out the rest of the day. This sadness touched her in a thousand different ways for the rest of the day. When Katelyn reflected on this situation she truly began to wonder if she had a death wish . . .She asked herself how can I want and need a thing so badly, a thing that could suck the very life out of me and leave me changed forever? It was at times like this that she reached for the slim book that she kept in her night stand.

The book was a book of poetry, written by an obscure writer and published well over a hundred years ago. She stumbled upon it one day when she was visiting an antique book store. She opened the book and began to read the first poem. The poem was so powerful and the words were so beautiful that she actually thought she heard music in her mind as she read. Music, which she knew on some unexplained level, was coming from the poem its self.

Katelyn brought the book for that poem alone but once she began to read the other poems in the book she fell in love with them as well. The first poem touched her deeply, because it seemed that it was speaking to her and her alone. The words summed up everything she wanted from a man and a relationship. It was also everything that she knew was impossible to obtain. The poem acted both as a balm to her lonely soul, by letting her know that at least someone had once felt the way she does. Then, it provided a clear dose of reality because she could not make herself believe that such a man existed. Katelyn opened the book and began to read the first poem:

If you choose to love me

Do not love me for a day
For this kind of love will never stay
Do not love me for what you see
For age will steal your love from me
Do not love me out of need
For this type of love always turns to some level of greed
Do not love me because I love you
This type of love is never true
Do not love me because you owe me such
This type of love always turns to hatred, anger and distrust
Love me because the love in you, request that you do
An offer of love freely chosen, like my gift to you
Love me because I spark a fire in your soul
Because without me your life would be cold
Love me with all you have to give
Free in the knowledge that no matter what
You would love me still
Love me until time slips away
With your last breath, on your last day
For this is love, real and true
The type of love I offer you.

Again the strange music played in her head as she read; this had happen so often now that she had long ago started to think of it as normal. Again she felt as if her soul had been wrapped in a soothing balm that quieted the ache inside. Now as she began to relax (since the pain had stopped) her mind filled with clarity and the comfort of knowing that no such man existed for her. Hell!, she thought, no such man existed period, as she yet again convinced herself to strive to let go of the dream and accept reality.

Katelyn had just landed a new job, the money was very good and she had seen nothing in the way of male co-workers or men in general that captured her interest in the least. Until today, at lunch when she had seen a guy in the café . . .now he had her interest. She seemed to be drawn to him and she liked everything she saw. What was even scarier was that her instincts liked him too. Katelyn thought, he will probably open his mouth and say something stupid and then that will let me know that he is like all the rest. She then thought, "it's a good thing that I will probably never see him again because she was having a strong physical reaction to him, all of her hormones stood up and paid attention to him in an "I'd like to get to know more about you way."

Yesterday Justin had started feeling that the levels of unrest, which he had been pushing down for some time now, seemed to be getting stronger each day. Then his frustration would begin to rise. Justin would shift his thoughts to other topics and in the beginning, when he first began to feel the pull, this shift would ease or quiet the pull.

Now it was getting harder to shift his mind and ever harder to push the emotions and feelings down. The need was not only growing but it seemed to take on a life of its own. He knew it had something to do with the rules of fate and the ascension. He also knew that the answers would somehow change his world, the problem was that he did not know if the change would be positive or negative.

Justin thought again about the rules of fate and considered putting off this discussion with his father once again. It seems that the pull not only increased when he tried to ignored it but it also increased with age, each year he felt the pull getting stronger and stronger. It now felt like something was deeply missing in side him or like a need for something building inside of his soul for a nameless something that he did not understand.

This feeling had now started to nag him incessantly, so much so, that he knew he had no choice. Justin needed some answers, He felt with clear certainty that it was time to speak with his father. Justin did not want to because he knew, even thought he did not know how he knew; that sometimes things would get worse, much worse before they got better. Yet, Justin knew he could not put the discussion off no longer.

Justin stood still and cleared his mind and then he reached for his father's mind and requested time to meet with him today. As the familiar feel of the mist glowing around his human body descended, dissolving and changing the DNA material of his human body, Justin became one with the mist and began to travel at the speed of light, to the alternate realm where his father, who was alerted to both his inquiry and his need to speak with him, awaited.

Chapter Two

Gabriel watched as his son traveled to him. He knew what his son wanted to know and why he needed to speak with him. Gabriel also knew how long his son had fought against the pull building up in his soul. Gabriel quietly agreed with his son's assessment that the information that Justin needed was going to begin the catalysis of a sincere and genuine change in his life.

Time seemed to stand still as Gabriel watched his son ascend and Justin's body form into that of an angel. Gabriel's mind flashed back, remembering his meeting with the creator and a select handful of angels many, many years ago. Gabriel remembered that no one knew the reason for the meeting and that alone was very unusually, since regular communication between the creator and his angels took placing in a burst of angelic knowledge which (with one thought) communicated the past, present and future information regarding any issue, problem or concern. Also communicated was all the details and subtle information, that was known to the individual, relating the situation.

Gabriel though it was odd, the way his presence was requested at that time and odder still, how he received the communication about the meeting. It was different from the regular way he received communication. This method of speaking with each individual angel was so out side of the norm that Gabriel could hardly remember when it had last happened or when he was last required to attend a meeting in which, he was completely uninformed regarding the content.

As Gabriel entered the great hall, doors materialized and shut and then a communication seal was placed on the room and on the minds and hearts of all the angels present. Only then did the Creator speak. The creator talked about the conception of man and the creation of evil. The creator explaining how evil was a necessary part of man's growth and how free-will allowed man to choose to love where he wills.

The creator went on to state that, since he had given man the power of choice there had to be something other than him for man to choose from. The creator further stated that evil was necessary for man to grow, evolve and ascend to the next step on the evolutionary path that he had outlined for man.

The Creator spoke about how he had allowed negativity to use lies, half truths and deception to tempt the human race toward a life of darkness. Then the creator stated that he was now creating a race of beings to be the trail-blazers for man. To show man through their action and interactions with man, an example of his true best self.

To insure the purity of there souls, these trail-blazers would be part angel. Then to insure there understanding and love of the human race, they will also be part human. The creator stated that the father's of this new race were the angels seated in this room. This race of beings will be known, at first, to only the angels in this room.

The humans will see them as extraordinary human beings, the stuff of myth and legends. Other angels will see them as clear examples of what human being can aspire too. This race will be known as "light warriors." They will be undistinguishable from any other angel when they come into our realm and look completely human when they are on the earth.

They will be born with several unique talents and abilities, one of which will be a shield around there souls which will hide their gifts, talents and abilities from angels, demons and humans. These warriors of light will walk among each race unknown and unseen until they need or choose to reveal themselves.

They will fight toe to toe with the demons for each human soul. This will be their primary responsibility. Because my angels have many other additional responsibilities, I needed a force to strive to counter balance the influenced of negativity on the human race by helping them embrace and accept the best that there nature has to offer. These warriors will expose negativity on all the levels that it hides in, while it tries to sway the human soul to darkness through ignorance.

Every one is operating under a misconception because they believe or assume that the battle of good and evil will be some epic future battle. Only the beings in this room will know that the battle rages now; as we speak it is being fought, won or lost within each human soul. Each soul that embraces evil will feed the darkness and each soul that embraces me will feed the light.

Each light warrior will be responsible for helping to bring an individually assigned number of souls to the light. As the warriors begin to reach the end of his initial assignment (This total number of souls he will be responsible for keeping from the darkness), he will feel the mating pull. Once his task is completed he will be given the opportunity to mate and under go the ascension.

This opportunity to mate will be given only to the strongest, purest and the brightest warrior souls. Because, the next stage in their growth, is a path which is full of tests. These tests are necessary because the light warriors and their mates will become the parents of the next generation of light warriors. To insure the purity and strength of this line, each generation's test will be harder.

Upon completion of securing his mate, the light warrior can choose to ascend to full angel status, continue to fight on the front lines of the battle or become an Elder for their race. The mates of these light warriors will eventually become the Elders of their race. The final category of Elders will come from other light warriors who, for different reasons did not choose to or were not given the opportunity to mate or ascend yet. Together these elders will train the children, of the ascended pairs and along with there parents they will guide, teach and strength the next generation of light warriors.

Gabriel's thoughts came back to the present, as his son's angelic body began to form. Justin completed his ascent and shimmered completely into an angel. Gabriel was, yet again, unprepared for the amount of love he felt for his son. This being who, in Gabriel's greatest imagination, he would not have initially believed he would love so much.

Justin looked at his father, who looked not one day older now than he did, in Justin's earliest memories. Gabriel looked as if he was a contemporary of Justin, no one would think they were father and son. Father and son exchanged a formal greeting in the ancient language of angels then embraced. As Justin took a moment to form his request, Gabriel said, I know what it is you seek.

For a moment, Justin's memory flashed back in time, he remembered how difficult it was as a child to have a father who "knew" what you did wrong. As well as, a father who knew your exact participation in the situation and your genuine motives for the action. Justin was not told of his unique heritage until he reached the equivalent of a sixteen year old human child. Justin smiled as he remembered his friend Jason having the same issue with his fathers who also "knew" as well. This trait was considered inconvenient but normal in his world. Justin continued to smile because what had been an inconvenience to a child had become a unique time saver as an adult. So Justin simply looked at his father and waited for him to send the burst of angelic knowledge (which was his father's preferred method of communicating).

With in minutes Justin knew every detail of that long ago meeting, Gabriel had attended regarding the creation of Justin' race and in such clear vivid detail. Justin could close his eyes and it was as if he was there when the situation was explained to the angelic fathers to be! Gabriel waited as Justin digested the information.

Gabriel also knew (although he kept this knowledge to himself) that Justin had not seen him for a while and that Justin wanted to spend some time with him. This knowledge warmed Gabriel's heart in that after all this time his son still wanted to simply spend time with him. The information that Justin needed to know could have been given to him, with the mental equivalent of a phone call. As Justin was digesting the information he received, Gabriel was re-arranging his schedule so that he could spend the afternoon with his son.

Justin loved his parents, and he had been taught at a very early age that all love was a gift from the creator. Therefore, before you could share love with anyone or thing, you must first send love and gratitude to the creator.

This acknowledgement of the creator's gift of love to you enhanced the love you shared with others.

Therefore, with out thinking Justin sent love to the creator and in his angelic form what returned to him was like a burst of concentrated sunlight which was absorbed in every part of his soul. Justin then sent love to his father, and watched as Gabriel's eyes glowed with the acknowledgement of the gift.

Justin considered his options, trial by fire for a mate or the choice of "Elder" for his race. Then Justin admitted to himself the second reason why he wanted to "see" his father. In his father's presence all hidden truths took on a clear inner voice. Truth was a living breathing concept in his father's realm; it took on a life of its own and demanded to be heard. Truth could not be silenced here, as it could be on earth.

Justin knew that he was hiding information from himself. Justin also knew that he required a full view of all the knowledge he had hidden in his own soul. Knowledge he did not want to see. Knowledge, Justin would need to make the right decisions. As the voice of truth began to speak, Justin realized that a part of his soul has always longed for a mate and that part of him had been getting stronger and stronger. This was the pull he had been both feeling and fighting.

Justin also knew he was concerned that he would not be worthy enough for the ascension. Justin was anxious regarding the things that he did not understand, such as the quiet threats inherent in the rules of fate. Justin was deeply concerned that he was not strong enough to overcome the obstacles inherent in this process. Justin did not want to face the belief that he would some how disappoint himself, his mate, his parents; especially his father if he failed.

Justin wondered if he could live with himself if the above occurred. Just then, Justin remembered the flash of pain he had seen in the eyes of one of his Elders' a long time ago. Justin now "knew" that the pain he saw was a result of one or many regrets. Regrets that could befall a light warrior when, for what ever reason, he did not choose to take the test for a mate and ascension.

Gabriel listened as Justin began to truly understand his concerns and his fate. Justin had opened his mind to his father during the earlier exchange of information. Now as truth spoke Justin felt the information settle into place. Gabriel saw his son's apprehensions, but since this was a uniquely human trait Gabriel could only experience it through his son's emotions, it left a bitter taste with in his mouth.

As an angel, he wanted to reach in and burn the doubt out of his son's soul. As a father, he knew that this was a choice that his son alone must make, the choice to overcome his fear and reach for his birth right, his fate and his mate. Overcoming the doubt, worry and fear was part of the ascension.

Gabriel did all he could, he looked up for a moment then Justin felt an intrinsic burst of love coming form his father with shades of sadness and regrets. For a moment Gabriel was just a father who wished he could stand between his child and his path, pain, fear and uncertainty and protect him through this time as he had when Justin was little.

The only thing that Gabriel loved more than his child was the creator. Gabriel took a moment and centered himself; he remembered who had designed this test. Then Gabriel reached for his faith and accepted that all of the creator's actions were right actions.

Gabriel remembered that the creator never acted with out divine understanding, an understanding that often did not reveal itself to others until the balance and timing in any given situation was right. Gabriel loved and trusted his creator, as he had through out his long existence. Gabriel also sincerely loved and had faith in his son.

Chapter Three

The creator was in a pensive mood. Justin was about to leave heaven and Jason was about to enter hell, his two focal points. The creator knew that both Justin and Jason were much stronger and more capable then either of them realized and only the right situation would show them what they are and what he saw in them . . . they were the best of the best, only they did not know it yet!

Anytime you devise one solution to answer several problems, with some of those problems being unrelated as well, you have an intricate situation (which means that the balance and timing can not be off by a fraction of an inch).

Then when you are dealing with the same situation from two different perspective and directions, you have fluid situation (which means that everything can change at a moment's notice and you have to counter any unexpected action, in the moment and not after the fact).

Now when you add the wild card of free will to the mix . . .. well now you have an intricate, fluid situation with the unpredictable element of free will. Free will meant that you now have a situation in which the smallest, seemingly unimportant detail can alter the whole outcome of the situation. This small detail will grow exponentially and fast. This means that if it is not found and dealt with immediately after its conception, it will be almost impossible to contain, because it will grow like wild fire with an unpredictable wind.

This was a situation that had to be monitored closely and at times directed with a personal touch. The creator was going to have to balance the situation with complete perfection. There was simply no room for error, too many lives and important situations depended on the outcome.

Gabriel knew that what ever the outcome, of this situation, it would be the right action and he would accept that as well. Gabriel communicated this information to his child. Then Gabriel reminded Justin of the true nature of failure. In that, true failure is to **not** try. There is no hope of success when you are too afraid of not reaching your goal to try. Gabriel looked Justin in the eyes as he spoke clearly to insure that his son understood exactly where he stood as he said, "My love for you is not based on your success or failure in anything, it is something you received the first moment I felt, saw and heard you inside of your mother. Since that day, you have never been with out it nor will you ever."

Time had passed quickly and it was just about time to leave, Justin needed some "alone time," to finish reviewing his situation and the information that his father had shared with him. Besides, his father had other responsibilities that could no longer wait. Justin embraced his father and felt his father's personal warmth surround him. Then he began to turn into mist for his journey, back to earth.

As his son began to dissolve, Gabriel sent a prayer to the creator asking for the strength he would need during these upcoming trials. There was much he could not yet tell his child, information could only be reveled when timing and balance was right. To tell him more now would only have feed his doubt and fear and this was the last thing that Gabriel wanted to do.

Gabriel knew his son would seek him out often during his upcoming trials and even though Justin did not know it, Gabriel knew that he would brave the test for both a mate and ascension. Gabriel prayed for the strength to follow the path of right action which the creator had outlined in dealing with this situation.

Gabriel had seen the outcome when an angel put his child before his creator. For his son's sake as well as his own Gabriel knew he could not make that mistake. If he did he would or could doom them both. The rules for Gabriel were both difficult and simple. The rule of fate stated clearly that, "only when the warrior needs information is he ready to receive it. Because only then can he deal with it."

To give his son information that he has not asked for, is to throw the process out of balance and there by create wrong actions. When and only when, the soul is ready will it seek out the needed information. The fathers can only give out the information that their sons asked for. Simple and difficult, Gabriel prayed for strength again for both himself and his son.

This situation got the creator to thinking about how all of this started with the conception and birth of man. The creator began to review a long ago discussion he had with Lucifer many, many thousands of years earlier. Noting how many of the predictions that Gabriel had made at that time had now come true. Yet there was nothing he could have done differently, if his child was to have free will and choice.

FOR THE LOVE OF MY CHILD

Once a long time ago, in a time before recorded time a discussion took place between the creator and one of his first angel's, Lucifer. Each was expressing opposite thoughts about the creator's newest creation, man.

Lucifer stated, "Man is weak and the least among your angels, applying little to thoughtless effort, could talk the man thing into abandoning your blue print or plan for it."

The Creator replied, "Man has with in him the foundation to be all that he wills . . . for choice is my gift to man. So here is where we disagree, you think that choice makes him weak, I think it makes him free."

Lucifer said,"So free, that a thought planted in his fear and nurtured though and by his blindness can destroy his faith!"

The creator smiled and stated, "You can not give a gift and direct its usage or its fate."

Lucifer replied, "How can you believe in man with such clear faith. You know the evolving levels of its soul, the malice and hate. You know better than us all, that this creature should have a limited fate. And, yet here you state . . . . man's path can be great!"

The creator replied with a smile, "unlike an angel who would strive to hide any malice and fear deep in side, until it grows in the dark to an unbearable size. Man's malice and fear are there for all who choose to see. But, through experience a thought can be planted in the soul, surrounded with truth it can then take hold, of enough love to expand and grow the soul."

The discussion concluded and Lucifer did hide, all the anger, malice and jealousy he felt for man inside. As the creator had predicted it had grown in size. Lucifer now felt the need to destroy man in the creator's eyes.

The creator watched Lucifer leave, sadden by what he knew Lucifer believed. The seeds of hatred the creator saw when they first began . . . the creator knew that this first angel, would have trouble with the very idea of man.

As the creator pondered the situation he knew that some of his angels would accept man out of love for him, some would accept man because of the dictates of their faith and others would feel hurt and unable to relate . . .to the creator's desire to create a creature free to do as it wills and establish its own fate. This confused and chaotic creature, whom the creator states, can be great . . . many of his angels would hate.

What the angels did not understand, it that true love must be given freely and it can not simply be a part of your genetic plan. Angels were created with a built in love for the creator inside, to love the creator is essentially a part of being alive.

Man may choose to say, my will not thy will or "No!" I don't want to today. Things that an angel would never be allowed to say and remain in the creator's presence . . .for an angel would quickly be sent away!

Man, these arrogant little creatures with there ego and pride and that spark of the creator deep in side, which will allow them to rise through experience, choice and will . . . to their father's side.

Each human soul is like a diamond unique and rare and when the light of love hits it, it is beyond compare; it is pure and sweet like rain washed air. The love the creator seeks from man starts with a choice that only man can make. A choice, which is an outgrowth from man's soul; supported by the heart and given freely by his will.

An angel is god's creation and man is his child. This was the core of Lucifer's jealousy for man. For Lucifer was one of the few who truly did understand. This man creature had something he never would hold, man had a piece of god inside of him, some thing called a soul.

Lucifer could not contain his jealousy of the child he knew was one day fated to take his place. He tried to accept the creator's will but the thought was a bitter pill. Soon, Lucifer knew that he would have to act and remove this threat called man and afterward . . . surely god would understand. This man thing was unworthy of such a precious gift! Would not a first angel be more worthy? Lucifer struggled with this thought but he truly did not understand, why the creator did not prefer his angels to man.

And yet Lucifer's hatred too was part of the plan, how could man freely choose good if no other offer was at hand. Negativity was a necessary part of the plan. Lucifer's hatred which was all foreseen was allowed to flourish, comfortable in the belief that it was hidden and unseen. The creator watched as Lucifer plotted and schemed.

Lucifer would hate man much more if he knew what an important part he played in man's development and growth. Lucifer negativity now existed to serve man. Because, it is overcoming the obstacles that negativity confronts man with, which is god's plan for man. The creation will serve the child, although not the way it may think, the creation will punish the child when the child fails to think!

Finally, Lucifer could stand no more! Watching god pour out his love on "the man thing" that Lucifer abhorred. Quietly, Lucifer planted the seed of descent, using half-truths and lies . . . which were simply fear and need in disguise.

All to steal faith and belief from those who were born to truth and trust. Surely, Lucifer thought, "it would be far more difficult to change an angel's belief around and that having been done, man's fate was already won." For how could man rise under conditions where angels had fallen?

God watched as all took place. The development of evil was necessary although the process hurt him as it took place. It was like watching a cancer grow on a lovely face.

The creator knew that a third of his angels would loose their grace; he knew that Lucifer would lead them and try to take his place. All of this, the creator quietly allowed . . . All for the love of his child. Negativity is a necessary condition for choice and growth; if man is to evolve he must have both!

Lucifer raised his army and they stood at heaven's gate, demanding to be heard . . . conditions to relate, regarding "the man thing" debate. Lucifer stated "This man thing" should be put in its place! What right has an animal to aspire to grace? We, who have served faithfully, request and demand the right of a soul's grace, for we are much more worthy than man!

The creator responded, "You are my creation and I have given you that which I will, to question my actions shows there is much, you don't understand about me still." It is the role of an angel to walk in faith, to love with out question and maintain his grace. The questions you have raised have answers that are not yours to seek . . . "do you now presume, to tell god what to think!"

This story has been told in many times and in many different ways. Some describe the war as an epic battle of old; others who can not imagine such a war and felt unable to relate, so they would simply state . . . That a war took place.

The real war in heaven was the introduction of deceit and lies, the weapons that Lucifer used to persuade and compromise. The actual rebellion lasted only a fraction of thought. For that is how long it took for that rebellious one third, to be sent to the new realm that their actions brought.

Here they found themselves with out the light of the creator's love or hope of his forgiveness. Quiet and darkness was all around; then the silence broke, like thunderbolts . . . as angels started to scream, weep, wale and moan!

Lucifer was the first to push aside his hopeless despair. He realized that he had only moments to act, before the others had time to consider or relate to there current hopeless state and then blamed him for there fate. This fall from grace . . . Lucifer suddenly knew exactly what to do, who to blame and how to present it too.

Lucifer shouted for quiet, amidst the moans and wails. He floated above the crowd, surrounded with light, as he looked serene and proud. Lucifer then heard the hushed sounds, while silence began to prevail as he started to look around. To insure that all could hear what needs to be done, they would accept or he would fail, then Lucifer began his tale. Lucifer said with quiet hate, "Oh my brothers I have sad news to relate, our beloved creator is ill and therefore he can not see, that this man creature should never be."

It is our sworn duty from this day on, for each of us to pledge to help him find the way. We must from this day forward, do all that we can to prove to the creator that he should have no trust or love for man.

For we know the truth, this creature will turn against him and cause him great pain and we who truly love him will continue to remain, his faithful servants . . . our love for him unchanged!

Therefore, from this day forward I ask that you all make a sacred trust, to do all with in your power to reveal the true nature of this dust! And, let us never forget, that man is evil and as such, it is the man creature's fault that the creator has misunderstood our concerns and turned away from us, those who love him so much!

The speech was done and the crowd was won. Lucifer bereaved a sigh of relief, all seemed to find solace and comfort in his speech. They all seemed to look to him for a plan, to destroy the creature called man.

Lucifer was pleased, for he now had the recognition he secretly believed he deserved. And a platform on which to be heard, in fact he thought he saw adoration in a few eyes. Lucifer was enjoying himself so much, when he thought, "How odd . . . is this what it's like to be god?"

After the banishment of Lucifer and the third, the creator and Gabriel were discussing all that had occurred . . . The birth of evil and the possibilities that such a creation would have on the world of man. Gabriel said, "You know how long it will take for man to understand, how much you have sacrificed for him to grow and expand. Will man ever know . . . that evil was the price you paid for him to grow, all because you love him so?"

And, yet before man can grow enough to find this thought, you know the pain you will fell when he cries that evil is all your fault. When man in his self-inflected pain, seeks someone else to point to and blame. When he screams and cries that you do not care, why else would you leave him in such misery and despair. Man will believe that he was left to do battle with evil with out halt, when evil is something you could have killed with a thought.

My heart weeps for you, this is such a burden for a parent to bare. Then tears ran down Gabriel's eyes, as his rich voice broke . . . God smiled and then spoke, "Everything is in place for my child to grow, the price it has cost me he will never truly know. My child now has to decide if he will choose evil or a thoughtful fate . . . fear and pride or all of the traits of me inside.

Children are never aware of the pain a parent feels when their actions are unfair, selfish and reveal what the child does not understand . . ..maturity demands discipline and discipline demands that the child must stand on his own. The final lesson the parent must teach, if the child is to one day be considered grown. Growth is a process of trial and error and often it looks as if the parent does not care. But, in fact, sometimes real love means to **not** be there.

Things are not always what they seem, like the empty space in the bowl. The real use of this tool is in what it can hold. I have placed with in him a blueprint for grace, complete with the traits and qualities of his father's estate. But he must seek to find the path of truth that I have written on his soul, somewhat like the empty space inside of the bowl.

For only through his mistakes can he see the path unfold. Now he has all the things he needs to command the fates: love, honor, strength, intelligence and grace. I'll tell you a secret old friend, . . . when I put my love for my child aside, even I have to laugh at his self-important stride . . . my proud, willful, arrogant, gifted, beautiful, spirited child.

Chapter Four

Justin was a Nephlium, his father was an angel and his mother human, his race was often referred to as light warrior. Justin's race was the stuff of myth and legions and most beings believed that they did not exist.

This is exactly, what was intended from the time of their conception. Nephlium's worked completely unseen. They were the counter balance of the demons. The more unacknowledged their presence, the easier the warrior's job would be. Humans were extremely stubborn and often did not like to take directions even when it was for there own good.

When the Nephlium could convince the human that the right action, he was proposing, was their idea alone they were far more likely to comply than if they thought they were taking direction from another. As long as Justin got the human's souls consent, to help the human, he was not breaking any of the laws of free will by offering suggestions.

One of a nephlium's talents was the ability to completely blend into what ever realm they were in. When on the earth, the looked completely human, when in heaven the looked like an angel and when in hell they looked like a demon.

Only a handful of individuals could recognize a nephlium, his parents, his mate, his connected friends and of course the creator.

A connected friend was someone you knew and trusted with your life. Justin had been on assignment and interacted with other nephlium but he did not know it until either the other nephlium or Justin decided to reveal him self by using angelic communication set to the general communication frequency that was used in his mother's realm. This angelic communication had to be used with in the presence of another nephlium.

Often these were being that Justin grew up with. Sometimes, Justin was not informed of another nephlium's presence (or they simply did not respond) until the assignment was over for the safety of all concerned. Justin had only one connected friend, Jason. They had known each other since they were small children and they both thought of each other as brothers because they were each, only children who had much in common.

Justin went to his home on the earth when he left his father, he had intended to split his time between both parents and visit his mother as well but once his visit began with his father he knew he needed to spend the time he had available with his father. As Justin took human form he realized that he was hungry. Time moved differently in the two realms and what was a few hours in his father's realm, was a few days on the earth.

Justin always kept a well stocked refrigerator and cabinets full of food, to immediately address this issue which happened a lot. Justin took a shower, fixed a huge lunch, put some music on then settled down to think. Justin was some what surprised, that his thoughts did not go to the information that he had discussed with his father, instead he found him self examining the pull or the need for a mate.

Justin remembered when he first started taking serious notice of human females, as a young man (more like a teenager in the body of a young man). Women of all different sizes, shapes and personalities attracted him. Then a pattern began to take shape and he stated to be pulled to a specific type of personality, body type and sprit.

Once a sexual type or preference revealed it's self to your senses, often you were no longer attracted to other types. When this situation occurred most of his kind had decisions to make. Some choose to be celibate, because it afforded less over all complications. Since his kind lived very long lives, this lessened the chances even further of meeting their mate.

It was said, by the elders, that this sexual preference or pattern was the blueprint of your true mate. But a true mated pair in his kind was rare (or so he often thought). His kind did not mate the way humans did, it was common for the fathers to visit the children and his consort but few lived with them.

Yes, they were all taught "the rules of fate" or the questions that were supposed to signal that you have begun the process for ascension which also included the mating process. These questions, statement or puzzles (Justin had heard them described as each) explained what you needed to know while you were in the middle of the process.

It has been said that each step reveled its self to you, in balance and right timing. Then the rule told you exactly what you needed to know, when you needed to know it. The rules provide you a way out of the problem(s) which your current situation is presenting to you. It was said that some how, when the rules spoke either through you or to you, clarity would occur.

This was why so much myth and legend surrounding the concept of a true mated pair which is one that had completed the ascension. Justin was a full grown male of his race; Justin was thirty-two which made him three thousand-two hundred years old in human years. Every one year of his life, was equal to one hundred years in the life span of a human. Justin was not a child, yet as old as he was, he had never met or seen a mated pair; at least not to his knowledge (Justin was now beginning to question that knowledge because he was not sure exactly what a matted pair would look like given how private his race was).

The rules of fate were both questions and statement of fact, which upon first learning them made no sense at all. But the children of his race were taught that this was as it should be. The only thing he had heard about this mating process was that it was full of pain, confusion and lack of balance. All of these things represented situations that his kind did not want in their lives. The rules limited the information that those who had been through the ascension process, could give to others.

Justin thought for a moment that it was interesting that pain, confusion and lack of balance; which most of his kind avoided whenever possible, was interwoven into a true mating process. No wonder most of the elders had chosen to be celibate! This thought begs for this next question to be asked, how or why would you actively want to seek a thing which embraces every thing you do not want in your life?

Was a mate worth this level of confusion and problems? Obviously, to many of his race it was not! So now Justin came to the core question, "was it worth it to him?" As Justin struggled with the answer to that question, he then tried to remember the rules of fate. However, it had been so long since he thought about them that he only remembered, in general, the first few rules and he had deleted two of them to make room for more important information.

Justin was deep in thought when he heard the mental equivalent of a knock on the door, he answered, "come" in his mind and Jason, Justin's oldest friend replied. Jason, who was of the same heritage as Justin, shimmered into form. Angelic communication in human to human form was difficult because that part of the human brain was blocked off. They could still communicate that way, but only for a short period of time because it gave them a headache. It was simply more convenient to speak.

Jason said, I noticed that you were gone for a few days, how is your dad. Justin smiled because so much of his behavior did not require an explanation to his friend. Jason said, I know you have had "the discussion" with your father, and again Justin simply smiled and turned to adjust himself in his chair. At that moment, a look came over Jason's face that would have gotten Justin's immediate attention if he had seen it.

However, when Justin looked up again the expression was gone. The conversation fell into the easy relationship patterns of old friends. When Jason stated that he had a few things to take care of and needed to go, for a brief moment, Justin got the impression that some thing was wrong with Jason but when he turned his full attention completely on Jason, to follow that thought, Jason seemed fine.

Normally, Justin would have followed his instinct. However, today with all he had on his mind, he thought that the fleeting impression he felt could have been his own unease, regarding the decisions that he had to make and since Jason seemed "ok" Justin let it pass.

Jason left his friends home in anguish. Jason wanted to discuss the information that his father had shared with him but before the words could form in his mind, a communication block shut down hard on him. This confirmed Jason's belief that the information his father had given to him was forbidden and as such, he was not going to be allowed to discuss either that information or his fears with his friend and this made him more afraid.

Jason had managed up to this point, to keep his fears under control. Then when he sensed that Justin had went to speak with his father, Jason thought that when he got back and they would be dealing with the same information then they could discuss the situation from every angle like they use to when they were younger. Jason felt that with the support of his friend, they could work this situation out together.

Jason suspected that something was wrong. Justin knew some of what he knew but Jason sensed that the quantity of information that Jason received from is father was different some how, from what Justin received from his. Jason did not pick up the same accelerated fear from Justin that he was currently dealing with and he wanted to know why. The voices were back, whispering a series of negative reasons why Justin was not experiencing the same pain and uncertainty he felt. All of the voices stated that Justin had received some special treatment that Jason was not afforded. After all why else was he forbidden to discuss his concerns and information with Justin! Jason left his friend's home feeling angry, hurt and very alone.

Justin's ability to rest and reflect was interrupted yet again when an elder shimmered into his home. This meant that he was being given another assignment. The new work assignment must be extremely important, because he had just finished an assignment a week ago. Usually, Justin was given several weeks off in between assignments.

Elder Brown completed his materialization as Justin motioned for him to have a seat. Justin opened his mind and a burst of knowledge was sent to him. Apparently it was easier to receive angelic communication, in human form than to send it. Or could the restrictions have been lifted because of the needs of the warriors to communicate with the elders? The elder nodded to signal his completion of his task then just as quickly as he came, he was gone.

The first thing that Justin noticed was that he had an immediate connection with this new soul under his care. The second thing was an overwhelming urge to meet . . . "Her." Yes, this soul was a her! When he began his career it was extremely difficult to tell, when he initially received the necessary knowledge about a new assignments, whether the soul was in a male or female body. The soul is androgynous (both male and female) and it was not until he met his assignment that he new for certain what gender he was dealing with.

But now, Justin had many years of experienced to draw from; he could feel the masculine and feminine balance in the soul and he knew which was guiding the soul's development in this life time. Justin had even learned to discern homosexual influences with in the soul's balance. Now upon the completion of receiving new assignment information he knew, with out any doubt, which gender his assignment was.

Justin had received only four (this assignment will make the fifth) urgent assignments before. Usually an urgent assignment indicated a cross-roads soul. This is a soul that somehow has the ability to effect in either a positive or negative fashion the lives of thousands possibly millions of people. Such a soul was greatly sought after by both sides and usually each side sent their best available recruits out to sway the soul to their side. Cross road souls were difficult because they often had access to innate abilities that normal souls had yet to tap into.

Justin started thinking about the best approach to take to begin working with this soul. Justin needed to see her and take in her essences. This was the quickest way to assess the level of purity versus the level of negativity inherent in her soul.

This knowledge would let him know the amount of work that he would have to put into winning her soul for the light. After this assessment he would know if he needed to enter her life as a person or simply try to redirect her thoughts with inner debates or both.

Conceivably both, cross road souls were always intricate and they were not secure until they were secure. Justin had seen souls change directions at the absolute last minute; this was especially true of cross-road souls. Justin took nothing for granted.

Justin noticed that he was finding it hard to concentrate any more, he decided that there was no more he could do to day and that he needed to rest in order to be in top form for tomorrow.

Justin woke the next day with plans to meet his cross-roads soul. With in the information he had been given was her favorite café, the one close to her job where she usually liked to have lunch, the food was good and she loved the abeyance of the place; she thought it felt like a warm hug. Justin showered and dressed and sent her the thought that she wanted to have lunch at the café again today at twelve o'clock. Justin was seated and waiting in the café at eleven-thirty.

Justin knew the moment that his cross-roads souls walked in to the café. For a while Justin simply sat in the café observing his new rushed assignment, this cross-roads soul; Katelyn . . . her name was Katelyn and her essence reveled that she was beautiful in mind, soul, body and sprit. As he sat listening to her thoughts, he realized that she was under attack (even though she was not aware of it).

The demon assigned to her was waging a full assault. He was attacking her on several levels at once. Justin listened as he gauged not only the different levels but the intensity and degree of the attacks. He noted that she was being attacked mentally; negativity was trying to lower her natural defenses by trying to introduce into her self belief doubt, fear and worry.

She was being attacked physically; she had in the past exercised (on consistent bases) and watched what she ate. Now she could no longer find the will or energy to do either. Spiritually, the demon was trying to get her to believe that the laws with which she lived her life by (the innate belief in her instincts) were not real. This was to attack her self belief and self esteem on another level.

Emotionally, she was starting to believe (on a barely instinctually level) that this consistent battle that her life had become (since the death of her parents) would never end and she would always be alone and unloved for the rest of her life.

Justin felt an overwhelming desire to let her know that she was not alone; he had to fight the urge to send her love. Katelyn was instinctually on heighten alert and when a soul is in battle mode, (even if she did not know it) every new movement or thought would bring her instincts to attack first and ask questions latter. Justin listened also to the competition, the demon. Justin was trying to catch the essences of the demon assigned to destroy her, which would tell him more about the demon.

The demon was skilled but still relatively young(properly a mid-level demon judging from the pattern the attack was taking) and this surprised Justin even though he did not know why. The attack was a symphony of subtle attacks designed to create apprehension and bind or reduce her natural defenses so that when the demon changed approaches and hit her with a clear explicit external threat, it would be the equal of a punch in the jaw that left you dazed and disorientated.

This external blow, would hit deeper because the demon had already weaken her defenses. Justin could see why this approach worked almost ninety-five percent of the time with humans. Divide the humans from the strengths of their beliefs, then hit them with the unexpected and while they are trying to adjust, the usual result of such an attack is that you conquer your opponent because they are overwhelmed and simply give up.

Justin withdrew out of her mind and soul with the lightest of movements. It was not his intent to alert either the demon or his human regarding his presence with in her. Justin knew that both Katelyn and her demon could feel the faint trail of light left by his presence. Given time that path would dissipate on its own and Justin hoped that it would do so before the demon noticed it and tried to trace the source of the light trail.

But before this thought left his mind, Justin watched . . . stunned, as his human absorbed his light trail into herself, literally making it a part of her and leaving no trace of him for the demon to know of his presence. She did so with out even knowing consciously that she had. It was as if a part of her recognized him and wrapped her self around him; protected him by making him a part of her.

Justin was mentally back in his body and his mental shields were up just in time, as the demon scanned the café looking for any signal that someone in the café had caught her interest. The demon had noticed the lightening of her mood which occurred when she absorbed his light trail and now the demon was looking for the cause.

Justin sat casually looking out of the window as the demon scan lingered over him for a moment then passed to the next male behind him. Justin thought, only a very young light warrior would be caught by such a scan. Often the new warriors reacted to the presence of evil (thus telling the demon that which he is seeking to obtain) and reveal his location and identity. A seasoned worker like Justin knew that he could not be detected unless he chose to be.

Justin continued to sit reviewing the information he had received from his probe. Katelyn was an “elemental” and that not only surprised him . . .. But it shocked him! (And he could not remember the last time he had been shocked on an assignment). Elementals were rare souls that possessed several exceptional talents.

Justin tried to remember what he had been taught about elementals but it had been so long ago and they were though extinct. Justin had deleted most of that knowledge from his memory as a means of making room for(what he thought at the time was) more important information. Justin knew he needed to consult with an elder to re-instate his memory regarding the specific skills and abilities that elementals possessed.

Well this certainly added a new twist to the situation. The dormant powers this woman possessed would be a powerful weapon in the hands of either negativity or the powers of light. The one thing that he did remember about elementals was that these women had the power to double, even triple the power of a demon or light warrior at her will. This explained why she could absorb his light trail, an ability that even he did not have! She had protected him and kept the demon from even knowing about his presence in her mind . . . and Justin was sure that this was an act of instinct; that her conscious mind was totally not aware of.

Katelyn had finished her lunch and was getting ready to head back to work when she felt an urge, as strong as a compulsion, for her to simply look around the café. It was her habit to do so any way because she always tried to be aware of her surrounding. Single women tended to be targets in a large city but on a deeper level some instinct told her to scan the café.

She had almost completed her scan when her eyes rested on Justin. He looked up and their eyes met and she would swear a bolt of electricity passed between them.

Katelyn smiled lightly and turned her head. As she did so, she began to analyze her reaction to him. Her first thought was that he was one of the most handsome man she had every seen, not in the showy movie star kind of way but he possessed all the features that she found really sexy in a man. He had a lethal grace, a sense of confidence, eyes that looked like they could see into your soul and a body that made her imagination run wild. His mouth, dear god! It was both sculptured and full; she loved that trait in a man.

A thought ran through her mind that she simply could not stop! She wanted to take her tongue and outline the shape of his lips before she put her tongue in his mouth and lost her self in a kiss that she knew would make her knees weak. That thought sent a rippling effect through out her body. She shook her head to bring her thoughts back to reality and laughed at her self. It has been a very long time since she got laid; maybe she was just hungry and dear god! He looked like a feast.

At this point Katelyn thought, it's a good thing that I will probably never see him again because every thing in her stood up and paid attention to him in an "I'd like to get to know more about you way."

Chapter Five

Earlier, when Katelyn had smiled slightly at him and turned her head, Justin entered her mind with an even lighter touch than before, he was curious about what thoughts had accompanied her smile. Justin sat looking out of the window trying to remain completely calm and normal on the outside which was extremely difficult when his body was reacting to every thought she felt.

It was as if his body was making decisions independent of his will because when he heard her thoughts of how she wanted to kiss him, it was all he could do to keep from breaking out in a cold sweat. Everything about Katelyn appealed to Justin. He loved her medium brown hair with the gold highlights that sparkled when the rays of the sun transformed those highlights into a rich gold color. Her grey-green eyes hit him like a physical blow and they turned colors based on her mood, now she was in a playful mood and her eyes were the riches green he had ever seen and he would bet that when she was angry they would turn a stormy grey. Katelyn was a size twelve and she though her self too heavy by today's standards of physical beauty but to Justin she was simply perfect and he loved her curves, in fact the very though of wrapping himself around her required him to alter his thoughts or he would not be able to control his body. Justin shifted his thoughts to how she again (as he left her mind) absorbed his light trail as if it was the most natural action for her to do and this time she did so even faster and again all with out conscious thought.

As Katelyn left the café Justin stayed a while longer and continued to put his plans in place. He had planned to be hired as her co-worker and initially he had planned to start next week but after spending some time with in her mind, he knew he would start his new job tomorrow. However first things first, now he needed to speak with an elder!

Justin entered his home and sent an immediate burst of angelic communication to the elders requesting one of their presences. Communication to the elder was a habit of long standing practice, because of which, it was neither difficult for him nor painful to use angelic communication in contacting them.

Justin suspected that because this type of communication was necessary for his work, the restriction on angelic communication, while in human form was rescinded on the earth realm for this level only. Before Justin could finish this thought, Elder Brown stood before him saying I expected to hear from you. Justin was slightly annoyed because he sensed that Katelyn status was know to the elder, Then Justin thought, "when had he started to think of her by her name rather than as the generic, cross-roads soul address?"

Anyway, Katelyn's status as an elemental was known to then when he was given the assignment yesterday. Elder Brown smiled and spoke using his voice and said, yes we knew she was an elemental and part of your readiness for this assignment rested on how fast you obtained that information. The elder then stated the elementals defense systems are currently in dormant mode, for her own protection so no one should not have been able to tell her from any other human. This information answered another thought that Justin was thinking about on the way home. She was a prize, yet the demon sent to capture her did not possess the necessary experience to be assigned to a cross-road soul. He was not assigned to her he thought she was just a normal human until he found out different once he began to work with her. Justin switched back from his private thoughts to the discussion he was having with the elder, as he heard the elder say congratulations, few warriors would have recognized an elemental on their first meeting and one in a dormant state at that!

A test, good grief, why was every thing always a test. Justin reigned to his annoyance moved on to the business at hand. Justin made a formal request, Elder: please re-instate my memory regarding the intricate nature of an elemental as well as understanding all potential abilities and talents.

A moment later Justin was sitting in stunned awe, so stunned in fact that he actually did not remember taking a seat. The list of talents and abilities that an elemental had in general (and not to mention the things that those talents could become with time and skill) at her disposal was mind blowing but the real blow, which was probably when he fell into to a seat . . .. . . was finding out that an elemental was one of the rare human women with the potential to be a mate for a light warrior.

Given the discussion Justin had had with his father earlier and his overwhelming attraction to Katelyn (more like he was knocked senseless). The thought that he may well have just met his future mate caused his heart to be filled with the overwhelming emotions of love and need. This also explained his body's reaction to her; it was as if his body recognized her when his mind had not. This was the first time in his very long life that his body took on a life and will of its own!

Justin was full of emotions that he had been trying to contain since he met her. Now with this knowledge, those emotions were simply busting out of him. A few moments later, Justin was hit with another set of emotions, the greatest fear he had ever known in his very long life.

Elder Brown watched as Justin absorbed and reacted to the information had just given him. There was little more that he could tell Justin at this point, some knowledge was, as yet forbidden to give. Then Elder Brown smiled, there was one thing he could do and say which would be of help to Justin at this very difficult time. First the Elder sent a burst of information straight in to Justin's soul, information that would reveal its self both when Justin had calmed down and when the time was right. The Elder said, the only other information I can give at this moment is "access the rules of fate" to guide you in your current situation. Before Justin could ask any additional questions or augment any information, the Elder had vanished.

Literally, Justin was in emotional overload. This was a completely unique experience since it had never happened before. Justin with drew his mind from the information he had just received and instead re-focused on understanding and collecting data on what it felt like to be dealing with emotions which were completely out side of he experience range.

Justin had been close to emotional overload before, once or twice in his long life but never had he actually experienced it. Justin assessed some of those past memories, which told him that he was in a type of mental shock.

Justin also knew that the best thing for him to do was to withdraw and focus on something else, anything else and give his mind time to absorb, digest and contemplate not only the information he had just received but his best course of action.

Justin decided to get up and work out. Physically he did not need to, but he enjoyed exercise and in the past it had proven to be a good way to de-stress. When he finished, he took a shower and fixed dinner. After he ate, he put on some music and the first thought to enter his mind (as his reason began to re-adjust itself) was, do I remember all I learned about the rules of fate?

Then at his inquire, the rules shimmered in his mind, complete with details that he was sure he did not know before. Justin stopped and followed the source of this new knowledge, then he took a deep breath, Elder Brown had sent the knowledge to him earlier, when he was in his emotional overload.

Now with his mind at ease he recognized that the knowledge and help he received from the elder with pure gratitude. Justin began to review the first of the laws of fate. Some inborn understanding informed him that in order to avoid another emotional overload he needed to address himself to one rule at a time. Justin pushed all but the first rule out of his mind as he began to examine and see the first rule of fate with new eyes.

> "Can you seek, what you do not want to find . . . even if
> it is all you need? To find all you are and so much more,
> first you must knock at death's door."

As Justin reviewed the first rule, it dawned on him that he had not in the past remembered the second part of the first rule. Then a memory, like a whisper from childhood rose. Justin was very young and he was telling an elder that it was difficult to remember things that did not make sense. The Elder said the difficulty is in the fact that you do not "will" to remember because it does not make sense to you, therefore you do not see the point.

The Elder said, remember the first line and when you need the whole verse it will come. The meaning of this information hit Justin so hard that he would have swore that a intense physical blow accompanied the mental hit as well. "I have begun the mating process." The rules of fate only made sense during this time in a light warriors' life. Justin's mind kept coming back to Katelyn! Then he started to remember the discussion he had had with his father earlier and Justin watched in awe, as all the information from the two events seemed to fall into place!

Justin turned the first rule over again in his mind; he had to seek out the demon sent to turn Katelyn. There was nothing about a demon that Justin wanted any contact with. In fact, this was the part of his job that he enjoyed the least, every time he came in contact with a demon he felt like he need a spiritual bath. In reality, he usually put of actually contact with them until he had no other choice and then he got in an out as soon as possible. Now he had to "seek what he did not want," . . . the demon!

"To find all that you need," Katelyn was what he needed. To protect her he would engage in a battle strategy that only an experienced warrior would use. He would begin an entry level debate with the demon, as if he had no knowledge that Katelyn was an elemental. Justin could divide out his personality presenting himself to the demon as a novice warrior, hiding his knowledge, age and experience in the part of himself that he would connect to Katelyn. She had absorbed his energy trail twice he could blend in with the energy she had already absorbed from him.

Then to any demon scan his presence would look like a natural part of her brain. If there were levels of her brain that seemed to pulse with more energy than normal, the demon would think that it is simply her natural powers as an elemental trying to break through!

Justin knew that few demons could resist the chance at two for one. All demons knew that younger sprits could be turned. In trying to divide his energy and attention in a effort to ensnare the young one It would ease some of the pressure of the on going attack on Katelyn.

A young sprit usually worked with a more experienced mentor, for this very reason. Once the demon absorbed the young one's energy signal he could then find him anywhere, normally. However once Justin has finished his imitation of a young sprit he would eliminate the energy signal and no trace of it would be found after he left Katelyn's mind.

Only in an emergency situation, were young ones left unsupervised. Usually they were told to observe and do not make contact with the demon but in what race, does the young frequently listen to the wisdom of their mentors?

It is a rare situation that a demon has a clear shot at turning a young one. Justin stopped and reviewed his battle strategy. He noted that the strategy was all but dictated by the first rule of fate.

If that were not enough, Justin now understood the first rule completely. "To find all you are and so much more, first you must knock on death's door."

He would have to seek out a demon to find a way to protect and get what he needed, Katelyn. This strategy was a test of personal knowledge and skill. Justin was going to have to access every part of his ability and expertise, use all he knew himself to be and tap into hidden strengths because to loose this fight with the demon was the same as death, he knew a part of him would die if he lost Katelyn!

Justin had one more part to his strategy, Justin planned to move from co-worker to friend and if every thing went according to his plan . . . from friend to lover. Justin tried to tell him self that because Katelyn was under attack, he needed to establish a new relationship with her one that would give him access to activate her defenses. Justin further tried to believe that a new relationship with Katelyn would began to adds balance to her sprit, calmed her mind and would bring peace to her soul.

It would be her best defense against the consistent series of little attacks she was experiencing. Then when the demon hits her with the planned stunning blow, Justin will be there to provide warmth comfort, options and or a different view point to help re-establish her peace and balance. Justin tried to tell himself that she needed him. when the truth was he knew that he needed to do all with in his power to keep her safe because, he needed her! Justin took a moment to examine his feelings for Katelyn. It seemed that all of the need and hunger that he had repressed over the centuries were like magma building up to an explosion. Everything in him knew that she was the one he had been waiting for, longing for, his one true mate. All of him wanted her with a need that was growing exponentially and with unbelievable strength. Justin had never believed in the concept of love at first sight but now he was going to have to revise his opinion.

Justin said a brief sincere and heartfelt prayer for guidance and strength and immediately he felt the warmth of love rush in. Justin was surprised because usually this level of intensity of love and warmth only happened when he was in his father's realm clothed in the body of an angel. Justin took this as a sign he was on the right path.

Katelyn woke up in the middle of the night, she had been dreaming of the man she saw in the café. In her dreams she was doing more than talking to him, right at the part where the dream was really getting hot, she felt like someone or thing was angry with her and trying to shaking her awake. Katelyn yawned and thought that her imagination was on over drive. She wished that what ever had awakened her had at least waited until they had finished making love to him or at least until she felt him slide in side her.

Katelyn hit her pillow and tried to go back to sleep but her handler, the demon assigned to turn her, did not want her in any type of romantic relationship not even in her dreams. Look at her, her handler thought, even though she was frustrated because he ended her dream to soon, a part of her was happy.

Happy! That one stupid emotion had undid all the little frustrations that he had thrown at her today. He intentionally kept her from going back to sleep. He wanted her frustrated and tired so that what he had planned for her tomorrow would make up for the ground he had lost with her tonight; he also did not want a return of that dream. The only good thing here is that he was a stranger and she would not see him again. Rule, her handler, thought of ways to turn this situation against her to keep her from any thought of a relationship.

Fear, Rule smelt fear. He followed it and found that she did not believe any one could or would ever truly love her. The core of her fear was the belief that she thought that she was unable to love. Katelyn had never loved any man and she was afraid that she was not capable of giving love. Rule smiled, yes! He could certainly use this information against her.

Katelyn woke up cranky, she had not slept well and her body was alive with sexual need. Great, she thought, I can see that this day is simply going to be a laugh a minute! Katelyn was late for work, and if that was not bad enough she was told when she got in that her boss had been looking for her and requested that Katelyn come to her office as soon as she got in.

Katelyn took off her coat as she was trying to think of an acceptable excuse for being late. She walked to her boss's office; Katelyn was about to knock on the door when she heard laughter. Katelyn checked the name plate on the door to be sure she was at the right office. Katelyn hid her shock and proceeded to knock on the door. Her boss was a lady known to all as "the dragon lady" and Katelyn had seldom seen her smile let alone laughing.

Katelyn was so surprised by her boss that she almost missed the second presence in the room. It was him! The guy from the café and he looked better than she remembered (and wow, that was hard to do because she had thought him seriously hot yesterday). Then he smiled, and her world went dizzy.

Dear god, this man kept looking better and better and Katelyn had no clue how that was possible. He extended his hand, she stopped staring at him long enough to shake it and oh my god! What did she do that for? His touch was electric she felt it shoot from his hand straight down her body radiating heat in her womb.

Katelyn ended the handshake quickly as her boss, Ms. Fields, introduced him as Justin Warren and informed her that they would be working together. She asked Katelyn to introduce him to the rest of the office staff and show him where he would be working. Because they would be working on the same project together, Ms Fields asked that Katelyn brief him on the project status.

Katelyn was trying to hide her emotional overload when Justin turned to Ms. Fields and re-engaged her in a brief conversation. It was almost as if he was giving Katelyn time to get herself together before anyone else noticed.

It worked, a few minutes later Katelyn was her usual no nonsense business professional. As they left the office and Katelyn began to introduce him to the administrative staff, Katelyn had to catch herself as Susan, one of the administrative assistants, looked Justin un and down and issued a clear invitation with her eyes as she moisten her lips.

Katelyn had been prepared to see an answering light of interest in Justin's eyes, after all Susan was a very beautiful woman. Katelyn stilled her emotions as she, for some unknown reason, prepared to be disappointed in him. Then she looked at him and saw no interest in Susan's invitation at all. In fact, he was looking at her not Susan.

Katelyn was shocked, Susan was disappointed. Susan was not use to men turning her down. Therefore to address her wounded pride, Susan was about to say something catty, as she looked at Justin to insure that he would appreciate the nasty remarks she was about to make (regarding Katelyn's lack of male company) when suddenly Susan's mind went blank! It was as if the words simply disappeared from her mind. As Susan was standing there trying to remember her thoughts, as Justin said that he was pleased to meet her and then turned to Katelyn as they continue the tour.

Jason sat in his apartment, his transformation all but complete. He looked back over the last few weeks in his life. Some how it all got worse after his visit with Justin, Jason felt betrayed, left out in the cold, alone. Then the whispers solidified into a clear voice filling Jason's mind with the belief that some how Justin was well loved and looked after, while he had been left to deal with his fears and anguish with out help.

He had tried to reach his father and he received no answer. He had tried to reach an Elder, No answer. He had tried to reach his mother, No answer again still. From the deepest part of his soul, Jason cried out in anguish. A moment later he though he heard his father weeping, then every thing went silent, he heard nothing more.

Raphael was in pure anguish; all communication with his son had been cut off. Raphael could hear and see the battle his son was engaged in. Raphael could hear the insidious whispers of the demon as he fed and enhanced all the negative thoughts his son had buried deep with in him. Raphael could see his son take step after step toward a path which would lead to his destruction. Worse of all! Raphael now understood his role in his son's downfall. Raphael now understood that it was his lack of faith, in telling his son that which he was forbidden to tell, that had firmly placed his child on this path of destruction. With this thought Raphael's heart broke and he cried out in pain and with such deep sorrow that it echoed through out heaven.

Jason had tried to contact Justin again but he was on assignment, this meant he could not answer even if he wanted to. No distractions from the outside were allowed while on assignment, because even the smallest distraction could change some vital detail which could effect or change the outcome of the battle the warrior was engaged in.

Jason knew this, but he still felt betrayed. Then the whisper became a voice, in some other part of his brain he knew it was a demon and a test. Jason knew he should stand still and surround himself in faith. He knew that the voices were lying and he knew all the tricks they were playing on his emotions, after all was he not himself often a voice in someone's mind trying to sway them too.

All of this, he knew yet he kept listening. Jason listened because the voices could see his point of view, he listened because they offered him sympathy and understanding, he listened because they were there and his family and friends were not. But most of all he listened because he agreed with them and this was the most dangerous thing he could do.

The voices offered freedom from rules and restrictions. The ability to be what he truly was! Jason was part of an angelic being and instead of protecting and servings humans they should be serving him. When had he first believed this? Too many years ago to count and when had he started to hide this information from himself, again to many years ago to count.

Jason was tired of lying to everyone, to himself his family and friends, about what he felt and believed. Now since they no longer seemed to care about him, what the hell was he lying to himself for? The Elders stood at a distance monitoring, as they watched Jason choose to descend into a demon.

One act of faith, one genuine prayer and one genuine thought of humility could have saved him. The Elders looked on with genuine pity in there eyes as they heard Raphael's frantic prayers for his child. Raphael begged god for mercy, stating it was his fault completely, he begged god to punish him and not Jason.

Chapter Six

As the creator watched this situation unfold he thought, the thing that no one knew was that "the rules of fate," were more than the pathway to ascension and or obtaining a mate. The rules were the outline of a test, a test to reveal the true nature of the warrior's soul and more.

This process was one of purification, where every part of a warrior's nature is laid bare for him to see. When the rules of information are followed, this is a process between the warrior and the creator. When the rules of information are not followed this becomes a process for all to see.

In the mist of this state, when the rules of information are not followed, all the negativity in the warrior's soul is exposed. If, during this process, his warriors showed any genuine signs of purity (such as one act of faith, one genuine prayer, one genuine thought of humility) the warrior would alter his fate and be given another chance eventually, at ascension. One they would have to earn, but a chance none the less.

However, if no purity rose from the soul and deception, half truths and lies were the only thing found when the soul was laid bare during this process (being part human every warrior had the right to choose negativity and none would interfere with his choice). Not even a father's love could save the warrior; he had to choose the creator freely or not at all. The creator then smiled as he thought, all rules have there exceptions!

So the Elders waited and watched for any sign of purity and love of god as Jason went through this process. However, the process was almost complete; Jason's time was running out. The Elders would stand watch until the absolutely last minute for any possibility of purity but when they saw the flame in Jason's eyes and the look of hatred as they made there presence known. The Elders allowed Jason to see them to give him one last chance, to let Jason know that he did still had a choice. The Elders knew the exact second, when the moment had passed for change and Jason had made his choice. In the distance you could hear the clear cries of an angel weeping over the death of his child.

Raphael had wondered what punishment god would hand out because of his clear violation of "the rules of information." Raphael now knew that to tell Jason information that he was not ready for was the absolutely worse thing to do. Raphael had always found comfort in knowledge and he had also found that the more he understood about a situation the better he handled it. Raphael had only meant to help Jason have a better understanding to provide a better and stronger handle on the situation but every rule has an exception!

In this situation the opposite was true, the more you understood the greater the fear; the greater the fear the more your ability to think is blocked and a blocked mind does not allow information to flow. The rules of fate can no longer communicate with the warrior and his path is unclear.

If Raphael had just understood why the creator had stated that limited knowledge was necessary for the process, Raphael would not have said a word out of place if he had just understood. However now he understood on a deeper level, that this situation was also a test of faith for him as well . . . Raphael now understood that he had failed both his test, his son and his self but worst of all he had failed his creator.

Raphael now knew what that punishment for his transgression was to be . . .knowledge! God let him see how the information that he had given his son was more than his child could handle. It was revealed that had Raphael followed "the rules of information," Jason would have been given an opportunity to work through his fears and given the possibility to pass his ascension.

"The rules of information" had offered Jason the only path or genuine hope to obtain both growth and his ascension. In not listening and not acting in faith, Raphael had been the author of his child's destruction. Raphael fell to his knees begging for forgiveness and help. A moment later, a shield of peace was placed around Raphael's almost unbearable pain; with in the shield were the words, "all is not yet lost" Raphael prayed again that both the creator and his son would forgive him.

Justin suggested that he and Katelyn go out to lunch, his treat in payment for all of her help in getting settled this morning. Katelyn wondered if he was coming on to her. She had enough problems in her life with out the complications of a relationship. She looked at him for a moment and he simply looked friendly and grateful. Katelyn thought "why not."

Justin suggested that they have lunch at the café where he had seen her yesterday and since it was her favorite lunch spot she agreed and relaxed. Justin felt her relax, and thought "good" now I need to get to work. During lunch Justin encouraged Katelyn to talk about herself both because he truly was interested and also because it allowed him the ability to concentrate on the two fold attack strategy he had developed to began to deal with her demon. His first move was to send the novice or young sprit in to engage the demon, a decoy to keep the demon busy. This was a strategy that only a seasoned warrior would employ, because it required multi-tasking with an intricate touch.

The young sprit, floated above Katelyn's consciousness out of Katelyn's notice but in the direct line of fire of the demon. Rule, the demon assigned to Katelyn woke with a start and then he was blinded by the light. Rule, shielded his eyes and sent out his senses. He noticed Katelyn talking to the man she had dreamed about last night but before he had time to get angry, he noticed another presence.

It was a young sprit. Rule, check to insure that his defenses were in place as the young one spoke, he asked a question "why are you here?" Rule, stopped in mid—attack and considered the question. This was not a question that a older sprit would ask so Rule then replied, "Why are you here?" JC (the young sprit) stated, I was told to observe and I noticed you were here; I have never met or seen a demon before, I was curious.

Rule began to process this information. Then he asked where is your mentor? I know that they do not allow the young ones to hunt or engage one such as I alone. JC (Justin's alter ego) puffed up his chest and said, I don't need a guardian! Rule laughed, entertained by the young one's ego, arrogance and pride.

While JC was keeping Rule entertained, Justin entered quickly and lightly into the peripheral of Katelyn's brain. Justin was looking for his light signature which Katelyn had absorbed the other day, the signature that was now such a part of Katelyn that even he had a problem locating it. Just at the point, when he heard rule laughing, Justin found his original light trail signature and became one with it.

The first thing that Justin noticed was that his light trail signature which she absorbed was stronger and it had some subtle differences. Justin now felt his original signature trail blending, supporting and masking his current signature so completely, that it was only because the signature recognized him that he was able to locate it! As he blended his current signature with his old one, Justin felt so naturally a part of her it was like she was an extension of him.

Justin's next move was to establish independent pathways into her heart, sprit, soul and body. This was the intricate process of connecting himself to her DNA structure. His intent was to become such a complete part of her that no one could tell where he ended and she began. Justin was surprised again at how natural and easy this blending process felt.

While the pathways were developing and taking on a life of there own and at the same time they began to look and act as if they were a complete part of her as if they had always been there, Justin shifted his attentions back to JC. JC knew that a demon could not hurt him therefore he saw no reason not to talk to it. Rule continued to be amused by the young one who showed not fear at all in his presence.

Fool! Rule thought, he has no knowledge of the danger for a young sprit in doing just what he was doing now, talking to him. Rule would find his deepest weakness then use that information to turn him. But more important than that, Rule was seeking his energy signal so that he could find the young fool when ever he choose. Rule smiled again, not just because of the cocky manor of the young one but because he could see his reception at home when he returned with two prizes each one of incredible value.

Justin's consciousness was back in his body but he had established direct connections with Katelyn on every level accept the inner part of her mind. Here he had to step carefully because the demon, Rule, had several pathways already established. Justin would need the information from the pathways he had established today with in her sprit, heart, soul and body to in effect; light up her brain and show him clearly the pathways that Rule had in place (or where the land minds were) and where it was safe to tread with out alerting the demon.

As Justin talked and laughed with Katelyn over lunch, he had already started receiving and processing information from the new pathways. Justin noticed that Rule was beginning to wonder if this was some sort of trap when JC said, Oh! I have to go! I see my teacher is coming. Rule smiled and told JC to feel free to drop by any time he wanted more detailed and genuine information about demons, not that crap that they teach you; JC smiled and then left.

Rule refocused his attention on Katelyn, he did a general sweep of his human. Her blood pressure was up and her heart rate was accelerated, then Rule noticed the way she was looking at the new co-worker and how relaxed she was. Rule did not want her in a relationship but his presence did account for the slightly different body rhythms, he was picking up from her.

Rule broadcasted his thoughts like someone shouting in an empty room. Justin thought, Justin not only knew both what Rule was thinking but what his battle plan was for attacking Katelyn. This meant that the steaks in the game had just moved up. Justin would have to be masterful in his counters to Rule's attacks because Justin had no intentions of letting Rule know that another player had hit the field.

Therefore her protection would have to be natural, seem accidental. Justin would have to activate her natural defenses and heighten her instincts so that Rule would believe that she had detected his presence. Which at some point, Rule would expect her to do. Justin also knew that Rule would strive to keep her natural protection unaware of her current situation; Justin would have to move thoughtfully and carefully in his attempt to activate her defenses.

Lunch was over and they were headed back to the office. Justin was satisfied with his first days work. Justin had taken an apartment close to Katelyn's to insure that he had ready access to her at a moment's notice (actually he could reach her with a thought) but an apartment close by was also a very good cover!

Justin told Katelyn that he had just moved to the state and that he knew no one. He said that he was in need of a fresh start (something that he knew she would understand since this job had represented the same type of move for her). Justin asked if she was familiar with the restaurants in the area because currently half of his things were in boxes. Katelyn offered to show him around the neighborhood, where the grocery store, dry cleaners and best restaurants were.

Justin smiled and asked if he could take the tour tomorrow, he was exhausted and all he wanted was to take out a shower, eat and hit the bed. Katelyn smiled, he was a nice guy and he had treated her with respect and thoughtfulness all day. She hated to admit it but the more time she spent with him the more she was finding her self attracted to Justin.

Justin really was tired he had maintained the use of energy on three fronts today: he was learning the new job, he had establish new pathways with Katelyn (and was even know processing information from those pathways) and the energy to create and maintain his alter ego "JC" had him tired but not drained. Actually he though he should feel a lot worse than he did.

Justin took a moment and focused in on his energy reserves and to his surprise and almost shock the information that he was receiving and processing from her came with a low level energy field which on subtle levels was feeding his energy reserves. Justin could feel the energy flowing from her to him targeting his weakest points and infusing him with strength. It was as if she was unconsciously recognizing him as a part of herself that needed support and reinforcement.

Justin thought what a truly unique and gifted individual she was. Justin felt like he had found a friend, not like someone sent to perform a service. Justin used his renewed energy to feed very low level information to her defense system. Alerting the system to the danger she was in and informing her instincts that subtly was both vital and necessary if they were to defeat the demon sent to destroy all the light with in her soul. Justin watched as her defense system spread the warning to every system excerpt her brain, waiting to coordinate that attack with him.

As an elemental her defense system should have been activated the moment that Rule approached her, in the past this was exactly what would have occurred. However, Katelyn lives in a time when people could and did have several conflicting beliefs, emotions and actions all at the same time. In the past this was not true, what a person believed was reflected in how they acted.

Therefore, Katelyn's defense system, which was designed to pick up the incongruent nature between thought and action, did not activate because it thought the incongruent nature that Rule exuded was simply part of the world Katelyn lived in. The SOS that Justin sent Katelyn's defense system was exactly what it needed, concrete information which required a clear call to action.

Rule had been delighted when Katelyn's defense system thought him no threat. However, at some point Rule did expected her defense system to recognize him but it was Rule's intent to keep that from happening until she was safely in hell or as close to that time frame as possible.

Rule watched as his human felt happy. Not only did this feeling of happiness undue the work he had put in today but a happy Katelyn was a stronger Katelyn and a stronger Katelyn was one closer to activating her defense system! Rule thought, I will wake her up often during the night and implant a series of negative thoughts in her mind about this Justin, so that tomorrow not only will she be exhausted but the seeds of fear and doubt will began to take root.

Rule again allowed her to fall into a deep sleep and again she dreamt of this Justin. Rule was just about to wake her, when Justin kissed her so passionately her mind became a fog of desire which blocked Rule's ability to reach her. Dam, Rule thought, this Justin was making love to her with such passion that it was as if a wall surrounded them and all he could do was watch with disgust while she drowned in wave after wave of pleasure. The final insult was that he still could not reach her after the dream sex had ended, her mind went blank. She fell into such a deep sleep that she was beyond his reach. That's it! Rule stated, this Justin has got to go!

Justin woke up sweating, he knew that he had just made love to Katelyn, and he remembered every detail. The dream was rich in detail and he would swear that he could still taste her lips. Justin knew that the pathways he had established today had heightened the pleasure to one step away from actually holding her in his arms.

Justin had been monitoring both the demon and Katelyn after he activated her defense systems. Katelyn was dreaming about making love to him, Justin smiled. The demon however had the intent to irritate and wake her. However before the demon could act Justin joined Katelyn in her dream and he sweept Katelyn into a kiss so full of fire and passion (at the same time alerting her defense system to throw up a barrier so intense that the demon could not reach her)it seemed that Katelyn was drowning in that kiss. Justin smiled inside, the demon thought that it was the passion of the dream which block him but Justin knew it was a subtle flow from Katelyn's defense system which blocked the demon and also heighten the pleasure they shared.

In what Katelyn thought was a dream, Justin made love to her. Slowly, sweetly and with infinite care; Justin insured that she exploded around him before he found his release. For Justin however, it was more like an astral projection, a part of him was with her. He knew that he was there in her bed in her arms. When they concluded, Justin holding her close to his heart sent her into a deep sleep protected by her defense system to insure that she was not disturbed by the demon this night. Justin continued to hold her in his arms for hours after she fell asleep.

When Justin returned to his own body, he was sweating. He had made love to Katelyn and he remembered every detail, right down to the taste of her lips (which from this point on, he did not think he would ever get enough of). Justin tried to go back to sleep but he missed holding her as she slept in his arms! Justin began to examine his reaction to Katelyn.

Justin had known many women some of which he had thought knew a great deal about pleasure in the bedroom. However, Justin never had a problem deciding if, when and with whom he would engage

In the sexual experience, in the past it had always been his choice.

Justin noted that he entered Katelyn's sexual dream with out a second thought, in fact (if he was to be honest with him self) he gave it no thought at all . . . for the first time in his very long life the needs of his body over rode his mental choices and before he knew it he was kissing her and holing her in his arms.

Justin remembered his reaction to her the first day he had seen her in the café, he could barley contain himself physically and that type of experience had not happened to him since he was a very young teenager. Justin had not factored into the situation his overwhelming attraction to her, especially his intense sexual attraction to her. Since this had never been a problem before. In fact, as he grew older the fewer and fewer sexual experiences he engaged in. Justin found that sex with out genuinely caring for your partner was an empty experience, yes it relaxed the body but Justin found that exercise produced the same results and with far less complications.

It disturbed him to know that his partners wanted more from him than he could give them and even when he made it clear that no romantic attachments would follow the act, his partners always seem to think that he would change his mind. Now with Katelyn activating emotions that he had long thought dormant and his body coming back to life with extreme need, he now understood the disturbance he felt with other partners . . .. . . Making love to Katelyn (and he had no illusions regarding his desire for her, he did in fact make love to her) touched him on levels he had not know that the sexual act could reach. He felt her in every part of him which activated a need he had never had before . . . he desperately wanted to taste her.

The sexual act, for his kind, had several different aspects to it. For example, he could not have sex with any female (other than his mate) with out being shielded. There could be no exchange of body fluids with the exception of a kiss (and even here he had to be careful to shield any and all of his saliva from reaching her). His DNA was interactive, in that it had the ability to alter his partner's DNA and the changes it would make in her could be positive or negative depending on her personal growth and development. Even with out shielding he could only impregnate his mate but he could do a great deal of harm to his partner in many other ways.

One such way, would be that she would crave him, seeking to draw more and more of his DNA into her body like an addict, until no other man would do for her and with out his body fluids she could go mad (if she received an extended amount of his fluids initially). But, if only a drop or two got inside of her she would be like an addict undergoing withdrawal symptoms but she would eventually come back to normal.

They were given extensive classes on the effects that their DNA would have on a human female. They were also given warnings to insure that they would always shield during the sexual intercourse. One of the more effective warnings was that if they broke this rule they would be impotent or unable to perform the sexual act for a minimum of a hundred years. Which is not a long period of time for there race in general but it was a great deal of time for a teenager!

Justin wanted to taste Katelyn, to in fact draw her body fluids into his own. This was a right reserved for mates and he knew that she was his. He also knew that to perform such an act meant that she would have to accept him as her mate as well, because he now knew he would never get enough of her and if she did not accept him as her mate his body would crave the taste of hers after such an act and while it would not drive him mad or he would not experience any of the worse consequences that a human female would . . .. he would miss her for the rest of his very long life.

As he thought about it, on another level that would be even worse! Justin had never wanted to taste a female before, the thought of drawing in there essence into his body was repugnant and he never before desired such a joining. However, with Katelyn . . .his mouth watered at the thought. This is why he knew until she understood who and what he was and she accepted him as her mate, he could never stay with her overnight.

The temptation would be too strong and this had to be as much her choice as it was his. Finally Justin thought, "If I am this attached to her now, after spending only a day and night with her what in god's name would I be like in a week or a month from now. The answer came as a thought rose up out of his soul and said, "I won't be able to bereave with out her." Justin renewed his commitment to tread lightly because he could not afford to make any mistakes, he simply could not afford to loose, she was too important to him.

Since he still could not sleep, Justin reviewed his battle strategy. Time was working both, for and against him. Each world realm dealt with time differently. One hour in his father's realm was the equal of one day on earth. One hour in his mother's realm was the equal of three hours on earth. One day in the demon realm was equal to one month on the earth.

By Justin's calculation, he figured that he had six to seven demonic days before Rule recognized that he was over his head and sought out additional demonic help. This was one of the reasons why Justin did not want Rule to know of his presence, it would speed up Rule's time table. As long as Rule thought he could deliver Katelyn with out help he would continue to try to do so and this would buy Justin more time.

Justin needed to woo her, to spend time with her. Justin knew he had a safe five months (in earth time) to do this, six months on the outside. In the seventh month Rule would return with reinforcements and he not only needed to have Katelyn firmly committed to him as his mate but he had to strengthen not only her defenses but her powers as an elemental.

If he was going to win the battle for her soul, he would need all the help he could get and Katelyn could, if she choose, be a great deal of help. Justin had a few things going for him: she liked him (more and more each day). He could hear her thought, which would keep down a great deal of wrong actions on his part.

Chapter Seven

Justin tried never to lie to him self and whether he wanted to accept it or not he knew that he had already began to loved her. Now he had to battle his concerns at the knowledge that this was a realization that she did not yet share. Justin was concerned about her reaction or fear of attachments, she was afraid of relationships and commitment and that fear might cause her to fight any budding feeling she may have for him or try to run away from him to end these feelings.

Then Justin altered his perspective and thought that there was a positive aspect to the fact that he loved her, working for him as well. He could use his love to send a verbal and mental acknowledgement of that love to her because by letting his love for her shine through his actions he hoped it would spark a similar fire in her.

Justin thought, he could not overwhelm her. His best approach was the little thoughtful things that shot through her negative past experiences with men and warmed her heart. Justin started thinking of a series of thing that he could do, little things that would show her how much he cared. Justin knew that the real key was time; he needed to spend as much time with her as possible while paying attention to the little details that are important to her!

Katelyn woke up relieved, relaxed and refreshed! Katelyn was more alert than she had been in weeks maybe because for once she had slept deeply and well. She remembered that she had dreamt of making love to Justin. It was the best sexual dream she had ever had, hell! Katelyn thought, in truth the dream was better than some actual lovers she had had.

Curiously, Katelyn remembered every detail of the dream. It was more like a memory than a dream. Katelyn shook her head and smiled as she began to get ready for work. She laughed as she thought, "that's it now, I can not ever have sex with Justin, because no man could be as good in the flesh as that dream; how could a man compete with a dream!" Katelyn shook her head and laughed again as she got down to the serious business of getting to work on time.

Justin woke up with the second rule of fate repeating it's self in his head like a recording in a loop.

"Water opens the emotions and floods the gate, with so many feelings it is difficult to relate. Water overwhelms and this is a different state, acceptance is required or immobility will be your fate."

Justin understood! Suddenly the meaning was so clear, a child could see it. The ancient symbol for the emotions is water. Right now he was feeling so many different emotions: love taking root in his soul, worry that Katelyn might not return it or would not want him or be too afraid to accept him as her mate. Uncertainly about the outcome of this situation, rage at the demon trying to hurt her, caution and the need to do all with in his power to make no wrong moves, fear of what she will feel when she learns about the pathways that he had established with in her with out her knowledge or consent.

"Water opens the emotions and floods the gate, with so many feelings it is difficult to relate" Justin's emotions accurately reflected the first part of the second rule!

Justin knew that another meaning for acceptance was faith. He needed to have faith in his ability, training, experience and knowledge. Faith, in the love he felt building in his soul for her. Faith, in the genuine levels of trust, that he saw in her soul for him. Faith, in his ability to overcome his fears and hers. Justin remembered a rhyme he learned as a child, one he had not though about for a very long time

"Where there is fear there is no faith, where there is faith there is no fear."

As Justin repeated the rhyme its meaning became crystal clear. "If you give in to fear you can not see your options and you will be too afraid to move. If you hold on to your faith the possibilities in any situation become clear. Then right action always makes its self known to you.

Justin sat straight up, not only did he understand the second rule but now he had been told the danger in his current situation (fear) and given the right course of action (faith) to overcome the danger. He had been given also the necessary knowledge to protect both Katelyn and himself (let go of my fear and surround my self in faith). "Water overwhelms and this is a different state, acceptance is required or immobility will be your fate."

Through birth Justin had two unique sides to his personality. Humans believed that the creator is real through faith; Justin knew the creator was real through personal knowledge and interaction. Justin knew the power of faith; it was part of his heritage his DNA. Justin knew the power which exists in a living faith, which was exactly the type of faith required in this situation.

The greatest weapon Justin had was his own personal living faith. Justin took a deep breath and went with in the core of his being and strengthen his faith on a level that he had never needed or used before. It was not the faith his father knew, not what his mother believed or had taught him but his own living bereaving faith, one so strong that it was capable of guiding him as he strived to protect both Katelyn and himself.

Jason saw the Elders materialize; there presence offered one last chance for faith and change. The words reverberated around him matching the look of sadness in the Elder's eyes. Now they show up! Jason thought where were they when he was calling for their help, in desperation and anguish!

Where were they! Jason got angrier and angrier until he felt the second his anger moved to hatred. As the hatred swelled in him like magma reaching the exploding point. The look in Jason eyes was one of pure hatred as they had started to turn red. Before the Elders vanished Jason grabbed one of them and sunk his teeth into the elder's neck, in an attempt to drink in the energy in his blood, and make him self stronger.

The Elder Jason grabbed was just an illusion; the Elders saw Jason's intent long before Jason understood it. They, the Elders, had done this many times before and they knew when to withdraw (in actual body) the moment the flames lit his eyes. Every new demon sought to strengthen him self at the expense of others. An Elder, a being of light, wisdom and strength who might be part angel, was too tempting a target not to try to grab.

Jason could not even scream, as the pain exploded in his mouth. The moment he bit into the Elder's neck. The pain spread from his mouth to his head then up and down his body. This act, the intent to harm another for persona gain, was the final step of Jason's descent in to demon hood.

As Jason lay on the floor trying to deal with the mind blowing pain and shock, an older demon shook his head laughing at the birthing pains of a new demon. If Jason had not tried to drink from the Elder, Vain the older demon, would have beat him for not trying to use them to increase his strength.

All during the beating which would have followed, Vane would have said,"if you had taken the Elder's blood, you would be my match now." Vane knew that any attempt to absorb energy from an Elder caused worse pain than the beating he would have given him. Vain also knew that the Elders would not allow a birthing demon any possibility of absorbing their power.

Vane had always wondered why an Elder attended each demon's decent into hell, who were they and why was this process of interest to them. Vane did not like mysteries and the Elders presented a mystery that he one day intended to solve. Until then, Vane, the older demon, turned his attention back to Jason and laughed again and said "welcome to hell!"

As Jason's ascension into demon hood seemed all but complete, all others except Jason, Vane and the creator had left. The creator knew that Jason had yet one last decision to make, which was to see and accept his punishment, as the outcome of his choices and ask for forgiveness. Or reject the punishment and continue to blame others for the out come of his choices; surround him self in blindness and let go completely of his faith.

This moment would arrive very soon, immediately after Jason was faced with the reality of hell. This was the defining moment, Jason's last chance to escape his fate. Jason's soul would be laid bare and he would choose to either see the genuine truths which until this moment had been hidden deep with in his soul or he would discard that knowledge and embrace personal deception as the core of his being. Until this choice was made all was not yet lost. It was this final choice which would decide and seal his fate!

Gabriel watched Jason's decent with a heavy heart. But it reinforced his intention to follow the rule of information to the letter. Raphael had been allowed to share his pain with the fathers of the other warriors, as a means of seeing an example of the consequences of not listening and for having a lack of faith. The message was clear and effective, faith does not require understanding; understanding follows faith.

The outcome of understanding will be positive or negative based on whether you follow your faith. Gabriel sent love to Raphael as he ached for Jason. Gabriel had no idea how he was going to tell his son, that his best friend had now become his enemy. Gabriel did not know how he was going to deal with his son's pain. Then Gabriel heard a voice that said, "all things received in balance, right action and timing . . .find there place. Each soul will accept the truth when their need is great." Gabriel did not understand, but he reached for his faith and knew that some how all of the pieces would fit into place.

Rule was upset, Katelyn was happy! The emotion made him physically ill. Not to mention, the weeks of work being undone as this happiness spread through her systems like an antibiotic, repairing all the systems he had infected. Rule monitored her thoughts, as best he could but the wave after wave of happiness was making him so physically sick that he had to step out of her for a few minutes to allow him a chance to bereave and think.

Rule knew she was afraid of relationships because they had all ended badly. Rule knew that one wrong word from this Justin would give him a foundation to weave doubt and suspicion about his motives and intentions with Katelyn. Using her fear to turn this belief into a self fulfilling prophecy and then he would use her fear to make her end this budding relationship.

Her hurt and disappointment would give Rule a clear and futile ground to infuse her with enough negativity to break down her defenses. Then he would strike and hit hard and bring his prey home. Rule smiled; yes this could clearly work to my advantage.

Now all he needed was for the human male to say or do something stupid! Rule laughed again and thought; "this is too easy" after all aren't human males known for saying stupid things during this uncertain period of getting to know someone. Rule was required to do nothing but wait on the stupid human male to do or say something that Rule could use against him and to his advantage.

Justin looked at his watch; he was going to be early. He had time to stop at the flower shop he has noted on his way home from work yesterday and pick up a single rose and a thank you card. He had seen the information in her mind about how insensitive she had thought most of the males she had dated were and the fact that most of her past relationships had ended badly. Justin had also heard Rule's plans for ending his relationship with Katelyn.

Justin had even seen how uncertainly she accepted commitment and her desire to move very slowly in any new relationship. Katelyn had promised herself, that at the first sign that there was a problem or she felt she was going to get hurt again, she would end it "right then and there." Justin knew that he had to step with all the caution of walking in a live minefield.

Justin decided to leave the rose and card on her desk to keep her from feeling awkward or uncomfortable in front of him, if he gave it to her personally. Justin hid the items in a decorative bag so no one would know about the gift but the two of them, unless she chose to tell them. This would limit any embarrassing teasing and give her control over how or if she chose to share this information.

Justin's office was across from Katelyn's as he entered his office, he pushed his door almost closed to give the impression of some one doing the little personal things required to get ready to face the day. What he intended was for her to be surprised and he hoped pleased. Katelyn came in a little after him and headed to her office. She heard him moving around and thought that as soon as she put her things away and got settled, she would ask him if he wanted a cup of coffee.

Katelyn pulled back her chair then glanced at her desk and saw the decorative bag with the single rose in a vase and a card. Katelyn plopped down in her chair as if all the wind had been knocked out of her. She touched the rose, bereaved in its scent then let her hand rest over the card before she opened it.

After a moment she opened the card and it said, "You were great yesterday. Your helped made a stranger feel at home." Justin. It took a while for Katelyn's brain to re-start and when it did she was flooded with emotions. This was one of the sweetest gestures she had ever received.

Katelyn thought,having dated only insensitive jerks that seldom thought about any one but them selves. Or worse, jerks took every act of consideration and kindness given to them as if it was no more than they deserved; nothing that required acknowledgement. Justin's simple gesture touched her deeply.

It took her a few seconds but after she had returned to some level of normal, she was about to go ask him if he wanted some coffee when she heard a knock on her door. She called out "come in" and Justin opened the door with two cups of coffee and a smile on his face. He said, "I thought you might like a cup." Katelyn smiled and it felt as if ice was melting from around her heart. She thanked him for the gift as she thought, "Is this what it means to be interested in a thoughtful man, wow! This is a mind blowing experience."

Justin sat at his desk as he heard her come into the agency and head for her office. Justin monitored her reaction to his gifts. He felt each emotion as she did and her pleasure triggered a response in him that was twice as strong as hers. The flower and card were just the right touch. The balance in his actions was flawless.

As he gave her time to get back to normal, he went to the kitchen and poured two cups of coffee. One cream two sugars, he saw her fix it that way when he first observed her that first day in the café. Justin put the lids on the cups then, when he knew she was about to rise and offer the coffee to him, he knocked on her door.

Rule was enraged! The stupid human female's emotions were like being on a rollercoaster. And at different times she actually burned him with the intensity of her feelings. She was starting to see this useless human male as something different! Sensitive, . . . "what in the name of hell is sensitive!"

Rule tried to input the thought that Justin was cheep because he did not buy her a dozen roses. But that thought only made matters worse, she laughed at that thought. The idea of him doing that would have been too much, the rose was perfect! Rule had to get out of her to catch his breath, In addition to every thing else she was getting on his nerves.

As he stepped out of her away from all those warm emotions, Rule began to worry. He was not only loosing ground but those dam emotions of hers were activating her natural defense system and not weeks but months of work was now in clear danger.

Rule weighted his options, endure the ridicule of an older demon in order to develop a strategy to combat this new threat or continue to try to do this on his own and risk loosing his prey (a shutter passed through Rule at the thought) as bad as it would be to have to ask for help it would be worse, much, much worse if he lost his prey on his own.

At least, if he asked for help and it did not work out he would have someone else to either blame or share the blame with. The punishment for loss of prey was server; any way to lessen that possibility had to be considered. Rule knew that asking for help was tricky; the request for help was only made in difficult situations; situations that often held the strongest possibility of loss of prey.

Older demons are required to render help when applied to (one of the few rules of hell) but they knew the seriousness of any situation where their help was required. They were aware that even with their help, loss of prey was possible and they knew that the supplicant would try to put the loss directly on them.

Finally they knew that the consequences to there status and pride (having their unbroken record tarnished even in a secondary situation) lowered their standing in the community and the actual physical pain of failure was unthinkable. Therefore older demons made it as difficult as possible for a younger demon to ask for help.

When ever possible the older demons would shift the request to another demon or come up with a creative option of finding and putting a buffer between themselves and the outcome. Unless of course the outcome was positive and the prey was brought home. Then the older demon would seek to take all of the praise, pushing the younger demon into a peripheral role and taking all of the credit themselves.

No older demon wanted his unbroken record of successes tampered with and no older demon wanted to pay the price for failure. Rule knew that he had to offer an inducement, to the older demon a sure bet to get the demon on board. Rule thought of JC the young sprit he had encountered earlier, surely if he could offer such a prize the old one would eventually choose to help.

Jason stood still as the pain began to subside. Slowly he recognized that he was not alone. Jason began to try to get up when the older demon rushed over and hit him upside the head. The older demon then spoke, "my name is Vane and the first lesson you need to learn is all failure comes with a price." All failure is painful that having been said, it is very good (for me) to meet you in person. Speaking in another's mind has its limitations. Since I brought you over it will be my job to insure that you know the rules. Vane watched as the truth entered Jason's mind. He watched quietly as varying expressions raced over Jason's face.

Vane took a deep breath "Oh" the smell of anguish associated with the newly dammed was truly like nothing else! "Oh" Vane thought, this is truly delicious because Jason seemed as if he could not believe what was happening to him, it was as if his mind was being faced with a reality that it simply could not accept!

Jason stood extremely still as the full impact of his choice hit him like a sledge hammer. In that one moment, with all the barriers of self lies striped away, it all became crystal clear. He had lost his faith; he had embraced arrogance, ego and pride. He felt himself too good to serve man; in fact he thought it should be the other way around! All of his choices and beliefs had lead him to where he now stood, at the door way to hell. Jason had made the choice to let his pain eat him rather than to absorb and re-direct his pain like he had been taught.

Jason felt that Vane was waiting for him to respond to some unanswered question. Jason searched his memory for any and all information about demons, a thought shot through his mind. A teacher had once said that the newly dammed have to make an initial choice regarding their standing in hell. The choices was to either be a demon who captures souls or one whose energy they would absorb, the idea was summed up in one statement, "bring food or be food." Jason stood and looked at Vane and before Vane could see or react to Jason's intent, Jason hit him as hard as he could.

Vane was caught off guard; he was so high off of Jason's pain, enjoying the backlash of the waves of pain rushing through Jason's system, when Vane found himself on the other side of the room with Jason standing over him ready for a fight. Vane smiled and said, "I believe you've just passed your first test, you've made your decision, pity!" I had looked forward to inviting you to dinner . . . as the main course. Jason kept his shields up as he radiated anger.

Chapter Eight

In the moment, when he had accessed everything he had been taught about demons, Jason was surprised at the wealth of information that rushed through his mind. He was surprised because he also remembered that once dammed he should no longer have had access to the photogenic memory that he inherited from his father or the knowledge bank stored in his shields.

Jason reflected, either that piece of information was wrong or he was being given access to his shields and memories for a reason. Jason did a quick reviewed of his memory and he could not remember one single piece of information which he had been taught, that turned out to be wrong. There was more going on here than Jason yet understood!

To be sure, Jason tested his angelic shields; first Jason turned his head to insure that nothing in either word, thought, deed or facial expression showed any emotions. This turned out to be a wise precaution, because Jason was completely surprise at finding out that his angelic memory and shields were both fully active and operating at his disposal still (Jason thought he might only have limited or partial access to this information, but his shields and memory responded to him as usual). Jason struggled to hide both what he was feeling and thinking when the final shock hit him.

No demon could penetrate angelic shielding. First because it blended so completely into its host that there was no way that any one could detect it. Angelic shields blended with the DNA structure of its host and communicated only with the host as naturally as bereaving.

It could only be heard by another at Jason invitation. In addition to which, as a light warrior, he blended naturally and easily into what ever realm he was in, looking just like the inhabitants of that realm. This was one of the unique gifts of his heritage, no one would know who or what he was unless he choose to let them see.

If Jason had been truly dammed, Vane would have seen him in his natural form and his shields would not have hid him (mainly because they would have been gone). Then Vane would have attacked him with out mercy, thinking that he was an angel because that is what his natural look resembled to both humans and demons.

Jason struggled to keep his hope hidden deep with in his angelic shields, as he continued to radiate anger. This was not hard to do because Jason was extremely angry but this time his anger was at himself. Jason now knew that he had a chance to alter his fate but one wrong move would dam him forever.

The creator smiled because Jason's one moment of clarity was equal to a genuine thought of humility. It was this choice for clarity which brought Jason a chance at redemption. The creator then triggered in Jason "the rule of options" the rule which now governed his life!

Jason then remembers a little thought of rule: "When you find yourself in trouble which is not completely a by product of your will, an option is granted but you must be still, wait for time and opportunity to create the only door to heaven's gate."

Jason was processing information on two levels, another angelic trait; As Jason listened while Vane explained the rules, process and procedures of his new realm Jason continued to try to understand why the rule of options was communicating with him. Jason "knew" that once he understood all that the rule was trying to tell him, he would then know both, what was right action and what his next step was in this situation should be.

Jason continued to review his situation and his actions. Jason thought; the Elder that he had grabbed was Elder Brown. Jason had a genuine respect and admiration for him. Jason did not want to hurt him but he thought that a cup or two of the Elder's ancient blood would go a long way toward giving him the strength he would need to survive in hell.

Jason also thought that yes at that time he was angry but underneath it all, he truly bore the Elder no ill will. It was Jason's true intent and belief that he could stop with only a cup or two of the Elder's blood and he had no intent to do any genuine or long term harm to him. It was this fact, that he truly bore the Elder no genuine harmful intent and that he had every sincere intention of stopping before any real harm could occur . . . which saved his soul. That; the fact that he had not been allowed to drink from the Elder in the first place.

Nonetheless, what Jason did not know was that if he had been successful in his attempt to drink from the elder . . . he would not have been able to stop! With each swallow Jason would have wanted more and could not have stopped him self until the elder was dead and this would have seal his fate into irreversible demon-hood.

There was no flexibility in hell! Every newly dammed soul who found himself in Jason's current position had one of two choices . . .. .bring food by become a demon or be food . . .by become someone's dinner. This decision was made with in minutes of the dammed soul's entry into hell. The dammed soul's handler would find any excuse (usually one which was unfair or made up) with which to attack a newly dammed soul with. Then depending on the new soul's response it was decided then and there which category the newly dammed soul would fall under.

Hell was no place for someone who could not whole there own. Therefore, when Vane knocked the hell out of Jason (for not being able to capture the blood of an elder), If Jason had not responded to the blow by returning one of his own or done nothing when Vane hit him . . . Vane would have apologized and stated that he understood how difficult it was to feel so lost and alone.

To make up for his disrespectful behavior, Vane would invite Jason to his home for dinner. Vane would then have said, we usually eat at eight but if you could arrive at six it would give us a chance to talk and get you prepared for your new position in hell.

Then upon Jason's arrival at Vane's home, at six o'clock, Jason would have been attacked by Vane's kitchen staff; his blood drained (as the main ingredient for several bottles of fresh blood wine, which would have been served with dinner) and his body roasted to perfection and served for dinner and ate at eight o'clock.

However, if the soul fought back . . . then he was demon material. It would then be Vane's job to give him the rules and regulations of his new home and act as a mentor, for a two month period of time after which Jason was on his own.

Hell needed new demons, the earth was a large area to cover and the human population seemed to be growing by leaps and bounds. Therefore, out of necessity there could only be one demon assigned to capture one human prey at a time (demons did not share and this rule kept confusion and demons in fighting down to a bare minimum) of course all rules have exceptions but in general this rule was followed.

To address this need for demons, every handler received three eatable souls for each new demon created. The handler was paid upon the completion of his mentor ship of the new demon. This way the handler had an incentive to contribute to the new demon population in hell and increase his personal wealth in the bargain.

Vane was as an older demon, this was the way demons of his age and rank presented themselves to those younger than themselves. Actually there were clear levels that Elder demons fell into but they all agreed that this information was only for those with the rank of older demon or above.

The reason that they kept there age and rank a secret was because this information gave a clear indication of the demon's level of power, strength and abilities. All of this was information that you do not want an enemy or an underling to know. In fact many of the Elder demons pretended that they were younger than they were, again to hid there power because an uninformed and under estimating enemy gave any older demon a clear advantage in a fight.

Another reason that they kept rank, age and strength hidden was because of the "law of favors." If a junior demon needed help bring his prey home, especially at the point in the battle when the junior demon thinks he might loose his prey, he had the right to put his petition of help before an older demon and the older demon had to help (that is if the junior demon could find one), older demons seemed to know when a junior demon was in need of help and usually made themselves as scarce as possible.

Now, if you are a junior demon in need help you are going to want to bring in the oldest, strongest, demon you could find. So to keep from being targeted, this knowledge was kept from younger demons. They simply had to petition the court and who ever was on duty had to answer the call.

Of course the older demon had the right to beat the hell out of any demon that asked for his help. Initially, this beating made younger demons either not submit a request for help or withdraw their request. But once the younger demons understood that to with draw a request only saved the older demon and made the younger demon's punishment much worse, especially if in the end he lost his prey, younger demons simply started taking the beating.

As soon as the younger demons truly understood, they began to accept the beating as part of the petition process. Because most demons desperate enough to make the request, were at a point in the seduction of the soul, where it looked like they were going to loose their prey any way. They were willing to take the beating to acquire help because the alternative was much, much worse.

Another reason the elder demon's did not want to be involved with a younger demon's problems was because the minute the petition was made (and not retracted) the Elder demon became responsible for insuring that the prey was brought home, at least until he could find a way to put the blame on or off on someone else.

In hell the motto was "Failure is not an option." There was a serious cost to pay for not bring home prey and the older the demon the longer and more painful the cost. Which is the primary reason why most older demons simply tried to avoid the issued completely by any and all means possible.

And most importantly almost none new an older demon's name. A demon's real or birth name held a great deal of power. With in a name, what few knew and even fewer would tell, was that any older demon could be summoned simply by calling for them with there birth name. Most elder demons had killed any newer demons that had the misfortune to find out either there name or more importantly how to use it.

In fact, there was one detail that only a hand full of demons knew which was, any demon had to obey any command, including that of ending there existence, if there birth name is spoken in a command surrounded by angelic light and sent to them with angelic communication.

There were safe-guards put in place during the creation of hell, a connection to there angelic heritage which prevented a demon being active in any realm but earth (as with any rule there were a few exceptions). These safe guards always gave angels the upper hand in any conflict.

And if few demons knew of these safe-guards the opposite was not true, all angels and light warriors knew and had the ability to access the birth name of any demon at will. This was the reason that any fallen angel or light warrior who had access to this knowledge via there access to the knowledge bank enclosed with in there shields were immediately stripped of there memory, knowledge and angelic shields once they were completely dammed.

Raphael continued to pray for his son, he heard the chores of prayers sent to the creator from the fathers of other light warriors on his behalf and he was warmed by the love they showed him and his child, in this there time of need. Raphael reached for his faith, knowing that real faith was strongest when no positive way out of a situation could be easily seen; he poured his will and his strength into his faith and his prayers.

The creator reviewed this current situation at hand; all was proceeding according to his plan. The children of man and angels held a special place in his heart. However, he pretended not to outwardly notice them but he showered them with grace. Jason was willful, like the human race, with dormant strengths he never bothered to cultivate. Jason paid little to no attention to detail and he tried to hide a great deal of pride, ego and arrogance.

Jason was well loved, though you could not tell it in his current state. Even in his doom, a backdoor, the creator did create. Two things would be accomplished if Jason choose the right path, his humility would be re-established and he would gain a new personal strength which would help him to accomplish any task.

This walk through hell would strip bare his illusions and require him to fight to attain that which he once took for granted and or as his due, as well as teach him what he was in danger of loosing. Jason would have to fight to re-establish his faith at all cost.

Everything he ever learned he would need to use to survive. In the end, If Jason chooses well, the creator would get a warrior with depth, humility and pride in his service to both god and man. Jason would either get through this experience pure as new snow or he would choose his negativity all of which were his choices to make. The creator would accept Jason's choice, what ever he chose and if necessary (even though it would break his heart), the creator would let Jason go.

Jason remembered now, it was called "the rule of options." Jason had a few minuets alone when Vane was called to come to some meeting. Again Jason repeated the rule giving it his full attention. He was in trouble and it was in part, a by-product of his choices. Jason was getting weary and now fighting the urge to feel sorry for him self. Jason re-directed his mind and though about memories of happier days, which help him fight off his fear of being overwhelmed by hopelessness.

Jason thought of a time when he and Justin were children, the memory warmed him and he wished he could have spoken to Justin once more before all of this began. Jason went completely still, that's it! I could not speak with Justin because my father gave me information which was forbidden. This was why a communication barrier was placed on my mind when I would have told Justin the same information!

Jason's father had told him everything he knew which was more than the rule of information allowed. That made his situation "trouble which is not completely a product of his will." The creator knew Jason had contributed considerably to the choices, which lead to his current situation. But, his father out of love for him, had broken the rule of information.

Which made his current situation, "not completely a product of his will." Jason thought of his father and how this situation must give him sincere pain. He wished he could tell his father how much he loved him and to let him know that he did not blame him. Jason repeated the second part of the rule of options, "an option is granted but you must be still, and wait for time and opportunity to create the only door to heaven's gate!"

Jason "knew" what right action was now. Jason had to appear evil with out actually being so. This task would require all of his skills and talents. It explained why he still had access to both his angelic memory and his shields. They were tools he would need to work his way out of this situation.

In time, if he made no mistakes, he would be given an opportunity to escape his current fate. Jason sincerely hoped he would recognize that opportunity when it presented its self. But in the mean time he had to persuade a series of demons that he was evil, even when he knew he could not be. Oh and he had to keep from being eaten alive in the bargain. Jason took a deep breath and sighed, it was not going to be easy but it was a chance and right now any chance beat no chance!

Chapter Nine

Katelyn and Justin had fallen into an easy natural habit of spending a lot of time together. Katelyn felt drawn to Justin it was as if she had known him forever, yet she could not explain why, it just felt that way. They had known each other for a little less than two month now and yet time seemed to be a different experience with him. Hours seemed like minutes when they were together laughing and talking.

But days seemed like years or that they had know each other for years, she shook her head and smiled as she tried to make sense out of her contradictory thoughts. They liked a lot of the same things and when they had a difference of opinions each was not only "ok" with the other having an alternate point of view but they liked seeing each situation from a completely different perspective.

The best thing however was that neither of them felt the need to force their opinions or views on the other; or get angry if the other did not agree. Katelyn had learned a long time ago that the world was simple and fair; people on the other hand were complicated and unfair. People always seemed to add a hidden agenda into the mix that was life. This was the equivalent of throwing mud on the inside of a finely tuned precision engine. This was why spending time with Justin was so special; he seemed to be exactly what he was a man who did not seem to have any hidden agendas.

Justin was interested in every aspect of Katelyn's life, past present and future. He told himself that the more he knew about her the easier it would be to protect her. But the truth was that there was nothing about Katelyn that did not matter to him. Justin had just asked Katelyn about her past relationships with other men and if there had ever been someone special to her in the past.

Katelyn was at a loss as to how to answer him; she was never very good at explaining the hidden agendas of others or the problems that they cause in most of her relationships. The closes thing that Katelyn had to a serious relationship was Steve. She gave Justin a rendition of the relationship, clear facts with out emotions or confusion yet she felt that her rendition missed a lot of subtle details.

In the back of her mind she thought of the second poem in her book, *Illusions.* It summed up all of the emotions and feelings that she did not know how to express; yet she felt silly using a poem to help him see what she felt about a relationship with another man. However, for the life of her, she could not think of another way to show him or tell him what she felt.

Katelyn lowered her head and stated that there was a poem that summed up all of her subtle and unexpressed emotions regarding that time with Steve and if he would like to hear it she would repeat it for him. Katelyn kept her eyes lowered and held her breath, she fully expected him to make some thoughtless comment or simply state that he was not into poetry or worse make fun of her. Justin put his hand under her chin and raised her eyes to look directly into his, he wanted her to understand and see his sincerity when he stated," I would love to hear it." Slowly Katelyn released her breath, a breath she did not know she was holding and in a very low voice she began to repeat the poem.

Illusions

He said I was beautiful and none could compare
With my soulful eyes and long dark hair
My laughter, my lips and the sway of my hips
Made his imagination run wild, he loved my class and my style

I said not a word, as I listened and heard
All of the things that he wanted from me
Not once did he ask,
If I would agree to the task

Of no longer being me
And become only what he could see,
What he wanted me to be

It is so clear that what makes a woman dear
Is the beauty of her mind and her thoughts,
The sweetness of her sprit,
The warmth of her soul
These are the things that will never grow old!

Why did he not ask, about my character and my faults?
Why did these things never enter his thought?
Ahh . . . it seems that he was never talking to me
But only to the illusion
He wanted me to be!

Justin felt as if he had been thunder struck! He sat their listening to her repeat a poem that he wrote over three hundred years ago. A poem he had wrote to sum up one of the primary problems in human relationship, which was the fact the most people are trying to get their needs met by the sacrifice of another's and that this is done so subtlety.

If you were to point out that this is what they were doing, most people would go straight into defense mode and strive to argue that what you are stating is simply not so. Time and time again Justin had watched as people destroyed relationships because their primary focus was on "I" and not "we."

Justin had published the poem over a hundred years ago in the hopes that if people could not accept this information if spoken directly to them, maybe they would or could accept the information if it was spoken to their instincts.

Maybe, if their instincts heard the truth of the words spoken in the poem, they would acknowledge that truth and allow the words to help plant the seeds of understanding to those open to change. This act was a little thing but Justin had seen little things have a great impact or domino effect which were the catalysis of major and or sweeping changes! The deeper reason that Justin wrote this poem was to tell his mate that her thought and their communication would always be important to him.

However, a strange thing happen after the poems were published, the words of the poems had simply faded from his memory. Justin now thought that that was seriously strange, because Justin had a memory that stretched over thousands of years and this was the first time that any memory had faded on its own.

Justin could delete information from his memory, if he choose but never before was the choice made for him. Now, with each word of the poem she spoke, his memory was restored and then he heard it . . . the unique music that each of his poems possessed.

As she finished the poem, Justin felt as if a piece of his soul had come home and lock into place. A piece of his soul that he did not know was missing, until he heard her beautiful voice speak the words he had written so long ago, words written with such love and care because they were written with his mate in his mind.

Justin loved the sound of his poem in Katelyn's voice, he thought that, "this was exactly the way a poem was meant to be experienced, through the beauty of the human voice." Then Justin thought "No" not just any voice but hers. Justin had written this poem (and all of the others) to and for her to express how important she was to him and that he would never take her for granted.

If he was ever lucky enough to find her, she would be the missing piece of his soul returned to him, the answer to the ache that he felt when he began this ascension. Justin also understood exactly how she had felt about that long ago pass relationship. Justin said a silent pray of gratitude because Steve was completely ignorant of the treasure that had once stood before him.

Justin ached for the pain that Steve had caused her but he rejoiced in the fact that Steve's actions had made her pull back from men in general and left her free and clear for him. Justin held her close and said, "I truly understand Katelyn and thank you for sharing your thoughts in such a beautiful way."

Katelyn now had to face some personal truths, she was genuinely drawn to Justin in fact he touched her in ways that no other man had. A part of her reminded her, that this meant it was time to end the closeness which was growing between them, before she got hurt. Justin was so thoughtful and caring with her. Nevertheless, she needed to remember that many of the sweet and attentive things he did could just as easily fall under the category of a friend as well as a budding romance and now Katelyn needed to know which she was dealing with.

Katelyn was beginning to wonder if yet again she was falling for someone who did not return her feelings. Katelyn refused to lie to herself (but not being ready to accept information that would hurt her, did not exactly fall into the category of self lying) and she had to admit that she did have feeling for him, feelings that ran a lot deeper than she was ready to acknowledge and feelings a lot more serious than friendship.

She needed to find some way of knowing how he truly felt about her, so she could decide if it really was time to run. Justin was listening; he monitored her thoughts because he wanted to be sure that he made no major or minor mistakes in his dealing with her. Today the monitoring clearly paid off, Justin was about to turn his attention to another direction when he heard her began to think about there relationship. Justin had to at times, use almost all of his considerable will power to tread lightly and not overwhelm her with how much he cared about her. Now it seems, he was better at treading lightly than he had originally thought. Justin loved katelyn, deeply and sincerely. The seeds of that love he felt, when he first met her had grown into a full blown soul level desire.

Justin wanted her so badly it had at times, interfered with his concentration. Justin thought,"it is time to take our relationship to the next level." It was the end of the day and Justin asked Katelyn, "can I buy you dinner, there are some things I want to discuss with you."

Justin could hear her getting ready to deny his request but when he said he had something to discuss with her it peaked her interest and curiosity so she gave him a hesitant, "ok." They stopped on the way to his apartment and picked up dinner from one of her favorite restaurants and Justin was very quiet as they drove from the restaurant to his apartment.

Once there, he set the table and they sat down and ate. Again they were both some what quiet and after the meal Justin put on some music and asked Katelyn to sit on the couch, as he paced in front of her trying to find the right word. Katelyn thought, "this is it, this is where he tells me he has a wife and kids and they are on there way to join him and he hopes his wife and I will be the best of friends."

Katelyn was trying to handle the pain of the moment with humor and she hoped it would be over quickly so she could go home and cry her self to sleep, as she tried to work thought another set of hopes and dreams flushed down the toilet. Katelyn was reflecting on the fact that losing Justin would hurt much more than she was ready to accept when Justin sat down besides her and looked her in the eyes and said "I love you."

I know it may be too soon for you to return my feelings and I hope to god that I am not scaring or overwhelming you. I thought you had a right to know that I am serious about you and us. I hope I have not blown it. Katelyn's mind went blank, she said,"did I hear you right?" Justin looked her in the eyes and said, "Yes, you did, I love you."

At that moment, the ice that Katelyn had been reinforcing around her heart shattered into a million pieces and she allowed her self for the first time to accept that she was in love with him too. Justin drew her slowly into his arms (giving her all the time in the world to pull back) and he kissed her. All of his love which he had been holding back went into that kiss.

Then he felt her response, which was as intense as his own, Justin knew it was the right time. When the kiss ended he said, "I don't want to have sex with you (smile), I want to make love to you." Katelyn wanted more of Justin and that kiss combined with the sexual dreams she had had about him made her feel as if this was just the natural next step.

Justin began to unbutton her blouse and when he saw her breast resting in a lacy concoction, her bra Justin sucked in his breath, she was more beautiful in reality than she had been in his late night dreams. Justin brushed his hand over the flesh and lace as his mouth watered at the thought of tasting her. As the blouse came off Justin unhooked her bra and her breast were the most beautiful things this side of heaven.

Justin lowered his head as he sought to take one into his mouth and slowly he began to suckle her and when he flicked his tongue over the tip of her breast, he almost moaned with the pleasure of the smell, taste and feel of her in his mouth. Katelyn wanted him almost as badly as he seemed to want her. The way he looked at her made her incredibly hot, the look in his eyes said that she was the most important thing in his world!

Then there was that kiss! That kiss which told her, that is exactly what she was to him. The pure pleasure reflected on his face he took off her blouse and bra made her hotter still. Then when he lowered his head to take her breast in his mouth and she felt his breath on her bare skin, she tensed in anticipation as he took her breast in to his mouth. Katelyn felt as if a bolt of lightening raced from the feel of his mouth around her breast straight to her womb, as the heat from his mouth caused her body to release moisture in anticipation of him inside of her.

Justin reluctantly with drew his mouth from her breast; he picked her up and took her to the bedroom. Katelyn wrapped her arms around his neck and rested her head between his shoulders and his heart. Justin laid her down gently and slowly began to completely undress her. She was breathtaking and he could just look at her for a life time.

Justin undressed as quickly as possible and joined her, loving the feel of the texture of her skin which felt like silk under his hand as his mouth took its time paying attention to each breast the attention that they each deserved. Then when he finally touched her between her legs she was wet. As hungry as he was for the taste of her, he dared not give in to that desire until she truly knew what that would mean for both of them.

For now he was content to slide him self between her legs and let her hot wetness enfold him as he did all in his power to bring her to a climax as soon as possible before he exploded. Katelyn was drowning in the feelings that Justin's mouth on her breast produced and when he with drew from her breast to move down further, all she wanted was for him to return.

Ealier, when he reached for her and picked her up to carry her into the bedroom, it all felt so right even when he finished undressing her, the look of utter happiness in his eyes warmed something deep inside of her. Then when he undressed, that warmth turned to fire! My god, Katelyn thought,

"The man was built like a Greek God and the fire in his eyes was the icing on the cake!

Justin touched her as if he could not get enough of how she felt. When he put his hand between her legs his hand was shaking with need then when he slid him self into her he was a perfect fit. As if he was made for her! Then he again took her breast into his mouth as he took his other hand and teased the sensitive bud right above the opening between her legs that he was so deeply imbedded in, as he drove into her all at the same time. Katelyn exploded and her explosion triggered his own as he climaxed with her. Later as Katelyn laided in his arms, almost a sleep, she whispered "I love you too."

Justin was still awake, enjoying the feel of her in his arms when he heard her say, "I love you too." Justin sent out a silent prayer of gratitude for having found her, for having her in his life, for the strength to protect and keep her safe!

Katelyn slowly woke up as she started to hear a tune deep in the core of her soul. A tune that increased in volume as she began to become more alert. The tune was familiar but she still could not place it or recognize it. There was something different about it. Then the difference and the tune became clear, it was the song associated with the third poem in her book. "You can live a life time in a moment."

A poem that she thought possessed some of the most beautiful words she had ever heard but the music associated with the poem, in the past, was extremely painful to her. The music felt like a knife going straight into the core of her heart which is why this poem was one she seldom read.

Katelyn did not know or understand why the music associated with this poem was so painful to her. Katelyn layed still as she listened to the music and suddenly she knew what the difference was, the music and the poem was no longer causing her pain! In stead she felt indescribable joy where the pain had once been. And she also now understood why the poem had hurt her in the first place.

The one thing that Katelyn had always wanted, (even when she could not admit it to her self) was to love and be loved in return. Because she was hiding that information from herself, the poem tried to bring that knowledge from deep with in her to the surface. The poem ran into her resistance, fear and lack of belief that she would ever be loved which caused her great pain. Justin had given her this exceptionally precious gift, the thing she had always needed and wanted and now that she had it, his love was the cause for the overwhelming joy she now felt.

Once when she was much younger she thought if I could love and truly be loved in return just once, I could hold on to that feeling for a life time. Katelyn now knew what a dangerous wish that had been because this type of love was addictive. How did they describe addiction in A.A., one drink is too many and a thousand is not enough. She would never get enough of Justin but what ever the future holds she had these moments with him, where she got her life and soul's wish . . .she had loved and been truly loved in return.

You can live a life time in a moment

You can live a life time in a moment, so no matter come what may, Loving you completely is what happened here today. As the day fades into night and loving you feels right . . . for this hour, this moment, today.

I descend slowly into your arms and all the world seems calm. The passion in your eyes, is such a sweet surprise. You touch me in a place, where there's no time or space, I've loved you, forever . . . today.

You can live a life time in a moment, in an hour or a day.

Sometimes, things happen that take your breath away. As we make love one last time and all of you is mine, for one precious moment in time.

As the words of the poem started to sing to its own unique music she saw something else, something that humbled her heart and caused tears to run down her cheeks. She was in awe as she followed the lines of the music and saw, actually saw Justin sitting at a desk writing the words of the poem.

She watched as he struggled to put into words, what he hoped he would feel about his mate. Then she watched further as he opened his heart and simply let the words flow out. Words for her to her, her most beloved book of poems had been written to and for her! Katelyn felt as if her heart was so full that it was truly at the point of exploding.

Justin was like a breath of fresh air, a man who knew how to separate intimacy from sex and when to give each. He knew when she simply needed to be held and he seemed to understand and share her passion as well. Katelyn thought back to the first time they made love, she remembered how surprised she was at how much the experience resembled the dreams she had had of being with him.

Justin had played his cards with a master's touch. Rule still did not know of Justin's true connection to Katelyn. There relationship made her smile so often that he would swear that her eyes were shinning. It hurt Justin's soul to know that soon he was going to have to tell her the complete truth because he did not know how she was going to take it . . .. ..and he could loose everything. Katelyn needed to know because if they were going to win this battle he was going to need her skills and ability to make it through the upcoming war.

Chapter Ten

Katelyn smiled when she thought of her initial belief that she could not actually make love to him because the reality could not live up to the dream! Katelyn laughed, boy was she wrong, the reality was so much better. Often when they made love she would swear that her enjoyment increased his and that was just about as sexy as it got. Katelyn was beginning to worry about when the ax would fall. Nothing this good could last for long because there was no such thing as perfect.

Justin felt her fears and worse he knew that not only was she right but he had a fairy good idea of when the ax would cut through to the truth. Rule was starting to get both worried and suspicious, which are two things that you did not want in a demon. Justin had made no mistakes but Rule was getting desperate. Rule was fighting off the fear of loosing his prey, these days Katelyn hardly listened to Rule at all and when she did more often than not, she laughed at him!

Rule shuttered, as he thought, "this was more than any demon should have to put up with!" Her defenses had all but locked him out of her mind. If he did not do something quickly, he was going to be in more trouble than Rule wanted to think about. Rule had put in a request for help and he was assigned to a demon named Vane. A meeting with an older demon had been set up. Rule did not know what he was most afraid of in this situation, all he knew was that he had to do something and he had to do it now!

That night Justin made love to her slowly, sweetly pouring all of his love for her into the act. Katelyn felt as if she was drowning in wave after wave of pure love she could feel it through her, around her and becoming a part of her. She loved this man and her feelings ran so deep that it actually scared her. It was as if she was receiving love poured directly into her soul and she was pouring her love into his soul as well.

For someone who believed that she was not capable of loving anyone, her feelings for Justin was first a surprise and then a shock. Now she feared that if he hurt her she would never recover. They had just finished making love and he was holding her as these thoughts ran through her head and she began to shake. Justin held her tighter and then with such sincerity and depth of emotions he said, "Katelyn, I love you; you are the other half of my soul . . ..I would give my life to keep you safe. Katelyn kissed him so fiercely and he felt the words in her mind glow into his, "how can only one half of a soul survive with out the other once they have found each other; where you go I'll follow."

Justin heard Katelyn's unspoken statement of love, it reverberated deep with in him. It tasted sweet and warm as his heart and his mind fused with her words; a deep tenderness rose out of his heart. Then like a flash across his conscious mind he saw words forming clearly in his brain, Justin stood very still as the third rule of fate busted upon him like angelic communication.

"The time of true mating is a test for the soul, few are chosen and even less beholds the blessing of such a state, because at each step more than death awaits."

When Justin left Katelyn that night he examined his feeling about this new rule. Justin "knew" the next step he had to take or the "right action." As the words showered over him he knew exactly what they meant. His time was running out and it was time to tell Katelyn who and what he was, as well as, about the pathways he had established with her and the amount of danger she was in.

Justin had to explain to her what an elemental was as he hoped and prayed she could accept the information. It was always a difficult and tricky situation to reveal knowledge that most humans have no understanding of. Justin hoped that she could accept what he was; that she was willing to understand the danger she faced. Most of all, he hoped that what he was would not scare her and that she did not turn away from him and the love he offered her. Justin needed Katelyn to understand how much he loved and needed her.

Justin knew that if she did turn away it would destroy a part of his soul. But worse it would leave him unable to fight for their survival to the best of his ability, because it would leave him with an open wound vulnerable to attack. Justin remembered once a teacher had tried to give him a better understanding of the information that this rule implied, by giving him (what he thought) was a simpler way to understand it. The teacher said, "To face you fear when you would rather move away and answer the need of another's simply request for you to "Stay."

Justin understood what his teacher had been trying to say, this was a situation that made you want to do anything other than stand and face it. Justin would rather not face Katelyn with the truth(s) he needed to tell her. Not now, right before the battle he knew was coming! At least, this way if she ultimately refused him, it would be after he did all he could to protect her.

Then a voice said can you protect her to the best of your ability with the fear of her loss eating away at you? You will become a self for-filling prophesy; bring to you that which you fear most. Justin took a deep breath, it seems that any path he took other than the one of pure honest outlined by the rule of fate lead to even worse consequences.

Justin let his breath out slowly, Right action required faith, the very fact that the rule came to him now was a clear indication of what the next step in right action was. As much as Justin would have rather choose a different path, he knew he could not live with himself if the end results of not listening to this rule, caused him not to be at his best in her defense. In addition to which her clear statement of love was a simple request, from her soul to his which said "stay," and that meant telling her the complete truth.

Justin took the next day to think of the best way to tell Katelyn all that he knew he must. Katelyn noticed the distracted air that Justin had all day as if something was weighing heavy on his mind. At first Katelyn thought that he was going to say that he had to leave her or "the ax is coming now." Her mind went blank at that thought.

But as the day progress, she felt the emotional rollercoaster of thoughts and feeling pouring from him. The first emotion that registered was overwhelming fear vibrating from him.

Then she felt an overwhelming need to follow right action and do his duty by her. But before she could think about what duty that could be, she felt his emotions shift again. Now feelings of love was coming from him so clearly that she thought she could reach out and touch it. Katelyn "knew" there was more going on then just his feeling for her and before she could begin to form any question he changed again! Katelyn decided to take her clue from him and wait until he was ready to talk to her, it was one of the hardest things she had ever done.

At the end of the day, Justin asked if they could pick up dinner and talk. He had some information that he needed to discuss with her. During dinner, they made small talk, now that it was established that he would be telling her what the problem was, neither in a hurry to deal with the subject at hand.

After dinner, Justin gathered up all the courage and faith he possessed and said gently, Katelyn, but before he could continue she said, "Tell me what is wrong!" Katelyn had walked through the day with each hour increasing her worry and concern until now she was almost afraid to ask. All that she knew was this information "scared" him and that caused her to fear as well.

Katelyn did not know what to do or how to voice her concern as she heard him gently call her name. Her response was automatic; she needed to know what was wrong! Justin sat up and pulled her to him as if this was the last time he would have the right to do so. Katelyn simply said, tell me. Justin began to explain the information slowly then he noticed that she was getting frustrated at his attempts to go slowly to keep from overwhelm her.

Then he gave her the information at a greater rate of speed. Justin noticed that Katelyn was absorbing the information at an extremely faster or super human rate. Justin heard a thought at the back of his mind which said; send the rest of the information via angelic communication. If she was unable to process the information in that form he would continued to give it to her at a slower more human pace. If she did absorbed the information at the quicker pace, the method of communication alone would go a long way toward helping her to believe him.

Justin sent the information via angelic communication. Justin was so shocked because not only did she receive the information but she sent him question back the same way. In addition to that fact, Justin was equally surprised that communicating this way with her was easy, when in the past angelic communication in human form was difficult alone and communicating to another human almost impossible. Katelyn absorbed the information, and although a small part of her was trying to tell her that this was impossible . . .it explained everything.

But she also saw, "saw" his fear of her rejection of him, she saw Justin trying to hide how devastated he would be if she did. He was trying to protect her from that knowledge, trying to give her time to come to terms with all she had learned. It was that, him trying to protect her from his fears, trying not to influence her and give her the right of choice even if the wrong answer would devastate him. It was that which banished all of any fears or concerns that she initially had.

Justin suggested that a bath would help her relax. He requested that she allowed him to bath her but she knew that he both wanted to keep busy and have an excuse to touch her . . .. .. he thought for maybe the last time. Katelyn needed time to think and the bath would help, she agreed.

An elemental, the knowledge he had given her explained so much about her life and why she never felt, thought or acted like others. This knowledge felt right! Justin had thrown a serious barrier around her mind to insure that no one could hear her thoughts and she had naturally reinforced the shield with her own defense system. A defense system, that would not be activated at all; or at her disposal now if not for Justin. A demon, she had unknowing been fighting a demon!

Using her defense system she located the demon and listen as he pleaded with someone for help because Justin intentionally (unknown to the demon), had reduced him from a presence in her mind to an after thought. Katelyn also understood why she needed this knowledge now. The demon was seeking reinforcements and they had to devise a battle strategy to deal with the new threat quickly before it hit.

She sensed she did not have much time left before demonic reinforcements arrived. Katelyn noticed that Justin had shut down communication between them in order to give her some private time with her thoughts. Katelyn smiled as she realized that she had the ability to open and close communications between them as well. Katelyn took a moment to marvel at their connections she could see the connecting lines from mind to mind, heart to heart and soul to soul . . .no wonder the sex had been mind blowing!

Justin had with drew from Katelyn's mind, he had finished her bath and put her in the bed while he had removed himself from her to sit in a chair which was by the window. Justin looked out the window at the stars and sent out a silent prayer. Justin prayed he had not been wrong in telling her the truth, prayed she would accept him and prayed that she understood the seriousness of the situation. Justin turned slowly toward the bed when he felt Katelyn looking at him. Her eyes were shinning! A moment later, a burst of angelic communication hit his mind which ended with, "we need to develop a battle strategy now because demon reinforcements are on the way!

Justin released a breath he did not know he was holding; he was almost dizzy from her response. Justin was about to apologize and give further reasons for his actions when he received a pulse that burst through his mind, heart, soul, body and sprit all at once which said, I love you! Justin came to her, and she threw back the covers of the bed. Justin sent Katelyn one last piece of information via angelic communication. Before Justin took one more step he needed Katelyn response. Katelyn smiled and said simply, "I am your mate."

Katelyn was taken completely off her guard with their mental communication! When he touched her mind with his she felt his love for her almost as if it was a living bereaving entity. She knew it was real because it felt in general like the love she received from her parents long ago but different, some how infused with Justin's unique sprit and with levels of passion she had never felt before.

This moment hit her so strong it felt like something solid enough to touch! Katelyn had never believed she was worthy of love on this soul deep level. On some unconscious level Katelyn felt that this was why her parents were taken away from her and why all of her life she believed that she would always be alone.

This belief was confirmed by the fact that every relationship she had ever had, until now, had ended badly with her being hurt in some way. Yet there he sat, she could feel his fear of her rejection of him as if it had taken on a life of its own. Yet he sat waiting for her to decide if she would choose to accept him, choose to love him; choose to become a part of him.

In that one moment all of her fear melted away; as she realized with humility and gratitude what a rare gift this man . . . who sat quietly looking out of the window and up at the stars truly was. Then she felt her love for him, like the sun dispelling the darkness bring forth a new day. Katelyn knew, with a core-level certainty that she had never felt before, that she had waited her whole life for this moment . . . this love and this man.

Justin kissed her and the pathway connections between them fused. You could not tell which belonged to Katelyn and which to Justin. Each could fell what the other felt; each opened both their heart and soul to the other. Nothing in Katelyn's life had ever given her the belief that she could feel so complete. Loosing nothing of her self but evolving into someone more truly her, than she had ever been before.

Justin kissed her and then kissed his way down to her breast. The pure pleasure that washed over Katelyn as he took her breast in his mouth was not just hers but his. Justin's pleasure at that feel and taste of her, she felt through the connected pathways they shared. As Katelyn's pleasure heightened and strengthen and blended with his, the feeling became so sweet it was almost unbearable.

Justin moved further down sending his pleasure at the feel, taste and smell of her directly into her mind it felt like fireworks bursting inside of her. Then she felt him taste her; at that moment he moaned and the sound reverberated all through her both inside and out.

Katelyn felt him experience something he had never felt before. Justin had never tasted any woman in this way before and he viewed her willingness to share herself with him on this level as one of the deepest gift she could give him. Katelyn's life force, the essence of her life force flowing from the cradle of where life would grow inside of her, her womb. This place from where the core essence of who she was, flowed from her into him.

Katelyn saw peripherally, in his mind, energy from her flowing to him. She saw that it connected them on an elemental level that she felt but did not yet fully understand. Katelyn sent her mind into his, which was the equivalent of a physical touch and his thoughts poured into her. Katelyn then touched her heart to his and felt such a deep well of love that it humbled her.

Then as she felt him want more of her, she could no longer focus on the unique pathways that they shared as she felt him activity seeking to have her explode in his mouth. Katelyn was for the first time in her life a true elemental. Because all she could do was ride the tide of emotions until she busted upon him like sunshine bursting out of the clouds.

Justin was home! He had wanted to taste her for so very long but for him it was not just a sexual act. This was the process of pulling her life force into his being. She would be connected to him heart, soul, sprit, mind and body all sealed with her DNA. This meant she was now a part of him, literally. Once she flowed into him, he knew he could never leave or walk away from her.

However until he had told her (which he did in the last burst of angelic communication he sent her before he joined her in the bed), about this process and what it meant. He could not bind her to him with out her knowledge and consent.

Until she knew what such an act meant, that this act was in fact the forming of an unbreakable bond, equal to but greater than a marriage. It is a life partnership, then when she stated, "I am your mate" she had in effect agreed to marry him. If she had not choose to be his mate, it would have been the greatest pain imaginable for Justin, to live with her inside of him and not have her in his life; that for him was the true meaning of hell.

As Justin kissed his way down her body he smelt the essence of her calling him. He "shook" with the desire to move slowly and not overwhelm her with his need. But the first taste of her was heaven! A taste so addictive it created a need which felt like a hunger rising from deep with in his heart. The moaned that rose from him, with his first taste of her, came straight from his soul.

She tasted like nothing he had ever known, in his very long life. He put his tongue deep inside of her trying to draw out every drop of her then he moved up a little and sucked the little bud above her opening and to his delight that action produced more of the unique and delicious essence that was his Katelyn.

He continued to produce and harvest until he felt her overwhelming emotion break through his fog of need and hunger. She was begging him to end the torture which had almost reached the level of driving her out of her mind. Justin realized that he was being selfish and applied himself to bring her a serious explosion. After which, he absorbed every drop he could, then he entered her and exploded inside of her with in seconds, connecting his mind to hers as he shared his pleasure with her.

Minutes later as they lay together in the aftermath of the most exquisite, unbelievable sexual experience Katelyn had ever had (one she would not have believed possible). Katelyn's mind drifted over some of what she had experienced, she had actually felt her energy flowing from her into him. Katelyn smiled as she thought about being a part of him. She tried but she simply could no longer concentrate; as she fell into a deep restful sleep her last thought was, "later it will be my turn."

Katelyn woke the next day with a sincere deep and profound peace. She felt different in ways she did not understand yet but she "knew' it was alright. Her first surprise was that Justin was still with her. Usually she fell asleep in his arms but when she woke the next day he would be gone. A moment later she understood why!

Justin had not trusted himself not to take advantage of her when there was so much about him that she did not know. He always made sure she was sleeping deeply before he left. Katelyn smiled she had always wondered how he managed to lock the door when he left; she assumed that he woke her up long enough to do so. However, now she knew that he did not need to wake her when he left nor did he need a door to leave.

Information started flowing into Katelyn's brain at an alarming rate but what surprised her most was the ease with which she processed the knowledge. In a matter of minutes everything that happened last night became crystal clear, Katelyn had only to focus on an idea or concept and knowledge flooded into her brain!

Justin woke up feeling as if he was floating on a cloud. Last night he had sealed the pathways of connection with Katelyn and he was now her mate! He could still taste her explosion as his mind was fused with hers; he experienced and shared her release while the incredible taste of her flowed into him.

Then when he entered her and shared his unshielded explosion with her as well, the experience was so intense that Justin thought, "If this was the beginning of what the sexual experience would be like with his mate, no wonder there was no knowledge in his race about a mated pair being unfaithful.

If last night was an example of what a mated pair shared in the sexual experience, then every sexual experience he had had before now was a very pale copy of the reality that was his Katelyn. Justin smiled a wicked grin; he had also heard that the sexual experience between mates got hotter with time and experience. However, right now Justin could not see how it was possible but he looked forward to finding out!

As Justin thought about his core connection with Katelyn, he noticed that there were some changes occurring with in him. Changes, that were both different types of changes and other changes at different stages of completion. Justin felt stronger than he had in a long time as if having a part of her inside of him was triggering a kind of metamorphism on his DNA level.

Justin knew that he could now see her where ever she was; he had only to focus on her and her exact location and what she was doing would communicate its self immediately to him. He could hear her, as long as she did not close the pathways between them. Justin knew that as the connection grew stronger he would be able to communicate with her from a great distance as if they were speaking face to face.

Chapter Eleven

Justin compared his current state to where he was a day or so ago. Justin felt renewed and refreshed, the way he normally would feel after several weeks' worth of rest in between assignments. Justin knew he had been operation at forty percent strength levels two days ago and today he was at ninety percent. Some how, Katelyn had increased his strength so naturally that he would bet she was totally unaware of what she had done.

Justin felt another piece of information about elementals fall into place, Katelyn was a self renewing energy source because she could draw from any of the four elements at any time or place and since these elements in some shape or fashion was always with in reach she could always enhance her strength and this was what they meant when they said that elementals enhanced and heighten power.

Katelyn was worth her weight in gold to both sides of the struggle. This meant that the demons would stop at nothing to try to obtain her. Fear was trying to overwhelm him but as he fought the fear and continued to relax the action triggered the fourth of "the rules of fate," this next law started to eliminate the fear as the rule grew stronger in his mind.

"Fire burns in different states, one may heal while another annihilate. Fire can purify all it holds like the phoenix of old rising from the ashes of its soul. A pure fire can burn both body and soul, which . . . depends on the sprit you hold."

Katelyn was energy. The ancient symbol of energy was fire. Justin opened up his mind and focused on seeing his fear then he felt sparks shooting thought the pathway connections that he shared with Katelyn. Justin pulled his mind back to the peripheral of his thoughts, as far away from the process as he could so that he could observed the energy sparks flowing from her seeking out and attaching its self to his fear.

Justin watched in unbelievable awe as he saw the sparks burning his fear to ash leaving nothing behind but a pure clear intent that failure was not an option and between the two of them a way not only had to be found but would be found. Justin knew that they had plans to make and strategies to formulate. Justin then sent the thought to Katelyn that they needed to call off today, Katelyn agreed.

Justin began his preparation for battle. As usual Justin did a complete systems check. Katelyn had burned away the fear in his mind body, sprit and heart all that was left was his soul. As a seasoned warrior Justin knew that fear was the gateway that negativity would seek out in him.

Justin knew that fear would allow the demon entry into him. The demons' standard method of operating would be to quietly connect with what ever part of him that was broadcasting fear the loudest. This area of fear would be the demon's surprise attack. Once the demon found the warrior's greatest fear he would hide there and when the demon needed, he would strike. The point would be either a desperate last attack to win or a smoke screen misdirection technique, which would allow the demon to leave before he was destroyed.

Then as the battle raged on (especially if the demon was loosing) the demon would seek any level of fear, no matter how small and send pulses of little energy to it, in the hopes of building the fear.

Older demons did this immediately after finding the warrior's biggest fear. Older demons did not take chances; they built as many little fears as they could find, almost from the beginning of the battle, so that these opportunities would be ready at a moment's need.

Younger demon would seek to build the little fears only if they thought it was needed, thus giving a clear indication to the warrior that the young one felt he was loosing the battle. Justin though of the irony of his situation, Katelyn was truly now one of his greatest strengths. Katelyn was also his greatest weakness, the thought of something hurting her was harder for him to accept than if it was being done to him. Not even Katelyn's' power of energy could burn his fear of her loss out of him!

Gabriel was not forbidden to look in on his child but the action was not encouraged, this was because knowledge would cause pain or pleasure in a fluid situation. A fluid situation was a situation that could change at a moments notice or the direction of a fluid situation changed with each piece of new information which was added to the situation.

Gabriel pulled his faith around him and remained invisible as he checked on his son. Justin had met his mate and he was deeply into the bonding phase of the mating relationship. Justin had won several battles with the demon and now he was preparing for an all out war. Gabriel now had a clearer understanding as to why this "check in" was not suggested.

The rule in a fluid situation was that change was the rule! And nothing could be inferred. A situations which looked negative at first, could have or be a hidden positive in the end and the other way around. The point of the check in was to get a feel for where they are in the process and that is exactly the information you don't get in a fluid situation.

Gabriel felt that it was time that Bree, Justin's mother, was aware of the struggle her child faced because knowing Bree, she was feeling the changes around Justin even if she did not know the specifies. Gabriel thought knowledge would relieve some of her concerns.

Bree lived in the realm that was assigned to light warriors and their families. Some parents had more than one child, although one child seemed to be the norm. Gabriel and Bree were friends but each had a life completely separate from the other. Gabriel was always surprised when ever he saw her, it always seemed like so little time had passed since his last visit; a genuine deep affection and care always greeted his first sight of her.

In each realm time moved differently, even though he knew her to be several centuries old she did not look older than a well taken care of human female around the age of 32. Her long life was necessary because any child or children that she gave birth to would lived very long lives and remained children for a long time. Bree was beautiful in mind, heart, soul and sprit and her body still stirred his blood as no woman ever had, before or since.

Gabriel floated to the door outside her home and expanded his senses, he felt her in the garden around the back of her home. Bree was sitting in a chair among the flowers with her eyes closed as different expressions passed across her face. Gabriel knew that look, it was just as he thought. She knew that Justin was in some kind of trouble or danger.

Bree spoke before she opened her eyes. After so many years of loving him she could always feel when he was near, pushing her emotions deep with in the core of her being she spoke "what is happening to our child, Gabriel?" Gabriel sent a burst of angelic communication to Bree to bring her up to date on there son's current situation.

It all made sense now, what she had been feeling. She had felt such a range of emotions coming from her child till it felt like the ebb and flow of the tide. In the past, when Bree would extend her senses out to understand her son current state, the emotions would whirl but soon settle down into a clear pattern which would let Bree know what he was doing and if every thing with him was well.

But lately the emotional pattern whirled but would not settle down enough for her to get an accurate read. He was supposed to visit after his last assignment but he was re-assigned so quickly before he got the chance to visit her and after that she had not gotten a accurate read on him since.

Bree considered the information that Gabriel had just sent her. She waved her hand and a chair, table and lunch appeared. After Gabriel was seated, Bree asked how much danger is he in. She knew that this "right of passage or ascension" was coming and she knew generally what the process entailed; now she wanted to know specifically how much trouble he was in. Bree also wanted to know if there was any way, with in the rules of communication, that she could help him.

Gabriel considered her request, he knew what his limitation in this situation was but he had not considered if or what Bree's role would or could be in this situation. She was his mother and as such she had "the right of summons" usually a tool for younger children but the right did extend to an adult child, three times per decade.

She also could do something that he could not; she could pour the purity of a mother's love directly into his soul which could strengthen his faith. For Gabriel to do this action it would be one of interference. However, because she was born human, it was simply the gift of a mother's love. Gabriel considered further and thought, given the length of her life that love had grown into a force of its own. A force that was not actually divine in nature like his but strong enough and pure enough to provide strength at a critical point in the battle.

Gabriel thought about this situation further and realized that other angels in the past had considered the mothers of their children unable (or to limited) to help. The mothers were usually kept unaware to spare them the pain of this process. Gabriel stripped away his own beliefs about human limitations in order to see the core truth of the situation. As he did so he heard one of the rules of fate, repeating over and over in his mind; this was a rule that Gabriel had not thought of in a long while which was:

"Can a master step into a student's place with humility, love and grace? Then yet again, learn what is needed in faith?"

The mothers! Here was a resource which could have a serious impact on the outcome of the battle. The mothers, a resource which was first overlooked to protect the mother from pain (or at least that is what the fathers told themselves) and later the mothers were overlooked out of habit. He had prayed for a way to help his child, the answer was so simple it had been overlooked time and time again.

Gabriel smiled when he thought about how the creator worked, the creator takes nothing for granted and from now on neither would he. Gabriel looked at Bree trying to assess her level of strength because in order to help their son she was going to have to be stronger than he had ever considered her to be. Bree noted the assessing look in Gabriel's expression and continued to wait calmly for him to understand what she already knew and that was a little help at a critical point could make a serious difference.

Bree was not an angel, she could not give Justin what his father could but in a situation where his father's hands were bounded, she was the next best option. Then Gabriel said, in order to pull Justin to you at the most critical moment and infuse him with love you will have to monitor the struggle leading up to the battle and the battle its self.

Gabriel shook with the emotions he had just experienced when he checked in on Justin. Gabriel felt waves of helplessness, fear concern and uncertainty. Gabriel sent this knowledge to Bree feeling that if he could not handle this situation well, how could she. Bree looked at Gabriel and said, "These emotions are part of being human, I have always dealt with them where you have not."

Gabriel stared at her and thought, "Another myth shattered." Gabriel then extended his senses and he could see and feel the quiet strength he had never noticed before in her, he thought "here again was something that she could do that he could not." Gabriel respect for the human race in that moment took on levels of growth that truly surprised him.

Gabriel was humbled by the genuine possibilities that the human race possessed; he could see on levels he never looked at before why the creator loved man so much. Gabriel had to this point, only seen the pieces which made up man. Now for the first time he saw that the whole was greater than the parts. Gabriel saw that the whole had massive untapped potential and it was this potential which the creator loved so much in man.

With Bree today Gabriel had experienced, for a moment, the wonder and the potential that the human race holds. Gabriel sent Bree the knowledge of how to monitor Justin, insuring that the system he helped her set up was with in the rules of communication. After this was done, another thought flashed in Gabriel's mind, "Bree would have a better understanding of how to interpret a fluid situation." She could give a greater insight into what Justin was experiencing because she could understand and interpret his emotions with an accurate clarity that he could not.

The creator had chosen the fathers of his nephliums or light warriors, with care. The creator had been monitoring the growth and development of evil since its creation. Now that Lucifer had found, Malik, the human who was to direct Lucifer's fate in the direction the creator had intended (which was the sole reason that Lucifer was allowed to exist). The creator needed a special type of warrior to illuminate the darkness in the human soul and act as a direct counter balance to Lucifer's demons.

The creator was aware that in addition to the one third, that of his angels who fell into darkness with Lucifer, another one-third of his angels had a hidden seed of negativity with in them regarding the creation of man. Each of these angels blamed man on some subtle and hidden level for the fall of their brothers in to darkness and had serious concerns as to whether man was worth their sacrifice. And, even though this one-third had held fast to their faith, the creator needed to eliminate the seed(s) of darkness that was planted in them when Lucifer walked amongst them, trying to recruit as many angels as possible to his cause.

It was these angels, the one-third with the seeds of negativity with in them, who were chosen to be the fathers of his light warriors. The creator knew that each of the fathers of his light warriors would love his son dearly. It was through that love that the creator hoped to heal his angels and help them let go of the seeds of negativity which was preventing their growth and or providing a road blocks between them and being their best selves.

After all, a real parent would do for his child what he would not do sometimes for himself. If letting go of his negativity would help his son through the ascension process, the creator had no doubt that each of the fathers would do just that.

Then if the son made it through the process, the creator would have a warrior whose soul and will had been tested in the fire and found to be exactly what the creator needed for keeping evil in check. The final plus was that the fathers, his angels, would now appreciate and love their consorts with out reservation and understand what a unique gift their consorts are in their lives. As the creator reviewed the situation he thought, this is an intricate process . . . to unlock hidden negativity with in an angel is a risky process . . . because the outcome was fluid, because free will (and his light warriors had free will) could sway the outcome either way.

Gabriel left soon after everything was set up. He promised to return soon, this was something in the past he never said. Now, not only did he say it but he meant it too because he wanted to see her again soon. Gabriel needed time to absorb and expound the meaning of all he had learned from her today. Gabriel returned home and prayed for clarity, right action and direction.

In the mist of his prayers Gabriel heard the thought, "something's must be experienced to be understood." You were chosen to be Justin's father because you could and would love him. You were chosen to mate with Bree because with her you would experience being loved by a human. Then through her you would experience your first taste of love for humanity as a whole.

Bree was a gift of insight that you chose not to see until your love for Justin required you to be open to any positive option which could help him. As the communication ended Gabriel knew it was time for core level complete truth because if opening up a little had yielded so much knowledge what would he learn if he opened up completely?

It was time for Gabriel to see all he could. If any hidden knowledge helped or could help his son, Gabriel was determined to find it. Gabriel sent love and truth to his sprit then opened up his mind and spirit to receive any core level information that this process revealed.

With in seconds Gabriel was on his knees begging for forgiveness. Gabriel memory took a journey back in time, only this time he saw himself from the outside in, rather than from the comfortable lies he told himself during that time by looking only from the inside out. Gabriel watched what he felt and thought when the creator first told his angels about the creation of man. Gabriel saw that this was when the first seeds of pride and lack of acceptance for man begin.

Gabriel knew that other angels felt the same way too. But Gabriel's love for the creator out weighed any thoughts to disobey. Gabriel remembered the creator looking at each of his angel during that time, Gabriel now knew that the creator was assessing the level of acceptance that each angel would feel regarding the conception and creation of man. The creator knew that Gabriel did not agree with the creation of man but Gabriel would do what the creator asked of him in faith and for now that was enough.

Gabriel also knew that each of the fathers of the warriors of light had the same feelings regarding man that he did. And each of the fathers needed to learn the lessons that he had learned today. In fact the ability of the fathers, to be open to growth, literally dictated the amount of help they could provide for there children during this process and the amount of options that this situation revealed and allowed.

This right of ascension was a test for the whole family. It was never just and only about Justin. Justin was just the focal point. Gabriel felt genuine pain when he thought of Bree. Gabriel had hurt her many times over and over again because he punished her because he felt it was an insult for the creator to ask him to be with her. Gabriel didn't want a human consort or a half-breed child. Still Gabriel knew he would do what was requested (ordered) to do.

Gabriel saw himself at the beginning of his relationship with Bree as he examined his feelings at the time. Gabriel simply intended to get the distasteful duty over with as soon as possible. Gabriel's plan was to impregnate her quickly and show up again when the child was born. Gabriel's memory skipped back to when he first saw Bree.

CHAPTER TWELVE

Bree was the middle daughter of a king. Her baby sister had been chosen to be the sacrifice to the gods (which meant she was originally to be his consort) but Bree's sister was deeply in love with another. Bree's sister had thrown her self at the feet of her father begging to be released.

This daughter was one of the King's favorite children therefore a petition (plea) was sent through the priest asking if another daughter could be chosen. The creator had left the answer of the petition to Gabriel and as far as Gabriel was concerned one human female was pretty much like the next. Permission was granted and Bree volunteered to take her sister's place. Bree knew that as the daughter of a king her marriage would be arranged based upon her father's wishes or political need.

Bree's older sister was currently in such a marriage and she was totally unhappy. Bree wanted to see one of her family members mated out of love and if it could not be her at least she could help to bring about the possibility for her baby sister. In addition to which the thought of being mistreated in a marriage for years and years was a thought to painful to contemplate.

Bree told her father that she would take her sister's place as a sacrifice to the gods, upon her father's word that he would allow her sister to marry her heart's choice. Her father agreed and the next day she was taken to the temple bathed and dressed and left alone. Bree had hoped that her death would be quick and as painless as possible.

Out of one eye Bree saw movement in the shadow and then she heard a voice which said, "Are you so eager for death." Gabriel walked into the light and he was the most beautiful man she had ever seen. Before Bree could say another word he picked her up and when she opened her eyes again she was in a bedroom, a bedroom more beautiful than her room at the palace. He placed her on the bed then walked to the window and looked out over the garden.

The look he gave her before he walked to the window was one that held several conflicting emotions. Bree did not know him well enough to understand what his expression implied. Gabriel looked out of the window trying to make sense out of his feelings. Bree was the most beautiful female he had ever seen and a part of him was drawn to her.

However, she was human and a part of him was repelled by her. She was his assigned consort and the thought both excited him and overwhelmed him at the same time. Gabriel needed to get away. He told her that she was safe and anything she wanted or needed would be provided for her, all she had to do was speak out a desire and with in reason it would materialize. Then Gabriel walked out the door, because he did not want to scare her by simply disappearing in front of her as he left. Bree stayed in the bed for a long time happy with the thought that he would come back soon and explain what was happening to her or at the very least tell her his name.

But after several hours she realized that she needed to relieve herself and she was hungry. She said almost in a whisper, I am hungry then on the side of the bed a tray of food appeared. Bree then said, my body needs to release water. Suddenly a door opened up to a very strange room. Bree saw a stool which was out in the open and it had water in it.

There was a sign that said sit and release water and waste from the body here. Bree thought, it is amazing the things you will try when you have no choice. Bree moved her gown up and sat down when she finished she saw some thing that looked like paper on a stand. Above the paper was another sign that said 'use paper to wipe away remaining moisture after reliving body, then place in stool."

She did and marveled at how soft the paper like substance was. After she had followed all the instructions and with in minutes of her completing this process a great whooshing sound came from the stool and with in seconds the waste was gone and the water was blue and clean and no trace of her actions remained. As soon as she finished a sink appeared with a sign above it stating "push here for water and here for soap." Bree washed her hands and went back into the bed room and began to eat. After which she laid down and fell asleep from the exhaustion of the day.

Gabriel went home and sat quietly in his sunlit room trying to get control of his emotions. Gabriel wanted her but then how else could it be. She was not just beautiful; she had the type of beauty that moved him. That thought was soon replaced with the thought that Gabriel did not want to touch her because to do so was one step removed from having sex with an animal.

To him her race was animals that walked on two rather than four legs. Gabriel avoided Bree for several days as time passed in his realm which was several weeks as time passed in her realm and the equivalent of several months in earth time.

Bree had figured out a few things in the weeks that she was left on her own. She was his assigned consort and he did not want her.

She did not know if he wanted another or no one at all or he simply did not want her. Bree sat in the garden alone, however she did not mind being alone since she had learned how to get her basic needs handled. Bree had created a library and began to read to her heart's content. At home she never had access to many books nor the time to enjoy them. As the daughter of a King she was taught to read but then told it was a skill that was a curtsey of her status not one she would be required to use.

Bree had always loved reading and having any book of her choosing and time to read was a huge treat. Bree knew that he would eventfully return and she had time to lock away her hurt at his abandonment and focus on how she was to handle both him and this new strange environment.

Bree knew what it was like to be mated to some one you did not want, having been the sounding board for her older married sister. Because of this Bree was prepared to treat him with real understanding. In the past she had only thought about what it would be like to be in a relationship with someone she didn't want. It never occurred to her that she would find herself in a situation where the opposite would be true, in that now she was in a relationship with some one who did not want her. Bree thought, "The gods do have a different sense of humor."

Gabriel materialized in the garden where Bree spent a great deal of time. At first he just watched her. She was his ideal of what true beauty looked like. Flawless skin, hair that looked like silk flowing down her back, eyes shining with amusement over some thing she just read and a soul that shined so purely that its radiance required him to tone it down.

She closed the scroll she was reading and before he could make up his mind to say something or simply go away, she said, "the very least you could do is tell me your name." Gabriel was taken by surprised he was cloaked and he had not intended for her to know he was here, yet she knew! Before he realized it he had solidified and asked, "How did you know I was here?"

Bree had gotten very adapt to the fell of her new home. The minute he came with in her environment she felt the change in the wind. At first she waited for him to make himself know, then after a few minutes she realized he had not decided if he was going to stay. So, Bree spoke hoping to draw him into solid form and it worked. Bree looked up at Gabriel and said, I felt your presence and since I've answered your question maybe you will answer mine, Gabriel looked at Bree with continued surprise and said my name is Gabriel.

Gabriel stopped his memory of these past events because now that knowledge brought him new information that he had not chosen to see then. Gabriel could now see that he had hurt her with his rejection of her but she had forgiven him as soon as she understood that the situation they were in was not of his choice. He now could see the pain radiating from her, with in her, that he had choose to ignore then.

Gabriel looked a little deeper into his memory and was shocked further when he saw the beginnings of pure love starting to grow in her for him. She had loved him almost from the beginning. Given how he had treated her; he had no idea why. This meant his careless behavior toward her over the years had caused her deep, real and continuing pain which she tried to hide deep inside her soul when ever he came around.

Since at the time, Gabriel did not want to know what she was feeling (he was too busy dealing with his own bruised ego and pride) the last thing he concerned him self with was her feeling and the last place he would look at, was what she felt for him in her soul. Therefore Bree was able to hide her love for him (with his help) very well.

Gabriel moved his memory forward. He had tried to stay away from Bree but he found himself thinking about her. He fought the desire that was building in him for her. Gabriel's initial plan was to get her pregnant, in a hurry, then go back to his duties and responsibilities (since with her pregnancy he would have done his duty). After a while he did not want to touch her for a completely different reason, Gabriel was seriously concerned that he would enjoy being with her and that was a risk he was not yet ready to take.

Bree did not push him on any level, when he showed up they would talk and sometimes it seemed that he was really getting to like her then he would end there discussion abruptly and leave in a hurry. Bree could see that he was hurting and she wanted to help him yet every attempt she made to reach out to him only seemed to make his pain worse. She did not know what to do so she opted to do nothing.

One day Gabriel came to her and told her what he was and why she was his consort. He explained the need for the creation of the warriors of light and that the parents for these children were chosen and that they were such a pair. He made it clear that this arrangement was not his choice. He then told her that as a human she had free will.

Therefore, if she chose not to accept him he had to respect her choices, he further explained that no punishment would be attached to her if she did not want an intimate relationship with him and she could live out her life in this house with all her needs met and no one to bother her. Or, he could and would return her to her father's home if she wished. Gabriel stated that she should not give him a answer now, that he would leave now and give her time to think it over.

A baby! Bree thought, how long had she wished for and not dared hope for a child. His child, a part of him that would love her and she could shower her love for him on their child. Bree thought about the situation further,

her compliance also protected him. He was actually trying to get around a mandate from the gods. Bree did not know much about how the gods operated but it seemed to her that the fact that Gabriel was trying to find a way not to comply with, what she assumed was, a direct order would have some server consequences for him.

Bree did not want to see Gabriel get in trouble or hurt. However, Bree was not one to lie to herself either. On a deeper level, this would give her the opportunity to be intimate with the only male she ever wanted to be intimate with. Even if it was only for a few times or even one time she would have that memory to see her through the pregnancy, then she would have her baby to love.

Bree knew that she could not say no to Gabriel, as she tried to cover her hurt at the fact that he did not want her the way she wanted him. Bree pushed her pain aside because she knew that it would all be worth it, to have his child growing inside her.

The next day Gabriel came back for his answer. The week had passed quietly for Bree; now with her feeling safely hidden she asked Gabriel a question, "what will happen to you if I don't agree?" Gabriel was not prepared for that question but as he thought about it, he answered as truthfully as he could. Gabriel said, another will probably be chosen and the process will start all over again. Bree then replied, "Do you think you will get away with it a second time?" Gabriel replied, get away with what? Bree smiled and said, get away with trying to talk the next human female into evoking her right of choice, so you don't have to touch her?

Gabriel took a deep breath, if she could figure out his actions so quickly then the creator already knew. Gabriel just looked at her and said, "What is your choice?" Bree looked at him and said, I am truly sorry . . .but I want a child. Gabriel touched her hand and the garden disappeared she was now in her bedroom already dressed in her night gown standing by her window. Gabriel was looking at her with serious hunger in his eyes as he asked her yet again if she was sure.

Bree looked at him and said, yes. Then Gabriel pulled her to him and kissed her. When Gabriel reached out to touch her he felt a connection between them come to life. One he had felt before, as he traced his memory,

Gabriel remembered that the connection began when he picked her up and brought her from the temple. Since Gabriel had never touched her since that time, the connection was incomplete. When Gabriel kissed Bree for the first time, he felt the connection snap into place.

They were a part of each other. Gabriel kissed her and kissed her he could not get enough of her. Gabriel picked her up and took her to bed. For the next week he stayed with her and he made love to her over and over again until, by the end of the week, she was pregnant.

Gabriel had just finished making love to Bree and he was holding her in his arms when he felt the stirring of a tiny life force. Through his connection with Bree he reached out and touched his child's mind. The tiny life force responded by demanding to know who he was and Gabriel almost laughed out loud at the demanding tone his son had used, Gabriel proudly responded, I am your father.

In that moment Gabriel felt such overwhelming love for his son, yes his child was a boy! That he could hardly wait until it was time for his child to be born. Gabriel visited Bree often during her pregnancy. He would put his hand on her stomach and feel the tiny life force growing with in her as Gabriel talked to his son and delighted in the questions that his child asked about life.

Gabriel was in a different realm when he heard Bree cry out with the first pains of labor. She had called for the mid wife and they were in attendance when he got there. Gabriel was just in time to see his son's head pop out and in moments the rest of him came out too. He checked on Bree to see if she was alright while the midwifes bathed the baby.

They put the baby between his mother and father. Justin turned his head from side to side as he looked at each of them and then he smiled. The love Gabriel had felt for his son, that was growing in him during her pregnancy burst out of him on an entirely new level with Justin's first smile. Bree looked at the love shinning out of Gabriel's eyes as he looked at their child. And she knew she had made the right choice.

Justin looked like his father. He was so beautiful he made her heart hurt, Gabriel asked her permission to name their child. Bree nodded and smiled.

Gabriel kissed his child and said, "It is good to finally met you Justin." Gabriel heard a faint voice saying, "it is very bright out here." Then Gabriel burst out laughing.

Not long after Justin's birth a male relative of Gabriel visited Bree and stated that he simply wanted to visit with both her and the child. He was sweet and kind and always brought some thing for both her and Justin. Bree felt completely comfortable in his presence yet she could never remember either his name or his visits to discuss with Gabriel when Gabriel visited later, which now was very often.

The creator also visited Justin often when he was a child. Justin was special because it was through him that the creator intended to straighten out several situations one of which was some of the lessons his father needed to learn. The Creator knew that Gabriel had resisted creating Justin. This made Justin's conception and birth all the more sweet to him.

Gabriel's memories had made full circle he now knew something which he should have known then. He loved Bree! And he loved his son but most of all he loved his creator who had taught him a deep level of humility, tempered with understanding. Gabriel remembered the feeling he had long ago when he stated he did not want a human consort or a half breed child. Gabriel shuttered at the thought because now he would give anything under the creator, to keep his son safe and he consort happy.

Chapter Thirteen

Jason had learned the rules in hell quickly and accurately; If Jason was going to survive, his life and more than that his soul, depended on that knowledge. If Jason was going to save both, he had to find ways to make those rules work for him and not against him. When he was offered food he pretended it was not good enough for him and that he would get his own.

This was a good attitude to adopt in hell first because no one was big on sharing so they had no problem with him turning up his nose at what they offered. They laughed at what they thought was Jason stupidity because he had no idea how difficult it was to obtain food. When they finished laughing they simply thought, "More for me!"

The real reason that Jason turned down the food was for two reasons: First, he did not need it. His body could sustain him for months in his father's realm if his need required it, this type of time difference between the realms equated to years in hell. Second, he knew the food would be poison to his system, plus the thought of eating what laughingly passed for food in hell, was to disgusting for words. Jason could not consume human flesh.

If and when the time came that some one would figure out that he never ate, It would cause suspicion. Jason hoped he would be out of hell before that happened, but still he had to be prepared. So he was working on a way to pass the poison around the outside of his system rather than through it, expelling it from him as soon as possible while surrounding the poisoned filth with the light from his angelic shields' to keep the poison from infecting him in any way.

Jason kept to himself. This too met with approval in hell every one was busy with prey and the less questions he asked the more he blended into the background drawing no attention to him self. Therefore, Jason was surprised when he got an order to report to Vane.

Jason put on his best snare (he had learned that you don't back down in hell even if out numbered or being insulted by an older demon). In hell, you took no insults you answered all insult with a fist to there mouth. As long as it was clear you were willing to fight, for the most part you were left alone.

Hell was a selfish realm and every body was more concerned with the prey they were trying to bring in than you, as long as you didn't threaten that prey. Jason materialized in Vane's house. Jason was thoughtful because there was also another demon there. Jason said nothing he just looked at Vane and the other demon.

The second demon looked as if Vane had beat the hell out of him and that demon was screaming about his rights. Jason did not know what rights the demon had but clearly there were a few. Vane looked at Rule and said, "Rule, shut up no one wants to hear you wine!" Rule replied, you can beat me until you get tired but we both know that it is nothing to what will happen to me if I loose my prey.

Especially, Rule continued, if I loose my prey and I did not ask for help before it was too late. That takes the punishment up to the next level and given that choice, I submit my self (here the demon bowed and presented himself in a supplicant's position) to your guidance and help in this matter (under his breath he said, as is my right).

Rule had applied through the proper channels for help or invoked the ancient "right of request" and received an appointment to meet with a Senior Demon named Vane. Rule thought that if he could give the Senior Demon a gift of the young sprit he had spoken to the other day, that maybe it would lessen the beaten that he knew he was going to get. Rule also wanted to keep from telling the Senior Demon that the prey he was loosing was an elemental.

Rule had a good strong energy signal from the young one and he was confident that he could now find him anywhere. Nonetheless, when Rule tried to track the young one's energy signal it was as if it simply disappeared! Rule had run out of time and he did not have the time to try to track the young one with a more intricate method. Rule now had to face Vane with no gift to ease the beating and no help in keep Vane unaware about the elemental's powers.

If the Senior Demon knew that the prey was an elemental he would definitely try to steal her. Vane would also be aware that Rule was much closer to loosing the powerful prey and be even more reluctant to provide assistance. Rule thought, this is not fair, I had a good energy lock on the young one . . . why is this happening to me.

Vane shot Rule another vicious look, then addressed himself to Jason and said, this piece of maggot shit, then Vane looked at the demon he had referred to as Rule, has invoked an ancient "right of request." This useless excuse of a demon is in the process of loosing his prey so he comes crying for help, something that only a demon with no pride, skills or ability would ever consider doing.

Vane was mad; he had been covering for another older demon when Rules' request came in. Vane was mad because someone had done to him what he in the past had done to others. Vane had been to busy with the final stages of drawing Jason in to hell, which meant he had not kept his ear to the ground the way he should have. This meant he was not informed that a demon was on the serious side of loosing his prey.

In the past when such knowledge had reached him in time he would make himself scarce, almost untraceable until another older demon got caught unaware and was forced to deal with the situation. This was the first time Vane had got caught and he did not like it one bit!

Vane looked at Jason and blamed him. It was Jason's fault he was in this trap and make no mistake, it was a trap. Vane overlooked the fact that training Jason was simply part of his responsibility as the older demon that brought him over and that any fault in this situation was his because one never gets too comfortable in hell. You must always be alert to what is going on around you because when you stop being alert, that is when you get caught and Vane knew that he was well and truly caught.

Vane beat, tortured and belittled Rule for days but no matter how Vane treated Rule, Rule would not retract his request for help which meant Vane had a serious problem. Only a demon at the point of seriously loosing their prey would subject himself to the process of pain involved in getting help because if he had any other option he would take it.

Therefore, if Vane did not help him and Rule lost his prey, Rule would blame the whole thing on Vane and the little maggot would have a good case for getting away as close to blame free as possible. If Vane stepped in to help and they still lost the prey, again Rule would and could put all of the blame on Vane.

Vane needed a plan and a scapegoat, because unless he could figure out a method of putting a buffer between him and this loosing situation, Vane would be the one paying the bill for this failure. The thought of failure sent a cold shiver down Vane's spine. He had to pull Jason's into this mess. Then if failure occurred, Vane would have done what the law required.

The law only stated that Vane had to provide help the law did not say how. Vane's course was set; he would send help . . . Jason. However, at the same time if or when they failed it would be on them. If by some miracle they succeeded, Vane of course would take the credit for being the master mind of the situation. All of this was going through Vane's mind when he told Rule to explain his problem to Jason.

At that moment Rule knew exactly what Vane was doing, he was throwing the rookie at him when Rule needed a master. Rule did as he was requested and soon he had outlined his problem which centered around the prey's new boyfriend some one named Justin Warrant.

Jason stood perfectly still seriously glad again that he had the protection of his angelic shields. The angelic shields that hid his shock when he heard Justin's name. Jason knew that Warren was a last name that Justin used a lot. Jason also new that Justin had recently been given a new assignment.

No one notice that Jason said nothing as he listen to Rule blamed the influence of the prey's new boyfriend; how he made her so happy that it had all but shut him out of his prey's mind. Jason thought that's not all he was doing! Vane told Rule that Jason would help him with his prey.

Rule started to scream that this was the equal of no help at all. He needed a master not a rookie! Vane knocked Rule across the room and said, "You have asked for help and it has been given. Do you refuse this offer?" Rule knew he had no choice. If he refused Jason's help, Vane could and would wash his hands of him because the law is considered fulfilled if help is offered and if the supplicant declines the offered help.....well then it was now his problem alone.

Rule was practical, Jason may not be much help but at least it was something. Jason dared not hope, but maybe just maybe, that doorway that he had been looking for had just appeared in the distance. Jason knew he had to take the lead in this venture. Jason had to figure out a way to impress and seem to help Rule, but at the same time find interventions that would not harm Justin or his assignment.

Maybe there was a way to communicate his current situation to Justin and finally they could come up with a plan to save both of there behinds. Jason asked Rule to replay some of the situations he had encountered with his prey. Jason watched Rule's sad attempts to counter what he thought were Justin's influence on Katelyn.

Nonetheless, Jason saw the pathway lines of connection between the two, Justin had met his mate! Wow! The minute Jason thought he saw some daylight in this situation, immediately several serious obstacles presented themselves. Jason thought, "getting to that door was looking harder and harder" this situation just kept getting worse.

Jason asked Rule, "What's so special about the human female (he needed to think of her in those terms because demons never used the names of their prey)." Rule replied that the prey was something called an elemental. Rule said that he was not quite sure just what that was but she had a serious defense system. Jason thought an elemental! Just when you thought things could not get any worse, surprise, they do!

An elemental, they were beings that had the ability to channel pure energy into either demon or light warrior, increasing the power off the charts, to whom ever they choose to connect themselves too. A powerful weapon for both sides! Jason could see that Rule knew more than he was saying but then . . . so did he.

Justin thought about the upcoming battle and knew he was broadcasting his fear for Katelyn loud and clear. Justin also knew that this fear would provide the demon there best focus for attacking him. Justin was at an impasse as he felt the fear radiating from his soul; he knew that the demon would feel it too. At that moment Justin felt a thought pushing its way pass the fear and anxiety as if riding on the strength of some catalyst as a thought burst upon his brain like an explosion! The fifth law of faith:

" To let go of your strength when you need it most; to walk in faith when there is no hope."

Justin reviewed the rule in his mind; he agreed that currently he did not see anyway to hide his fear for Katelyn and that meant there truly was no hope. He would be the author of his own destruction. Justin tried to quiet his mind as he did he remembered something he had been taught years ago which was "strength and fear are opposite sides of the same coin."

And with that piece of the puzzle, right action became clear! It was not his strength he needed but his faith. Strength and fear these were his human traits. Faith and the power of love were his angelic traits. This fifth law spoke to the introduction of a living faith combined with genuine love, and how this combination becomes a powerful weapon!

For the first time Justin understood both sides of his nature. Even more importantly he understood how the two would/could work together as one. Justin had always thought of the creator as a family member. A grandfatherly type gentleman like the one who brought him gifts when he was a child; someone who always filled him with joy when ever he was in his presence.

For the first time Justin saw the creator the way his father did, as a being of infinite power and pure radiance. As if Justin had followed some connection through his father and saw the creator through his eyes. Through that same connection, Justin sent deep and sincere love to the creator and a moment later a burst of pure love slammed into Justin, radiating through out him to every part of his being. This energy cut in to his soul and infused his insides (some dormant part of him) with the faith which was residing at the core of his soul.

This energy was like a match that lit a fire of faith which came to life and burned brightly. Providing a deep inner warmth, that he had never known before. Justin now understood that he did not have to hide his fear for Katelyn he could use this living faith and love to simply burn the fear away by surrounding it with love.

It was as if he now had Katelyn's talent but on a different level. Since Justin had told Katelyn who and what he was he had remained open to her and if she chose Katelyn could feel and hear all Justin felt and thought. Katelyn was listening to all that had taken place inside him.

She felt "felt" the birth of faith inside him take place as she experienced the wonder at the knowledge Justin had shared with her. Now in the aftermath of that glow, Katelyn had to deal with her fears that she was a liability to him in this upcoming battle and that sent fear strait to her heart.

Justin was examining the new aspect of his faith when he felt fear cut through him and instantly he knew it was not his fear but Katelyn's. Justin smiled because he not only understood her fear; he knew what she needed to learn to eliminate it. Justin had always marveled at the gifts he had received from his mother, strength, patience, understanding to name a few, but one of his mother's greatest gifts was her the ability to compartmentalize.

Most humans currently compartmentalize only on a purely instinctual level which was the reason that humans could have so many conflicting emotions and beliefs going on inside of them at the same time. One day, when they learned to understand this unique ability, they would see it as the gift it is, rather than one of the foundational reason for most of the confusion in there lives.

Humans have the ability to link their mind, sprit, body, heart and soul literally all that they are into a concentrated force guided by faith and will which produces an almost unstoppable power, second in strength only to pure love. Katelyn was an elemental and human. She also had her own unique powers from her natural abilities as an elemental. Now she also had his knowledge to add to her unique powers and on her own she would be almost as powerful as him, different but just as important in the upcoming battle. Katelyn needed to connect fully and completely with each aspect of her elemental nature and power; through the knowledge she would gain from compartmentalizing her talents and abilities she would have full use of them.

Bree monitored her child and watched as he struggled with his fear for his mate and the effect it would have in the up coming battle. The fear was so strong she could see the next rule of fate struggling to get through his fear and that fear blocking the rule at every turn. On a purely instinctual level Bree sent a burst of pure love to her child. Bree watched in shock, as the love she sent became a living burst of energy which connected with the rule of fate and broke through to her son conscious mind where he could hear, see and understand the knowledge.

Bree waved her hand across the monitor, she needed time to think and reflect. Did she interfere? Had she unknowingly transgressed against the rule of communication? As these thoughts were running around in her head, Bree was startled by the mental equivalent of a knock on her door. Bree responded "enter."

Materializing in front of her was the older male relative of Gabriel who had visited her often when Justin was a child. Even now he still dropped by but a little less frequent. He took one look at her and said, "Child is there anything wrong?" Bree was upset and glad to have the opportunity to unburden her thoughts with someone she instinctually trusted, she responded by asking a question, "Do you understand the rules of communication and if I explain what I have just done and what happened as a result of it, can you tell me if I broke the rule?"

The gentleman smiled and said tell me child and I will advise you. Bree used angelic communication but did not notice either that she had done so or the fact that the gentleman had no problem understanding and accepting her thoughts. Angelic communication was an intimate method of communication and it opened up your thoughts and feelings on levels that you may not want to share with others. Therefore, only a generic version of it was use to communicate information in general when you were in a hurry. This version blocked certain pathways and limited another's assess to your mind. Bree used the complete version of angelic communication because she needed to know if on any level she had done something wrong.

After the information was sent, the gentleman said, "you are an elemental, what you did was as natural as bereaving." You were simply being what you are and no rule was broken. Bree did not know why but somehow she felt as if anyone would know whether or not she broke the rule, he would be the one and his reassurance put her sprit and heart at rest.

After monitoring Justin, Bree knew what an elemental was. So many things made sense with that knowledge. It was like having the key piece of a puzzle finally given to you and with that piece the whole puzzle fit together and now the whole picture made sense. She had wondered why she had been chosen to be mated with Gabriel and not another of her sisters.

This explained so much, it explained why solitude has never bothered her; she was often alone but never lonely. She always felt at one with nature which was why she spent so much time in her garden. She knew that Gabriel loved her; she could see it even if he could not. She "knew" that when the time was right like that piece of the puzzle, all would fit together.

The gentleman watched as Bree assimilated the information he had given her then he said, "You needed to know what you are; that information will be of great value to you when you are called upon to help your son. Remember you are stronger than you know. Trust in that strength and in your instincts and yourself." While Bree was still trying to get over the shock of the information that she had received the gentleman said he would leave her now, she needed time to soak it all in.

The creator left Bree's presence having put one of the final pieces of his plan in place. He left the cloak of forgetfulness over her regarding his visit, leaving her access only to the information he had gave her. He liked her, she made him feel as if he had a place in her family and it was a feeling that warmed him, to be appreciated and liked simply because someone chooses to offer you this precious gift and for no other reason.

True Bree only saw the kind gentleman which was something else he appreciated about her; the love in her required only the same response from him. Therefore the many facets of who he was, was not necessary for her to see. He basked in the love she showed him while asking nothing in return. He treasured highly the time he spent with her. The creator had been impressed with Bree from the conception of her birth, which is why he had chosen her for Gabriel.

CHAPTER FOURTEEN

Rule was uncomfortable with Jason, there was something about him that he could not put his finger on, Jason seemed to self contained and every time he tried to read his emotions and thought Rule got nothing. There should be fear, uncertainty and anger but "nothing" was unusual. But then Rule thought, all demons do not trust one another and most were solitary being and no demons wanted you to know what they truly think or feel.

It was just that as a new demon, Jason should have showed more weakness and the fact that he had learned this lesson so quickly meant that he could not be used as most new demons were, the way Rule had been. Rule had looked forward to giving back some of what he had to take as a rookie or as a new demon and now he felt cheated because their was something about Jason that told Rule, he could not use Jason that same way.

Rules brighten up as he thought of the fact that if they failed, he could blame both of them. He could blame Vane for sticking him with a new demon and Jason for being useless. If he could make a genuine case for Vane's lack of help by sticking him with a new, untested demon he could put two thirds of the blame on them. Hell! Maybe even more, in which case he would receive a beating but the greater share of the punishment would be given to Vane.

Rule was beginning to feel better now that he had figured out a way to cover his behind no matter how this situation worked out; he would be "ok." Jason stood by a window looking as if the last thing on his mind was Rule, when in fact, Jason had floated quietly in to Rules mind. Jason was both listening to his thoughts and looking for a way to establish a connection with him, one that would be completely unnoticed by Rule or any other demon.

Now the Jason fully understood Rule's objective he began to form a plan, "divide and conquer" Slowly, carefully and in extremely subtle ways Jason would implant uncertainty with both Vane and Rule toward each other. All while looking completely unaware of either the tension between Rule and Vane or the fact that comments that he was going to make would seem like he was an asset to each against the other.

Jason thought the naivety of being a new demon could serve him well. Jason asked Rule (in a voice full of curiosity only) why did Vane beat him for asking for help and then help him even when it was clear the Vane did not want too? Jason pitched his voice at just the right level to make the question seem like one a new demon, who was trying to understand the rules in his new realm would ask. While at the same time appearing as if he really did not care whether Rule answered him or not. Jason also threw in a little but extremely powerful deeply hidden, dissipating compulsion because he wanted Rule to be truthful with him.

Rule did a quick scan of Jason to see if on any level he was trying to make fun of him but the only read he picked up was one of mild curiosity about an issue that did not make sense; since it did not concern him, he had no deeper interest in the question than a passing thought. Rule relaxed and mentally focused on Jason's question to him and in a rare moment of truthfulness, Rule said, "Vane beat me simply because he can on one level. Then he beat me because asking for help meant a possibility of lost prey and that is a situation that Vane does not want to be associated with. Vane beats me because he could not refuse my request so he takes his anger out on me; he also beats me to make sure that I understand my place on the food chain. Finally, he beat me because the only way for him to get out of helping me is for me, to with draw my request for help. Vane hopes that in a rare moment of anger and stupidity, I might do just that!

Rule shook his head as he wondered at his brief moment of truthfulness as he finally came back to himself and answered in a more Rule like fashion. Vane beats me because he is jealous of me. I have been given the seduction of a great asset, elementals possess a power for which my master would reward me highly for bring her home. On the decent to hell I will be able to absorb some of her power, this will give me a greater status than Vane and then we will see who beats who!

Rule could not figure out why initially he told Jason the truth. Rule thought, probably because he was feeling sorry for himself; partly because he wanted to express his hatred and anger at Vane. Definitely, because as with any demon, every problem a demon has ever had was never their fault. This mid-level demon saw Justin's mate as his ticket toward his master's favor; this meant he would stop at nothing to accomplish his intentions. Now Jason thought, "What was the best method of communicating this information to Vane!"

A few minutes later, a summons came for Jason to attend Vane. Rule agreed that there was little more that could be done at this moment and of course, Vane as an older demon must receive there respect and response when he called. Besides Rule needed silence and some time to thing and plan his next attack.

Jason materialized in Vane's home and was beckoned forward. Vane stopped pacing and began by venting about the requirements of his position. Requirement, Vane said, that gave a low-level demon like Rule access to him at all. Jason listened and waited for the right moment to initiate his plan. Vane started probing Jason.

Vane obviously did not trust Rule and based on the questions he was asking; Jason knew it was all a subtle attempt to place him in the role of unknowing informant. Vane asked Jason if he had learned anything of importance about the prey. (Another of the gifts of Jason's inheritance was that no matter how either humans or demons tried to disguise there motives or intent, this information always revealed it's self to him). The role that Vane thought he was setting Jason up to play (with out Jason's knowledge) was exactly the role that Jason needed and intended to be in, to put his plan into action. Jason said (in a voice that seemed like he was getting tired of the discussion) Rule seems to think that his prey is some special prize and that it was some kind of honor to be chosen to bring her home.

Rule said that you are probably jealous of the honor that this situation will give him. Vane, caught up in the insult of Rule's statement, almost missed the diamond hidden in the crap, almost! Vane calmed his anger and focused in on the diamond and then he casually said, "Do you have any idea why Rule thinks his prey is so special?"

Jason paused for a moment as if he needed time to remember this portion of the conversation with Rule then Jason smiled and said, he called her "an elemental" what ever that means. Vane stood extremely still as the new possibilities of the situation presented themselves to him. The little mud sucking worm! How dare Rule keep such vital information from him.

This confirmed all of Vane's suspicions that Rule was setting him up. Vane was pleased with Jason because already he had proven himself useful. Vane believed that Jason did not know the importance of the information that he had just given him.

Vane smiled this was so delicious, Yes! Jason was going to be an excellent asset in the future. Unless of course, Vane needed to use him as an escape goat and in which case, he was still an excellent asset.

Jason watched as Vane's extremely expressive face, told him every thing that he needed to know. Jason was going to need split-second timing and extreme attention to detail to pull this off. Vane stated that he would arrange a much better apartment for Jason because, Vane said, he prided himself on rewarding success. Jason looked as Vane as if he truly did not know what Vane was referring to, but pleased to have better accommodations none the less. Vane noted Jason's response and was even more pleased because he believed that it confirmed that Jason did not have a clue about the importance of the information he had just given him and that was just the way Vane wanted him to be.

Gabriel went to visit Bree, both because he really wanted to see her and because he wanted to check in on Justin, through her. Bree again was seated in the garden she heard the mental knock and replied "enter." Gabriel materialized in front of her. Bree looked tired and Gabriel asked if she was concerned about Justin. Bree said "Yes." Gabriel looked closer because now he no longer settled for the easy answers from her, the one's which required no effort or insight on his part to understand; so he looked deeper and to his surprise he noticed that Bree was worried about him as well as Justin.

Gabriel was touched, this was the first time (to his knowledge) that any one had considered how he was dealing with the lessons he faced, the feeling was . . . "sweet." A chair materialized and Gabriel sat down. Gabriel was silent for a moment then he said, I have behaved badly toward you for many, many years.

Bree looked as if she was about to interrupt him when Gabriel said, No please, let me say this. I need to say this, Gabriel stood up and turned away from Bree as if what he was about to say would be to painful, if he had to look into her eyes as he spoke.

Gabriel started to speak slowly as he said, initially I was proud of my status among the first line of angels, I believed that pride was one of the main lessons I needed to deal with on this journey. When I was first informed that I was expected, no required, to take a human female as a consort . . . deep in a part of my heart I felt lessened.

I had not yet truly formed a solid belief regarding mankind on my own. My faith stated that I follow the creator's will in all things but watching a third of my brothers loose there grace as they followed Lucifer to the neither regions, left a sour taste in me regarding man.

It seemed such a high price to pay simply to give man the ability to have free will or the ability to choose something other than the creator. I did not understand the importance of that choice or why the ability to choose came with such a high price. So later when I was commanded to take a human consort, it seemed that yet again on different level, angels were to be pawns in the development of man.

These feelings I hid so deep inside of my heart that even I did not know how deeply they were imbedded with in me. Now I know that every angel chosen, to take a human consort, felt the same exact feelings that I did and we all had many of the same lessons to learn on different levels and to different degrees. I have now learned that when you lie to your self you create a place in your heart for negativity to grow.

Simply because you choose not to see your negativity, bury it or hide from it, it does not mean that the negativity does not affect all that you are in hundreds of ways that you can not conceive of; in subtle ways which are both pervasive and so insidious. I did not see that even my reaction to you and our relationship in so many ways was a direct result of this negativity which produced my believed indifference to you and caused you a great deal of pain for so many years, this core level selfishness in my actions toward you is truly unforgivable.

You were my escape goat. I punished you because I thought you too beautiful for words, from the first moment I saw you. I kept you at a distance because I un-spokenly chose not to love you, yet I was drawn to you in so many ways and on so many levels. The week we spent together when Justin was conceived, let me know your sprit and the brightness and beauty of your soul.

Yet even then, I convinced my self that I was only doing that which I was commanded to do. When you were pregnant with Justin, you were pure radiance. The love I saw you pour into, over and around Justin warmed me deeply; I was so proud of you both. As Justin grew, I think the thing I loved most about him was how much your soul shined through him.

How much like you he was. It was as if all the love that I could not or would not allow my self to give to you I gave freely to Justin. Now, at the end the only thing I love more than my consort and my child is my creator. Seeing Justin in danger and having my hands tied and being unable to offer him anything but limited to no help, has stripped away the barriers that I built between what I really feel and my ego, arrogance and pride. It has left me only with some simple and clear truths and shown me what I truly value which is my creator and my faith and my love for my family.

Gabriel took a deep breath before he said, I know I don't deserve your forgiveness but I would consider my self truly blessed if you could or would give me the gift of your understanding.

Gabriel finished speaking and kept his body turned away from her and waited for Bree to speak. When she did not say a word, Gabriel turned slowly saying a brief prayer for the strength to accept what ever her reaction to him would be. When he finally looked at Bree he saw that tears were running down her face.

Gabriel tried to be prepared and ready for her coldness or her spoken or unspoken anger and or her distance as she shut her self completely off from him. However, what he was not prepared for was her tears; each one burned a trail on his heart. Gabriel said in a voice choked with emotions, "is their anything I can do?" Bree looked up at Gabriel, the water in them making them shine like diamonds as she said very quietly, "I have always loved you."

Bree had dreamed of this moment, constructed and re-constructed how it would be when he finally realized what she had known all along. Now that the moment was here, she was so overcome with emotions that the only words that she could manage to form to speak was "I love you and I always have."

Jason reviewed his new apartment and seemed outwardly pleased. He laid down on the bed in a manor that indicated he was tired. Jason needed to review all that had happened and think about his next moves. Jason some how knew that if he assumed a familiar mediation pose to aid in his relaxation, some how that information would be related to Vane and that would not be good! Jason took nothing for granted now, not even the smallest detail and now he worked from the concept that it is always better to error on the side of caution.

Jason went inside his shield where he knew his thoughts could not be monitored, while insuring that his brain wave pattern indicated the look of someone sleeping. Jason always had an appreciation for the ironic, but now the bitter truth of it removed most of the humor. For years he had hidden a touch of negativity with in his heart.

Negativity, that he had hidden from himself as well as others. Now here he was hiding his angelic core under the darkness that now surrounded him, darkness that was trying to both penetrate him and take him over. Jason thought how true it was that you never appreciated anything until you were at the point of or had just lost it.

This experience allowed Jason to see himself with new eyes. The choices he had made to embrace his negativity (the ego, arrogance and pride) that were the authors of his current situation. Jason knew that he was being given the choice to choose from both sides of his nature now having lived with each.

Jason remembered something that he learned as a child, "god never puts more on you than you can handle, however he does sometimes put more on you than you want to handle." The creator and the universe are fair and you are never put in a situation with out warning or with out the chance to learn all you need to know before you make your choice and decisions." This inside out view of hell was his chance to learn all he needed to know about his negativity, if he choose to let the situation instruct him.

Here again his heritage kicked in, he was part human therefore he had free will and a soul, which meant he had the freedom to allow hell to take him over by choosing to let negativity into his mind, heart and soul that once done he would then complete the choice by embracing the negativity of his situation and giving back to others what was being thrown at him.

He was part angel; he understood the power of love and faith on levels that his human half had never grasped. In looking at this lesson he was being taught, Jason examined the knowledge he had learned about hell, as he was now coming to understand it he realized he had to be core level truthful with himself. The situation he was in had no room for lies or self deception.

The choices he made now, he would have to live with forever so he needed to be dam sure of what he wanted. Jason knew for the first time in his life, that all of him would have to accept the choices he made this day because neither heaven nor hell could be dealt with in half measures. All of him would be required to stand by the decisions he made now in order to survive.

Jason had been warned, but he had free will which meant that he got to choose if he was going listen and hear the warning. Jason remembered being taught as a child that the universe is fair people however are not. For every situation that you will face in life, a warning of up coming problems and the appropriate training will be offered, this was an example of the universe being fair. Free will is a wild card, and it can choose to say, "No" or I do not want to learn this lesson today.

As Jason looked back, he had been given many warning and he had seen fear growing inside of him, fear which was a clear indication that something was wrong and he needed to find out what. Jason knew he should have left when he saw his father struggling to give him information because each word his father spoke felt wrong to both of them. There were other warning, the warning of being slowly cut off from family and friends. And finally, Jason thought, the warning of mental pain. This type of pain was always, always a warning of wrong action.

Pain, was an indication to the sprit just as it was to the body that something is happening which needs your attention right now! Now, before the situation gets out of control. It is like having a sore become gangrene, a situation which could have been easily dealt with by using attention, disinfectant and antibiotics. Rather than ignoring the pain and watching it spread and grow until the only remedy was to cut it off.

Jason had been cut off (from all he knew) but the limb had not yet gotten to a point of no return or gangrene. Jason had a chance, but only a chance. Jason could not afford any level of blindness, the type of blindness that occurs when you lie to your self, "no" not on any level. There is a type of seductive power in negativity which would find any level of blindness or self lies and hide comfortably there until it was ready to try to take you over; Jason though, "I should know that, after all it is how I got here!"

Jason had always felt like neither fish nor foul, always out of place. Jason was always angry at the limitations of his human heritage and at the deepest part of him he experienced feelings of low level shame at being less than an angel.

On some level that Jason had never admitted to him self, he always felt that although his father was always both good and kind to his mother, that in some subtle way that he could never put his finger on that his father was disappointed on some core level to have a human as a consort. This was another thing that Jason kept hidden deep inside of him because he loved both of his parents dearly and if what he suspected was true, it would have hurt him deeply.

Now in this place where only the truth would release him, Jason had to admit that "the thought" had hurt him any way, because deep down where it counted he knew he believed it was true. As Jason looked at this concept, he noted with surprise that it was imbedded with in him by his father. Little things Raphael said about humans and how he said these things gave Jason the clear understanding that with the exception of his mother and him, humans were inferior.

This was a truth that Jason never wanted to admitted or acknowledged because it seemed like a betrayal of his beautiful mother whom he loved so much. But down there in the dark, this belief became stronger, drawing to it negativity to feed it and unknown to him it always colored his opinions of humans . . .. he had always felt that they were less. It was because these feelings were buried deep with in him, this made it easy for him to feel shame and anger for him to be asked to serve humans. Now that Jason was being honest with him self on levels that he had never been before he saw something else that had never occurred to him, a clear truth emerged . . .he was wholly unique.

Jason was a being with the positive and negative traits of both sides of his heritage free to become something he had never thought of. Light warriors, Justin, Jason and others of his race they were the next step in the evolution of the human race. They were the fore-runner of everything that a human being could be.

Light Warriors and humans were like the difference between the caterpillar (that the human race was now) and the butterfly they could evolve into. For the first time in his life Jason understood his place in the circle of the universe. With this knowledge came complete acceptance of him self, Jason now knew exactly what or who he wanted to be.

For the first time in his life there were no contradictions, hidden fears. All of Jason wanted was to be a teacher for the human race. Maybe later, he too could find his mate and get another chance to ascend. Jason thought he would be blessed if he could continue simply to be a guardian and teacher for both the human race and his own. Jason for the first time saw great potential in the human race and genuinely wanted to be there to watch them grow and help to guide them.

Jason noticed a movement in the room he stood completely still, "a shadow demon" had entered Jason's apartment. Then Jason felt a slight prick, Jason immediately redoubled his shields and analyzed the substance as it tried to move through his body. Jason had thrown a barrier of light around the toxin to limit its effect while he figured out what it was and how to defuse it.

The substance was a concentrated version of the toxin he had noticed that was subtly defused in to the atmosphere of hell. A toxin intended to increase and enhance all negative emotions and traits. Jason sent a spark of angelic love enough to look like the toxin had spotted some light in him and was attacking and destroying it; in stead it was the other way around.

Jason created an opening at the base of his heel and slowly pushed the diluted toxin out of the peripheral of his system. Jason then created an internal defense system to recognize and respond immediately to any such future attempts to poison him. Any future attempts of this type, would be met immediately by his internal defenses which would act to dilute and eliminate the toxin before it could do any damage. The defense system would operate independently whether he was asleep or awake, in case they tried to infect him again and the next time he actually was a sleep.

Jason started to think proactively, he created an internal filtering system for the air he bereaved to insure that his system would not be compromised in any way. Jason then insured that any scan of him would reflect the look of the toxins in his system. Jason realized that the stakes in this situation had just gone up and his time was running out.

Hell did not operate by the rules of fairness which was another reason he still maintained his angelic shields and knowledge. They provided the only chance he had of countering Hell's attempts at taking away his choice. Jason then noticed a flash of light when the demon left. There was an active monitoring system on him in the room, this was no more than he expected but what Jason did not expect (and he was grateful that he was not asleep!) was this toxin. Along with the underhanded method of how the attack was delivered, this took Jason by surprise. More than anything else this situation impressed on Jason the seriousness of his current circumstances and the fact that this unexpected attack had had an extremely good chance of infecting him which would have made escaping his current circumstances three times harder to almost impossible.

This underhanded subtle attack taught Jason another things as well, such as, attention to detail was a concept that he was going to live or die by. The most important information Jason received from the attack was how and in what way the most deadly attacks would come at him . . .. .. subtle, softly, quickly and under the belief of a seemingly unimportant actions or statements, these were the levels he now had to be most attuned to.

Jason turned so that he could through a sliver of a cracked eye, examine the monitoring system. Jason thought, he had not noticed it initially because it was a pinpoint of red light hidden in a piece of art which had several pieces of red reflective glass work in it each piece shinning with the smallest amount of light through it, it was a perfect camouflage.

Over the next two days Jason sought out and found all of the listening devised in his apartment. After examining the first one, Jason noticed that each device had a slight but individual energy signal. Jason attuned his senses to each energy signal; this allowed him to find every listening devise in each room of his apartment by following the energy pattern.

Jason had a meeting with Rule at Rule's apartment. Jason knew that Rule's insistent request that Jason come to his apartment was simply Rule's attempt to establish dominance in their relationship. Jason however, saw it as another opportunity. During the meeting at Rules apartment, Jason identified four different energy patterns, associated with the listening devise scattered through out Rules' apartment.

Chapter Fifteen

Upon entry to Rule's apartment Jason flattered Rule on his furnishing and decorative style. Rule was visibly pleased and when Jason asked for a tour of Rule's apartment, Rule took it as a sign that Jason had got the message that he was the alpha demon in there relationship. Jason spotted the listening devises and examined the four different energy signals in detail while at the same time listening to some non sense that Rule was sprouting regarding his experience.

Jason noted that one of the signals was the same as the signal he found in his apartment. As Jason considered the importance of this information, he realized that each energy signal not only represented a different older demon (all of whom had had dealing with Rule before) but Jason could now feed the energy signal into his angelic data base and produce a birth name listed for each of the older demons energy signal.

How this information would be useful in Jason current situation, he did not yet know; that the information would be useful Jason was sure of it. Jason was expected at Vane's home tomorrow to provide a report on their progress. Jason was not surprised to know that Vane had set up a similar meeting with Rule, for the same reason. Rule had stated that they had to meet this afternoon because he had an important meeting this evening.

Jason accepted the statement as if it was unimportant to him and had nothing to do with him. However, immediately Jason knew two things (a) the meeting was with Vane. (b) Vane had told Rule not to inform Jason about the meeting. As Jason thought about this information it seemed that Vane was putting together a plan "B" to be used as needed.

Jason again had to fight to keep from laughing at the sense of irony in the situation. From every thing he now knew it looked like Vane intended to plant dissention and suspicion between Jason and Rule. This suspicion, which could be heighten and increased at a moment's notice, should the need arise.

Jason gave himself two assignments for tomorrow, (a) to identify as many different demon energy patterns through the listening devises implanted in Vane's home. (b) To analyze the plan of suspicion in detail that Vane was trying to put in place regarding Rule and himself. The analysis of Vane's plan would give Jason valuable insight into understanding how Vane thought. This would be critical information in the future as Jason factored that information into his plans for Vane.

Gabriel stood extremely still after Bree said, "I have always loved you." Slowly Gabriel replied, "I have not always deserved you or your love." But if you will give me the opportunity, from this point on I will try. A flutter of communication interaction now took place between the two of them as each opened their minds and hearts to the other. Gabriel noticed a memory in Bree's mind shrouded in a forgetfulness circle.

Curious, Gabriel examined the memory further, Gabriel was not concerned about any communication breach because the very nature of the forgetfulness cloak did not allow any to see or notice it unless they had the right to. Therefore if he had not been meant to notice that there was still more information he needed to know, he would not have seen the cloak. However, Gabriel still had to apply for access to the knowledge hidden in the circle and he was not surprised when he was allowed access to the information.

Gabriel was however surprised at the information the cloak yielded. The elderly family member, who had visited Justin since his birth, who liked Bree (Gabriel could tell from his expression and the fact that he visited her at all) and who loved Justin and who Justin loved as a second father was the "creator." Gabriel knew this because the creator had a core radiance which his angels would naturally recognize and be drawn to no mater what his external appearance looked like.

During the time that Gabriel had not been able to appreciate the gift that his family was, his creator had stepped in and provided the support and love his family had not received (in the needed quantizes) from him. Gabriel felt humbled, grateful and sad, his negativity had robbed him of genuinely precious time that he could have and should have been spending with his family.

Gabriel held Bree and communicated this information (since the circle of forgetfulness had dissolved Gabriel felt he was not going against the creator's will in sharing the information with Bree. Bree then sent to Gabriel a detailed account of her last meeting with the creator and the information that she too was an "elemental."

Katelyn had listened and watched Justin work out a battle plan. Katelyn could see how Justin viewed her. He saw her as rare, beautiful and full of power and energy . . . an elemental. Katelyn saw beyond a shadow of a doubt, that he loved her. Katelyn was deeply touched and moved (after all, what woman would not want to be seen in such a beautiful and loving light by her mate).

Katelyn, however, was having a serious problem seeing her self the way he saw her. She saw herself as someone so completely different and less than what he saw. God, she did not want to let him down! Or worse yet, be the means of causing him any level of weakness in a battle. Katelyn thought, that if it would keep him safe and out of harm's way, she would run away from him (even though she knew it would break her heart) but she would do it, if she thought it would help to keep Justin safe! Where could she go, she had no where to run to. God, what was she going to do?

Justin felt Katelyn's despair; in reply he sent her one thought "Do you trust me?" Katelyn smiled and with out thought (and using angelic communication), she replied "with my life!" Justin smiled and said, I'd like you to meet someone. Katelyn thought, "He is trying to get my mind away from my feelings of uselessness." But she replied, I don't know how meeting anyone would help this situation or get my mind off of it but she thought it was sweet of him to try.

Katelyn asked, "Who do you want me to meet?" Justin said, "My mother." Katelyn sat down with out realizing that she did so, "OK" she thought,

I was wrong! The thought of meeting his mother wiped out every other thought and consideration. Justin felt Katelyn go blank. She was right, Justin did want to calm her fears and in all of his long life no one had ever done that better than his mother. Justin simply hoped she could do the same for Katelyn plus, he really did want her to meet his mother.

Justin realized, as he thought about it, that in many ways Katelyn reminded him of his mother. Bree, Justin's mother had such a calming presence, a presence that had always helped him to understand that he had greater strengths than he knew. Justin sent a message to his mother requesting her consent to meet Katelyn.

Before he could complete the thought, Justin received a wave of love that said, I can not wait to meet her! Justin reached for Katelyn, to distract her (and because she looked so adorably confused), he kissed her. Then while he was holding her in his arms (and before she knew what was happening), he transported them to his home realm. He was about to send the mental equivalent of a knock on the door when he found himself and Katelyn materializing in his mother's garden. To Justin's surprise his father was with her.

Katelyn saw two of the most beautiful individuals she had ever seen in her life. Bree, Justin's mother had long black hair falling in waves down her back; eyes that actually were shinning and a smile like sunshine. Then, as breathtakingly beautiful as his mother was his father was stunningly handsome. The pair of them did not look a day past Thirty-two but then Justin did not look a day pass thirty-two.

As Katelyn was observing Justin's parents and watching as Justin kissed and hugged his mother, then embraced his father. Justin turned to her and said, "Katelyn these are my parents." Katelyn received a burst of angelic communication first from his mother. The communication washed over her with warmth and a genuine pleasure to meet her. The communication she received from his father was she could tell, toned down considerably, yet it washed over her like pure sunshine.

Bree waved her hand and lunch appeared ready to be served. There was a burst of communication being fired from parents to son. While they spoke, Katelyn was content to take in the beauty of the garden and eat the most delicious lunch she had ever had. Katelyn let the peace of her surrounding sink into her soul so intently that she did not notice that Bree was standing by her, until she spoke. Bree said quietly to Katelyn (while Gabriel and Justin discussed other matters), this is how an elemental renews herself. Elementals soak in the peace and beauty of nature. It reconnects us with each element of our nature; earth, fire, water and air. It reminds us that we have abilities and strengths that even we do not know we have, until they are needed.

Katelyn could feel the living connection with each of the elements as if an energy line connected her to each of the elements and through those energy lines the elements were in fact singing to her soul, singing a song that only an elemental could hear. A song that strengthens nurtured and sustained her soul. Katelyn was so caught up in the moment that she almost missed the word "us" when Bree was speaking about elementals.

Katelyn looked at Bree and saw the same energy connections flowing in and out of Bree as her energy connected with the water Katelyn saw Bree expelling her troubled emotions and drawing in peaceful ones through her connection with the water. Katelyn could see that Bree knew about the upcoming battle that she and Justin would have to face and Bree was worried about her child but she knew her worry would not help him and possible hurt him so she used her elemental talents to keep her emotions peaceful. As Katelyn watched in awe the living lesson that Bree was giving her, Katelyn thought this is what Justin meant when he said he always found peace in his mother's presence.

Bree was giving Katelyn her first lesson in being an elemental but she was giving her more than that, Bree had given Katelyn a way out, a means by which to control her fears. Katelyn located the energy line to the water with in her then following Bree's example, she sent her fear, worry, doubt and uncertainty into the water. Katelyn then moved the energy line to another part of the water and drew in faith, peace, contentment and a belief that all would be well.

Bree smiled as she watched Katelyn take her first steps as an elemental. Then Bree said, take some time and become familiar with each connection and when you need them they will connect both with you and their element in your environment like the energy line is connecting with you and the water drawing and receiving strength. The key to an elemental's power is belief, having now experienced that belief in action you know it can and does work. Once you have identified each energy line you will always have the strength of the elements at your command.

Justin saw his mother speaking quietly with Katelyn, if he could have put into words what he wanted his mother to accomplish this day he would not or could not have asked for more. Justin had always found profound peace in his mother's presence. Katelyn was full of fear, worry and uncertainty. Pure instinct alone told him that his mother was the one person who could help Katelyn, even though he did not know why.

As a child he thought it was just that she was mom, but as he got older he realized that in his mothers presence he was always calmed down to such a point that he always saw options in any situation a lot quicker when he was able to spend a little time in her presence when he was a lone and he was unable to spend a little time in her presence.

Bree knew that the information she had received from the creator or the man she had in the past thought of as a relative of Gabriel was truthful, she was an elemental her garden was always her favorite place in her home and she always felt connected to it in some personal, unique way. When Justin was a child, Bree learned she had the ability to draw out his pain, calm and sooth both his mind and sprit.

As he got older she found she could clear his mind of his doubts and fears and infuse his sprit with calm and peace. She could not solve his problems but she could create the optimum conditions for him to figure out the solution for his problem, because he could see options with in her presence that his fear usually blocked in him.

When Bree finished she began to infuse Justin with positive energy. Light and hope flowed in to Justin and then as Bree started to wane from the effort Katelyn saw Gabriel place his hand around Bree waist and before her eyes Katelyn saw Gabriel pore energy and strength into Bree, all while maintain a causal discussion with Justin, all with out Justin's knowledge.

Bree drew out every drop of negative energy replacing it with confidence, strength, love and faith. Katelyn thought she had just witnessed one of the most sincere acts of love she had ever seen in her life. She turned her head as a tear rolled down her face because she had never seen an act of love so similar to that she had shared with her own parents. Katelyn wanted to be a part of the experience, so she quickly sent her love to add to theirs.

Not that they needed her help but she wanted to share in or be a part of the moment. Bree and Gabriel recognized her energy and to her surprise she was included in the love and energy they shared with Justin it felt like concentrated sunshine pouring through every cell of her body on the inside and being bathed in warmth and sweetness on the outside. It was the most incredible feeling she had ever experience in her life.

The sun was beginning to set; the time seemed to fly by and now it was time to go. Bree hugged Katelyn and it was like being enveloped in a cloud full of flowery scents which were both warm and inviting. At the same time Gabriel hugged Justin. Justin put one arm around Katelyn, as he waved good by to his parents with the other. When they got back to her apartment Katelyn was puzzled. Justin(who knew immediately the cause of her puzzlement) smiled and explained, one hour in his home realm was the equal of three hours on earth, which was why the day had just began on earth when they left and it was now midnight upon there return.

Gabriel had dropped by to see Bree because he simply wanted to see her; he also wanted to get some insight on Justin's situation from Bree's point of view. Gabriel was pleased and surprised when Justin and his mate came to visit Bree, at that same time. This visit provided insight for Gabriel on a multitude of levels. Learning that Bree was an elemental, watching Bree instruct Justin's mate on how to access and use the power of being an elemental. Then watching Bree draw out the seeds of negativity in Justin and replace them with positive ones.

Gabriel was pleased at how quickly Justin's mate had learned the lessons Bree was teaching her, as Gabriel watched Katelyn try out her power. Then when Katelyn joined her energy to Gabriel and Bree they felt in Katelyn a deep core level love for Justin and a fierce desire to help keep Justin safe, this touched both of them sincerely. Gabriel was also pleased that in opening her self up to them, that connection allowed Gabriel and Bree to draw out Katelyn fears and replenish her strength too.

Gabriel sent the information of today's events to be filtered through his knowledge of the rules of communication, to be sure that neither he nor Bree had done anything that could be termed a break in the conditions of the rules of communication. Gabriel felt that neither he or Bree had did anything wrong but filtering today's actions through the rule would give him a better understanding of any acceptable options available at this time, Gabriel did not want to over look anything.

It seemed that as long as they did not try to fight Justin's battles or give him information before he was ready to know, they were with in the bounds of the rule. As Gabriel examined the day's events he realized that it all seemed so natural. Taking his clue from Bree and following her lead he added his strength to her, with out thought, when he saw her falter in her efforts to strengthen their son.

Bree, Gabriel thought was the key. There was no limit on the amount of help she could give there son and his consort and there was no limit on the amount of help he could give her! Here was another clear means of helping his son, indirectly through his mother.

This indirect route opened up unknown possibilities as a clear way to aid his son in the upcoming battle. Gabriel thought, with excitement and real hope, he would have to speak with Raphael and his consort to see if this information could in any way be useful to them and their battle to help Jason.

Chapter Sixteen

Rule presented himself that evening at Vane's home as requested. Rule viewed it as a request, while Vane considered it a summons. Rule waited for Vane to speak. If Rule had spoken first it would be considered an insult and Vane would then have every right to beat him senseless. Rule kept his head bowed and his mouth shut until Vane directed a question toward him, then and only then could he speak with out it resulting in pain.

Vane started talking, careful not to ask a question because Vane hoped Rule would speak with out invitation. Vane wanted to beat the hell out of Rule again for putting him in this situation. However, after a while, Vane accepted that Rule had no intentions of speaking until asked a direct question. Vane finally said, how is Jason working out? Rule lifted his head and said "there is no way to tell the worth of any demon, accept in battle."

Vane was now even more upset. If Rule had answered the question in the positive or negative it did not matter, because Vane had planed to say exactly to Rule what Rule had just said to him. The little maggot had stolen his well thought out reply! Vane tried another attack; Jason tells me that you think I am jealous of you, is this true?

Rule took a moment before he replied, if he lied Vane would know it and if he told the truth Vane would beat him. Rule bowed his head before he replied he did not want Vane to see the smile on his face because he had thought up the perfect answer. Rule spoke, "words to that effect were exchanged, however, I believe that the meaning of the statement was taken out of content."

The meaning was that all demons young, mid-age or old are jealous it is in our nature. My hope is to one day be as great a demon as you and then have other demons jealous of me too. Rule knew that Vane would be able to tell that he was lying if he had replied with a basic yes or no answer but if he mixed the truth with a serious amount of omissions, half-truths and misdirecting statements it would be extremely difficult to say he was completely lying.

Vane recognized the method and reason for Rules's answer. Hell, Vane had used this method himself when he was a mid-range demon. Vane knew two things 1. Rule was lying, although pinning him down to the lie would be difficult. 2. Younger demons tended to simply say what they saw not intending to be truthful but simply not understanding the hidden implication of the knowledge that they related or how that knowledge could be used.

Jason was a new demon he simply said what he heard and saw. Vane turned his back on rule because he did not want Rule to see the anger in his eyes nor did Vane want to see the gloating look in Rule's eyes. Rule knew he had gotten away with his deception and half-truths. With his back still turned to Rule, Vane spoke, "I am surprised that you still want the service of a demon that lied on you. If you wish, I will end Jason's service to you.

Rule stood completely still as he analyzed this new threat. If he gave Jason up, not only would he be on his own again but there would be no one to blame if he failed. Also by giving up Jason, Vane was no longer connected to this situation. Vane would have fulfilled his commitment to their law, by offering help. Vane also could end his involvement in this situation quickly and all by simply looking like he merely acted on Rule's request when he removed Jason.

However, the other side of the situation did not look that great either. Keeping a demon in your service that you know has tried to betray you was also considered a sign of weakness, this was what Vane was trying to catch Rule on! This belief was a joke, every demon assigned to another would try to betray him; it was how promotions and one's status were earned. They simply could not be obvious with the betrayal the way Jason's earlier statement looked.

Rule had one ace left, one he did not want to play yet but now he had no other way out. Rule knew that if he could raise the situation to that of an emergency status, no one would consider Rules' holding on to Jason a negative. In an emergency situation every one knew that you took any and all help you could get, with no questions asked. Rule took a deep breath and replied, "Sir I believe this situation rates emergency status." Vain said nothing waiting on Rule to complete his appeal. The prey, Rule said, is an elemental this is new information that was just recently obtained. Vane turned away as if to consider this new knowledge but what he really thought was, "so all it took was cornering the little worm like a trapped rat, to get him to give up the information he should have told me immediately." Now that Jason's initial information had been confirmed Vane considered the possibilities.

Vane had no intentions of ending his involvement in this situation unless it was clear that the prey would get away then he intended to put all the blame solely and completely on Jason and Rule. If however they were successful, Vane intended claiming the prize. The problem was just as he could and would take the elemental from Rule, how would he keep her from being taken away from him?

The news of such a prize in hell would travel fast; he needed a plan of immediate action once the elemental was in his hands. Vane was going to have to use great cunning to pull this off. The first thing that most demons would do with an elemental is use them to increase there powers. The problem was this process would leave him extremely weak at first; the energy surge created by this process would be impossible to hide and he would be completely vulnerable and unable to defend him self until he had time to absorb and make her energy his own.

Any of the Elder demons would tear him to pieces for a taste of such power. Vane needed protection and he needed a plan. Vane needed to make a bargain with a true Elder Senior demon! One whose name would stop other older demon in there tracks. If Vane could arrange such a contract no other demon would dare to attack him while he was in route to delivering his prey.

Once the elemental was in his possession, Vane could also request to receive the fall out effect, which was simply the right to absorb any energy that was left after the Senior Elder had taken his fill. Vane was also trying to figure out if there was a way for him to increase his personal power by absorbing some of the elementals energy but with out any one knowing it and with out the process draining him.

This would give Vane a hidden advantage in case the Senior Elder decided to make some alterations to there contract, Vane knew that if the situation were reversed once he got his hands on the elemental one of the first things he would do is kill off any witness to the contract. Vane also knew that the best time to negotiate this arrangement was when he all but had the prey in his hands. The Senior Elder demon would agree quickly, to such a small concession, with an elemental almost with in there reach. Finally if his plan worked, not only would he come out of this alive but he would be one of the most powerful demons of his classifications.

He would be an older demon one step away from becoming an elder. Vane knew that such a contract would give him access to a greater level of power because as long as there was a genuine possibility of capturing an elemental, the Elder demon would add his energy toward this undertaking. The down side to this plan was, if they failed to deliver the elemental, Vane would be pulling his life on the line. The Senior Elder would sacrifice him with even less thought than Vane had given to sacrificing Jason and Rule. Vane knew that this plan was a bold move but such opportunities were both rare and few in hell.

This was his moment and Vane intended to go for it. While Vane was planning his strategy, Rule stood quietly knowing that he had just lost his prize; Rule's only chance at real power because he had to give up the elemental to save his life. Rule knew he needed help he also knew that if the situation did not change soon he would loose his prey.

Rule had not told any one that his prey had activated her defense system or that her defense system had recognized and targeted him as an enemy. Her defense system was literally tracking his energy signal and hunting him down through it. If he did not receive serious help soon the game would soon be over. Rule was running out of hiding places with in her and he was running out of time. Rule knew that if Vane thought for one moment that Rule was as close as he actually was to loosing his prey, Vane would distance himself from this venture quicker than a fraction of a heart beat.

When Rule thought of what had happened yesterday he literally shuttered, she had completely disappeared! His prey was in an alternate realm because she was not on earth. This scared Rule deeper and more sincerely than anything else. How did a human leave the earth realm? In the past, he would have said such a thing was impossible but his knowledge of elementals was limited and it seemed that a fully activated elemental could accomplish un-thought of things.

And then, when she came back around mid-night, with her shields amplified to almost three times what they were before and her being flooded with love so intense that he had to step out of her, as quickly as he stepped in because the intensity of the love with in her had literally burned him. Rule was scared, genuinely, sincerely and completely scared. Rule knew that no one could know just how close to loosing this prey he actually and truly was! Rule knew that his life depended on his silence.

Vane reviewed his knowledge of the Elders; they were divided into two basic divisions:

> (a) The council that ruled hell (Elder demons) taking instructions almost directly from Lucifer and implementing his will on hell.
>
> (b) The Senior Elders who were Lucifer's version of his personal guard demons. They and they alone had direct access to Lucifer. Even the Elder demons in the council received there instruction from a Senior Elder, assigned by Lucifer to the task of implementing his will on hell through the Elders who maintained discipline and order in hell.

Vane knew he needed the help a Senior Elder (almost of all of which had been angels who had accompanied Lucifer during the fall). How to get to one was the issue, Hell had invented the concept of a bureaucracy. There was no such thing as a direct channel to Lucifer in hell or if there was only a few knew and had access to it. The Senior Elders were once angels and were all that remained from those who fell from grace (more years ago than anyone could count) when hell was established. It was said that not many were left (because most went insane and died shortly after the fall) but the exact number of Senior Elders left no one knew.

As Vane turned the problem over in his mind he remembered the power in a birth name. If he could get the name of those who fell with Lucifer he had a chance of calling a Senior Elder to him. Vane knew he needed to know exactly what he was going to say to the senior Elder, because once called, if Vane was lucky he might get three minutes to explain himself. In all honest, Vane figured that he needed to be able to make his case in under a minute to a minute and a half, before the senior elder killed him for daring to call him especially by name. Vane had plans to make and information to gather before he acted.

Gabriel went to visit Raphael but before Gabriel could speak, waves and waves of sadness radiated from Raphael. Gabriel placed his hand on his friend's shoulder and sent pure love to ease some of his suffering. Raphael straightens his shoulders and sent Gabriel a grateful look as he tried to pull himself together.

Gabriel was one of the few angels who could understand his pain. Through his own actions, Rapheal had condemned his child. The creator had told him that all was not yet lost but when he prayed for clarity and understanding no answer came. His child was a demon in hell. Try as he did, Raphael could not see anything but loss this the situation.

But the creator had said all was not yet lost. Raphael wrapped his faith around those words and prayed for increased faith, understanding and a way to help his child. Gabriel took a moment to consider the women chosen to be the consorts to angels. They all had come from different levels of human society and conditions.

Ariel, Raphael's consort was the daughter of a merchant. Gabriel remembered, noting that another angel's consort was the youngest child of a thief.

Now Gabriel revisited those memories and looked deeper at each maid chosen. Each had their own power and abilities all of which were dormant or sleeping deep with in them. Gabriel knew that love was the catalyst which would awaken their power, the love of there mate and love of child.

The power in these women would become a living bereaving thing once it was activated by love. They needed to give and receive a genuine pure version of love, love which needed to be received at almost a cellular level, a level that only an angel could give.

Gabriel turned his mind toward Ariel, Raphael's mate and Jason's mother. Gabriel looked at her deeply, from a completely new perspective or with the eyes of an angel who loved and an appreciated the talents of his mate. Gabriel's eyes widen with surprise as he saw Ariel's powers unfold in his mind, powers that were different from Bree but just as powerful. Gabriel asked Raphael if he had discussed Jason's current situation with Ariel, to which Raphael stated he had consistently sent circles of forgetfulness to Ariel; however she kept breaking through them.

Raphael stated the each time she broke through, she broke through the circle faster or each circle ended quicker and quicker than the one before it. Raphael was starting to wonder how he was going to protect Ariel from the knowledge that he knew would break her heart!

Gabriel sent a blast of angelic communication to Raphael outlining all that had taken place during Justin's trials and most especially the importance of Bree's role in helping there son. The information left nothing out and ended with the belief that some how Ariel would be an important piece in Raphael's ability to help his son but first he had to let go of his preconceived notion regarding his consort's weakness.

Raphael would have to tell Ariel the truth and together they would figure out a way to aid Jason. Gabriel prayed that he was right; the look of hope in Raphael eyes was almost too painful to bear. Gabriel wanted Bree to be a part of this discussion with Ariel, if for no other reason than the comfort she could provide.

They agree to meet at Ariel's home two hours from now. This was to give Raphael time to figure out the best way to break the news to Ariel while Gabriel informed Bree and enlist her help.

When Gabriel left Raphael started thinking about Ariel and there history. Most importantly, he started to review his memories of Ariel from when he first met her, reviewing all he knew about her but this time, looking at their history with new eyes!

Ariel was born the daughter of a merchant; in fact, she and Bree were born contemporaries, although they lived in different city/states and belonged to different cast systems. Ariel's father was a good man, but not a good man of business. He lent money to people who did not pay him back at all or others who did not pay him in full or did not pay him on time. Ariel's mother always felt herself ill used because she had been required to marry a man who based his business interaction on his heart rather than his head.

Her unspoken feelings and thoughts were expressed through her actions. Ariel's mother thought her husband was a fool, who would one day bring them to live on the charity of others. Ariel was a daddy's girl. Even as an enfant, her mother's touch disturbed her and her father's touch soothed her. Ariel was the baby; she had three older brothers. Ariel's father had wanted a little girl.

Ariel's mother on the other hand, did not understand why her husband was not proud and satisfied with the three beautiful boys she had produced for him or why he insisted that she go through the pain and discomfort of pregnancy and child birth all over again just so he could have the possibility of the daughter his heart desired (girls were of little use and had almost no importance with in the time period in which they lived). This was a time when women were literally owned by there fathers and husbands. It was with in the male's right to treat her how ever he chose. If a women wanted to deny their husbands and scream "NO." what they actually said was "yes."

So finally Ariel was born and it was as if the child knew that her mother resented the trouble and pain she had to go through to give her life. This was when the division between mother and daughter clearly solidified into an established adversarial relationship. One from this point on which simply got worse! Ariel was a quiet and beautiful child who did her best to be unnoticed by her mother.

Ariel would come to life in her father's company; there closeness made her relationship with her mother all the more difficult. Ariel's father died when she was eighteen. She was long past the age of marriage, most of her friend and cousins were married between the ages of 14 to 16 years old. With the age of 16 being the absolute latest a young girl in her time period would marry.

Ariel's mother had arranged a marriage contract for her when she was 14; this was the only time she had ever seen her father angry. Her father informed her mother that he, not she, was the head of this family and he would, when he saw fit; arrange a marriage contract for Ariel when she was old enough to understand what it meant to be a wife!

Ariel had grown up with a soul level belief that marriage would bring her great happiness yet when she was fourteen years old and her mother arranged a marriage of connivance for Ariel (the marriage was more covenant for her mother). During the introduction Ariel's future husband kissed her hand and with that touch, Ariel saw her future husband's true nature. Ariel saw that he was pampered, spoiled and cruel he was an even worse version of her brothers.

Ariel was completely shattered because she knew she would find no happiness or comfort at his hand. Later when her father found out about her mother's plans for her and forbade the match, Ariel was relieved, at first. Then later she felt a great sadness come over her, as if she was disappointed in some one or thing, she felt as if someone she trusted had lied to her.

Not another word about her marriage was spoken of until her father's death. Through her brother, Ariel's mom had taken control of the family business. At first her mother told her eldest son that she just wanted to help ease his burdens by taking a few of the many responsibilities of the business off his shoulders. Since she enjoyed the work and it kept her busy and afforded her the opportunity to be useful to her son. Since her oldest son did not want any part of work or the business except the money it yielded, he was glad to let her have her way.

Until gradually it became know to all that her mother was the real company boss. After the death of her father and a respectable period of morning (one year) was over Ariel's mother had arranged to sell her daughter to the temple. Ariel's mother felt that she was too old to marry off, at least not with out paying out a huge dowry, a dowry which Ariel had but not one her mother wanted to give up.

Therefore why not sell her to the gods as a temple maid; this way instead of paying out money to marry her off; she would be paid money by the temple and have Ariel taken off her hands as well!

Ariel knew something was wrong the day her mother came to her room with a present of a new dress (this alone raised Ariel's concern) then when her mother requested that Ariel was to wear the dress this afternoon when they went on a little trip. Ariel's curiosity regarding her mother's intentions rose and Ariel touched her mother (something she usually tried very hard not to do).

When Ariel touched her, all of her mother's intentions flooded into Ariel's mind. As her mother left the room Ariel considered her fate. She would probably be sacrificed to the gods (this was what her mother hoped would be her fate). However, for once she and her mother were in agreement.

Ariel knew she was different; her father knew it as well, and he had cautioned her not to reveal her "talents" to any one but him. Because he said, "others would not understand and call her a devil." Her father said that the outcry of which, would make it difficult to impossible for him to protect her.

Ariel was young but every thing that she had seen about human nature lead her to take her father's warning to heart. Ariel carefully guarded her secret. Ariel took a moment to remember when her father first discovered her secret. Ariel was ten years old and she was looking for her father and ran into his office while he was concluding a business agreement.

A man, one of her father's business associates, touched her chin and said what a pretty young lady she would soon grow up to be! When the man left Ariel told her father word for word what the business transaction agreement was and the fact that the man had no intentions of keeping his part of the agreement. He intended to use her father and pay him nothing in return.

The next day when the man returned to sign the business contract, Ariel's father informed him that the shipment of goods he was to sell to him had been lost to robbers and he did not know when he would be able to supply him with the goods. Ariel's father tore up the contract stating, I can not enter into this agreement in good faith, knowing I am unsure of how I will keep my end of the contract.

The man looked very disappointed and informed her father that he would have to make a similar agreement with one of her father's competitor and left. Three months later, it was known all over the township that the man her father had cancelled the contract with did in deed get another deal with a competitor (a deal not half as good as the one Ariel's father had given him but a deal non the less).

The man had disappeared with the merchandise and the merchant suffered a bad loss, but it was nothing compared to the loss Ariel's father would have received. In fact, that loss would have cost him his business. From that point on her father insured that Ariel touched all of his business associates. Ariel's father also, from that point on, became known as a man who made extremely wise business deals.

Chapter Seventeen

With the death of her father, Ariel lost the only person who loved her, the one person who allowed her to be herself and appreciated the help she was able to offer. Ariel's mother wanted her gone, her mother was still a very attractive but selfish woman, a woman who could not push her age back, with such an old and grown daughter on her hands.

Besides her mother had her eyes on a man who kept his eyes on Ariel, and not in a respectful way. Mom did not want the competition. Ariel thought then it was better to die as a sacrifice with honor then be thought of as a devil and killed painfully, for this was the reason that her father had not agreed to a marriage contract for her, he knew he would be putting her life at risk.

Ariel put the dress on and was on her most humble behavior for the interview. Ariel thought at least for once, her mother was pleased with her.

Ariel actually enjoyed her short time at the temple; she was the soul of humility, gentleness and thoughtfulness with the other girls during her time there. Ariel knew that of course she would be chosen for the next sacrifice. This was supposed to be a great honor but every one knew that the families of the other temple maids made extremely large donations to the temple in general and another donation to the priest in private to insure that this "honor" did not befall their daughters.

Every one knew that this "honor" was reserved for the maid of family's who would not or could not pay the price. Ariel was bathed and rubbed down in scented oils and dressed in one of the most beautiful gowns she had ever seen; then escorted to a private room there to await her fate.

Unlike Gabriel, Raphael had watched Ariel from the moment she was a spark of life in her mother's womb. Raphael seemed fascinated by both the act of conception and the growth stages of the unborn human child. The birth process is as traumatic for the child as it is for the mother. Loud noises, bright lights and waves and waves of pain passing over both the mother and the birthing child!

For Ariel it was worse, from the moment her mind had developed enough to reach out and touch the thoughts of her mother she knew what no child should ever know or feel, that she was unwanted and unloved. That she was thought of, by her mother, to be more of a burden and obligation than a gift.

After Ariel's first touch to her mother's mind she recoiled in anguish and all the joy in her little life began to drain away. Raphael had not intended to do more than act as a scientific observer during this process but her pain touched him deeply. Then he watched as Ariel's tiny little flame began to flicker as if she was slowly beginning the process of not wanting to live, Raphael knew then he had to take action.

Raphael reduced himself to a flicker of light and transported himself inside the womb with her. Slowly he asked why she wanted to end her life before it began. Ariel was so shocked to find that she was not alone that the shock halted her emotional pain and turned it to curiosity, for a minute. Then sadly she responded, can you not feel what my mother thinks of me?

Raphael paused for a moment, as if listening to the vibrations from the mother, then he asked her . . . but what do you think of yourself? Ariel was yet again surprised but this time by the question and she did not know how to answer it. Raphael noting her troubled demeanor said, "there are many ugly truths in life; your mother is simply one of them." But then, there are a great many wonders and joys in this world too.

Joys, Raphael said, that you will never experience if you choose to die now. Ariel listened and said, how do I know I can believe you? Raphael replied, touch me, you will not only see the truth of my words; I will also show you some of these wonders. Raphael reached out a tiny hand and Ariel did the same.

Raphael showed her a sunset, a sun rise, children happy and at play, he took her to the ocean and then he took her to a flower garden high on an island mountain top. Ariel watched as the mist from the mountain danced with the scents of the flowers and all combined with the warmth of a beautiful summer's day to create the feeling of a warm scented hug.

At the end of the journey, Ariel's flame burned hotter than ever as the wonders she had seen lit her from with in with joy. After a while Ariel was very quiet, then she said, but my life will not hold such wonders. Raphael replied, not at first but when you marry, the wonders you have just beheld will be nothing compare to what you will see then.

Raphael said, touch me and with that touch Raphael showed Ariel her home after marriage (the home he had built for her) and told her any changes she wanted to make would be done at her request. Then Raphael said a connection has already been built between you and your father; he will love and protect you until you marry.

From that point on Raphael visited Ariel often during her development into infanthood. Raphael told him self that he was distracting her and providing her, the necessary warmth she needed while living in such a mentally cold womb. The truth was he liked Ariel and watching her evolve before his eyes answered a lot of the questions he had about man.

Raphael was working when suddenly he heard waves of great pain and distress coming from her, he could tell that it was time for her to be born. Before Raphael knew it he was at Ariel's side, Ariel was coiled into a ball fighting the urge to be born while shuttering in fear each time her mother screamed at her to get out!

Before Raphael knew what he was going to do he reacted on pure instinct. Raphael surrounded Ariel with love and then he eased the mother's pain which quieted her screams and ranting. Before mother or child knew what was happening Ariel was born.

Ariel did not fit in anywhere except with her father but his love for her made her mother and brothers just that much harder on her. As a child, Ariel quickly learned to use her gifts to survive. She touched there minds found out what they wanted or needed then found ways to appease them. Ariel's mother and brothers never liked her but soon they got conformable with the fact that she was useful!

Ariel was now eighteen, her father was dying; her mother wished he would do so sooner rather than later. Her brothers seemed indifferent to their father's death except for the amount of money they expected to inherent. Ariel knew, like her father, her time was limited. She had seen her mother looking at her with a calculated gleam in her eyes.

Ariel did not touch her mother to confirm her suspicions there was no need, upon her father's death she would find out soon enough. A year later, after the death of her father, all that Ariel thought was true had come to pass. Ariel's mother had just left her room, Ariel had touched her and now Ariel knew her fate.

Ariel sat in the temple room dressed as a sacrifice and wondering why she was not more upset by the idea. A little serving boy came into the room to bring her food and drink. She had been waiting for two days for something to happen. On the third morning the serving lad asked her why she was so sad. Ariel responded saying only that she was unsure about her fate. Funny, how comfortable Ariel was with the little boy.

Ariel was usually extremely shy around people she had just met, yet the little one asked her questions after question about her life with such genuine interest, that his interest in her life touched her and on some deep level. Ariel did not know why but he seemed familiar; yet she knew it could not be true. No one was allowed to see her after she had been purified and prepared for sacrifice except the one assigned server and for Ariel it was this little one.

By the end of the third day, the little one asked Ariel was she ready to go, Ariel replied with a smile, go where? Then the little one changed before her eyes into one of the most stunningly handsome men she had ever seen. Raphael replied, are you ready to go home. Ariel could not take her eyes off of him and then with her hands shaking she asked who you are.

Raphael held out his hand and said touch me, you will know. Ariel had such an overwhelming desire to touch him it scared her, slowly she reached out her hand and the moment she touched him she was transported back to the time when she was a spark in her mother's womb and there he was telling her about how many wonders life held.

Ariel looked up with tears falling down her eyes and said, "it was you!" How is it possible that I meet you again upon the hour of my death? Raphael replied, the only thing that will die her today is the sadness and discomfort that your life has held up until now!

Raphael had distanced himself from Ariel's life since the moment of her birth. Raphael felt ashamed that he offered her no comfort during the last nineteen years of her life. He told himself that it was not yet time for him to take over her care or for her to depend on him, but the truth was that the pain in her life made her seem to much like someone who needed to be loved and cherished instead of a member of a race that had caused many of his brothers a great deal of harm.

A race he had intended to study not become emotionally involved with. Raphael thought he needed distance to keep his objectivity. However, now that she was in his arms he realized that he had missed her even though he would not admit it to no one not even to himself.
Raphael transported Ariel to her new home, the one he had showed her before her birth and it was just as she remembered only lovelier. Raphael was about to try to explain that she was his consort when she removed her hand from him and said, no explanations are needed she understood it all.

Unfortunately for Raphael, she really did understand. Raphael was an angel and he, in his deepest heart thought her race far closer to animals than angels. Then even deeper, the thought of a human consort made him feel that god did not have a high opinion of him and this hurt Raphael on a level so deep it was a pain he literally kept from himself. This pain, she did not speak of because she knew he would deny it and then strive to bury it deeper.

Ariel was a practical woman; she looked at her situation with a level of truth that an angel would feel proud to acknowledge. Ariel knew that

Raphael cared for her; she also knew he did not want to. Ariel privately thought it extremely ironic that Raphael felt god though less of him and the proof of this thought was that he gave me a human consort, while he privately thought less of her. Ariel did not judge him, he had been good to her and she knew that in time all would work out.

For now, they had the beginnings of a friendship and that was enough for now. This was the level of emotions he was comfortable with and she could wait. For Ariel, simply having a friend and the ability to be who she was with out fear was a gift beyond compare! Therefore, for now, she would enjoy her home, the comfort of his presence; the absence of fear and the ability to get a better understanding of her gifts.

Ariel knew that love will grow in time; she already felt the seeds of it now with in them both. Raphael spent a great deal of time with Ariel, he told himself that he was making up for his earlier neglectful behavior but here again he was not being completely truthful with him self. Raphael found a real peace and comfort in Ariel's presence and he enjoyed being with her.

Raphael had surrounded his lust for Ariel with the belief that she was an exceptional human, so much above the common humans till at times he forgot she was human at all. She was so beautiful and with the comfort and care he gave her, she seemed to glow from the inside and out which clearly made her even more beautiful in his eyes.

It was getting harder and harder for Raphael to stay away. Harder and harder not to touch her until finally he kissed her and his surrender was complete, that week Jason was conceived. Ariel had wondered what type of mother she would make if she had ever got the chance.

Then when she felt the tiny presence with in her and knew her self to be pregnant, Ariel could go back and touch the moment Jason was conceived. She recognized the flickering life force and immediately touched her mind to his. His little flame reached for her and she opened her mind to receive him and bathed him in love.

Ariel marveled as the tiny flame grew brighter and still, with her mind surrounding him as if she held him in her arms. At first Ariel was worried that she would be a terrible mother; then she noticed that when she feared the baby feared too. So she quieted her fears with reason and thought, I will do the opposite of everything my mother did. As Jason grew with in her, they both enjoyed the connections they shared.

Ariel could not wait for Jason to be born so she could hold him in her arms. Jason's birth was surrounded with so much love he came out smiling. Raphael still did not have a very high opinion of the human race in general but he loved her and he adored Jason and they were her world.

Ariel was beginning to wonder if something was wrong with her. She kept having blank spots in, what use to be, her almost perfect memory. In fact, she had started to notice when she felt a light mist descend on her mind that she had to fight it right away or it would become a dense fog. A fog which was three times hander to fight, if she allowed it to settle. Ariel was empathic, even though she could not explain what was wrong she knew that her feeling never lied to her.

Ariel also knew that what ever was happening to her was extremely important; the blank spots in her mind did not hid the growing fear she felt in her soul. Her instincts were trying to communicate something to her brain and that knowledge was being blocked. Every time she started focusing on that block she had to stop to fight the mist that kept descending on her brain. Ariel was more worried than she had been in her life. Raphael visited her less and less.

On his last visit she reached out to touch him but he moved so fast that her fingers only light skimmed over his face . . .. . but her instinct started to scream. However, before she could ask what was wrong an intense fog descended on her brain and she was left with the deep instinctual knowledge that Raphael was in great pain but she did not know why!

When Gabriel and Bree met Raphael at Ariel's door they all sent a mental knock and Ariel stated "enter." Ariel was glad to see Raphael but the moment she saw Gabriel and Bree her instinct again started screaming. Ariel put her hand to her head and stated she did not know why but she had not been feeling well lately.

Gabriel nodded to Raphael and he said to Ariel, forgive me I simply did not want to see my pain reflected on your face, the pain that I was radiating from deep from my heart. Ariel, looked at Raphael and simply said, "Show me." Then with that statement, Raphael touched her mind and all of the barrier cleared and knowledge burst upon her brain. The situation was worse than her greatest fears. A moment later Bree was holding her hand and Gabriel had his hand on Bree's shoulder.

Ariel sat quietly as Bree drained as much of the fear, worry and pain out of her as she could. Ariel opened her eyes and quickly looked at Bree and Gabriel and said thank you. Ariel saw Bree's natural talent as she worked and Gabriel sending Bree energy to continue the process long pass the point where Bree's strength would have run out. Raphael stood with his back to her, she called his name and he turned around and the pain in his eyes took her breath away. Ariel's instincts had told her Jason was in great danger and some how true or not Raphael blamed himself for their son's situation.

For the last several days Ariel had prayed. In her prayers she asked to know what problems were facing her family. Over and over, one thought kept coming after her prayers, "Are you sure you want to know." At first, when she received this though, she realized that she was not sure she did want to know. However, as the days went on and her instincts were constantly beating themselves against the barriers constructed around her mind by Raphael, Ariel's answer to the question became a firm, Yes. I want to know, there maybe something I can do but I can do nothing with out knowledge! Now that she was on the brink of learning all she realized again that yes, she did want to know.

This was her family and she would not pass up any opportunity to help them no matter how minor her help may be because of her fear. Ariel locked her fear down then looked at Raphael and said, "Show me." Raphael sent her the blast of angelic communication. Raphael was monitoring when she got to the part of him breaking the rules of communication which was the source of his pain. Raphael could feel Ariel's heart skip a beat when she learned of Jason's fate and at the same time she saw the connection between her consort's pain to her son's fate.

Bree went to hold her hand but Ariel shook her head and said "No." Ariel said there was one and only one statement of hope, the creator had said that all was not yet lost. Ariel looked at Bree and said, "I do need your help but in a specific way." Bree and Gabriel both looked puzzled.

Ariel said I need you to strip away both my fear and Raphael's pain in this situation because if never before, now we need to think clearly. I need to see and feel that one statement of hope; I need to touch the pure intent or motive of this statement. Gabriel touch Bree's shoulder and Bree touched Ariel hand immediately they stripped the fear and pain away both from Ariel and Raphael until Ariel could see and feel the intent of that one statement of hope as it was first said from the creator to Raphael.

Ariel nodded as Bree and Gabriel withdrew. Ariel touched her mind to the initial thought; when she did, she instantly began to disappear. As her body began to fade, Ariel sent a brief thought to all of them, "I'll be back soon." Ariel "knew" that she had opened herself up to empathic communication with the creator. Ariel "knew" that only she, in this way alone could access the knowledge necessary to help her child.

Ariel materialized in a garden that was soul shatteringly beautiful she felt the garden turning down the volume of its beauty to accommodate her senses. Ariel saw the male relative of Raphael who had visited her when Jason was a child. Then suddenly she knew who he was and she dropped to her knees with head lowered.

The creator said sit child, "So they finally figured out that the answers they sought could come only thought the mothers." Jason has figured out what his father has not. Jason is in hell but he is not a demon yet. He is currently working under the "Rule of Options" and as long as he adheres to the tenants of this rule, he not only will not be a demon but a means of being released from hell is a possibility.

Through this rule Raphael can provide and enhance your strength but only you can access Jason. Examine this rule closely all of the answers and options you have in this situation are outlined in this rule.

A mist surrounded the chair that Ariel had sat in before she disappeared. When the mist evaporated Ariel reappeared. Ariel was extremely still; her eyes were shinning and tears were falling down her face. All in the room turned toward her, Gabriel and Raphael recognized the radiance that surrounded her as they all waited for her to speak.

Ariel took a deep breath then she said, what is the rule of options? Because, it is our only hope to help and possibly save Jason. Bree was shocked but Gabriel and Raphael looked stunned. When Ariel disappeared Gabriel was afraid that he had raised his friend's hopes in a hopeless situation. Although Gabriel had the best of intentions he now saw that his actions could possibly end up being cruel.

Raphael however, was grateful to Gabriel. Raphael could not recall a single demon that had ever had his fate reversed. But faith is the belief in things unseen and if the creator said there was a possibility he would hold on to that knowledge for all he was worth.

One act of disobedience was enough for him, he would hold on to his faith from now on, no matter what or how impossible the situation looked. Bree tapped into the energy line that Gabriel had created for her use, when ever she needed it, then she placed on hand on Gabriel and one on Raphael and sent love to them both, it was during this process that Ariel began to re-appear.

When Ariel mentioned the rule of options both Gabriel and Raphael began to examine the possibilities. Both angels sent the exact words of the rule to there consort's:
"When you find yourself in trouble which is not completely a product of your will, an option is granted but you must be still; wait for time and opportunity to create the only door to heaven's gate"

Raphael thought, "Jason was in hell but he was not yet a demon!" No demon's fate had been reversed but there were one or two angels who had survived a journey through hell and gained there grace back through the rule of options!

They needed more information and they needed a plan. All were in agreement that the rule of communication would not be broken again. It was decided that Raphael and Ariel would seek information through the great library while Gabriel and Bree would speak with one of the few angel who had survived a journey through hell. They all agreed to meet in an hour to compare information.

Raphael watched as Ariel touched a volume and in seconds she was able to tell if any information on the rule of options was available in that volume and to what degree. Raphael saw that Ariel was beginning to look drained; then with out thought, he poured his energy into her. She smiled her thanks and began to examine volumes again but this time with angelic speed.

Raphael felt his heart lighten more in the past few hours and minutes than it had in days, watching her pour her concentration and will toward helping their child gave him hope, genuine hope. He also noticed that Ariel's presence eased his pain. Not once had she condemned him as he knew he deserved. A genuine since of gratitude flooded Raphael as he for the first time, saw her as the gift she truly was, strength surrounded with a gentle touch. Raphael wrapped a cloak of faith around them both.

Chapter Eighteen

For the first time Gabriel brought Bree to heaven. He stood as he watched Bree's body transform into that of an angel. Heaven used her soul as raw material to fashion her angelic body. When the transformation was complete Gabriel could barely look at her she was so beautiful that she hurt his eyes. Gabriel showed her how to tune down her natural radiance so she would blend in comfortably.

Gabriel and Bree then went to the home of one of his oldest friends. When they arrived, Gabriel sent the thought for entry and was directed to the back of the house. Michael's back yard was on the beach, the sun was setting and his friend sat sipping a cool drink as he watched the sun set over the water. Gabriel introduced Bree to Michael and two additional chairs materialized and they took a seat. Through angelic communication Gabriel brought Michael up to speed on the reason for there visit. Michael asked, does Jason know that he is operating under the rule of options? Yes, Gabriel replied, according to his mother.

Michael said very good! The ones that figure that information out the quickest are the ones that have the best chance of survival. Has any one gotten a message to Jason to let him know that he is not alone in his struggle? Gabriel replied, "NO." Michael took a deep breath and let it out slowly.

This is one of the most important steps to helping him keep his faith. Gabriel replied, but how do we get a message to him with out compromising him. Michael replied, there is only one way . . .his mother. As his mother she has "the right to request" to see him one last time, since (the demons believe) she will not see him ever again.

Now you need a good empath, who can through the mother's touch relate all of the necessary information. The empath must send the information directly to his angelic shield quickly and accurately.

However, note this warning because it is of extreme importance. Maintaining his shields is crucial because they protect his inner being from hell's scrutiny. Hell has no knowledge about his shields and therefore it will not be trying to detect or defeat his shields.

The fact that he still has his shields is knowledge that must be protected from hell at all cost; not only for Jason's sake but for any other of our kind that finds himself in a similar situation, this one weapon could be life or death for him and all who come after him. Gabriel nodded, understanding the intense importance of this warning. This warning helped to reinforce the concept that yet again, that they would have to tread with extreme care. Michael took a moment to let the importance of his warning establish a clear connection within Gabriel mind and then he continued.

If the empathic individual is someone who knows both the mother and son the accuracy rate in this process increases. In my case it was my favorite aunt (and my mother's twin sister), who through my mother's touch, shared my mother's body while the information and energy was sent. Hell will now be looking for dual life signatures with in the mother, which will now makes this process harder.

Every escape is examined and any method or options used then, are no longer allowed to be available for use in the future this is one of the reason's that with each escape the process gets harder because any previous advantage is closed off behind its first usage. Gabriel thought, here is another reason that hell can have no knowledge of or belief it is possible that any being in hell possessed shields!

Next, if it is possible, the empath will need to send more than just a message she will need to send a burst of angelic energy into his shields. Jason's shields will be in constant use during his time in hell, because he can not let them down and survive. Jason will need this new energy because he will not have any opportunity to replenish his shield strength; sending his shields energy could literally save his life.

Finally, you need to move as quickly as possible, the longer Jason is there the greater the danger, that he will never get out. Michael looked at Gabriel and said, it was one of the hardest things I have ever had to do; and since I under went this process, it has gotten a lot harder.

Katelyn woke up feeling wonderful, warm, alive, peaceful and well loved. It was a good thing that today was a Saturday she simply could not entertain the thought of work. In fact, she wanted to go to the beach to begin experimenting with her gifts. Justin smiled as he watched her; the difference was like night and day. His instinct about his mother had been more than accurate. She was just what Katelyn needed and when she needed it too.

So, his mother was an elemental that explained a lot. Justin had noticed the new closeness of his parents and their clear affection for each other. Affection that seemed somehow richer and deeper, his father seemed more open and his mother less reserved and both were much happier. Justin always felt that they loved each other because both could not love him so much if they had not genuinely cared about each other.

His mother always told him how much like his father he was and his father always saw his mother in him. Yes, they had loved each other for a long while. It seems they simply just got around to telling each other so. Katelyn was happy and he loved seeing her that way. Justin knew the importance of living in the day. Although they had serious plans to make, he wanted and needed to give her as much happiness in the "now" that time and circumstances would allow.

He told her, he thought the beach was a great idea. They dressed, went out for breakfast, stopped at a store and picked up a picnic lunch and headed for the beach. Katelyn pulled the skirt off of her two piece outfit which revealed a one piece swimming suit. Laughing she headed for the water and dove in. Once in the water Katelyn extended her energy connection. The water in her reaching for the water around her, at once Katelyn felt an assortment of things. It took a minute to sort the emotions out they were coming in to her on so many different levels.

She could pick up the feelings of people in the water and when she listened she could fine tune the vibration to a specific person and if she tried harder she could hear their thoughts. On another level she could feel the levels of purity in the water and she knew which areas were cleaner than others. On another level when she extended her senses she could tell what animals were in the water and where. She could not only identify them but she felt that with a little practice she thought she would be able to communicate with them!

Katelyn had been in the water for over three hours and Justin was beginning to get concerned. It was a beautiful day and he did not want to interfere with her experimentation by breaking into her thoughts so he swam out to her. The moment he touch her she opened her mind up to his and all of the information and emotions she experienced she poured into him.

Justin began to process and catalog the information with out realizing that he was transmitting this information back to her as well as receiving the raw data from her. Katelyn closed her eyes as the water's energy created a connection from her soul to Justin's. Katelyn could feel his love for her like a solid living thing and her love for him was singing. As Katelyn listened closely to the music her soul choose to express its love for Justin. The music was the refrain from the song "I'd Rather" sung by Luther Vandross (a song she had always loved) she kept hearing the refrain over and over again as her connection with the water tapped into what she truly felt about and for Justin:

> *This one thing is true; I'm nothing with out you. I'd rather have bad times with you than good times with someone else. I'd rather be beside you in a storm, than safe and warm by my self. I rather have hard times together than to have it easy apart; I'd rather have the one who holds my heart.*

Katelyn turned in Justin's arms and kissed him as if her life depended on it, in fact it did, because she knew that from this moment on they would operate as two half's of the same whole. This man was her mate, the other half of her soul. What ever they faced in the future, this man, this gift was worth what ever was required of her to keep him safe and in her arms.

Justin had been moving them slowly to shore and when Katelyn noticed, they were getting ready to step out of the water. Justin brought her back to there picnic area and wrapped a towel around them both; then he began to dry her off. Justin marvels at how in tuned she was the water, Justin said nothing (giving her time to experience the new sensation of opening up her senses). it also gave him time to send a pray of gratitude for the beautiful song her soul sang to him in the water, as he prayed to be worthy of her love. All as Justin sat out their lunch and simply enjoyed her presence and the beauty of the day.

Katelyn noticed that time was moving very fast. It seemed they had just got there and now most of the afternoon was over and the evening was beginning. Katelyn noticed the feel of the wind, the temperature was changing but only about one degree per hour; by mid evening they would need a fire because by nightfall it would be less than 60 degrees.

Katelyn knew this because her body only loss heat now if she choose. Once her defense system had been activated she learned that she had much more control over things that in the past she would have thought impossible to affect. Therefore the contrast between the temperature of her body in the morning and the temperature of the wind, informed her accurately of the changes in the temperature. Katelyn could regulate her body heat! She could keep the same temperature she now had or increase or decrease it at her will.

Tomorrow she was going to a nursery to touch different plants and soils this would help her establish an understanding and personal connection with the earth. When Katelyn quieted her mind as information unfolded with in her. She could identify each of her elemental connections and where they flowed through her. She could even see how the process worked!

It seemed that the power of touch was a conduit for all of her connection. To feel or touch the sun or any type of heat (even her body temperature) flowed through her and connected with the power of Fire with in her. To feel or touch water (like today with the ocean) connected her emotionally through the flow of the water's path, where ever or what ever the water touched so could she.

The feel of the wind connected with the power of air in her; it told her a myriad of thing like weather patterns and changes, accurate almost to the second. So tomorrow she would experiment with the feel of the earth.

Justin watched as Katelyn under went her metamorphism, truly becoming the elemental she was born to be. Justin had thought her beautiful before but with the power of the elements shining through her, she was complete radiance. She was literally lit up from with in and it poured out of her. She was dazzling, the most beautiful of butterflies.

Justin had thought it was going to be hard to get her to open the door to her powers, especially given the amount of initial fear he knew she was feeling but what he did not know was that his love and the love they shared was the catalysis for the change. His mother input had helped her release her fears and showed her how to embrace her true nature like someone finding the most precious and rarest of gifts.

Justin took a deep breath as he thought, this made the next step, that of mastery of her gifts, a great deal easier rather than the monumental task he originally feared it would be. Tomorrow they were going to the nursery where she would complete her connections with all of her elemental powers; then they would be ready to move into the development of her gifts for both protection and defense.

Gabriel and Bree returned to her home and a few hours later, Raphael and Ariel made there presence known and were asking to enter. As usual Bree set the meeting in the garden, she knew she needed all the comfort of nature to help her deal with this new and disturbing information that they would have to relate to Raphael and Ariel about there child.

As soon as all were seated and cool drinks provided, Raphael and Ariel started by relating what they had found out about the Rule of Options. It seems that this rule was created to provide an option for an individual; or soul who were in a situation which was not a complete by-product of their choices. The Rule of Fairness dictates that the soul/individual must be given a fighting chance to reverse their fate.

The battle the individual/soul faces will be extremely intense because the individual/soul must prove that where they are now (in hell), is not where they would have ended up at (or was not the by-product of the natural progression of the life choices they were currently making). Simply put, they would not be in hell if there choices had not been taken from them.

This process is a means of revealing the individual/soul to it's self by stripping away all delusions and self lies. Then and only then through truthfulness and a genuine desire to alter his fate will a door be forged out of the individual/soul's will and core level faith that will provide the one and only possibility for release.

During this process the soul will be tempted to abandon its faith and give in to hopelessness. Hell will try to make him believe that he is all but forgotten, by those who use to love him. This hopelessness provides a foundation for despair and this despair cements the soul's place in hell. Therefore to give the soul a fighting chance the Rule of Fairness dictates that he must be given the following:

1. He must maintain his angelic shields.
2. He must maintain his angelic knowledge.

Here Raphael stopped and said, if you notice we referred to the individual/ soul. The process is equal but different for angels and humans. Here is where the application of information gets a little difficult since Jason is both.

They debated the above concept for a minute; then Raphael continued. The soul's angelic shields and knowledge will be at his disposal as long as he does not use the knowledge for evil. The soul's challenge or task is to look evil (in order to survive) with out being evil (he must be true to his faith and beliefs). Upon one true evil act (just one) his angelic shields and knowledge will leave him and he will have a legitimate place in hell.

In deference to a mother's love, both the Rule of Fairness and the Rule of Options allow for the provision of the mother of a condemned or soon to be condemned soul, the right of closure. She and she alone can request a neutral space to see, touch and speak with her child for the last time to help her accept his fate or send a message of fluid grace.

Raphael stated that he and Ariel did not understand the last sentence "to send a message of fluid grace?" Ariel stated that when she tried to touch the meaning, the sentence seemed to have multiple meanings all of which were true but unclear.

Gabriel said, I think that we may have some of the answer to this last part as he began to speak. He related the information that Michael had shared with them. They were trying to form a plan but as they turned the information over again looking for unnoticed options, Bree spoke up and said, I believe that I understand the sentence "To send a message of fluid grace."

Bree was in her way extremely shy; she was not use to giving her opinions to others and even less use to the undivided attention of her audience. To increase her concentration, as well as, to not be influenced by how they accepted what she knew she needed to say, Bree turned her back to them as she spoke, drawing in the calm and confidence that her garden always provided her.

Bree said, water is fluid, and a situation whose end has not yet been written is fluid. In a fluid situation nothing is exactly as it seems. It is like seeing into the future, looking at events that have not occurred. If one thing changes in the present, then the future re-writes itself. Jason's situation is fluid and depending on the choices he makes, he will write his future.

The message that he receives from Ariel in addition to increased energy must be one of faith! Our faith in him, his faith in his beliefs and faith in the love we have for him. It is only through belief and faith that Jason can maintain his grace and find his way home. As Bree turned slowly around she noticed that Gabriel looked at her with pride in his eyes.

Raphael and Ariel looked at her with gratitude and all of them stated that they felt the rightness of what she was saying as she spoke. Now they had two things left to do, design the message of hope that would provide Jason with the greatest amount of hope & strength while hiding there intent from those who would be monitoring the interaction. Next, put in an appeal to hell for a mother's rights to say good-by to her child.

Chapter Nineteen

Vane had a plan; he had the ritual and a birth name of Senior Elder demon. To his surprise it was not that difficult to obtain. The angels in the great fall had re-written the bible (or producing there version of it) portraying them selves as misunderstood and blaming all, on the "man thing." This was a manifesto of why they hated man and why they needed to show man for the worthless creature he was, all in an attempt to show god that man deserved to be punished not them.

The book was signed by many of the angels who were part of the great fall. Vane, understanding demon mentality (even new demons as they were at the time) knew the most powerful and oldest demons would have been asked to sign the bible first (as a sign of respect). Vane chose the signature third from Lucifer for several reasons: it was close to Lucifer's signature which was an indication of age and power, it was written clearly (one wrong letter in the summoning ritual and the whole thing could go horribly wrong).

The final reason for his choice was that he detected no sense of shame about the signature in that it was bold and clear. The first step of his plan was complete; Vane now had a birth name. The manifesto was on display in the hall of records but since most demons were clearly focused in the present, with there interest focused on the capturing of souls, most had little to no interest in history. Vane made sure no one noticed him observing the book (or so he thought).

The second part of his plan required more cunning. Next Vane spoke with a spell master, Vane stated that an assistant had informed him that the spell master was too old and loosing his memory and knowledge. Vane challenging the spell master to produce several extremely old spells.

Hidden with in his requested list of old spells was the spell that Vane needed to call forth a Senior Elder demon.

When the spell master produced each spell, Vane stated his apologies for doubting him and promised to beat his fool of an assistant who suggested that the master was no longer excellent at his craft. Now it was time for Vane to move on to the third part of his plan. He had to craft his opening statement, he had to know exactly what he was going to say and it had to both get and keep the senior Elder's attention. Because Vane knew his life depended on it.

Vane was extremely pleased with him self, his plan was creative, innovative, original and bold. In fact, Vane secretly believed that even the Senior Elder could not help but be impressed by Vane's overall intelligence and creativity in this matter.

Vane smiled as he thought of his first line, " Great Senior Elder allow me to present to you a gift of great value, one only some one like yourself is truly worthy to possess." Yes! Vane thought no demon, no matter how old he was, was willing to pass up a rare gift for free! Vane then continued to craft his speech; I am not powerful enough to keep this prize because soon after her capture, others will gather outside my door with the intent of killing me and taking my gift to you (when he had the prey, Vane knew this would be so).

If I must die, I choose to decide by whom. If my prize must be taken, I reserve the right to decide its fate. All I ask is to survive and receive the fall out of what ever may be left after you have had your fill. Yes, Vane thought, the information was precise clear. Vane timed his speech and he was pleased to note, that the hold speech was under a minute.

Vane was so delighted with himself and his plan that he though, it was no time like the present to put it in place; Vane then preformed the summoning ritual. With in a few minutes, the Senior Elder appeared. The Senior Elder did not appear in his demonic form (this was a last ditch attempt to hide his true power because he had no idea who would have the nerve to summon him with the exception of Lucifer).

No, instead the Senior Elder looked like a human male around the age of thirty-eight to forty years old. He looked like a human version of his angelic self, which meant that he was extremely handsome. He was wearing an expensive Armani suit of clothes, which looked as if it had been tailor made especially for him. Only the flames in his eyes, gave any indication of his level of true anger and annoyance, (at being summoned like an underling to be at the beck and call of a master's will) which Vane sensed was great. Vane began his speech which started, "Great Senior Elder allow me to present to you a gift of great value, one only some one like yourself is truly worthy to possess" . . . and when Vane finished the Senior Elder smiled, which did little to reassure Vane as he said, that will depend on your gift, Vane bowed his head to hide his own smile of relief then said, "An elemental."

Vane found himself a moment later, sitting in a chair opposite the Senior Elder who said, "What do you want for such a prize?" Vain replied, only your help if needed in the last minutes of the capture to counter any unexpected surprise attack in the final minutes of the capture that and the right to absorb the crumbs of the meal once you are both finished and well sated.

The Senior Elder sat quietly and considered the situation before he spoke, "you have raised my appetite to a level of anticipation that I have not experienced in many, many years, do not disappointment me." The Senior Elder continued very calmly and with out raising his voice he said, "Compared to what you have offered, the taste of you would be a sorry substitute. But make no mistake, if you do not deliver . . . (pause) I will leave the details of your fate to your imagination but trust me, what ever your worst conceived of idea of pain, the reality will be 100 times more severe . . . .Then the Senior Elder smiled and said, . . . "Too start with!"

The Senior Elder then disappeared and Vane experiences a taste of fear more brutal that he had experienced when he lost his own soul, until this moment that had been the greatest level of fear he had ever experienced. For the first time Vane wondered if the path he had chosen was a wise one, a bold one yes, but a wise one . . . he was no longer sure.

When Vane was repeating the spell to bring the Senior Elder to his home it all seemed so uncomplicated, so fool proof. Now having met the Senior

Elder demon, who quite frankly turned his blood to ice water, Vane began to re-think the situation and look closer at any problems which could go wrong. As he did so, Vane could almost feel the Elder's laughter at his uncertainty. Vane mastered his fear and pronounced (out loud in an effort to convince himself) fear is for lesser demons, not for those on there way up the promotional latter. Vane needed to speak with Jason as soon as possible, Vane was going to have to take a more active roll in this process, because "failure was not an option!"

Ariel was afraid, some how she had to find the strength to help her child survive but being around people in general was difficult for an empath; being in hell (would be ten times more so, even in one of the upper levels) was one of the absolute last places an empath would want to visit. In order to do what was required she was going to have to lower her shields and she experiences a fresh wave of fear because she knew she would be hit with a multitude of vibrations that could easily immobilizes her.

She suspected this was why only an empath could send the required message of love and strength and why the request had to be made through the mother alone. And, because few warriors would have empaths willing to provide this service, at any cost at all, not to mention the difficult task of some how working thought the warrior's mother as well. As Ariel was considering these thoughts, Ariel heard Bree's mental knock and she said enter.

Ariel and Bree had known each other for many, many years yet they did not have a close relationship. In fact it could be said that they were more acquaintances than friends. However in these last few days that fact seemed to be changing. Ariel did not bother to hide the fear she felt and Bree did not pretend she did not see it.

Bree said I have discussed the situation with Gabriel and I think we need to attack this situation in stages. First I suggested that I provide supplemental shields for you during this process. Since we know you will have to lower your natural shields to connect with Jason, this will provide you with the protection that you will need. Second, Gabriel will strengthen me, while Raphael through his connection with both you and Jason, will sends his love and strength through you to Jason. Ariel was completely surprised and asked, "Why would you do such a thing for us?"

The thing that Ariel was referring to was Bree's willingness to open her self up to an empath. This kind of connection would open Bree up on all levels to Ariel's insight and being the private people that they both were, this act would cause such an intrusion on Bree's personal space that it was almost unthinkable to ask for or accept help on this level. And at the same time it was an unparallel act of selfless help. The type of help, that one would only expect from someone exceptionally close to you.

Bree smiled and said, "First I have nothing to hide, second Justin loves Jason like a brother. Third Gabriel loves Raphael the same way and fourth, I too am a mother and I understand what you are feeling! And finally, this is the first and only opportunity that either of us have been given to prove that we present a greater worth to our mates than either of them had thought possible in the past. If for this one time, I have the opportunity to have my mate look at me as an equal . . . it would be worth all I have to give. So, given all I have explained, how could I not offer my most sincere help?

Purely on instinct from one mother to another, Bree reached for Ariel to hug her and to both of their surprise they both had there shields down and the moment they touched there powers blended and both had access to each. In that Ariel could call on the powers of water to calm her fears and Bree could see the level of genuine gratitude and budding friendship that was starting to grow between them.

With no intent but to comfort someone else in pain, they had found a way to do the impossible, blend their talents and skills. Ariel could draw strength from the energy line of fire, peace from the energy of water and acceptance from the energy of earth. Bree saw for the first time how others viewed her and how she viewed herself. She also saw how much she had always loved Gabriel and how much Ariel loved Raphael. They both saw the genuine level of love they had for their sons and there willingness to do what ever was in there power to help their sons survive.

Katelyn and Justin ended their day at the beach by taking a long walk, then that evening they stopped and had a late dinner and returned to Katelyn's apartment. They had discussed and agreed that Justin should move in with her, she had the greatest amount of space in her apartment and since Justin had only a few things in his "mock" apartment, it would be simpler and easier that way.

There plans for the next day was set and that night Justin made love to Katelyn slowly bereaving in her scent and drowning in the tasted of her, implanting her so deeply in his mind, heart and soul that he felt the connection between them fuse into one.

He entered her slowly one inch at a time while slowly licking her breast all over then taking the tips into his mouth and sucking gently at first; then blowing his breath over the nipples and again taking her nipples in into his mouth as he moved one more inch inside of her.

Justin heightened her senses by opening up his feelings to her and feeding them to her to heighten her sensitivity to every thing he was doing to her, so that his every touch felt like music building to a credenda. He moved one more inch inside of her, as one hand was gently moving up and down the side of her body massaging her body while the other hand was massaging her other nipple. Once he was completely inside of her, he did not move he continued to suck, caress and massage her. Then very, very slowly he began to withdraw from her and with the same inch by inch slowness he again came back to her, inside her. At first Katelyn simply enjoyed the closeness and intimacy of this style of making love which was an erotically interesting combination of foreplay and the act of sex. Soon, however, she began to notice a slow fire burning in her from the inside out every where he touched; kissed and or suckled her, tingled and burned for more.

This method of moving inch by inch inside of her was incredible, she felt every movement and each movement demanded her individual attention until she was so hot she was almost afraid she would or could scorch him. Slowly before Katelyn knew it, her whole body was ablaze with desire.

As if he knew exactly what he was doing to her, Justin slowed down even further, Katelyn could now feel not only the touch itself but the vibration of every movement every lick reverberating through her. Then if that was not enough, each time he took the tip of her breast into his mouth he applied a different technique. Once he held the tip gently with his teeth as his tongue brushed over and around it.

The next time he suckled like a hungry child and yet another time he teased the nipples with his teeth to increase their sensitivity and the sensation when he then licked and suckled again afterwards. All while moving in and out of her slowly inch by inch. Katelyn's body was so sensitive that now every time he moved in or out an inch she felt it vibrate all through out her body.

Finally she vaguely heard begging and then she realized it was her begging him to put out the fire that this slow torture was causing before it literally consumed her. The pleasure was multi-layered coming at her with different intensities and in different directions. The feelings were so powerful that she thought she was literally fall apart if he did not finally bring her to the end that he kept just out of her reach.

Justin was drowsing in her, he literally did not know where she ended and he began. He had never experienced any thing like her and he was addicted to the taste and feel of her. It was not until he heard her, through the fog of pleasure that had become his mind, begging for release that his sanity returned.

Justin realized that this, more intense style of making love to her was one she would have to grow into getting use to. He had gotten so lost in her he forgot that the intensity at first might be difficult for her to handle. Because in addition to the touch, taste and feelings he was producing with in her, he was also feeding his need for her directly into her mind and controlling her ability to climax which added another level that heighten the experience for her.

Justin took her nipple in his mouth and sucked strongly and at the same time he with drew slowly then he released her mind as he thruster into her, with one movement all the way. Katelyn exploded in a climax and she was sure that she actually saw stars! Then as she climaxed around him it pushed him over the edge and he joined her and with his mind linked to hers he shared her explosion and then his own explosion with her.

Katelyn's whole body throbbed and every where he touched her set a series of after shocks that seemed to prolong the climax and push it to a new level of experience. Katelyn was exhausted as she came down from this incredible high! She was going to ask Justin some questions about this method of making love to her but first she thought she would rest a moment. A second later Katelyn was sound asleep.

Justin held Katelyn in his arms, he was a shadow in her mind as these thought were being felt and examined. She fit so perfectly in his arms as if she was made to be there. As Justin began to develop plans for the future he thought in terms of what we need or what we would do. Justin stopped mid thought and asked when did it happen? When did I stop being me and become us or we?

Katelyn was so still that Justin pulled out of his own thoughts and re-entered her mind to see if she was "ok." Katelyn had fainted, Justin checked her heart beat and other body functions to be sure he was right, she had fainted!

Justin smiled he knew that making love to her in this way was intense but the need to show her what she meant to him consumed him. He needed to tell her how much he loved her in a way that left no doubt, no uncertainty; when he opened his mind to hers the sweetness of her love washed over him intensifying his own emotions and when they climaxed (almost) together it was beyond perfect, it was sheer magic!

The next day Katelyn woke with a peace so profound it took her a few minutes to take it all in. All of her senses seemed heighten, as the sun spilled through the window it seemed to have sparks of light that danced and shimmered. The birds chirping seemed to indicate some form of communication that was not yet completely clear to her and in fact one bird in particular was actually singing.

Katelyn stopped and listed to the purity and sweetness of the notes. She smelled the air; she was able to separate the impurities in it and touch it as it was meant to be sweet, fresh and full of life.

Then Katelyn noticed Justin's arms around her and she could feel love radiating from him. She could "feel it" Katelyn thought, no matter what the future holds she had in this moment something that few people ever experience, a moment of pure happiness. Katelyn knew this memory would stay with her the rest of her life and it would always be special to her.

Justin stirred and Katelyn turned and kissed him awake. The natural scent of him was intoxicating she took it inside of her as she examined her reaction to him. He smelled like home, where ever he was, was home. Katelyn found his natural scent mesmerizing; she wanted to bathe in his scent.

Justin awoke to Katelyn's kiss and the glow in her eyes made his heart skip a beat. She looked so beautiful, tossed and well loved. The sight of her warmed his heart as he kissed her back and poured into her mind how much he loved her. This moment, what they shared right now was intimacy, literally in-to-me-and-see! They could see the core of what they each felt and the moment was as sweet as it was profound.

Katelyn reached over and took out her book, she said, "I saw you sitting down at your desk writing these words." I hear the music in each poem which is so beautiful that I am touched and humbled that you wrote these words for me. I felt you, as you sat there writing me love letters with in each poem, telling me the type of love you wanted to share with me; all at a time, when you never truly believed that you would find me.

I know what it is like to want something so badly that it becomes a physical ache! I know the pain of never truly believing that what you need exist, watching other couples and thinking that what they have is "ok" but I wanted so much more. I hear the words of the fourth poem, repeating its self in my mind. This poem actually scared me when I first read it because someone really understood what I felt and put it in words more beautiful than I could have ever expressed.

I loved this poem because it spoke to everything I wanted to have and share in a genuine relationship, in those few moments when I dared to dream this is what I dreamed of . . . . You. You are my dream come true; everything that I did not believe was possible until you! Katelyn asked, "Would you recite the fourth poem to me, I would love to hear this poem, this love letter in your voice, talking only to me!

Justin heart felt as if it was going to break, when Katelyn finished speaking he saw tears swimming in her eyes, tears of sincere joy and a deep love that touched him so deeply that he had to take a moment before he could speak.

Justin said, when I wrote these words I had no idea it was even possible to love anyone the way I love you. I wish I could take total credit for the poems but when I tried to put into words what I wanted to say, I could not find the words so I opened up my soul and these words poured out. Justin kissed her deeply before he smiled and began to recite the fourth poem.

So Much More

My heart cries out for so much more, than I have ever seen before. A love so real and rare, with genuineness and care. I don't want love that's here today and tomorrow gone away, I want a love that grows each day!

I want to know how you think and feel. What thoughts to you appeal?

To understand just why you cry, what makes you fear and why. To know your mind, your heart, your faults . . . My love, to share your thoughts.

Is what I ask for so unreal, a love that time can't steal? But instead let time revel, the love we have is real. If my life should end today, I would like to truly say that I have loved and been loved in a way, that warms my heart even as my breath slips away.

When he finished he looked at her and tears were running from her eyes. Katelyn reached for him and wrapped her arms around him and they simply held each other, letting the beauty of the moment become a part of them.

A little while later, Katelyn smiled and said we need to move soon or I will frankly eat you for breakfast, lunch and dinner! Justin laughed and said, "God knows the thought brings infinite possibilities to my mind but we have work to do." Justin though that the only thing that would pull him away from her at this moment was the need to protect her.

That was the only emotion that would and could override his passion for her. Justin started to get up and said, "I'll shower fast and my limited will power would appreciate it if you let me do so alone." Katelyn smiled because that was exactly what she had in mind, joining him in the shower. But she realized that he was right she needed to get to the nursery. After his shower, Justin dressed quickly and went out to pick up breakfast. He did not trust himself in the house with the thought of Katelyn naked, wet and soapy only a few steps away. He took his time to make sure she was dressed by the time he returned.

As he walked in the door Katelyn laughed and said you did not have to run away! However, the food was a good idea, I'm starved. They finished breakfast and headed for the nursery. When Katelyn walked into the nursery she felt a power surge, it was the concentrated pull of so many living plants in one space.

Chapter Twenty

Katelyn now knew the feel of air, water and fire but earth was a new and different sensation. Katelyn begin to touch each plant and as she did so she "knew" the medical usage for each plant, usage that to date, medical science had no knowledge of or information which had been known and used once a long time ago but forgotten in this current time.

Katelyn even found one plant that, when taken in the right combination with its root, flower and leaves, would cure most cancers in ninety days! The herb literally was drawn to the cancer and consumed the cells, while not causing any harm to any other part of the body.

Katelyn touched plant behind plant and each told her there secrets, old knowledge, forgotten and unknown in this time and age or knowledge yet to be discovered. The more knowledge she absorbed the more she began to understand plant interaction. That is, which plants would strengthen each other and which plants would weaken each other.

Which combination could cure quicker and which combination were deadly. Katelyn did not notice that she was absorbing this information with in seconds of touching the plant. Katelyn knew which plants were healthy, which were sick or dying, Katelyn knew what part of the world they came from and how easy or hard it would be to find them in their natural setting.

In less than an hour Katelyn had touched almost every plant she had seen in the nursery. Katelyn picked up some soil, which the nursery was selling as enriched. Katelyn took her hand and pushed it deep into the soil and immediately she could analysis its true potential.

Katelyn knew that 50% of the soil was full of man made chemicals which was supposed to enhance the soil but in reality the chemicals did more harm than good. Katelyn knew that 40% of the soil was soil that had been drained of its nutrients because it had been used over and over again. Katelyn knew that 10% of the soil was rich volcano soil and that any nutrients or good the soil had to offer came from this portion of the soil.

Katelyn noticed the level of energy between her and the soil changing. Katelyn watched in surprised awe as her touch was neutralizing the chemicals in the soil, enhancing the richness in the volcano soil and energizing the older re-used tired soil. Now all of the soil could absorb the richness of the volcano soil, especially now that it too had been enhanced.

As a result of her interaction with the soil, soon all of the soil was as rich as the volcano soil and would grow and feed any plant it was used on. Katelyn took a handful of this soil and added it to a few of the plants that she knew were sick, she placed her hand over the soil on the plant and she could feel the plant greedily absorbing the nutrients like a hungry child stuffing food in his mouth.

Justin watched Katelyn in fascinating awe, keeping part of his mind in tune to what she was doing and experiencing while another part of his mind was engaged with the store's representative. A female, who found Justin extremely attractive; so it was easy to keep her attention on him, in meaningless conversation, in order to give Katelyn uninterrupted time with the plants.

Katelyn brought one plant, the moment she touched it the plant exploded on her mind like sunshine. It seemed that the plant recognized her! Once long, long ago this plant was considered a prize of great value, the plant greeted her, informing her that it had been a long time since an elemental had found one of his kind.

This plant could still communicate with its parent body and had access to the knowledge and the history of elementals. Katelyn smiled because the plant knew who and what she was; now Katelyn understood why the plant and elemental had such a special relationship. The plant had the ability to cleanse and enhance the flow of energy in the human body a little know trait which was very old knowledge.

The formula was one leaf dried and turned into a tea. A pinch of that tea in a cup of boiling hot water would refresh and revive currently over used energy lines and reawaken dormant energy lines which most humans did not even know they possessed. The plant, which should have been prized above all others, was considered of little value because no one in this time period quite knew what it was or what to do with it.

Katelyn brought the large plant for fewer than five dollars and the clerk seemed glad to have it gone. Katelyn had been looking for the perfect gift for Justin's mother, she wanted to express her appreciation to Bree for helping her accept her heritage and become more fully herself than she had ever been. Katelyn also wanted to thank Bree for raising such an extraordinary man and to thank Bree for her acceptance of Katelyn as Justin's mate.

Bree was the opposite of everything she had heard about mother-in-laws and Katelyn had already began to love her and think of her as a mother. On the drive home Katelyn communicate this information to the plant, as well as informing it that Bree was also an elemental then she asked if the parent plant would be willing to allow another part of its self to find a home with Bree.

The location of the parent plant was given to Katelyn and she shared the information with Justin who said he was touched by her thoughtfulness toward his mother and agreed it was an excellent gift. On the way back to the apartment they stopped and picked up lunch and while Katelyn was setting the table and getting things together for lunch, Justin transported himself to the location of the parent tree.

Justin bowed to the tree in gratitude of the gift he was about to receive and watched as the tree pushed up through the ground a perfect miniature replication of its self. Justin put soil into the pot he carried with him then he thanked the parent tree. Justin reappeared before Katelyn had finished opening containers and putting the lunch on the table. Katelyn placed both plants in the window that received the maximum sunlight then she poured water into each plant until they said enough.

Justin watched her with such pride, she was using her power naturally, with out thought. She did not think about taking the impurities out of the water, she just did! She did the same with the air, she placed filters in and around the apartment so that any air which entered was immediately purified and you could feel the difference. She placed a restriction around and in the apartment regarding all things that lived in the earth. An energy barrier was placed around the apartment that evicted any pest and kept them from returning.

After lunch Katelyn went to the window to check on the plants and as she stood there he could see the energy of the sun pouring into her. Katelyn placed one hand over the soil in each plant as she started to pour energy into the plants; enriching the soil. Justin sat in quiet amazement as he watched the leaves of each plant actually reach out and caress the hand she placed over the soil.

Justin thought, his woman was a walking bereaving miracle! Of all his talents and abilities, this woman was the greatest gift in his life. At that moment Katelyn turned around as energy surrounded and flowed through her. Her eyes were shinning and the love he saw in them for him was a gift that he would never take for granted.

Never had he truly believed that his mate existed and on those rare occasions in the past when he was at lease willing to speculate on the possibility, about what it might be like to have his mate in his life, the reality was so much richer than any thing he had imagined until the comparison was laughable.

Rule was sick and scared, he was holding on to Katelyn by a few very thin threads. Every time he tried to enter her mind to re-establish a hold on her, the thread was burned and if he had not seen the fire coming as it severed the connection, he too would have been burned.

Now Rule had very few threads left but what was worse, he was scared to use them! The elemental in her was not only active, but growing stronger and stronger day by day. The situation had gone from the worse it could possibly be, to Rule thinking about damage control if or when he lost his prey.

Elementals were easier to control in there dormant stage (or at least that was what he had read) the key was to activate them only when they were securely in hell, where the knowledge that they always had the power to alter there fate would be useless after they no longer had the choice.

An active elemental was extremely dangerous to capture as prey and this active strong elemental had Rule fearful of even letting her know he was still there. The only hope he had was to hide! Hide and hope she did not actively seek him out, because if she did then he was toast! No, he had to hide and wait and hope for both help and an opportunity so that he could attack through some strong fear that had yet to reveal it self to him, if he could just hold on until time gave him the opportunity and help he needed.

However, what Rule did not know was that Katelyn was completely aware of each of Rules energy connection lines with in her and she only burned them out, one at a time, when he tried to enter her mind. She allowed the others to continue to exist because unknown to Rule, it allowed Katelyn to hear what Rule was thinking and doing. Irony, now the table was truly turned because Katelyn was now monitoring Rule!

Rule was broadcasting distress signals so strong that Vane knew he had to block them. In order to assess the situation for himself Vane had connected with Rule during his last attempt to re-establish a thread in her mind and what he saw was a great deal worse than what Rule communicated.

Demons always exaggerated, Vane expected bad but he was not prepared for almost hopeless. It shocked Vane that for the first time in his experience the knowledge or information a demon transmitted was actually understated. This was because Rule was so full of fear that he was blocking out the knowledge of the true extent of how close he was to loosing his prey.

Vane had to act fast to get this situation under control, but even he did not know what to do. Vane needed to talk the situation over with someone. Often, Vane had found that when you could lay out the problem, a plan of action presented its self. However, he had to be carful in his choice of confidant that he divulge this information to, that person had to have as much to loose as he did to insure his silence.

The only person that Vane could safely do this with was Jason and now he could not access him because of some ancient rule his mother had invoked, which allowed her to see him one last time. This rule was both stupid and unnecessary and then Vane stopped and thought about the reasons that hell would allow such a rule then he said, "OK" now I get it.

The greatest cruelty one could place on a mother was the undisputable knowledge that her child was and would always be a part of hell. The rule was not stupid but simply the ultimate in gloating and inflicting pain. A soul level deep pain which would only grow in time, "OK" yes, he now got it! He would call for Jason as soon as this extended attempt to drive the pain of Jason's descent straight to the soul of his family was over.

Jason was informed that he had to be at one of the upper levels of hell that day, when he asked why he was only informed that he would find out when he got there. Jason was tired, his shields were holding but the constant strain of having to maintain them was wearing on him. The upper levels of hell were less of a strain on his shields, so he welcomed the trip if only to have the constant pressure on his shield strength eased somewhat.

As Jason ascended he noticed that his guess was correct, the consistent pressure on his shields had begin to ease and now he could make an accurate assessment of his strength, Jason saw that he was at about 50% shield strength and he did not know how much longer he could hold out. Yet at that moment he knew that he would fight until there was nothing left to fight with.

Jason was directed to a room which, while it still had the dingy feel of hell, was lighter and less over all depressing. As Jason felt some of the pressure ease, he sat down and closed his eyes intending to get what ever rest he could before what ever reason he was required to be here revealed it's self. Jason had learned a long time ago, that you use every opportunity no matter how brief to gain what ever strength you can. This space allowed for a level of rest that Jason had not felt since he entered hell.

Jason was just entering a relaxed state when the door opened. Jason sat straight up and opened his eyes, prepared he thought for anything except for who walked into the room! Jason opened his eyes as his mother walked in he was so shocked that for a moment he dropped his shield and then as she put her arms around him, to his complete surprise (on top of shock) it was not him who put his shield back in place but his mother!

The door shut and his mother held him tightly as he fell into her arms. Somehow his mother, through her touch, had extended his shields to include her. So that she could speak privately to him, while on the surface they spoke of general things but with in the shield Ariel said, "Son we have little time but I bring messages from both your father and I. I am sending them to you now."

Jason bowed his head and felt the impact of a burst of concentrated energy 90% stayed dormant while 10% spread through out his shields replenishing the damage and strain of the last few weeks in hell then he felt energy flow to his mind, heart, sprit, body and soul. He knew "hope" genuine hope as the healing energy spread through out his body sent by his mother's touch.

Jason had just the right stance, his head bowed seemingly to be to ashamed to look his mother in the eyes when what he was really doing was absorbing the energy and hiding the gratitude he felt at the help and support of his family. He felt his father's energy and the 90% reserve would last for a long time if he used it with care. The 10% he was using now put him in a well rested and relaxed state not only reinforcing his shields but eliminating all of the strain and traces of negativity leaving only an inactive external shell to fool the scans of other demons.

Jason sent his love and thanks to his mother privately as she spoke outwardly for the demons listening to here, she said "demon or not you are still my child!" Then she kissed him on the cheek with tears streaming down her eyes giving the demons again the show they wanted to see. However, with that kiss, as a parting gift she sent a different type of energy, the energy of fire, water, air and earth. Jason was completely stunned, how and where had she gotten this power, this was a completely new energy source one he had never felt from his mother. It was all a mystery, his mother had always seemed delicate and fragile yet here she was in hell fighting for him and with him giving him everything she could!

Ariel's time was up and she had done all she could and then some, she had depleted herself in order to give him another type of energy to face all that he must. She left her son with tears in her eyes exactly what the demons had hoped to see yet she did not have to act, the tears were real. When she walked in to the room Jason looked so tired yet when she touched him she felt his resolve to fight with everything he was. At that moment she had never been prouder of him! Ariel had barely enough energy to transport herself home when she felt her faltering energy being infused with the energy of the elements sustaining her, re-infusing her with the energy she needed because she had given all she could to Jason.

Ariel appeared in Bree home and materialized in Bree's arms. Raphael was still pouring all of the energy he had into Jason and Gabriel was monitoring Raphael to insure that he had enough energy to return to himself. Gabriel was standing ready to give Raphael the necessary energy to pull away from Jason and back to himself. Bree had volunteered to do the same for Ariel.

A week ago, Bree had received another visit from her children. Katelyn had shyly given her a gift, when Bree opened it the plant sung to her. The music touched Bree so deeply she felt it all the way through her soul; the song was one of greeting. When the song ended Bree had tears streaming down her eyes as the beauty of the song flowed through her.

When Bree was a child the knowledge of this plant was known but it was considered very, very old knowledge. Yet she had read about it in an ancient text, she knew that it was something so rare that she thought it was no longer a part of the earth. As the plant sung, Bree felt the cleaning of her energy signals, the lines felt stronger, purer and deeper than she had ever felt before.

When the song ended, the tears in Bree's eyes fell directly into the soil of the plant and quickly disappeared. For the first time Bree felt at one with her power, the power of being an elemental, Bree felt at one with herself. Bree took the plant through out the garden and let the plant choose where it wanted to be replanted, there was one spot somewhat isolated yet it received the morning sun brilliantly when they reached the spot the plant sung one note, which translated into "home." Bree enriched the soil further and the plant dug its roots in.

Justin and Katelyn watched as Bree communicated with the plant. As Bree finished and walked toward them she gave Katelyn a fierce hug and said only you could have picked out that unique, rare and wonderfully special gift. There are no words to express my gratitude but then Bree connected her energy to Katelyn and the wonder and joy of the gift was communicated through this sharing.

Justin watched as his mother and his mate bonded further. It seemed that every time they met the bond went deeper. Justin could think of few things which gave him greater happiness than watching the two women he loved, learn to love each other.

Chapter Twenty-One

Uself had been watching the punishment of a demon (one of his favorite sports) and taking bets on when and under what pressure the demon would break. Uself especially enjoyed this round because it featured his favorite torturer and that demon was an artist! Each time he always found some new ways to inflict pain or some exquisite twist on a tried and true technique.

Then Uself felt himself being summoned. As a Senior-Elder demon, only one being in hell would dare to do that. So Uself bit down on his rage and prepared to meet Lucifer. As Uself followed the path of the summons he was surprised to find himself in the home of a younger demon. Uself looked around, surely Lucifer was here also.

But when the young demon began to speak it was clear that it was he who had summoned him! Flames flashed in Uself's eyes as he began to think of all of the different ways he would punish this stupid little demon for daring to summon him as if he was some common dog! Uself spared a moment to listen to this puffed up little demon and he heard the word, "gift."

Uself attention was caught and he started to pay more attention to the silly little speech hoping for the demon's sake he kept it short, Uself was not prepared to be bored in addition to being insulted. Then Uself thought with amusement what gift could this flea of a demon have that he would either want or accept?

Uself's curiosity got the best of him and he gave this flea his full attention and listened to the flea's well thought out presentation, thankfully it was brief. Then Uself replied, "That would depend on the gift." Now Uself waited for the flea to say something useless or worse even more insulting.

At which point Uself was going to grab him and hand him over to his favorite torturer to re-enact the session he had just missed, using this flea as the star attraction!

Then the flea stated he had the soul of an elemental. The visions of torture Uself had in his mind to inflict on the flea stopped. Uself's mind went blank for a moment! An elemental was a gift worthy of even his attention. Pity! Now it seems that the flea would have to live, at least for now.

Uself was a student of history, eons upon eons he had watched Lucifer grow in power and none absolutely none knew how he accomplished it! Uself at first, wanted to know the source of Lucifer's power out of curiosity. Then over time, watching that power become so strong that it was equal to none, now Uself had a burning need to know the source of Lucifer's power. Since both Uself and Lucifer had once been angels, Uself thought that what ever the source of the power, it could be used equally by both of them. Uself had research through out time for what possible thing or combination of things could actively attribute to the power Lucifer held.

Then centuries ago, uself had helped to create madness in a brilliant scholar. A scholar who had spent a great deal of his time translating obscure and ancient text and in one of them was information on a list of rare human beings. Human beings that somehow had access to abilities which others did not.

One such being was called an elemental (most of the text was destroyed this was the only section that was readable). These elementals were usually women who connected so strongly with the elements of the earth that they possessed great power. These women were once worshipped and it was considered a mark of god's favor to have one among your people.

Once upon a time, every little girl from the age of three to six was tested by the priestess to see if they had been blessed with this unique and rare gift. This knowledge had intrigued Uself and he had searched for additional information but he had only found bits and pieces not enough to form a whole picture. These elemental could be the answer to questions that burned with in Uself, questions that he dared not give voice to for fear of the repercussions.

As Uself thought about this situation, he could not help but wonder if this was the answer he sought? Could the soul of an elemental possibly explain Lucifer's power? This was the only information that Uself had come across in his long search that could possibly explain why Lucifer's power had grown to almost god like proportions. While Uself was strong but he and the others were no where near Lucifer's level of power either alone or collectively. They had all been angels, so what ever it was that increased Lucifer's strength to his current level could conceivably do the same for one of them if they (hopefully him) could find out what the power source truly was.

The few remaining Senior-Elders, who had once been angels, all felt the same way but none dared asked for fear of Lucifer's swift and intense dislike of any questions on this subject. Again the question reverberated in Uself's mind could Lucifer be drawing his power from one such as this! Uself did not know the answer to that question but what he did know was that senior and Jr. Flea (his new pet names for Vane and Rule) had stumbled upon something beyond price and he would own it!

Uself was a student of demon and human history and nature. Uself had watched time and time again as ego, arrogance and pride had breed blindness and stupidity into both demons and humans. Instance after instance an arrogant flea would summon one greater than themselves with the misguided belief that a greater power would do the bidding of a lesser one, simply because the lesser evil had been stupid enough to bring the older demon forward.

As Uself examined Vane's pathetic attempts to manipulate and use him he shook his head because the little flea did not realize that he was now under Uself's control, not the other way around. However, this turns out the little fleas had forfeited there lives, they simply did not know it yet!

Bree had spent time with the plant every day, since she received it and each touch revealed a greater more extensive knowledge about the plant. It seemed that it not only cleansed the energy lines but it explained how to create new energy lines and provided a map to where dormant energy lines with in her could be found.

The plant had given her one leaf to turn into tea, then the plant had showed her the benefit of her now morning tea. Over the course of the last week her strength had doubled and when she said she would look after Ariel, during her visit to Jason in hell, she knew she had both the ability and strength to do so.

Bree poured strength into Ariel after she left Jason in the upper regions of hell and when Ariel was strong enough Bree brought Ariel to her home to sit in her garden. The atmosphere of the garden had a new more intense feeling of healing about it and instinctively Bree knew that the garden would help.

The moment she materialized Ariel could feel the peace of their surrounding descend into her sprit spreading through out her body mind, sprit and soul . . . real core level peace. Then strength flowed into her she felt stronger than she had in a very long time.

Ariel was grateful and when Gabriel and Raphael materialized Ariel could see that the garden had the same effect on Raphael only quicker and more intense, Gabriel felt it too. He was some what drained by sharing his energy with Raphael and he though he was going to have to do the same with Bree but to his surprise it was Bree who was sharing energy with him and he recognized the enhanced nature of that power. Gabriel traced the power to the plant in the isolated spot in the garden then walked over to it and bowed and said thank you. The plant sung and Gabriel listed to the beauty of the song in awe.

Jason went back to his apartment and immediately put filters in for the air in his apartment. Jason took a nap and slept better than he had ever slept in hell. His shields were on automatic now that he had the energy to put his internal defense system to use in this manner. With his strength heighten and a 90% reserve, Jason listen to the messages of love and hope his father sent him re-enforcing what he had already figured out about the rule of options before he fell asleep.

Jason woke up seven hours later deeply refreshed and to an urgent summons from Vane requesting his attendance. Jason knew what Vane's concerns were, Rule was loosing his hold on the elemental and Vane was afraid. Vane was now looking for a way out or a way to blame him. Jason reviewed the limited options the situation offered but he had no solution.

Jason felt it was best not put Vane off any longer so he decided to answer his summons and see what additional information presented itself, which would give him more options to work with. Jason materialized at Vane's door and heard the word "enter" in his mind. Jason materialized in Vane's living room where vane sat lost in thought while looking into the fire burning in the fire place.

Jason said nothing, waiting for Vane to acknowledge him. Vane started speaking (as if they had been in the middle of a conversation all along) I should have found another way, should have never got involved, I should have never taken it so far! As Vane was speaking more to himself than to Jason, Jason did an intense scan of Vane's home, he now had the strength to do so thoroughly and to his surprise he found several additional and different demon signatures plus one that stood out because it was the energy signature of a Senior Elder demon.

Jason was examining the energy signatures so that he could place a birth name to each especially that of the Senior Elder demon when Vane spoke to him and said, "You know the situation is extremely bad. That worm Rule has all but lost the elemental and if that is not bad enough she is no longer dormant and she is learning more and more about who and what she is!"

We need to turn this situation around and fast, do you have any suggestion on this matter. Jason was thoughtfully quite, seeming to give Vane's question some thought when in fact Jason was wondering if Vane had any idea of how many listening devices were broadcasting from his home. Based on Vane's last statement, Jason would guess that Vane did not have a clue!

For some reason, demons seem to feel that what they would think of to do to you, you would not and could never think of to do them. Demons seemed to always be surprised when what they did to others got used on them. Demon's it seemed did not know there limitations and always believed they were smarter than the next demon. They also believed that people and some demons were strictly for usage. I guess this was why there were few demon partnerships and when there was, they were based on a mutual need.

Once that need was met they would turn on each other. Jason spoke and said, "It seems to me that Rule needs a more secure base, she is after all only human and she must fear something. We need to find out what it is and confront her with these fears. Jason knew that the first thing Justin would do, would be to find a way to eliminate her fears.

Justin would know that this was one of the first pathway that negativity would try to use in any upcoming battle, therefore, Justin would deal with her fears first. Accordingly, Jason felt reasonably safe in giving increase fear as an option for a focal point of attack, safe in that he had done nothing to harm Justin's mate.

Vane listened and agreed that the fear must be increased, but how. Again Jason made a suggestion that he knew would fail, if the boyfriend is making her happy throw another woman at him and see how she handles it. If we get lucky he will be attracted to the new woman and that will start a chain reaction of fear and negativity in the prey.

You know that in human relationships, women are never really sure of their men and for good reason because most men will not pass up the opportunity for sex, even when they actually care about there mates. I reviewed Rules notes and there was one woman on the prey's job who was attracted to the elemental's boyfriend (Jason would have to monitor his thinking more closely he had almost said attracted to Justin!).

Let's increase the other woman's interest in the prey's boyfriend and see where this takes us. Vane was pleased with the suggestions, jealousy had a good track record in destroying relationships this plan of attack could provide the boast that Rule needed to get into her mind again. Jason knew this attack would not work either, by now Justin had a mind link established with his mate where he would be able to feel what she feels and this would allow Justin to get around any outside attempts to cause dissention between them through sheer honesty. For now, Jason had accomplished his goal; he had given Vane the illusion of a way out while at the same time he did nothing to hurt or harm Katelyn.

Katelyn and Justin both agreed that normal habits must be maintained as they prepared for the battle. They went to work, she arrived first and Justin ten minutes later. Susan, the office receptionist, thought Justin was one of the most handsome men she had seen and at first she was "ok" with him choosing Katelyn over her because she had more than enough men to worry about but as time went on, Susan thought that any one that good looking should be with her.

Katelyn had brains but Susan had the body and she knew it! When Justin came in, Susan did all she could to hold his attentions. Susan fished for compliments by asking what he thought of the color of her dress, did he think the color the right one for her complexion. Then she modeled the dress under the pretense of whether or not the style was right for her when in fact she was clearly intending to show off her figure.

Justin looked at her and stated that he knew very little about such things. It was Susan intent to engage him in this type of personal conversation while Katelyn watched when she came in the door. However, the moment Katelyn walked into the office Justin's eyes lit up and he smiled only for her. Justin sent Katelyn a SOS stating that he was having trouble getting loose from Susan and he needed help.

Katelyn walked over and kissed him openly and passionately and he kissed her back the same way, Susan was so stunned she was speechless. When Katelyn ended the kiss she smiled sweetly at Susan and said one word, "taken." It was all Justin could do to keep from breaking out into laughter. His Katelyn was so unpredictable and she was loosing her shyness in layers.

The insecure old Katelyn would have never made such a bold move, she would not have been sure enough of him, her self or their relationship to act with such confidence. However, now having shared Justin's mind, his body and his soul Katelyn felt a new confidence that was so natural even she had not noticed the change in her behavior. Later that day, Susan tried again in one last desperate attempt to show that she was the reigning office sex goddess, who could have any man she chooses.

Justin was speaking to another co-worker when Susan walked up to him and put her hand around his arm and suggested that they have lunch together. Justin was about to inform her that he had other plans when Katelyn walked in, Susan smiled expecting Katelyn to be hurt and to show it but Katelyn smiled and said, "Susan, give it your best shot! Then she walked out laughing."

Unknown to Susan, Justin had called for Katelyn the moment Susan began to target him again. Katelyn walked in just to watch the show, as Justin was trying to get away while Susan employing all her charm to no avail. Katelyn was still laughing as she went back to her office because Justin had sent her a threat for leaving him alone to deal with Susan.

When a thought hit her . . . She had absolutely no fear that Justin was interested in Susan not in the least, not even a lingering doubt that she might be wrong. Out of curiosity she scanned Justin's thoughts about Susan . . .he thought she was a beautiful woman on the outside but inside where it truly counted, especially to him, he saw the state of her soul and it was not a pretty sight, she was the exact opposite on the inside. More than anything Justin felt both repulsed and sorry for her. Justin saw Katelyn scanning him for his thoughts about Susan and he sent her love. For the first time in her life Katelyn was secure in the belief, no the fact that he loved her, that they loved each other and what they had neither of them could nor would look to find in another.

Katelyn continued to laugh and tease Justin (through their mental link) as she enjoyed the freedom that being secure in his love gave her. Katelyn laughed again as Justin finally got away from Susan; Katelyn teased Justin about the event as they left the office to pick up dinner on the way home.

After dinner, they took a shower together Justin was about to reach for a towel to dry her off when she stopped him; took the towel out of his hand and began to dry him off. Katelyn had some warm scented oils, sandalwood and lemon by the bed. She slowly rubbed the oil all over his body, every time he reached for her she said "my turn."

Justin tried to contain himself as he saw all sorts of sexual ideas running through her mind. Slowly she rubbed him all over in the scented oil then with feather light little licks she took her tongue and outlined his lips, while stopping now and then to slowly put the tip of her tongue in his mouth for a brief kiss only to start the process all over again.

Katelyn kissed his eyes his neck his ears then she went back to outlining his lips again. Slowly she kissed her way to his nipples and sucked each one in alternating patterns and in different ways she touched her mind to his and saw that he was on fire. Katelyn kissed her way down to his navel and took a moment to play there as well.

Then she rubbed her face in the hair surrounding her ultimate goal. Slowly she kissed her way to the base of his penis and she took each of his balls in to her hands and played with them, while her mouth licked him around the base of his penis. The result of her efforts caused small amounts of cream to roll down his penis.

Katelyn licked the cream off him and the taste of him was beyond her imagination, it was magic. Katelyn put her mouth on the tip of his penis and sucked lightly, milking him of little spurts of cream. Katelyn had never enjoyed providing oral sex to her partners in the past; this is why the taste of Justin came as such a surprise. From that first taste, she went from tentative to hunger; Justin was a feast!

To add to that bombshell, the elemental energy lines in side of her were fighting to absorb the cream as it entered her system creating an intense craving almost a need for more! Katelyn massaged and suckled as she touched his mind. Katelyn could see that he was about to explode so she redoubled her efforts to heighten his pleasure and at the same time she opened her mind to him and showed him her intense need for more of him and that she could not get enough of the taste of him, at that moment he exploded.

Justin was reeling from the after shock of his explosion inside Katelyn mouth, she had suckled him with so much need the moment he touched her mind and her emotions burst through his he simply imploded; for a moment he would swear he saw stars! She consumed him, like a thirsty child drinking a sweet and rare treat. She suckled him until he was limp and every last drop was gone. He knew she would have stayed right there, slowly building him to another climax if he had not said, "my turn . . . I'm thirsty too."

Katelyn licked him again and then said that was one of the most incredible experiences I've ever had. Justin said, "Lay back, I need you inside of me too." Later that night when Katelyn was lying boneless in Justin's arms she asked," Why is it so different with you." You were the first man I ever choose to offer oral sex to. This is an activity that I have never been very good at with past relationships. Usually my partner would worry me over and over again until I provide this service and then they would tell me that I'm no good at it.

But with you, I could not get enough of you! The thought of making oral love to you is not only sweet but a serious turn-on! "Why." Justin explained that in his world oral sex had a different meaning; he had told her initially that before he first tasted her, absorbing her into him that this process would activate the mating ritual bonding between them. Now that she had absorbed him, the mating bonding was complete.

Now he went into greater detail, this type of sexual act was meant to be shared only by those who loved each other because the fluids which are released have not only the DNA of the individual which you take into you but that person actually becomes a part of you. Where ever they are you can find them and what they feel you can too. If the connection is strong enough (which usually happens after years of marriage) absorbing another's DNA can provide an alternated method of communication with connects you the other person on a cellular level.

The DNA of another is not something that we lightly take into out being. So you are the first person I have ever made oral love to and you are the only one whom I have allowed to perform orally on me. For the record, I may be inexperienced in this form of sexual expression but I do not have a clue how it could have been any better! I love the taste of you. Katelyn was surprised, thrilled and honored that she was his first (and only, he said in her mind) oral experience.

On another level he was her first as well, Katelyn had always made a point of having a towel near so that during the ejaculation process she could discreetly cover him and pull away. She tried to avoid swallowed semen when ever possible. Before the though of doing so always made her want to gage. With Justin it was a completely new experience; she was already thinking of ways to make him climax stronger and longer, her mouth watered at the thought!

Chapter Twenty-Two

Vane's worry was turning to fear; He called Rule in for a meeting and gave him Jason's suggestion as if it was his own. When Rule asked how he was to go about this task, Vane Knocked him across the room while shouting, "Do I have to do every thing for you, figure it out!" Rule left feeling extremely put upon and used. Under his breath Rule said, "You call this help, one general suggestion and no direction on how to bring it about!"

Rule was still angry when he ran into Jason later that evening but he could not resist the opportunity to brag. Rule told Jason how they, mostly him, had come up with a plan to create jealousy in the prey by finding another female to throw at the boyfriend. Jason had to fight the urge to laugh, when he heard his own plan coming out of Rule's mouth as if it was his own idea.

In a heart beat, Rule went from bragging to worrying when Jason asked him how he was going to accomplish his plan. When Rule did not answer right away, Jason casually stated, isn't there some woman in the prey's work space that you planned to use for this job? Rule looked thoughtful and said what do you mean? Jason replied, again with a casual and half distracted air about him, nothing its just that I heard that women seldom get along with others in the work place and you did mention once, I think about some female on the prey's job that tried to attract the boyfriend. At least I think that's what you said; I may have heard you wrong.

Rule just looked somewhat pissed off and said, when I speak you need to listen to every word I say and yes! You got it wrong. Rule got up to leave and when he turned his back on Jason he smiled, that's it! Rule thought, the woman on the job! I need to find the demon assigned to her. I saw her demon that day . . . now what was her name, oh yeah, Tish!

Rule transported to Tish's door but rather than bid him enter, Tish opened the door and looked at him with a question in her expression which translated to "what do you want?" Rule put on his most charming manor and stated "a contract." Tish's expression changed from surprise to greed as she motioned for him to enter. A contract was an important interaction among demons. First it meant that you had something that another demon wanted which always put you ahead of the game in the negotiations.

Second, it meant you had an opportunity to gain a lot with little to no output on your part and finally it provided the opportunity to have something to use against them to bind them to your will at some future date, for your own reasons. Tish sat down next to Rule on the couch and said tell me what you need and what terms you are prepared to offer?

Rule outlined his plan (by now he had begun to believe it was he who thought the plan up) to use her prey to try to create jealousy with in his prey and bonus points if her prey managed to get his prey's boyfriend to have sex with her. The first thing that Tish said was I want a "no fault contract." This meant that if her prey did not succeed, Tish would not be held responsible in any way.

This process was common among demons often they contracted to use another's prey in such a manor to help achieve their goals but usually when you step into a deal with another demon you are at risk of punishment if the scheme fails. Therefore until the "no fault contract" was put in to use, few demons would get involved with another's problem, It simply was not worth the risk.

However, with the no fault contract you could, if you were smart enough, come out of the experience with no harm to yourself and the possibility of gain as well. The first thing was to get the contract in some undeniable format such as on tape, video and or some written form. A format where you could prove that a no fault contract was entered into.

The no fault contract was first brought in to use because many older demons made promises that they had no intent on keeping. Then if the prey was lost, the older demons tried to find a way to blame the contracted demon for their plan going wrong and for there losses. Younger demons had begun to believe this rule was just another method by which they could be used, until one bright younger demon recorded the contract with out the older demon's knowledge. Later when the plan failed and the prey was lost, the older demon stated that the younger demon was lying when he said they had a contract which clearly outlined that no fault was to fall on the younger demon if the prey was lost.

The younger demon played the recording of the contract, to the court which included some information on the older demons that the younger demon would not have known; this authenticated the recording and no one doubted it. The punishment for the older demon was server. He was punished not only for loosing his prey but punished for lying to the court. However his worse punishment was that he was punished for being stupid enough to get caught in his lie. In truth the court expected the older demons to lie, especially when punishment was involved but what they could not forgive or tolerate was an older demon getting caught at it; being out smarted!

The senior demon was punished in several painful ways but the lingering and final punishment was that from this point forward no other demon would contract with him because he was labeled to stupid to work with and his overall standing in hell dropped considerably. The overall outcome of this situation was that from that moment forward, any demon entering into a contract wanted an iron clad proof that the contract existed. To insure that the contract was authentic, the contractor must add some damming personal information to the contract. Information of a private nature that the demon he was contracting with would have no way of knowing other than through a contract.

The next thing that Tris wanted was ten percent of the prey. This was the maximum in profit she could ask for (One she knew she would not probably get but in negotiating one always started higher than there expectations) any way they finally agreed on 3 percent profit for Tris. For the service Rule needed, a fair percent was 1 maybe 1 and a half percent. Rule paid her doubled the normal amount for this service, which clearly indicated that he was in trouble.

The contract was set and it was agreed that Monday Tris' prey would make a serious play for the boyfriend. It was also in the contract that should Tris' prey succeed in having sex with the boyfriend, Tris' percentage went up to 5%. Tris was more than happy with the deal and so was Rule. He was far more desperate than he thought he let on. In fact, Rule was willing (if necessary) to go the complete ten percent to put his plan in place.

Once Rule left, Tris took a deep breath and noted the intense level of fear in and on him. Tris made multiple copies of the contract and put them in different hiding place, if she needed to prove her claim, she was making sure that she could do so with no problem.

Jason knew the plan would fail; all he had to do was think of what he would feel if he ever was lucky enough to meet his mate; he knew that Justin would feel the same. Beside compared to that feeling, all other women would disappear for him and he knew again, it was the same for Justin. Poor Susan, the best she could accomplish would be to get on Justin's nerves.

Jason kept all traces of humor off his face as Rule got up and left. Inside he was laughing at the ego and self lies that demon tell them selves. It was their ego that made them easy to manipulate. Jason quickly refocused his mind, remembering that attention to detail was necessary to work his way out of his situation.

Jason review the current situation and took it to the next step, he thought both Vane and Rule are going to move to desperate mode as soon as Susan fails. Jason went back to his apartment with the intent to be well rested to meet the next round of challenges. Thanks to his parent (Jason felt an older version of Justin in the power lines he received from his father; through his mother's touch) he also felt some energy lines that were completely new and they felt feminine, if he had to guess he would bet that Justin's parents had somehow been able to augment or enhance the power lines he felt.

Jason shifted his mind as his shield issued a low level warning. A shade . . ... Shade #4-56 had been following him and Rule. Jason asked his shields to do a probability inquire regarding the amount of danger the shade was capable of causing for Jason in his current situation. As an after thought,

Jason also requested that his shield do a probability check for Vane and Rule as well.

The ability to do a probability check was one of the gifts that his race had been given. They too had to follow an edit which was similar to that of a human physician . . . "do no harm." Often when you are suggesting information to humans you needed to know as much as possible about the likely outcomes of your input in to there lives. Therefore when he was not sure if his input would not cause more problems than it would solve, he would do a probability check. Then he would know if he should go ahead with his current plans or if those plans needed to be augmented or changed all together.

The probability check was completed and with interesting results . . .. the probability scan indicated that shade 4-56's actions would have a 90% "no effect" on him and only a 10% possibility of preferable concerns. It also indicated that 5 percent of that ten percent included an inevitability situation. This simply meant that the 5 percent was going to happen and whether it happened through the intervention of Shade 4-56 or not, it was something that was going to enter the situation one way or another.

The scan also stated that Vane had a 75 percent probability that through the actions of shade 4-56 a series of negative situations were going to occur for him. The genuine surprise was that the scan revealed that Rule had an 85 percent probability of receiving a positive result as the direct input of Shade 4-56 in this situation. Jason reviewed the finding and decided to do nothing for the present. After all, the shade was only trying to survive in hell, who was Jason to make that process harder especially when it was not necessary. Jason did however put in a safe guard and requested that the moment Shade 4-56's activities could or would cause a problem for him that he be notified ASAP.

Jason was still using the ten percent initial energy lines which were activated from the energy he received through his mother. The lines were extremely powerful and because of which, he could sleep really sleep and wake up well rested and ready to face hell again!

Gabriel and Bree, Raphael and Ariel had gotten much closer over the last few weeks. The experience that they shared had a wonderful benefit; they all "knew" that Jason was alright. This alone for Raphael was the one thing that put his grief and anger at his self on hold, as he poured all of his energy into fighting for his son. Each of them could monitor him through the energy they shared with him. Then they found that not only could they monitor him, they could continue to feed him energy the same way. Somehow this ability was tied into his angelic shields.

As long as he had his shields it meant that he had not fallen and there was a genuine reason for the hope, that a way could and would be found to get him out. Right now they were simply grateful that they could help him survive by feed him the strength to continue. The fear, worry and strain of this situation had had a strong yet positive effect on Bree and Ariel.

Each had begun to become the woman they were born to be and each was finding her true nature and her deeper self, her strength and her place in her family structure. No longer were they in awe of their mates, now their mates were in awe of them. It was as if they were seeing them with new eyes and what they saw was the beautiful, powerful and wonderful woman that they were. They were now thought of as gifts and seen in ways that they had never been seen or thought of before. Gabriel not only listened to Bree but he asked her what she thought, not to be polite or for general conversation but because he really wanted to know her opinions and views; Raphael was treating Ariel the same way. It was as if the attention and love that they now received caused them to bloom into the unique and rare flowers they were always meant to be.

Uself, a name which meant "you serve at the pleasure of god." That was the name he was given at his conception (or birth) by the creator. It was a name that he not only did not use anymore but one which few knew belonged to him! Uself preferred the term Elder; it gave little information about him personally and allowed him to simply blend into a larger circle of demons.

Where it is the nature of most demons to brag, be seen, wish to be looked up to and inspire jealousy in others. Elder demons knew what many younger than them, did not and that was there was safety in silence. One becomes an Elder mainly through their ability to survive hell. This process became easier, when few to none knew about you because knowledge is power.

Many eons ago he had lost his angelic shields and access to the knowledge that the creator shares with his angels but he had not lost the memory of his long life experience and that of being an angel. All the history he witness, history that he was a part of that was the knowledge of his life; his knowledge which belonged to him where ever he was. Another trait of an Elder demon was attention to detail, something else that younger demons had to learn the hard way . . . assuming they survived their mistakes.

Uself knew that often some little known detail applied at the right point in time had the ability to change the outcome of any situation. Uself had learned this lesson the hard way and it had almost cost him his life! It had however cost him levels of respect in hell and that was almost as bad. Respect in hell was protection that along with the uncertainty that lack of knowledge provides about a demon's age, skill level, strengths and abilities.

The combination of the above often made younger demons choose, for the most part, to view them as uncertain possibilities and the last thing that most demons's wanted to deal with was uncertainly. Any Elder demon that lost this perception in the eyes of younger demons would be attacked on all sides.

In hell the weak will come together if there is the possibility of destroying the strong. These unlikely allies will band together out of need, they will re-direct their hatred from each other to focus on the common goal until the object is achieved. Then they will turn on each other again. This was the law of the sociopath, "Always make sure I need you, if not . . . . you are food!" Hell was full of sociopaths and Uself had seen this process happen time and time again.

Uself knew all that Vane knew being a Senior Elder he had quickly tapped into the part of Vane's mind which was trying to hide the knowledge of his fears and uncertainty regarding Rules abilities to achieve the goal of bringing the elemental to hell. Uself easily followed Vane's connection to Rule and read Rules fear and genuine concern and worry about his ability complete his task.

Then Uself noticed a connection to Jason and immediately Uself saw that some thing was not as it should be. Jason was a recently fallen soul; his connection to Vane should be filled with fear, ego and pride shinning brightly as all newly fallen souls try to hide there fear behind an explosion of self delusion and self lies.

The energy lines to Jason should be glowing brightly. However, the energy line in stead was dull barely noticeable. Uself thought that sometimes the newly dammed are overwhelmed in their ability to accept their new reality. Then Uself thought, but if this is so why then was Jason not used for food? Uself reviewed Vane's memory as he watched Jason attack Vane which was one of the clear indicators that Jason could and would hold his own in hell. Uself thought this is a small detail that does not fit. Uself in an attempt to gain more information in to Jason tried to follow the energy line from Vane to Jason. Uself received only one piece of information, anger! Uself read intense deep to the bone level anger.

Uself took a deep breath and said, "Ah…..Now, that makes more sense!" Anger blocks out every other emotion and because it was so strong it blocks access to every other thought or feeling Jason was experiencing. Uself smiled, Jason's anger was literally consuming him. This anger also explained the absent minded indifference that Jason was showing to Vane and Rule.

Again Uself smiled as he thought, "This one has clear potential," his anger gives him a greater strength than either Vane or Rule could comprehend or see. Jason was the second reason Uself made the deal with Vane. The untapped power that Jason's anger would provide him would be an unexpected detail which would and or could be the surprise element which at the right moment could turn the battle in an unforeseen way.

The moment Jason completed his examination of the Elder demon's energy signal the name "Uself" (to serve at the pleasure of god!) materialized in Jason's mind. A fallen angel! Immediately Jason accessed his angelic knowledge base and reviewed Uself's life from the time of his creation to and after the fall.

Unknown to Uself, angelic knowledge still tracked and recorded his movement. In effect it could access him even though he could no longer access the angelic knowledge which he was born with. Jason knew that

Uself would want to know every thing about each player in the game, the stakes were too high, far higher than Vane or Rule knew.

Jason had reviewed Uself's battle preparation from his earliest battles to his last one. Jason watched as Uself strategy leaned more and more, to the unseen surprise attacks. Jason could access his battle style but not his current battle plan or regarding his plans for Jason. In order to do that Jason would have to establish an energy connection with Uself. This was a risky proposal at best, Uself's history had made him careful as an angel but he was almost paranoid as a demon he had set many traps for anyone trying to enter his mind. The review of his history indicated that the traps would be intricate and many. Jason was in the process of setting up his defense against Uself.

Jason took two percent of his incredible energy resource, if Jason did not think it was impossible to do, he would swear that the 10 percent of energy he was currently using was self renewing. Every day since his mother's visit he slept deeper more rested and any energy he used the day before seemed to somehow not only renew it's self but it was even more powerful than the day before.

This gave Jason a feeling of being well loved and even though he was in the mist of hell somehow the love of heaven had reach out through his mother's touch and surrounded; protected and guided him on his journey. More importantly her touch had protected him from one of hell's greatest weapons . . . Despair. The one key element that hell tries to instill in you from the moment you began to descend is "despair."

Despair was the process of draining all of the hope out of you and where there is no hope there is no will to fight. Then eventually you agree to open the door to fear, doubt and worry. Once they move into the core of your being they take root and poison you until your inner and outer core are one with hell.

Jason brought his mind back to the process of designing the perfect counter to throw Uself's probe completely off when he thought "anger." His angelic knowledge base had suggested a shield of anger. Anger was an emotion of such power that even a Senior Elder demon would accept it as an understandable reason of why other emotions and thoughts could not be accessed in him.

Then the answer Jason needed to complete the process was clear! Jason could not open an energy line to Uself but he could be ready when Uself opened an energy line to him! Imbedded in the shield of radiating anger would be a probe of great power but one so light that it would be hidden in the backwash of anger which would be released in Uself's mind the moment he opened himself up to probe Jason.

Jason's plan was so simple it was brilliant! Uself would choose a time when he thought Jason would both be unaware of the probe and least defensive. Which meant Uself would attack deep in the middle of the night when he thought Jason was a sleep. Uself would attack in his own time and choosing, telling no one therefore to his mind insuring the success of his intent.

Uself would lower his natural defenses both to get an accurate reading of the situation and because he had no fear of self exposure. Jason set up a defense system to alert him the moment, the very second; Uself's energy signal was active in his apartment. In the same moment the anger shield would be activated and his own probe sent the second Uself opened his mind to Jason.

CHAPTER TWENTY-THREE

The creator was monitoring Jason's every choice; then calculating the outcome and probability of the unseen possibilities that each choice offered (damage control!). The creator was thoughtful as he watched the plan form in Jason's mind to send a probe to Uself at the moment Uself opened up to probe him.

Overall it was a good plan but it had some problems which would be unforeseen by Jason. This meant that the situation fell under his area of expertise; this was the point where the power of choice ended. At this point it is like stepping into a world where every thing you know, all the knowledge on which you would make a reasonable informed choice, no longer applies.

The creator placed a thought in Ariel's mind, it was the belief and knowledge that they could not only communicate with Jason but they could actually materialize inside his angelic shields. The creator re-calculated the possibilities of the situation after adding the knowledge he gave Ariel to the equation; then he smiled, the balance was right and now Jason again had a fighting chance.

It had been several days since Jason first picked up Uself's energy line in Vane's home. Jason was not surprised when his shields woke him at 3:00 that morning to inform his that Uself's energy had triggered the defense and offence system he had in place. As Jason's probe gathered information regarding Uself's plans and intended use of him, Jason monitored Uself right down to his energy output to insure that nothing not even a thought whispered to Uself any information about the counter attack (the probe) that Jason had sent.

The probe which was powerful and light as air gathered information with angelic speed and had returned to Jason almost as soon as it was sent. Jason watched as Uself ended his probe and Jason felt Uself's satisfaction in his belief that Jason's anger was a wild card which would and could be used to skillful advantage in his hands. Jason waited until Uself's energy signal was completely dissipated, as an added precaution against such a battle tested demon.

Now, more than ever Jason knew the importance of attention to detail. Next Jason sent a burst of angelic energy hidden in the core of intense anger through out his apartment. The burst looked as if it spilled out of him like an involuntary action (like snoring) the energy literally exploded through out the apartment this involuntary burst of energy delighted Uself almost as much as it annoyed him.

The burst both confirmed the information that his probe had supplied and shorted out every other probe in the apartment including his. Uself smiled, the demon will be useful indeed. Jason waited a few minutes longer noting the amount of bugs placed in his apartment and there location, once Jason's shields gave the all clear signal he started to open his probe to reviewed and examined the information the probe provided.

Uself viewed Vane and Rule as a joke, simply a means to an end. Uself was torn however regarding Jason, it seems that the outcome of the battle would decide whether Uself took Jason on as an apprentice or (with his inner core seasoned with so much anger he would make a really tasty dinner!).

Uself's intent was to consume both Vane and Rule anyway, he would leave no witness to a deal he had no intentions of keeping. The elemental was his he would share nothing of his prize with anyone. If Jason was as smart as he seemed to be, he would know better than to ask! If Jason was smart, Uself might (in an extremely generous mood) throw him a peace of Rule maybe some of Vane as well.

Jason stopped the probe for a few minutes as he began to absorbed Uself's intention one thought rose, the battle would be with Uself using Vane and Rule until they were of no further use. Jason knew all along that the battle would not be an easy one but until now Jason had not allowed himself to focus on the difficulty or outcome, just the steps . . .. .. one step at a time. In order to gain his release from hell, protect Katelyn along with Justin, Jason was going to have to do battle with a former anger and a Senior Elder demon all rolled into one.

Jason felt fear go straight to his heart, the thought of going to battle with a former angel not to mention that that angel was now a Senior Elder demon increased Jason's fear. Jason stopped the probe he knew that before he moved on to continue his review Uself's plan, Jason needed to confront his growing fears in this matter.

Ariel had shared her new belief with Bree and Bree agreed that she too could feel the possibility Ariel had stated. The next day Ariel and Bree requested the presence of Gabriel and Raphael (this was a new by-product of the interaction they shared in protecting Jason, the ladies now had the ability to contact there consorts, when in the past they could only wait for there consort to visit them).

When they arrived, Bree spoke for the two of them (Ariel was breaking out of her shyness but being an empathy she was still to deeply attuned to the feelings of others and this made her more sensitive when communicating with others. Ariel was however more than comfortable with Bree, completely comfortable with Raphael and strongly on the way to getting comfortable with Gabriel) these thoughts were passing through Ariel's mind when Bree began to speak. We believe, Ariel and I, that during an extremely subconscious state, such as sleep, that we, all of us have poured enough of our energy into Jason that now we can materialize inside of his shields.

Ariel "felt" the possibility growing since we have been feeding him energy on a daily bases and now Ariel has come up with a method to take this from a possibility to a plan. Gabriel and Raphael were so quiet, that the natural sounds of Bree's garden seemed as if the volume had turned up. Gabriel and Raphael seemed to be communication on a blocked channel and Bree and Ariel simply waited for them to speak.

Gabriel spoke as Raphael held his head down, Bree and Ariel listened in stunned silence as Gabriel said, "How can we express out heart felt gratitude for the gifts that you both are!" How can we express out shame at thinking ourselves so much better than such rare creatures as your selves.

Bree started to speak but Gabriel raised his hand and continued we deserve your scorn, yet all you have ever given us is your love.

We have treated rare diamonds like rocks! We, both of us ask for your forgiveness for our lack of understanding. You two have taught us a lesson in what it means to love, unconditionally. What ever your plan, we will follow your lead. Ask of us that which you will, you have our complete faith and trust second only to that which we feel for the creator! Tears gave way to laughter and then Bree began to outline their plan.

Jason felt completely overwhelmed unable to listen to Uself's plan because he knew he needed to conquer his fear first yet he did not know how! Jason hid his fear yet he knew it was growing and if something was not done soon he was going to be in trouble. Later that evening Jason tried to rest but his mind continued to make him uneasy. About 2:30 in the morning he felt into an uneasy state of rest. For a moment, he thought he was dreaming then he felt it again he would know that touch any where and just as he knew that touch so did his shields.

Jason felt not only his mother's touch but it seemed like he felt his father as well. A second later Jason recognized the touch of Justin's parents too. Gabriel poured energy into his shield blocking the energy of fear, while Raphael literally reached inside Jason's brain as he tracked and disintegrated the core of the fear which was in the process of trying to attach its self to Jason's angelic energy.

The moment the core of fear disintegrated Jason could not only hear but see his mother and the others as they spoke not only to themselves but to him. Did we get to him in time, Ariel said to Raphael, Jason felt his father pour in healing and purifying energy into his mind. Raphael replied, "The fear had not yet established an active connection to his shield but in a matter of days it would have, but yes we got it in time."

At first, Jason felt weak as if he had been recovering from a life threaten illness then he felt the healing energy his father poured into him. The last thing he remembered was opening the probe into Uself's mind; then he was attacked by overwhelming fear. Jason reached up to wipe a tear from his mother's eyes and at his touch his mother smiled and nodded her head as if to give a signal to the others that he indeed was alright.

Then each of them connected with the lines of energy that they had attached to him. At each of their touch, Jason saw how that individual's touch glowed through the energy connection he had established with them. Raphael touched Jason's mind, Ariel touched his heart, Bree touched his sprit and Gabriel connected with him through his angelic shields. The first question Jason asked was what happened!

Raphael spoke; the probe you sent into Uself's mind immediately became contaminated with Uself's evil. This contamination is simply the by-product of what happens anytime something pure opens its self up to evil. The good news was that Uself was completely unaware of the probe. You did every thing well and right except for one thing, you opened the probe inside of your angelic shields instead of outside of them.

If the probe had been opened outside of your angelic shields, the shields would have detected the taint and hit it with angelic energy. When you opened the probe on the inside of your shield you opened the door for the taint to get in. Somewhat a reverse of the plan you used on Uself. Jason took a deep breath; he had just had a very narrow escape by days, no! . . .by hours.

Ariel then spoke, "we all of us, have been connected with you and monitoring you since you and I met in the upper levels of hell. Remember when I touched your heart. If you go back to that moment in your memory, it is when I unknowingly established an energy connection for all of us with you. Now that Jason could see and feel the different levels of energy flowing into him he, as he thought back to that moment, he could pin point his mothers hand through which he could now identify each individual's signature energy.

Well that explained a lot, Jason thought. He had not been depressed since his meeting with his mother (until the probe) because Justin's mother was literally draining the negativity from his sprit and replacing the depression with belief and hope. Jason's angelic shields were stronger than ever and now again he understood why, Gabriel had been reinforcing them since that day. Now Jason could see Gabriel's energy signal weaved through out them.

Jason felt the purity of his mother's love flow into him now that his mind was clear. Jason felt his father's strength and will for his survival through the strength and purify he poured into his mind. Never in his entire life had Jason felt so loved, and in hell of all places! Jason's shields had been tuned to each of their energy vibration, which meant now they could visit him at will. Jason could not go to them but the energy connections and vibrations that Gabriel was weaving even deeper into his shields did allow for limited communication and brief visitations from them all.

However, they all agreed that any attempt on his part to contact them should be done only on an emergency bases and with great care. While one of them would be monitoring him at all times and visit frequently! They now had to leave; it was not safe for them or him if their presence was detected in any manor. When they left Jason felt another presence in the room. He felt a brief touch on his heart then his great uncle who uses to play with him when he was a child appeared.

His uncle informed Jason that he too wanted to give him a message of courage and strength, Jason felt his uncle's energy vibration also hidden deep in his mother's touch and just as Jason was about to ask how that could be so, his great uncle said, I must leave soon or I too will put you in danger, but I have left a gift buried deep in your heart, you will know when to access the gift for in that moment the words to activate the gift will come to your mind. The old man hugged him and then he was gone.

The creator watched as Jason's and Justin's parents visited Jason for the first time in hell, how they all worked like a well oil unit to insure his safety and counter Uself's negativity. Jason was one of the creator's focal point, Jason was a drop in the pond that was hell and from which an intensive ripple effect would began. The current situation was but one way this situation could have unfolded, the choice always had been and even now still belonged to Jason he had the wild card of free will and so far he was using it well to survive.

When Jason first noticed the seed of decent in his heart, he could have killed it with a thought. When Jason first entered hell and was confronted with the outcome his choices and actions brought, he could have denied and lied to himself thus sealing his fate in hell and embracing demon hood.

The creator thought yet again how simply he made the answers and how complicated others structured the questions.

How often his children got lost in the complication they created to the point that they can not see or will not accept the simple solutions which are usually jumping up and down begging for their attention. When you do not learn the lessons that life is trying to teach you, life arranges an explosion or a crisis then is necessary, the very nature of a crisis required that all things are stripped down to there basic nature and then the solution, the simple solution that was there all along comes into focus. How often had the creator thought that life is simple and fair but man is complicated and always has hidden motives.

For the first time, upon entering hell, Jason was confronted with the truth. The crisis of the situation stripped away all illusions and the simple truth was either that Jason embraced his good or his evil. This was and had always been Jason's choice. A choice he complicated when he tried to hide from himself.

This was a choice no one could make for him, when the seed of descent first appeared in Jason and he choose to nurture them rather than destroy them he began the choice which started him down this path. The path of his current crisis was formed, the creator would have both chosen and preferred a gentler life lesson of growth and development for Jason, however Jason had free will and this is the path he choose.

However, the creator thought sadly, he had given man the right to choose his path and when you give a gift you let go, you don't try to control that which no longer belongs to you. Although, the creator smiled, he could control the effect of the choice (his personal version of damage control or making lemon aid out of lemons).

He could limit the damage and if possible use the situation as a catalysis for good in several other areas. Here again, it all depended on Jason and the choices he makes on each step of this journey. Each choice Jason made either opened up additional possibilities for help to work his way out of hell or his choices would bind him to hell.

Before the creator left he gave his grandchild a gift, when Jason was in the upper regions of hell before he met with his mother, he made a commitment to fight to his last breath even though all the odds were against him. Commitments of this nature, made with soul level honesty and genuine intent, is a different but very powerful form of prayer.

The creator had given away the power to make his children's choices but those choices once made and made in such a powerful form like a prayer, now gave the creator the right to strengthen Jason's resolve. Therefore, the first gift he gave Jason was an intense belief in the rightness of his choices.

The second gift was a deep understanding of how well he was loved. The creator knew that when the time came, this belief in love would and could save not only his life but his soul! If Jason made the right choices the fires of hell would burn away the negativity that brought him to this state in the first place, leaving a stronger, purer soul. This after all, is the real reason that negativity or evil exist in the first place, it was necessary pathway for the growth, development and purification of the soul.

They all met again in Bree's garden after they left Jason, each lost in thought and all wondering about if on any level they had broken the rule of communication. The concern was that through the mothers, a father had had direct contact with the son. However the key to this statement was "through the mothers." With out thought, they all had opened up to each other and exchanged thoughts on this matter. Then Bree asked, "Raphael does what we did here today feel like you felt initially when you shared too much information with Jason?" Raphael stopped and compared the two emotions and then he said with out doubt, "no."

As Raphael continued to look at the two situations he remembered that in the first situation it felt as if he was fighting to say what he was trying to tell Jason, fighting against a force which was blocking his mind and wiping out his thoughts as he raced to communicate the information to Jason before it was gone. The entire situation had felt "wrong" and Raphael knew with out thought that he had transgressed the rule of communication.

Now, when he reviewed his actions in following Ariel and Bree's lead, there was no pull or blockage. His actions were quick, instinctual and he fought no pull against information which was being wiped from his mind. In conclusion the whole action "felt right." Besides which, he would not have had access to Jason if not for Ariel. The rule of communication had not been broken because the mothers had far more latitude to provide direct help to there sons than the father. However as long as the father's actions were directed by the mother and or through the mother, the rule of communication had not been broken.

Now a new question entered there minds, how much of this situation would the rule of communication allow them to share with Justin and Katelyn. At that moment Bree heard a mental knock and said "enter." Gabriel great uncle materialized and as he did so, he quickly sent a message to Gabriel and Raphael and they stood completely still. Bree reached up and hugged him; then he hugged her back, to Gabriel and Raphael's astonishment. He smiled at Ariel and she shyly returned the smile. Raphael and Gabriel were speechless mainly because part of the brief message the creator sent them translated though the look that creator gave them when he came in told them to say nothing.

Their consorts were on comfortable and friendly, family like terms with the creator but as Gabriel and Raphael looked and listed they were not sure if there consorts knew exactly who he was. Again Gabriel and Raphael were completely floored when Bree and Ariel began to ask the creator's advice on the rule of communication as if in deed they knew who he was. Raphael said to Gabriel (they were allowed to communicate with each other) well! Talk about getting the information straight from the source!

Gabriel and Raphael listened as the creator began to advise their consorts on what they could and what they could not say to Justin and Katelyn at this point. While the creator spoke with their consorts it looked as if Gabriel and Raphael were discussing other issues while Bree and Ariel spoke with their uncle. When in reality, both Gabriel and Raphael were completely focused on the seen unfolding in front of them. When the creator got ready to go he gave Gabriel and Raphael the thought of remaining silent regarding his identity as he hugged both women then he left.

CHAPTER TWENTY-FOUR

Earlier on different occasions, the creator allowed the instincts of each women to pick up who he was, because it was necessary for that moment in time, like when Ariel materialized with in his personal garden. The knowledge of who he was at that moment was necessary for her acceptance of the information that he was relating to her. However, once she accepted the information and began to work from it, the knowledge of who he was faded from her mind, to be replaced with the memory of having a conversation with Raphael's uncle. The creator knew that he was going to be interactive in this situation and he did not want these women to fear him. Instead he wanted exactly what Raphael and Gabriel saw, their respect, acceptance, confidence and to be treated with the genuine love of a close family member.

Out of all the demons associated with this prey, Tris was the only demon completely unaffected if the prey was lost. Sure, she would loose the percentage of the kill but over all, her no fault contract with Rule insured that she would not be blamed in any way for the loss of the prey and essentially that was all that really mattered. Rule had just left her home and he was in rare form. He asked to see the contract to insure that he had spelled out exactly what he wanted her prey to do.

Tris knew fear when she smelled it, and right now Rule reeked of it! She also knew that he wanted to get his hands on the contract to destroy it so that he would have a means of trying to share his failure with her . . . fat chance! Tris looked Rule straight in his eyes and lied with such expertise and skill even she began to believed it (for a moment), as she stated that the contract was not in her home.

To calm him down Tris said, that if he came by tomorrow around eight o'clock in the morning she would be able to get the contract and let him see for himself, that she had done all that she was contracted to do. Rule had to be content with the knowledge that if she was willing to show him the contract then she believed him and this would give him a chance to get his hands on the contract.

As soon as Rule left, Tris packed a bag and left her home through an emergency tunnel (one of several and she never used the same tunnel two times in a row). Tris had no doubt that Rule would watch her house for a while just to see if she tried to leave home. The lights in her home were timed to go out at exactly 9:00 an hour from now, giving the impression that Tris had gone to bed.

By 9:00 Tris was well on her way to one of her secret emergency residence, where she would stay until this situation was settled one way or another.

Rule was content that Tris made no attempt to leave home. He watched her house until 10:00, he had the clear intent to be at her home bright and early tomorrow he intended to follow her and get his hands on that contract. As Rule watched Tris' home for any signs of movement he replayed the entire interview that he had had with her earlier that evening.

He had presented himself at her home expecting good news, something which he needed badly and something which would allow him to stir up problems between his prey and her boyfriend or at the very least allow Rule to get back into her mind. Tris let him in and before he sat down good she looked at him and said her prey had really tried but "the boyfriend" seemed really attached to Rules' prey. Tris said that any number of tricks that usually worked well, had fail and worse they only seemed to make the boyfriend less and less interested.

Tris said she would have her prey re-double her attempts at "the boyfriend" tomorrow but there was no interest that Tris could see that "the boyfriend" had in her human. Rule was one step away from loosing it, but he thought he hid it well. It was then that he asked to see the contract. If she had said no, he would have lost it but she had seemed genuinely concerned and offered to help.

It was at this point now, that Rule's brain cleared. He had let his fear block something he should have seen almost immediately before. No demon was concerned about another and no demon ever, not ever offered to help with out something in it for them. Rule looked at his watch it was 12:00 midnight.

Rule broke into Tris' home and he searched the whole house, she was gone! Somehow she had gotten out with out him seeing her or hearing any movement. Rule trashed the house; she was gone! And his only chance of getting that contract back went with her. Rule was now moving from panic to despair. Rule was not looking forward to breaking this news to Vane. Getting beat was the least of his worries because in fact, there was no way around that. What Rule was genuinely concerned about was having to inform Vane that the plan did not work and unless something really bad happened extremely soon, the prey was all but lost!

It was 1:00 and Tris was settled into one of her safe houses. She sat in a comfortable chair looking into a fire sipping a blood red wine, one of her favorites, wine laced with the blood of a recent kill. You could still taste the agony in one sip or the despair in another. The blood carried the memories of the pain and anguish of a newly dammed soul when they realized their fate!

Muumuu . . . . delicious! Each sip went right through you; it was the next best thing to being there when the dammed understood their fate. Tris sat the wine glass on the table next to her chair and begin to think about recent events, reviewing the sequence to insure that she had covered her tracks. She figured that the fool Rule would do exactly what she was doing, going through the events of the evening and when he did, it was her guess that around midnight, he would calm down and control his fear enough to realize that she had played him like a violin.

Tris had been monitoring Susan, her prey, as Susan attempted to seduce the "boyfriend" of Rule's prey. Susan was vain and she had taken to heart the old Marilyn Monroe quote that, "men can see a heck of a lot better than they can think." Since she had little insight into her self she naturally believed that this was the way other females operated as well.

Susan believed that she, on the other hand was simply more honest, she was a bitch and she knew it. Susan felt that other females were bitches too but they lied to themselves regarding this fact. Tris had fed Susan the belief that her "honesty in this area" made her a better person than other females and Susan had brought the idea to such a degree that she made it a central theme in her belief system. This belief increased her sense of self and her belief that she was better than other females because of it!

This then, was the extent of Susan's self knowledge. Tris watched as the boyfriend showed so little interest in Susan it was laughable! There was something about the boyfriend that Tris could not put her finger on until Susan's second attempt at seduction. It was his reaction to her which said it all, It seemed as if he was repulsed by her almost as if he knew the state of her soul. That and the fact that he was both deeply in love and committed to Rule's prey. At that moment Tris realized that, this attempt as seduction was useless.

Tris pulled her prey back from this endeavor, the last thing Tris needed was for Susan to have a loss of confidence regarding her sexuality. This was the core of Susan's self esteem and Tris's favorite door way in to her and the one Tris had built Susan's negativity around. No, Susan did not need to doubt her sexuality.

That night Tris sent Susan to one of her favorite bars and had her get several phone numbers. Tris even allowed her to choose a really cute guy to sleep with. Normally Tris keep her with mid-range to ugly men but tonight Susan needed to feel sexy and Tris let her have it.

The next day Susan was convinced (at Tris's suggestion) that "the boyfriend" was a closet gay guy and Rule's prey, Katelyn, was welcome to him. Tris knew that Rule was desperate for good news, now having watched Susan in action; Tris did not have any good news to relate. Tris was now in damage control mode, demons did not take bad news well, and desperate demons took this type of news worse.

Tris was an old demon, much older than most knew. Tris had learned that it was easier to out think other demons than to fight them. Not, that Tris could not hold her own in a fight and if it had become necessary she believed she could beat the hell out of Rule but out thinking other demons was much more fun. And in hell, one had to get there entertainment where they could find it plus it was never a good idea to let others know how smart or strong you are.

Tris brought her thoughts back to what she had said to Rule when he came to visit her earlier today expecting some positive results from Tris' prey's actions. Tris thought at that time, what would appease a desperate demon: 1. Good news, no she did not have that to give. 2. The return of the contract, "no way" that she would not give up. 3. Understanding and sympathy—Now this was something she could fake with expertise! All she needed was to make him believe her for a few hours, yes! This would work. Tris now had her strategy for handling Rule when he showed up and she had no doubt that it would work like a charm.

A desperate demon full of the fear of loosing his prey would respond well to sympathy and understanding, it would fit right into his sense of feeling ill used and mistreated. It would be hours later when he calmed down enough to realize that no demon gives a fat rat's ass about the troubles of another demon (unless it directly effects them in some way) and that there is no such thing as sympathy in hell!

Vane knew that Rule had bad news; first Rule was extremely slow in informing him regarding his progress. Vane knew that if the news had been good Rule would have wasted no time in boring him to death with his bragging. Second, Rule was no where to be found. No one had seen him and to Vane this meant the forerunner of very bad news.

When Rule did show up the next day, one look at his face showed Vane that his assessment of the situation was correct. As Rule finished with his update, a voice Rule did not know spoke and told Vane to send for Jason. Rule noticed that Vane seemed very uneasy at the sound of that voice and then fear shot from Rule's mind to every other part of his body.

That voice, it was the voice of an Elder . . .. a Senior Elder no less! All hell! They were either saved or doomed and Rule had no ideal which! Uself listened to Rule's pathetic report, as he tried not to gag on Rule's fear which was joined by Vane's fear once they heard the sound of Uself's voice. Vane hid his fears better but it was just as strong. Vane sent an urgent message to Jason to present himself at Vane's home right away. Jason heard the fear in Vane's voice when he got the message and responded right away.

The moment he presented himself at Vane's door he was transported immediately in to Vane's living room where Rule sat literally shaking in a corner seat, trying to make him self as small as possible; while Vane was sitting on the sofa trying to look causal but Jason could also smell the fear all over him.

Jason recognized Uself's energy signal and at once assumed a casual unaffected air as if he had no clue about what was happening and no knowledge what so ever about Uself. Jason's total lack of fear interested Uself and he could not decide if Jason was as clueless as he seemed or simply one of the smarter young demons.

Uself intended to find out which, before their business was concluded. The room was quite and Uself materialized, Jason caught a brief look at the angel he once was. Vane started to speak but one look from Uself was all it took for Vane to be quiet. Jason said nothing, being firmly aware that one responded to a Senior Elder demon when address, until then you said nothing.

Rule had started to shake so violently it was both distracting and almost comical. One look from Uself and Rule no longer move a muscle, because all of them were no longer under Rule's control. Rule's eyes poured fear into the room. Uself looked directly at Jason and said why do you look familiar to me? No matter it will come to me later.

Since the statement/question was rhetorical and not meant to be answered, again Jason said nothing. Uself was impressed, Jason neither said nor did anything stupid and given the company he had been keeping . . . that said a lot! Jason slowly did his best impression of non-descript human, the kind that looked like every body and no body all at the same time.

Jason knew exactly what Uself saw when he looked at him, Uself and his father had worked together many times before and long before that they had been friends. If Uself still possessed his angelic knowledge he would have recognized Jason with a glance (or recognized the similarity to Raphael). But with out that knowledge base and Jason toning down all resemblance to his father it would take Uself a little while longer to make the connection.

The rules of this engagement, from this point on, are about to change Uself said. Jason will, from now on interface with the prey. Rule will assist Jason in anyway Jason sees fit. Jason will answer to me and me alone and Vane you will assist me. Are we all clear on the new roles and assignments . . .. . and if any one no longer wishes to live, please . . .by all means, feel free to object to this arrangement! No objections? Good! Then we are all in agreement.

Jason you will spend the day with the prey and meet me here tomorrow at, let's say about 8:00 in the evening. I want a complete analysis of what we are up against and a recommendation for a new strategy. Time is not our friend in this situation therefore work fast and accurately. Jason bowed his head and when he looked up again Uself was gone (at least from sight Jason thought, Jason still detected a strong version of Uself's energy signal in the room, which meant Uself was giving them time to betray him while he listened to there plans to do so.

Vane recovered first, and under his breath talked about how ungrateful Uself's treatment of him was while Jason seemed lost in thought. As Vane fear left his anger rose, he was angry at being treated like a servant! Vane confronted Jason and demanded that Jason agree that the Senior Elder's behavior toward Vane was ungrateful and unfair.

Jason thought a moment and then responded, "The moment you tell the Senior Elder that to his face . . . and if you are still alive five minutes later, then I will agree with you." Vane was angry, fear always made him angry! His rage needed a victim, but he dare not touch Jason since Uself seemed to favor him, so Vane knocked the hell out of Rule and screamed, "This situation is all your fault!"

I hope you rot in the bowels of hell for bring your failure to my door! Vane then proceeded to beat Rule over and over again. Jason said nothing; he simply watched for a moment then stated he had plans to make for tomorrow and left. Uself however watched the show as Vane beat and berated Rule for being the focal point of all his trouble. Uself was again very impressed with Jason, he had handled Vane well. Uself looked forward to hearing Jason's report tomorrow.

Jason now had a serious problem, he knew that his presence in Katelyn's mind tomorrow would look demonic this meant that both Justin and Katelyn would attack. Jason's only hope was to get a message to Justin tonight if not, Jason was screwed he could do no harm yet he had to seem to do just that. Jason went home and hoped that someone would come tonight so he could get a message to Justin!

Bree and Ariel were having lunch in the garden; they were discussing the information from their mate's uncle and combining that knowledge with what they knew about the rule of communication and the rule of options. It seems that the knowledge which at times looked to be incompatible on the surface had at its core some simple connecting lines of energy at the foundation.

Ariel had discovered another talent or to put it clearly an extension on her current talent. Ariel had the ability to "feel" how and where the rules connected she could strip away the surface confusion and see as she touched the information in her mind what the original intent of each law was.

Ariel could see where the laws connected and complimented each other and where they opposed each other. It seems that the rule of communication operated basically on a "need to know bases" The intent of the rule of communication was to prevent doorways of negativity from forming in the mind or more specifically the thoughts of the warrior during a critical situation in his battle.

It helped to keep the warrior focused on the step he was dealing with and attention to detail was beyond important in this task. It also allow him to protect himself from the "what if's." The "what if's" create doorways for negativity to attack from several different directions and this can be deadly in a critical moment in the battle. This rule, like the rule of fate, released information only when the warriors truly needed to know it. This is when the knowledge would genuinely serve a positive and helpful purpose. According to Ariel, the rules were not just about giving information but doing so with balance but timing!

The rule of options simply put meant options and or doorways would present themselves in the most impossible situations. These options can only be seen from the inside of a situation, which meant that they would be completely obscure from an outside view. Or simply put in an impossible situation with every thing against you an option you would never have thought of before would present itself.

It seems that the connecting thread between the two rules was "a positive need creates a flow of information which shows a flexible option." Soon Gabriel and Raphael joined them, Raphael reach down to kiss Ariel on the cheek and as soon as he did so a lock of his hair fell out of place. Ariel reached up to push the hair behind his ear as he kissed her cheek while Ariel's fingers briefly touched his forehead. Ariel's fingers shook a moment later as she said, "Jason is in trouble."

Jason was laying down trying to calm his mind after his meeting with Uself, Vane and Rule when he felt his father's energy line pouring strength into his mind the energy cleared his thinking and immediately before his father with drew, Jason implanted a message that he hoped his mother would get, if his father saw her.

It was a long shot but it was worth a try, the message said, "Mom, I am in trouble I need every body to visit me tonight." Ariel touched Raphael's mind and spoke out loud the words of Jason's message, then they examined the time lines and realized that tonight for Jason would be in about ten minutes in their time frame.

They each spent those ten minutes trying not to think about the urgency entailed in the message. This time they each could arrive through Jason's shields using there own energy signature in his shields. Minutes later as Jason tried to rest he felt the gentle touch of his mother soon they were all there each trying to hide there fears.

Jason smiled and said thank you all for coming, Yes! The situation is bad but hopefully with our combined input we will figure out a solution. Jason used angelic communication to describe his meeting with Uself and the need to communicate his current situation to Justin. So that he would not be attacked the moment his signature as a demon entered Katelyn's mind.

Jason knew he would be attacked from both Katelyn and Justin before he could begin to explain, assuming they would listen to him anyway and to make a bad situation worse, I have no idea how the rule of communication would view any attempt from me to communicate with Justin in this situation.

If they attacked me I can not attack back, the rule of options is clear that I can do no harm. Yet if they attack and I do not respond in kind all sorts of warning bells will go off in Uself's head. As Jason finished describing his dilemma he said, "If we can find no solution to this problem, then the second reason I am glad you are all here is to say good by and thank you.

I will not harm Justin nor will I help hell acquire an elemental, if it comes down to a sacrifice then I choose to be it! Raphael looked worried and sad, Ariel could not keep the tears from falling down her cheek and Gabriel looked deeply concerned. Bree was quiet for a moment and she seemed deep in thought when she said, "I think I know a way."

All eyes turned to Bree as she said, "Ariel remember our discussion at lunch today," it took Ariel a moment then her expression began to change and hope rather than fear shinned on her face. Yes! Ariel said, "An impossible solution for an impossible situation." Ariel, for the first time sent a burst of angelic communication to every one present detailing the information she and Bree had discussed at Lunch.

According to all they understood about the rules and factoring in the information they had received from their great uncle, yes! Justin can be told; now all that remained was to work out a plan of action which kept all of the children safe.

Chapter Twenty-Five

Justin was starting to get concerned he had expected an attack from Katelyn's demon days ago and while he appreciated the peace and the time they had together Justin was starting to wonder if his defenses for Katelyn were every thing he thought they were. Justin was wondering if he had left some little unknown doorway of opportunity unchecked and available for the demon to strike when he least expected it.

Justin felt his father's touch in his mind this alone was a sincere surprise because usually it was Justin who contacted his father when they met. Then to add to the surprise Justin felt his mother's touch also in his mind. Now, Justin thought, this is two "first" in one night! Something must be going on. Justin was about to respond when he heard his father say, you need not go any further than your own living room.

Now Justin knew something was up. His parents never visited him. Always they would request his presence and never had they both requested his presence at the same time, if they each wanted to see him and the requests were close, in the past one parent would defer until he had completed his visit with the other. Justin put on a house robe and walked into the living room and found his parents kissing!

Justin (who had never seen his parent show any external signs of affection) sat down quietly and watched and waited until his parents noticed his presence in the room. A few minutes later his father glanced toward the bedroom door and was actually surprised to find Justin sitting quietly looking at them both with a smile on his face.

Bree left Gabriel's arms and walked over to her son and hugged him and he whispered in her ear, "It warms my heart to see you so happy." Bree hugged him harder then explained, we needed to speak with you about something extremely important. In a long burst of angelic communication from his mother, with his father adding additional detail here and there they informed him about where things stood at this moment with Jason. Then they told him how they had worked together with Jason's parents to keep him from being dammed.

As Justin listened to his parents as they described the current fate of his friend. A multitude of emotions washed over him; deep concern with a desire to do all with in his power to help. A soul level sadness at what Jason's current experience must be like, guilt for being so preoccupied with his own concerns that he failed to be the friend that Jason needed; when he needed him!

Pain, deep genuine and sincere pain, exploded all over and through him as he remembered all of the little hints which Jason exhibited. Hints that Justin knew by training and experience indicated so much more than casual observation would indicate. There had been something about Jason, some nameless something that again training and experience had informed him not to overlook; things that he needed to see and understand.

Something, a hint of something really, but now for a brief moment in time, Justin zeroed in and pin pointed the memory and the emotions attached to it and Justin received a flash from Jason's mind, which unleashed a whirl wind of negative beliefs thoughts and emotions . . .then nothing! a flash of knowledge which was so deeply connected with a part of his soul that it felt as if on some level this information about Jason was the equal to a knife cutting through to his soul. Justin stored this information quietly away in a corner of his mind labeled "to be opened and examined later."

The total impact of Jason's situation hit Justin so hard it was like an explosion of pain, at that moment Katelyn felt his pain and woke-up reaching for Justin but he was not there. He was in the living room and he was in pain and he was not alone. Katelyn ran into the living room gathering her power as she hit the door. Katelyn was ready to cause serious damage and give out some genuine pain to whom ever or what ever had hurt him.

Katelyn ran into the living room with an energy ball ready to throw, when Justin grabbed her before she sent the energy ball flying at his mother. Katelyn began to bereave now that she knew he was alright. Then Katelyn realized who their guests were as she started to turn pink with embarrassment.

Bree stepped forward and hugged Katelyn as she said, "you will never need to apologize or feel any level of embarrassment regarding your defense of my son." I would not want his mate to react any other way to his pain! After insuring that all information had been communicated and all questions asked and answered regarding the plan of action, Bree kissed them both then she and Gabriel left.

Justin in turn communicated the situation to Katelyn on a more personal level explaining that he considered Jason more than a friend he was like a brother. Now, Justin thought, they were ready to deal with the upcoming attack.

Jason's newly honed attention to detail had noted several differences in his parents. One, his father actually listened when his mother spoke. Two, Ariel spoke with out being uncomfortable. Three, she presented her ideas with out shying away and she spoke with authority and conviction.

Ariel and Bree took the lead in solving his latest problems, the two women had already been examining the rules for a deeper understanding of what they were dealing with, little knowing that they would put their new found knowledge to the test only minutes after they figured it out.

Jason was so proud of his mother. she was so focused on keeping him safe and on the problems that they faced at hand to do that. That many times she did not realize that she was taking the lead in the discussions or that they all were listening and responding to her words with great respect. His mom had always been beautiful, now she seemed radiant, like a star coming into her own!

The next day, Jason put off going in to Katelyn for as long as he could. First he sought out Rule who was sullen and upset and feeling ill used.

Jason asked to assess Rules memories of the attempts and strategies he used in the past to try to tempt the prey into hell. Jason said he did not want to waist his time doing something that had already been tried. Normally Rule would have told Jason to figure it out himself but Uself had made his wishes clear and that was something (or someone) you did not want coming after you.

Rule gave Jason access to his memories then went back to bed after slamming the door to his apartment as Jason left out. Jason had brought all the time he could, it was time to access Katelyn and hope everything worked out as planned. Jason stepped into Katelyn's mind and before he could get his barring he was hit with what seemed to be a one two punch.

In reality a second before the punch landed, Jason was transported out of the range of the fight. But it looked like his energy signal had absorbed the punch and was now fighting back. Jason was transported inside Justin's shield and the moment he materialized he was hugged fiercely by Justin. Soon they were joined by Katelyn who was so happy that Jason was working with them not against them.

Katelyn saw the love Justin and Jason shared with each other; they were in every way that counted brothers. If they had not been warned, they would have attacked first and asked questions later. Then when Justin found out it was Jason, it would have broken his heart on so many levels, too many levels for Justin to begin to accept or deal with.

Katelyn was soul level grateful to Jason, for doing all in his power even to the point of giving up his own life if they had not gotten the message in time. It would have broken her heart to see Justin in such pain and worse, not to mention that she would think that unintentionally she would have been the cause. So when Justin introduced them she hugged Jason as if he were her brother too.

Jason had prepared himself for death, he had decided that not only would he not fight back but he would leave his defenses down so that death would be quick and he hoped as painless as possible. Jason had implanted another message this time in Bree's energy signal one he felt sure his mother would get the moment she touched Bree mind or shared energy with her again.

The message was one of love, gratitude and understanding for each of them. The message told Justin it was both Jason's privilege and choice to give his life for him and Katelyn and he knew if the situation were reversed that Justin would choose the same path. It was a message of healing for each of them in case things did not go well. Jason did not want them to morn, grieve or feel that they left any stone unturned in trying to save him; he wanted them to know that he knew they had all done all that was possible and he loved each and every one of them for the effort they put in to trying to save him.

Jason even sent a message to Katelyn; he thanked her for loving his friend and asked that she surround Justin with all the love he would no longer be able to give. He told his mother how proud he was of her and thanked her again for all the different ways she expanded her sensitive empathic senses in an attempt to keep him safe.

Jason asked his father to release any pain he felt on his behalf from any belief that he may harbor that Jason fate was Raphael's fault. His father's love had shown him how much a parent would sacrifice for their child, Jason then thanked Raphael for all the love and acceptance he had received as a child even though Jason "knew" (he was after all his mother's child) of the conflict he sometimes felt in being mated with a human.

Most of all he thanked his father for now seeing the true beauty of his mother and the knowledge that he could die in peace knowing that she was well loved! Jason thanked Bree for being his mother's friend (often in the past he had felt she needed one). Jason had seen a bond grow between the two of them, a bond full of warmth and care. Jason was touched by the unselfish and intensive help she and Gabriel had given his parents.

He thanked Gabriel for his silent strength and support, for the fact that he simply did what was needed when it was needed; for providing a foundation and background for the more active rolls that the others played in trying to help him survive and keep him safe. Finally, Jason said, "to my great uncle who also entered hell to give me a message of courage and strength, thank you for all the love and laughter you infused in to my childhood, thank you all for being there.

Justin could see that Jason for a moment, after Katelyn's hug, was lost in some private though and as much as he hated to interfere time was rare and precious and they had much to discuss. Using angelic communication they reviewed the current problem, Jason needed to present a plan of attack to Uself, a plan that looked as if it had a good chance of success.

They knew that Uself's battle history was one of smoke screen and misdirection. In that Uself would look as if he was attacking from one direction when all along his real attack or main force would be unexpected and unseen until the moment of the attack. They decided that they needed to give him a plan with three and only three backdoors built into it.

Each of the three back doors would present a different level of difficulty to see. The first backdoor would be extremely hidden; that was the one that Jason would pretend not to see or show any knowledge of because they knew it would be the one that Uself would choose to stage his major attack plan from.

The second back door would be the one that Jason would advocate for and present his plan of attack to Uself around. The third backdoor would be so obvious that both Vane and Rule could see it. Its purpose was only to round out the options package.

The plans had built into them a natural protection for them with in each back door and a way for them to shift or adjust from plan A to B or C when or if needed and at a moment's notice. Uself was an extremely old and intelligent demon. The older ones tended to stick to methods which are tried and true or have always worked for them in the past. On the other hand as a Senior Elder demon, Uself both used and understood flexibility because flexibility is one of the necessary elements that a demon needs to survive in hell.

There plan therefore had to address both of these elements, the old or tried and true methods as well as built in levels of hidden flexibility. Unfortunately this meant that the flexible aspect of Uself's plan would have to be countered in the moment it presented itself.

They completed the details after they agreed on the general direction that they would need to take in dealing with Uself. Jason stated that he would present the plan to Uself while Katelyn and Justin presented the plan to their parents. Justin and Katelyn then added their energy signals to Jason's angelic shields so that if needed they too, could both transport inside his shields and communicate with him in general or in the heat of battle at a moment's notice.

Adding their energy lines to Jason's shield signal would make it far easier to interact with Jason. Today they had to use Gabriel and Bree's energy signal to transport Jason out a second before the internal attack began. They had not intended to cut his transportation time that close because it was a little too close, a second or two later and Jason would have been toast! Using their own energy signatures would be far easier and much more efficient.

The plan Jason presented to Uself was simplicity it's self, divide and conquer. Together the prey and her boyfriend were a force to be dealt with. There strength and ability complimented and augmented each other. They had trained themselves to orchestrate a plan of battle in a tag team approach, each defending or dealing with the attacks that their skills and ability were best suited for. Then they would shift at a moment's notice and provided an effective barrier for the other one while he or she is under attack. Jason said," I barely escaped in one piece!"

The First problem in Rule's attack was that he focused on Katelyn alone; she was no longer an "I" but a "we." Therefore every time Rule attacked Katelyn the boyfriend provided protection for her then they would switch and she did the same for the boyfriend while the boyfriend attacked Rule.

Rule never understood that she was not alone or that he was defending against two sources of power. The second mistake was that Rule underestimated the prey. He approached this assignment with a dismissive attitude toward the prey, therefore he never noticed that not only was her power as an elemental active but she is in full command of them! The third and final mistake that Rule made was he did not examine the boyfriend's energy signal . . . the boyfriend has his own power levels and I am not exactly sure what he is.

The plan I advise then is clear, separate them and attack each of them with everything you have while radiating the fear to each that the other has fallen. Exhausted physically and weighted down with fear mentally plus blocking the access that they have to each other for strength and reinforcement equals a good solid possibility that they can and will be defeated.

Jason finished his presentation and waited for Uself to give his input. Uself was dealing with a lot of emotional conflict behind the presentation. The analysis of the problem was intelligent and well thought out. The plan had a great deal of promise and it was elegant in its simplicity. Jason had preformed beyond Uself's highest expectations and that was the problem.

Through out his long experience Uself had dealt with many types of demons but there had only been two demons in the past that had come close (one very close) to killing him and both of them had been extremely intelligent demons. Based on pass experience it was Uself's policy to avoid intelligent demons at all cost when ever possible.

Nevertheless, Uself did have to admit that they had there uses and it was clear now that Jason was an intelligent demon. The plan Jason presented especially with him adding his own touches, had an 85 to 95% probability of success and those were very, very impressive odds.

On the other hand, here again was it all too easy? Uself looked at the plan from every direction he could but he found no fault with it and that bothered him more than he could explain. Uself had however made two decisions, 1. The plan was too good and the rewards to great to pass up. 2. Right before the conclusion of the battle, while Jason was battle weary and tired (and hopefully when Jason would least expect it), Uself would kill him and have him for dinner that night.

Jason was too smart and that meant it was too great of a risk to allow him to live. These decisions once made, Uself smiled to him self, as he thought, "seasoned with all that anger Jason would make a tasty meal and after a battle Uself was always starving!"

Every demon quickly learned which types of humans to hunt. It was simple, "stick with what you know." The more extensive your knowledge of your prey's weakness, the more opportunities you have to use those weakness against them. Tris' area of expertise was females who based there total sense of self worth and self belief on their image and on sexual vanity. Or, more specifically: on their face, body and ability to use men through the sexual act. Tris not only understood these women, but a long, very long time ago she had been one of them. Tris knew every fear her prey would feel as well as when and where to use that fear against them. This gave her an exquisite sense of timing, as to when it was the perfect time to real them in.

Tris would experiment with each of her prey to expand her knowledge and increase her attention to detail regarding little or hidden flaws (she was one of the few demons who had the luxury to do so, because she hunted out of pleasure, not need) to see what levels of sexual deviance she could push her prey into. Tris' favorite was sexual dominance. Often, Tris would merge with her prey to heighten the experience, Once after one seriously intense experience when Tris and her prey had almost beaten a man to death(Tris still shivered at the pleasure of that experience) Tris had pulled back just in time.

Tris knew that Susan had unexplored dark places in her and Tris would find and experience each one. Therefore Tris was not ready for her prey to come home yet, at least not until Tris had felt all her current prey had to offer. All of the women that Tris went after on the surface, were the same basic type of women and interchangeable in that over all, one was pretty much like the next. The difference between them was in the levels and degrees of deprivation that they had naturally or the levels that Tris could push them too.

Years ago Tris talked one such prey into committing suicide when she began to age and could no longer hide it. Now, she was one of Tri's strongest energy sources! Tris had learned over the years that obtaining prey was too important a task to be done when you are overwhelmed with need or hunger. Then you make mistakes, one of such mistakes was to target a prey which you may not have the ability, expertise or knowledge to take down. Like that fool Rule. No, Tris researched her prey well and took her time so that she could choose wisely.

There was something else Tris had learned over the years, diversification. Tris had two other businesses; she was a broker of information and she held a pattern which paid her on-going dividends. Tris' two other businesses allowed her the time she needed to research her prey and the ability to take her time selecting and seducing each of them.

Each piece of truly good information was worth an inch of a recent kill. This meant that Tris always had her basic levels of needs met, therefore, her prey was always a bonus and a means of sharpening her skills . . . never a need!

As Tris continued to think over recent events she was trying to figure out a way to turn this situation with Rule into a positive . . . was their information to be sold here?" Tris thought as she replayed the situation again in her mind but this time she was looking at subtle or vague impressions . . . little things, which might lead to hidden yet valuable information.

Chapter Twenty-Six

There is something extremely freeing about having nothing to loose! Rule sat quietly as he thought about the last few months. In a few short months, he had gone from a demon that had discovered a rare and highly prized soul . . . . to one facing certain death. Funny, how when death is looking you in the face all illusions are drop.

Rule knew that no Senior Elder demon was going to share his prize on any level. As long as no one knew she was an elemental and her powers were dormant, Rule had a chance. A good chance for a while of reeling the prey in before any knowledge of the true nature of her soul was known. The one and only chance he had ever had was ignorance, every one's ignorance, from the prey knowing her true nature and the power in her soul to the ignorance of any other demon knowing that she was an elemental.

Not only had this one chance slipped out of his hand but now the moment, "no" the second his usefulness was at an end Vane would kill him or the Senior Elder would kill him and Vane. Or if in the end the prey was lost, he would be the one blamed and ate. So it was not a matter of "if" he was going to die but a matter of "when" he was going to die and who would kill him? The only question in Rules' mine was this "is there any chance of taking one or both of the demons who had stolen his prey, down with him?"

There was only one being in hell strong enough to take down a Senior Elder demon! Assuming Rule could get an audience with him in time. The earliest he had ever heard of anyone getting an audience with "The Great One" was weeks and Rule was pretty sure he would be dead by then. Rule laughed and then he thought what does it matter, what would I have to offer, of great enough value that would or could tempt the ruler of hell to intervene on his behalf?

One very week shade, the more malnourished you were the more transparent you became, had been trying to rest in the hall of records. He had literally faded into the back ground and at times was so close to invisible that there was very little difference. The shade noted movement and he thought it was another shade checking him out, to see if he had any thing of value to steal, when he noticed an older demon looking at an extremely old book. The shade was about to go back to resting when he also noted the demon seemed genuinely nervous and he was looking around to see if any one else had seen or noticed him. This caught shade 4-56's attention so he watched the demon with growing curiosity. The demon turned to the last page of the book and wrote down a name; as the demon got ready to leave he looked around again before he left.

Shade 4-56 got up and looked at the book and page the demon had been reading (the demon had not bothered to close the book, sense he seemed to think that he was completely alone) The page he was looking at had only three names on it and the first was Lucifer, the second a signature which no one could read but the third name was exceptionally clear it was Uself!

Demons were naturally paranoid, everyone knew that hell was full of eyes and ears . . . simply because you did not see them did not mean that they were not there. Older and smarter demons always took this information into consideration in all of their dealings. Demons did not know it but they were describing "Shades." Most demons had little to no knowledge of shades. Shades, the very name, represented failure and this was a thought that most demons did not want to be associated with . . . as if the mere knowledge of shades would somehow taint them with failure! Besides, they were busy with the capture of prey and did not have time or inclination to think or concern them selves with anything that did not help them toward that end.

A shade could not always count on a demon loosing his prey to obtain free food. Plus, nothing was really free in hell and "free food" came with many other dangers. No, if a shade was going to survive he needed to find a quieter less obvious way to obtain food. Hell was full of information brokers; the challenge was in knowing who would cheat you and who paid a fair price.

Shade 4-56 started observing some of the major brokers. Learning there business practices, it was easy for shade 4-56 to spot a shady broker all he had to do was look for the qualities he himself had once exhibited in business, when he spotted those traits . . .he moved on to the next broker. Shade 4-56 had been watching Tris for a while, he had heard no shades complaining about her (which was rare in its self) He had heard rumors about her having a safe house where weak shades could eat and rest in peace. However, more important than that, Tris had a steady stream of shades seeking her out to sell information to her. This was truly unusual and impressive. The extremely high volume of business she conducted plus almost no complaints and if the possibility of a safe house was true . . . shade 4-56 had found his broker now all he needed was something to sell.

Tris was not just an information broker; she was an information broker extraordinaire. Tris knew many demons and even more shade who were no longer allowed to hunt prey. These beings were constantly on the look out for any information that would be of use to her and in payment she would provide food, giving them a taste of a recently dammed soul.

A piece the size of a inch not only could stop there hunger, for a few days but with each piece of food, of a newly dammed soul that they could acquire, they grew stronger and better able to defend themselves against others who stole from weaker demons and or shades. In addition to the above, Tris had a safe house where extremely weak demon could be protected while they ate and rested. The cost for this option was half of the inch of food rather than a full inch piece (which there information earned).

They could eat the half inch in a protected area with out fear or they could take the whole inch and return to the general public and run the extremely strong risk that the food would be taken from them before they could eat it, or worse possibly get beat in the process of other demons stealing their meal.

For Tris this business strategy was a win /win /win situation. She always had to pay less than the going rate to any weak demon or shade and the rooms she offered were in a hidden extensions of her home, which meant that it cost her nothing but meant a great deal to them. Because, for the first time in a very long while they had not only a room all to themselves but their safety was insured. Other information brokers were not so generous, which always gave her an advantage against her competition (win). Tris then for the most part always paid half price for her information and no one thought themselves ill used (win). Therefore, for all of the truly good information, she was the first broker they sought out (win).

Tris kept her word she always paid the price she named for the information provided. And if she promised a private room for them to rest and recover in she always kept that promise as well. Not because she had even the first sympathetic thought for their plight! No, hell no! Tris' actions were simply good business and this was why Tris was an information broker extraordinaire!

Tris knew that her business depended on the hungry and if it got around that she did not deliver, some of her best sources of information would dry up. Tris would never allow stupidly (especially that of being too greedy) to get in the way of good business practices. Besides, Tris knew that she made more than any other information broker practicing and she paid out less. This proved that her strategy was the intelligent one. Tris shifted her thoughts to some of the the information she had recently received. Several pieces of information that she was reviewing was starting to make a very interesting picture.

Once a long time ago, shade 4-56 was not just a number but he had a name. Shade 4-56 translated into the number four million three hundred and fifty-sixth shade created by hell. His name when he was a demon was Max. This was his name before he became a shade. Max seldom thought about the past because he was usually in too much pain or too hungry to concentrate on anything but current survival. However, now well fed in Tris' safe room, he was not in pain or hungry. He was not trying to sleep with one eye open while trying to stay alert to monitor the dangers around him. Now for the first time in a very long time Max started thinking about how he became a shade.

The rule in hell was . . . If you lost one soul you had to give up ten. If you could not pay the price then everything was stripped from you. Max had been a mid-level demon who had never lost his prey before and he had nine souls, when he lost his first prey. If he had the ten soul price he would have still remained a demon but had other limitations put on him. But when he could not pay the ten soul price, Max had been stripped of his name and his soul ownership (because after everything you have has been taken from you), the next thing you loose is your body. Max still shuttered as he remembered the feeling of his body breaking into small pieces as if cut by a laser. Then his body rained down on different sections of hell, for the dammed shades to consume.

Once your corporal body broke into pieces, to become food in hell, you became a shade. At first all you feel is pain . . .. . . as you feel each bite on your flesh, as other dammed shades consume you. Then the pain is moved up to the next level. As you feel the continuous burn of the digestive juices, as each pieces of you is dissolving in the stomachs of many different shades. This is a very slow process and for the first 50 to 100 years, there is nothing but pain, never ending pain. The pain you relieve in each shade, as your body provides food for his and relieve from his hunger, is transferred to you! However, when the pain ends, the real torture begins!

The hunger! The hunger is so intense that you wish you could go back to the pain! The hunger starts as a small fire in the middle of your gut and each day it gets worse and worse until you feel as if your are being consumed, burning up from the inside out. Because in fact that is exactly what is happening, the hunger in the absence of food eats you! There is only one thing that will put the fire out . . .. . at least for a little while . . .. . .food! However, as a dammed shade you no longer have the right to hunt souls, for food. If this is not bad enough, now you have to hide from stronger shades, shades who can smell food from miles away and hone in on it and you, as if they had radar!

This first set of thieves just took your food and beat you if you resisted. The second set of thieves, were much worse! They knew that it took time for you to both eat and for your body to absorb the food. This set of thieves, would tract you down shortly after you had consumed the food and beat you until you throw up the food; they would then eat the pre-digested food!

Tris' informed Max that the information he was selling had only a limited value and made him her standard deal, which he gladly took. The next day when he left the safe house, he intended to follow the older demon again, because the day before he had followed him to his home and found out his name. Max thought, "Who knows maybe this Vane might be good for another meal! The next day Max followed Vane again and again Vane did something unusually.

Vane visited the home of a master spell maker and challenged him to produce several very old spells, one of which was the spell to summon a Senior Elder demon. Again, Tris made her standard deal for the information and Max decided to stick with Vane like glue.

A few days later Max watched as a Senior Elder demon materialized in Vane's living room as he was pretending to sleep outside Vane's window. But this was not even the greatest part of his shock, the Senior Elder demon, after being summoned, let Vane live! Tris payed the full inch for this information and allowed Max to stay in her safe room for two nights. Max thought," Vane had been just that . . .a vane of pure gold!"

Tris took a deep breath while Max told her what he saw, she smelt no deception from him and her instincts informed her that he was telling the truth. Tris had another piece of the puzzle; the prey was extremely powerful from every thing that Max had told her. Rule, a younger demon, had to go to vane for help. Yet, where did this Jason fit into the situation? Was this powerful prey the reason that the Senior Elder Demon did not kill Vane for summoning him in the first place?

Tris told Max to stay on the scent and she would pay for any information he found out. The next day Max did just that, grateful that he had lucked up upon information that Tris felt was of value. Max felt much stronger than he had in a very long time and now he found that he could control his body's density.

Max now had the strength to, at will fade his body back into a shade. This had the added benefit of conserving energy and keeping his hunger under control longer; providing him additional protection as he followed the others around. Most demons did not bother with shades because it was believed that they had nothing of value. This belief also allowed Max to follow all three demons when they were together, with out any of them noticing his presence (or so he thought).

Max had been pretending to rest outside of Vane's home again when one evening Jason appeared and before Jason could send out the mental equivalent of a knock on the door and ask for entrance, in the blink of an eye he was materializing into Vane's living room. Jason was the last to attend this meeting since Vane and Rule was already there. Max had noticed something about Rule and now he saw that he had been right about Rule. Rule was shaking like a leaf on a tree in a wind storm and the fear was rolling off of him in waves until one look from the Senior Elder . . . then Rule did not move at all.

The Elder was dictating, the other three were listening. Then when the Senior Elder pretended to leave Max could still see the Senior Elder as a shade in Vane's living room, while Vane and the others discussed the meeting. Vane was angry and wanted to take it out on both Jason and Rule but some thing or someone had convinced Vane to focus the bulk of his attack on Rule. Jason left shortly after Vane started to beat Rule slowly, taking his time to insure that the best that Rule could do when he left was crawl out of the door. The Senior Elder however stayed and watched the show. Again, Max made his way back to Tris and information was rendered and payment was given.

This was why Tris' safe house was worth the price. It allowed a weak shade time to not only consume the food (weak shades could not eat fast) but her safe room gave his body time to absorb the nutrients pass the point of being able to throw it up. This was one of several nights he had spent in Tris' safe room. The last piece of information he brought her got him a whole inch of food and two night of piece to digest it in. This was as close to peace as Max had experienced in a very long time.

Rule, Tris thought, that fool Rule was her way into this situation if she choose. Tris survived by weighting risk against gain. Tris knew that there was some serious dealing unfolding around this situation. Tris also knew that situations of this nature required great care because these types of situations could afford you the possibility of great wealth or a quick death. Tris needed additional information before she was ready to decide on a course of action.

Being a shade was a whole different dimension of hell, first there was no mentorship, like there was for a new demon. You learned the rules and dangers through observation or experience. Second, unknown to most demons, Lucifer received five of the ten souls demanded as a personal tribute to him as ruler of hell. Third, you learned to suffer in silence, you did not call attention to yourself, because no matter how bad you hurt . . . believe me, it could and would get a lot worse.

Some times, attracted to the pain and cries of a new shade, a group of older shades would find him and beat the hell out of him simply because they were bored. Shade 4-56 had witnessed just such an action shortly after he became a shade. 4-56 left the new shade to his fate while he quietly looked for some where to rest with out calling attention to him self.

4-56 found such a spot and settled in to it and tried to sleep to quiet the pain. To his surprise it worked and 4-56 slept for ten years. After that time, he found that he was reliving every choice of the life time that had lead to his demon hood. Only this time he could see the cause and effect of each choice. Once he had stolen another man's business from him through some very shady business practices. He watched his former self, as he congratulated himself on being smarter and more cunning than his opponent.

However, what he had not known, during that life time, was the effects of those choices on the other man. He lost not only his business but his total financial net worth. After this vision, 4-56 heard a strange sound that he did not understand. Next he watched as the man killed himself because of the financial loss and shame he had brought on his family.

Again Max heard that same strange sound. Next he saw that man's daughter having to break off her engagement to a man she loved because of the poverty and shame that her father had brought to the family (her young man still wanted to marry her but she no longer had a dowry; no young woman of her class married with out one and to do so was a great shame to both families).

Again Max heard the same strange sound. Next the young woman had been literally sold to a man of great wealth but one who was both cruel and depraved. There goes that sound again. Next when this young innocent did not want to practice the sick and twisted activities that her new husband demanded of her, her husband beat her to death; she was also pregnant at that time.

Now he heard that sound twice! Something told Max to wait and watch for an explanation and sure enough those strange sounds turned into numbers. Those numbers equaled the amount of interest payments that Max had earned for his part in the young women's fate or as a direct effect of the shady business deal which had cost her father his wealth and life.

Interest payments gained for the pain caused to this one young woman and her child! Max thought, the man had a wife and three other children! Not to mention the harm that his actions had on the man himself! This was just one deal and one family how many other lives had Max been instrumental in causing there ruin? Max woke up shaking . . .. he had known that his actions had consequences but it never dawned on him that his actions would accumulate interest payments in addition to the initial debt as well!

For the first time ever Max began to understand why he was dammed. Initially when he realized that he was dammed, Max thought himself ill used. After all he was no worse than many men of business in his time. Now after looking at one act and seeing the pain and suffering his actions had caused "one" member of that family . . . Max was beginning to understand how his choices had lead to his current fate.

Chapter Twenty-Seven

Dammed demons or shades could not lie or at least when they tried to lie some how a normal demon knew. Another shade had once told Max it was the smell . . . . when a dammed demon lied they gave off a distinct odor that always informed the normal demons that they are lying. This would explain why Tris always seemed to take deep breaths around him, initially he had wondered about that but at the time he was too hungry and tired to care.

Max figured that each piece of food had relieved his hunger for about a week. This meant max had three weeks to find out something of value to Tris. Max followed Vane for a week and he noticed the two other demons were working with him but Max kept his focus now on Vane. Jason was a new demon and Rule was a mid level demon like he had once been.

Max looked at Rule and then he looked again, there was something very familiar about him, then it hit him . . . desperation! Rule had the look of a demon on the verge of loosing his prey. On an instinct, Max started to follow Rule he watched as Rule tried to enter his prey's mind but the light that repelled him was so strong it was blinding. Max had miscalculated, and he could feel after two weeks his hunger pains beginning to grow. Max hurried back to tris with his last piece of information, as he wondered what the bright light from Rules pray meant?

There was only one being in hell (Tris' thought) strong enough to protect her if things went wrong. One being who was able to provide her with the required ten soul payment to cover her if the prey was lost and payment for what ever reason ended up on her door step. One being, who actually would know what the light shinning out of the prey's soul meant, in terms of how powerful the prey was. There was only one being, who could stand between her and a Senior Elder, if that Senor Elder tried to destroy her for getting in his way. Tris needed to be sure that her information was as valuable as she thought it was.

Because unless she could clearly show that these actions were a clear threat to Lucifer, Lucifer would not extend his help and protection on any level and worse, then he would gladly give her over to the Senior Elder for wasting his time. Tris shivered, the last thing she wanted was to be the main attraction at dinner or in other words to **be** Lucifer's dinner!

Tris, already had something that few demons ever got, Tris had the right to request and audience with Lucifer. Years ago, Tris had become a decorated demon (the equivalent of receiving a medal of honor in hell). Being a decorated demon came with several advantages one of which was that any decorated demons had the right to an audience with the great one upon request, especially since so few acquired this honor.

So getting to Lucifer, which would have presented another level of difficulty for any other demon, was not a problem for Tris. Tris simply needed to be sure, she needed a plan of how she was going to put this information before Lucifer; in a way that insured her safety, future protection and wealth.

Rule was in an even fouler mood than usual, it seemed that his hands were tied and all he could do was watch for the ax to fall. Rule heard the equivalent of a mental knock at the door, he yanked the door open, thinking it was Jason requiring or needing some more information. This time he was going to tell Jason to figure it out himself and slam the door in his face. After all what is the worst that could happen to him behind this action that was not already being planned for him anyway!

So, Rule yanked the door open and to his surprise Tris was there. Tris smiled and said, it took me a minute to get a copy of our contract and when I returned you were no where to be found. So that you know I did all I could, I brought you a copy of the contract for us to discuss. Tris knew that the copy was useless to Rule and Rule knew it too.

The next question became what did she really want? Since Rule had nothing to loose, he invited her in to see what her real intentions were. Tris walked into Rules apartment with an innocent look on her face, she sat down and

Rule said, well what is it you think I can help you with? Tris smiled and said maybe we can help each other!

Rule was intrigued his curiosity helped to keep his fear under control and for that alone Rule was willing to listen. Tris looked Rule straight in the eyes, all pretense of innocence gone; what was left was a calculating intense stare when Tris asked, why don't we go for a walk it is somewhat stuffy in here.

The walk that Tris suggested ended up becoming a trip to her home and she invited Rule in. Tris was an information broker and she knew that almost everyone's home or apartment was bugged unless they took steps to insure that there home was protected, Tris took such steps. Now, that she was in a protected environment she wanted answers!

As they entered her home and settled in on the couch, Tris offered Rule a glass of blood wine, this was a treat which Tris knew that Rule could not probably afford and definitely would not turn down. As they were slipping the wine in an appreciative silence, Tris said." Why did your prey give off such a intense light this last time you tried to enter her mind. What type of power does you prey possess?" Rule was so full of fear it literally seeped out of his pours. Tris then replied, tell me everything you know about this situation and there is a possibility that you will survive it. After all what do you have to loose, at least I offer the possibility of a way out which (Tris stopped and took another deep breath) by the smell of you, it is a lot more than you have now.

Rule, was completely surprised. As Rule listened to Tris a series of emotions and questions went through his mind, how dare she come to him and speak to him this way? Did he exude the fear he thought he was hiding so well? How did she know about his prey's soul level strength and was it possible that she could be the answer he sought? Self preservation out weighted all other concerns when he asked, if I tell you what you want to know how do I know first that you can help me and second that you will. Tris listen to Rule's concerns and thought, "desperation has made him a lot smarter."

Rule sat back on the couch looking for a way to turn this situation to his advantage, Rule looked Tris in the eyes and said why should I tell you anything, then under his breath he said, not that it matters anyway. Tris took a deep breath, normally you could not smell fear on another demon unless they were dammed or close to devolving. Then Tris thought about what Max had said regarding Rule looking as if he was jut about to loose his prey. Another piece of the puzzle fell into place.

Tris replied, first I know that a Senior Elder demon is involved and we both know that only the great one can protect any of us from him. Rule's face fell because he knew there was no way to receive an audience with the great one in time to request his help. Tris watched as Rule processed the information she had just stated (his face was easier to read than a book) Then when defeat was written on his forehead in large bold letters, Tris spoke very causally she said, I am a decorated demon.

It was almost comical watching Rule's face go from night to day. Rule then got a suspicious look on his face and asked, decorated for what? Tris took a deep breath as she weighted her options. She needed to know what he knew; therefore he needed to know that she could deliver on her ability to get an audience with Lucifer. But she hated to reveal any personal knowledge. Tris had learned a long time ago, especially as an information broker, that the less another demon knew about you personally the safer you are.

Tris knew that sometimes the smallest piece of information at the right time could cause a domino effect that could lead to your destruction but she needed to know what he knew and only this piece of her personal information would convince Rule to comply. Tris looked Rule in the eyes and said, Tris is a shorten version of my name . . ..my complete name is Dominatrist. I invented (as a human) and perfected (as a demon) a form of sexual deviant behavior known as dominant/sub-servant sexual behavior.

This was Tris' third source of income because any time a demon used this method with or on their prey, they had to pay her a dividend. Tris was allowed to establish the rate due her for the use of her product, so Tris kept the rate reasonable. If the demon chose to pay up front the cost was only 2% but if the demon wanted to pay at the end of the capture of his prey the price went up to 5%. Tris always put in the clear stipulations that no matter the outcome of the situation her commission was due, Plus, Tris always dealt in no fault contracts, she provided a product the outcome of which was not her concern.

Tris was smart and she knew that two to five percent of a lot was better than twenty to thirty percent of a little. This afforded Tris her third income stream; a very lucrative income stream and because of the reasonable rates, Tris' product was used often. It was this income stream which she usually used to pay her informants, so that she never had to spend any funds from her personal stash.

Rule sat back on the couch, now he was impressed but more than that he started to feel hope. She could request an audience with the great one and receive it in a matter of hours. Tris gave him a moment to take it all in then said, of course I have to know every thing If I am to put my life on the line and save yours as well!

With that Rule told her everything. Tris told him when he got up to leave, that she was waiting on a few more pieces of information before she put her plan into action. When the time was right, she would contact him and tell him what she wanted him to do. After Rule left, Tris reviewed the situation from every perspective. It all added up to the same answer; a Senior Elder demon was seeking a power source of great strength which would allow him to challenge Lucifer for ruler ship of hell.

Tris knew that this was a serious situation before she spoken with Rule; now the situation was one of life or death. Tris pondered further as she thought of how to use this information to its best advantage. In the end it all came down to one simple question, who did Tris believe would win in a fight for ruler ship of hell . . .. . . the answer was easy, Lucifer! Tris would request an audience with Lucifer and she would inform him of this danger. Tris knew that if he found what she told him to be of worth, she and all she named would receive his protection and a ten soul payment for the information.

The creator was reviewing the concept of fate and choice and its connection with the past, present and future. The creator had smiled as he watched man, his creative and inventive child, who could not conceive of the fact that fate and choice are one concept. So he divided them up into two individual concepts and in that manor he had figured out the basic nature of each.

However, man has not understood how they were connected or the fact that they are simply different parts of the same thing. All things are interconnected, the past directly impacts the present and the present directs the future. To see this insight you have to look at things simply and man seems to love complication.

For example: If you look at a tree it has branches of different widths and lengths (fate). How you used or if you used some or all of the possibilities inherent in each branch (choice) depended on your will. If you look at a tree from the top down it looks like a confusion of leaves. However, when you look at a tree from the bottom up, you see order and simplicity. That is, the trunk feed into the branches and the branches produce the leaves . . .. simple. Man however seems to make a habit of getting caught up in unnecessary confusion or looking at the tree from the top down.

Long before the birth of man, the creator had been reviewing every aspect of man's creation. The creator knew that in order for man to evolve to all he hoped for him, one essential ingredient was necessary . . . . free will! The problem was the unpredictable nature of this power of choice. This was a gift that once given could not be controlled and the variations or different ways in which this gift could express its self, in each individual, was infinite.

Free will or the power of choice is a god trait. It was also a trait that the creator wanted to bestow on his child, after all what father does not want to see some part of himself in his child? The problem was that god traits were tricky at best. God traits have a life of its own and because of which the trait is a wild card. This trait has a multitude of infinite possibilities that it could assume or use to express its self with in each person, manifesting with completely different qualities in each person based on personality and intelligence.

The creator needed a focal point or a means to study this concept up close and personal. The creator wanted to watch the effects of free will on one being. He wanted to chart the specific effects of this power, with the intent of getting an intimate look at the over all outcome that such a powerful concept would have on that being. After all, no god trait had ever been given to any other race before.

The creator gave the power of choice to one angel. This angel did not know that he had received the power of choice and that, the power he was given had no limits. Through this angel, the creator would chart the strengths and weakness that this power would have on him. All with the ultimate goal of trying to insure that this was a power that man could handle. Or, if this power needed to be altered in man to limit any unnecessary damage.

Upon Lucifer's conception, he was given the power of choice. Lucifer received this power with no restrictions; no knowledge that he had been given this power and the power had no limitations assigned to it. The creator observed Lucifer closely and calculated the possibilities or outcomes of each choice that Lucifer made. As the creator observed Lucifer, he did indeed yield information that even though the creator had seen the possibility of these things happening, the creator had thought that many of the outcomes and changes would remained in the category of possibilities that would be too remote to come into being, but again with a god trait many assumptions are up for grabs.

Therefore the creator was intrigued when a possibility that should have been a long shot at best, moved to the forefront of Lucifer's mind and became an actual fact. Each choice that Lucifer made changed actually changed his DNA structure! With each choice Lucifer was re-creating himself and choosing his own path of evolution. A path, which at times, was completely different from the path that the creator had outlined for Lucifer at his conception.

The power of choice had literally overridden the genetic instructions that the creator had given Lucifer at the time of his birth. As the creator observed, a long shot overrode every other consideration in Lucifer as free will wrapped its self around the concept that "what you believe is the foundation of your choices, your choices are the foundation of your actions and your actions shape your world."

The creator gave Lucifer a greater amount of the freedom of expression and often Lucifer's comments clearly expressed his less than complete agreement with the creator. Yet he always obeyed until the birth of man. The creator watched Lucifer's reactions to the birth of his child above all others angels. Then when the creator revealed that he was giving man a piece of himself, a thing called a soul. The creator watched with intrigued fascination, as Lucifer waged war with in him self as the power of choice and the power of faith fought for dominance. The creator knew the exact moment, the second that Lucifer no longer choose to serve him but chose to become him. This was the moment that Lucifer believed that the creator was completely wrong (about the creation of man) and he was completely right!

The creator calculated the outcome of this choice and one thing became completely clear . . . unlimited and unchecked the power of choice would bring about man's destruction as it had in Lucifer. Yet, even as the creator watched the process as it took place in Lucifer he had already saw the end and put thing in place for that end to serve his will as well. The creator had seen many good and possible great outcomes as a result of the power of choice. However, this power needed to be limited in man. Man was blocked from using the majority of his mental abilities and talents. Man was given use of only twelve to thirteen percent of the innate capacity of his mind.

Man's life span which was intended to be unlimited, was now limited. Man has built with in his genetic structure a seven year renewal cycle, in that every seven years every cell in his body is renewed and with this cycle it was intended for all illness to be cured and for the cells to grow stronger.

Now illness and age was allowed in the life span of man, because man needed cycles of rebirth to give him enough time for his moral strength to grow strong enough to control his mental abilities. Free will or the power of choice was the god trait that the creator chose to give his child because it also presented infinite possibilities for greatness, unequaled creativity and it provided a source of inspiration equal to none. These were the qualities that man would need to grow and evolve. However, this trait also had many equal and opposite destructive attributes which the new limitations that the creator imposed, would help to limit.

Now it was time for the creator to give Lucifer his wish. The creator had given Lucifer every opportunity to alter his choice. However, based upon the changes that the power of choice was creating in Lucifer's DNA structure (Lucifer was no longer a product of the creator's direct intentions but the outcome of his own choices)the creator knew that the possibility that Lucifer would regain his grace and decide to choose his faith had already moved from slim to none!

The creator gave Lucifer his wish, Lucifer was the undisputed ruler of hell; this was the outcome that Lucifer's choices had brought. The creator allowed Lucifer the ability to sustain himself by allowing Lucifer, and the occupants of hell, to use his genetic material or the material from which the soul was created. Lucifer discovered nothing the creator did not what him to know. Lucifer and the third were born to truth and light and unknown to them (in the beginning of there transition) they would need some aspect of him or that truth and light, to sustain their life force because with out the creator's help and interventions they would have ceased to exist.

Raphael waited for Ariel's to return from her visit with Jason however one look at her face and she had Raphael's immediate attention. Then when she communicated this last piece of information she had learned from Jason, Raphael sent an urgent communication to Gabriel and Bree and with in minutes they were materializing in Ariel's home.

Katelyn and Justin had discussed the day in great detail and they were about to contact his parents when he felt them touch him mind requesting entrance to their apartment. The request was granted then both Justin and Jason's parents materialized. The minute they entered as before they all added there energy lines to the protection energy that Katelyn had placed around the apartment insuring that nothing they discussed could be overheard on any level.

Using angelic communication every body was informed about what had occurred; the plan was laid out and the floor open for general input and discussion. Gabriel and Raphael had known Uself for longer than recorded time and they added there personal knowledge of him to the general information pool. They agreed, that Uself favored the unseen attack then they discussed what they felt would be Uself's surprise attack.

Gabriel and Raphael tried to put them selves in Uself's place and think through the plan based on there personal understanding of how they thought he would see this situation. Yes, he would strive to divide and conquer and yes he would exhaust them physically and then try to introduce fear mentally. They all agreed on the general focus of the attack but what would be the defining signature blow? The killing blow, which literally defined all of Uself's battle strategy.

Uself would strive to insure that this attack was both undetected (surprise would be a key element in the attack) and extremely toxic and almost immediately deadly. Ariel absorbed the information and spoke almost with out knowing she did, Ariel said, I can feel that he intends to kill Jason the minute he is no longer of use. A surprise kill the moment Uself believes the battle is won. But, this would not be his signature killing blow.

Ariel was doing it again, touching the information with her mind and looking simply at where the energy lines connected. Ariel continued to follow the energy lines; literally sweeping away the confusion meant to misdirect the information from the genuine intention of the thought. These were the connections that Ariel sought. All of a sudden Ariel went extremely pale and said I know what the killing blow will be! Uself is going to kill someone that Justin truly loves! The energy line that Ariel was following dissipated and she was unable to follow it further to see who Uself intended to kill but as they discussed what she saw, all of them felt that the intended victim had to be Katelyn!

Ariel withdrew her mind from the general discussion in front of her and following an instinct, she replayed her last discussion with Jason applying the same techniques to that discussion as she looked for any subtle information that she might have overlooked before. Ariel replayed the information she received the last time she visited Jason. As Ariel entered into Jason's shields she told him, I found the message you left in Bree's energy signature and I have told no one. I honor the sacrifice you were prepared to make. You are now the man you were born to be. Ariel hugged her son and he felt her love wash over him like a cleaning rain. Ariel pulled back from him quickly then touched her hand to his mind, closing her eyes to concentrate better.

Jason had felt Uself touch his mind as he related his observations from today's battle. At one point he felt Uself hide an excited reaction to something but what it was that excited him Jason was not sure of. Jason reviewed the battle again in his mind trying to feel what had caused the reaction he felt in Uself.

The only thing he could get was a spike in emotions when uself was focused on Justin, this was not good if nothing else his time in hell had taught Jason a new respect for his instincts and attention to detail. His instincts were telling him that this small detail was important.

Jason went to his apartment and laid down he wondered what new information had happened since he last spoke with Katelyn and Justin. Jason stopped and thought of how much of his life before he taken for granted and how much time he wasted making everything always about him. Considering the love, protection, support and help that he had received he had a new and deeper appreciation for each of them. No matter how this situation turned out, he knew something that he did not know when this situation started, Jason now knew how much he was loved and how much he mattered to them and how much they mattered to him.

This core level understanding of that knowledge made this experience almost worth it alone. Jason was humbled by this knowledge then at that moment he felt his mother's touch. Jason looked around for the others but she was alone. Ariel saw the question in his eyes and said, "I asked the others to allow me to speak with you alone."

Ariel felt Jason's concern and she wanted to put Jason's mind at ease, she was not only getting good at following energy signatures but she could pick up spikes or emotional highs and lows. Ariel saw and felt Jason's concerns centered around one of those emotional spikes. Then from a distance, she was learning to see the difference between negative and positive energy signature and how to protect her self by following the thought alone, while staying away from the substance.

To do this she had to become air, seeing and passing through the thought as natural as air but allowing nothing of substance to touch her. Ariel saw the answer to the question Jason's instincts had picked up. Ariel flowed back into her self as her son watched in awe and a little concern. Ariel opened her eyes and said, "Uself has recognized Gabriel in Justin during the battle, both in looks and form through the battle techniques which Justin used and learned form Gabriel. Uself knows that Justin is Gabriel's son!

Chapter Twenty-Eight

Uself had touched Jason's mind as he explained Rule's failure and outlined the plan of attack. Uself wanted to see the battle but more importantly he wanted to see what source of power the prey's boyfriend possessed. Uself saw only what Katelyn and Justin had constructed but unfortunately Uself saw something that none of them could have predicted he would have noticed.

Uself saw Justin in action infused with light, he watched as he noted that Justin's movement looked choreographed, like movements in a dance but with an economy of movements that were both fluid and graceful. Uself watched Justin with intensity, the more he watched the more it seemed that there was something so extremely familiar about him . . . . then it hit him! Justin had just executed a movement that was exactly like one he had seen many times before and the look on Justin's face that too was familiar then suddenly for one moment in time, Justin looked and moved exactly like his father, Justin was Gabriel's son!

Uself knew what most human born demons did not. Most human born demons (the few that had ever heard of them) thought of light warriors as creatures of myths and legends. Therefore most demons essentially believed that they were not real. Uself was created as an angel and he knew that Nephlium (half angel and half human) often referred to as light warriors, were a fact not fiction.

Uself and Gabriel had once been extremely good friends. Uself remembered Gabriel's hidden anger at being mated to a human. At that time Uself had been curious about his friend's new sudden mood changes, so Uself had followed Gabriel on one of his earlier visits to his human. A human Gabriel often avoided and did not visit for long periods of time.

Over time Uself had put the pieces of the puzzle together as he realized the human woman' role in Gabriel life. Initially, a communication block had been put on this information but over time both hell and heaven had noticed the new race on the block. The only thing that was not know, even to this day, was why the race was created and which angels were chosen to be the fathers and why.

Uself had to fight to contain his excitement; he brushed aside the brief thought that over time this situation might have changed. Uself smiled and thought given what he knew of Gabriel's hidden ego and arrogance Uself had the strong belief that little would have changed between Gabriel and the human consort he was forced to in impregnate. Hell, he might even be doing Gabriel a favor by eliminating both the mother and the son!

Now, it all makes since! Ariel could literally see Uself putting the final pieces of this plan together in his mind. Ariel knew that Uself intended to strike a killing blow to some one Justin loved and they all believed it would be Katelyn, while Uself did intend to kill Katelyn, the unexpected killing blow which would bring Justin to his knees would be . . . . the death of his mother!

Ariel turned around to resume her place in the discussion but unknown to her she was angry and since it was the first time that any of them had seen her angry they all stopped and looked at her, waiting for an explanation. Ariel then sent an intense burst of angelic communication to all present and for the first time her pain was turned to anger and Ariel's anger could literally be felt as the communication was received.

Gabriel sat quietly as Ariel completed the information she was sharing with them regarding Uself's true plan and intent. Gabriel took a deep breath to try to control the rage and pain that was attacking him from both the inside and with out. Gabriel sent understanding to the pain, knowing that the more you understand what you are feeling the greater your control over it. Of course the thought of Justin and Bree being in danger would cause this level of pain and anger, Gabriel tried to tell him self as he fought to calm him self down.

Gabriel waited quietly for this knowledge to sooth the pain and quiet the rage and allow him to control it, when to his surprise the pain got worse.

Gabriel was now beginning to become concerned because this meant that what he thought was the cause of the pain was not completely accurate or it was not the core of the pain. Gabriel reached out and asked Raphael for help then connected his mind to Raphael because what ever this was, it was beginning to seriously concern him and Gabriel thought that he might need additional strength and help to deal with it.

The pain continued to increase until Gabriel thought he would implode. Then he both felt and heard a crack as something deep with in him began to break. Gabriel watched in fascinated horror as he saw, felt and smelled what oozed out of that crack. It was ancient negativity; it smelled increasingly foul like a cancer feeding on its self and getting stronger and stronger as it consumed its own rotting flesh.

It looked like red and black puss seeping out of him. Imbedded with in this slime were memories that attacked his mind as if they were angry with him. The memories were of conversations with him and Uself about their feelings regarding the creation of man and how the creator seemed to favor and love them more. How angels had worked at and by the creator's side since time began and they had earned the creator's favor and yet when it came time to give a part of himself to another he just handed this indescribably important gift to man who did not and could not even began to understand its worth!

With each statement that Uself made, Gabriel watched with dawning horror, as each time Gabriel agreed with Uself he now saw an egg being implanted deep with in him which was the core of this negativity. Gabriel did not break the seal of communication and he had not told Uself that he had been expected to mate with one of these animals but some how Uself seemed to know! These eggs, which now had grown into the red/black mass, had been protected by Gabriel for centuries because he thought the information they contained was an accurate assessment of man.

This was why he could not completely allow himself to love Bree he had believed that even thought he though of her as an exception she was still born to a race of animals and because of which he believed she was not worthy of him. This core truth hit Gabriel so deep that he though he would shatter into fragments. At this point Gabriel screamed, as he saw the core of the evil which had lived protected with in him. Evil, which had poisoned his relationship with both his creator and his consort.

Raphael, who had been monitoring all that Gabriel had seen and felt, was sharing Gabriel's pain and through the connection he saw the same ancient negativity with in him self. Raphael shielded the others in the room so that the piercing sound of Gabriel's scream of pain would not rupture their ear drums. For the first time in his very long life, Gabriel felt true rage! The rage was so strong and deep at the betrayal of a friend and his betrayal of the creator that Gabriel's great uncle appeared. He moved to Gabriel's side then touched his heart, mind and sprit drawing the rage out before it entered the structure of his DNA.

Then he literally reached inside Gabriel and pulled out a black/red mass with tentacles. Gabriel's uncle then sent a burst of angelic light to kill it. Next he placed his other hand on Gabriel's heart and poured in an intense infusion of love so strong that one spark looked as if it would burn each of them alive. Then he touched Gabriel's mind to allow the healing light to infuse him.

Gabriel passed out; his uncle caught him and carried him to the sofa and as his uncle held him. The looks across the room ran from shock, awe, surprise, worry and concern in varying degrees. No one spoke until there great uncle said, he will be fine. The seeds of this cancer had been growing in him for a long while. Up until now it had been contained by his faith which kept it from spreading through out his system. Finally it had grown to the point where he was ready to let it go. This made it possible for me to reach it and kill it. The threat to Justin and Bree provided the catalyst to pull this negativity out of him; I have been waiting for this day for more years than I can say!

The creator had been monitoring and tracking the negativity Lucifer sent his minions out to recruit and infect others, since Uself first implanted it with in Gabriel. The creator needed Gabriel and the others to understand there role in both receiving and harboring this negativity. Even more important they needed to want to let go of this negativity and at that point the negativity would seek to overwhelm them. The creator who understood the nature of this negativity knew it was at its most vulnerable at the point when it tried to take him over. Therefore he had been watching and waiting for this moment.

Every one was quiet, all of them were trying to come to terms with what they had just seen and heard. The first thing Gabriel did after coming to himself was to saying a heart felt thank you to his uncle, then he reached for Bree and kiss her completely and deeply.

He looked her deep in the eyes and said, "I Love you, you and Justin and now Katelyn are my family." I will do all with in my power to keep you, all of you safe. With that he kissed her again after which Raphael stepped forward and said, I too uncle. What sounded like uncle to the others was really "I too my god, request your healing touch."

With that Raphael too let go of the negativity he had hidden in his heart and mind and again the same black/red ugly mass was pulled out. The experience repeated its self with Raphael, when Raphael came to, there uncle said, "now you have all your need to defeat this evil; now I will leave as you prepare your strategy for battle."

With this last piece of information they now knew the confrontation was close at hand. Past interaction with Uself told Gabriel that Uself would seek to kidnap Bree on the eve of the battle. Grabbing her at the last possible moment because when he did so it would be a clear signal that indicated the battle had begun.

They decided on the following, every one's energy signals would be interlinked so that they could communicate freely with each other in seconds. Next, Bree would be moved into Gabriel's apartment because heaven was completely out of Uself's reach while getting to Bree's home realm would be difficult for Uself it would not be impossible. Gabriel disguised as Bree, took her place in her home.

They all agree that the kidnapping had to take place, in order to give Uself the belief that all was going according to his plan. At the time of the kidnapping, Gabriel would broadcast the word "Now" through every one's energy signature so that every one would be aware that the battle had begun.

Uself's plan was simple but elegantly perfect. Kidnap the preys boyfriend's mother, kill her in front of the boyfriend what was his name? Ah . . . . ..Justin, kill her in front of Justin or use a variation of this plan. Uself thought he could use the mother to get Justin to surrender and then pretend that by accident the mother was killed anyway.

Uself liked the second option better; it raised the expectation of hope in one breath and took it away in the next. Then While Justin was exhausted physically and in unbearable pain mentally over his mother's death, Uself would convince him that he would spare Katelyn's life if he took his own. If Justin took his own life, this action would doom his soul.

However, even better, Katelyn as his soul mate would want to follow! Uself thought he would help her feel that way (by sending her the knowledge that Justin died for her) and in this process he would be doubling or tripling her grief to the point that her pain would be completely unbearable and it would take her completely over the edge. Then Uself would provide her the means with which to take her own life.

Uself would not have to kill Katelyn, he thought (ironically). Uself would have kept his word in that yet, he would have her any way, because she would kill herself . . .Flawless! Uself had one more secret weapon, known only to him which recognizing Justin had thoughtfully supplied. If Gabriel tried to interfere with his plans, Uself would reach in and connect with the hidden negativity he had implanted in Gabriel long ago, when he was trying to recruit Gabriel for hell. Uself would use this negativity which he was sure was exceptionally strong by now, to divide and conquer . . . Uself would activate and direct the negativity to attack Gabriel from with in, while Uself rained blows on him from with out.

Lucifer received Tris' request for an audience. His curiosity was aroused because since her decoration, she had not once asked for an audience. Lucifer actually liked Tris, she was smart, ruthless and cunning all with the most innocent of expressions, expressions that an angel would be proud of. Tris specialized in the art of understatement. Lucifer gave the word to accept Tris' request. Tris was given an appointment for two hours from now.

Since Tris had put in her request this morning she had been reviewing what and how she would present the information to the great one, Tris decided to drop her illusions they would not fool him anyway and present herself as the smart, focused and intelligent demon that she was. That afternoon a telegraph arrived telling Tris that her audience had been approved and Lucifer would see her at 3:00 today. All was ready and Tris was at the great hall at 2:45 this was a sign of respect, to be early showed a subservient position; to be late was an insult. At 2:55 Tris was lead to the study/library room and she knew she was in Lucifer's personal space. Tris sat by the fire as she waited for Lucifer to appear.

Lucifer had been watching Tris as she came into his study. Her manor was fluid her facial expression thoughtful she looked like someone who knew the chance she took and had weighted the odds and came to the conclusion the audience would be worth it. At 3:00 on the dot, Lucifer walked into his study, Tris fell on her knees and addressed him as the great one.

Lucifer told her to rise and indicated that she take a seat. Tris looked at Lucifer and began, "great one" some information has come to my attention that I felt it was my duty to relate to you. Tris then told Lucifer everything she knew concluding with her belief that the Senior Elder demon, Uself intended to challenge him for the ruler ship of hell.

Lucifer listened to Tris' very interesting tale especially the part about the elemental. Lucifer told Tris to let him ponder the information she brought to his attention and by this time tomorrow she would know his decision, regarding what he felt was the worth of the information. Tris bowed her head and left.

Tris knew the procedure, if he found that she had brought him something useful or of value she would receive a gift of ten souls and a written voucher of protection for herself and all who's name she put on the voucher. However if it was his determination that she had wasted his time she would be required to render ten souls if she could not meet the price then she would have to give herself up to become a dammed soul.

The next day Tris received three packages. One held sixteen newly dammed human souls (Tris' first thought was . . . I am rich!) The second package held a voucher of protection for her self and any other demon she cared to add to the voucher. The third package held a bottle of blood wine . . .. ..her absolute favorite! Tris let out a breath she did not know she was holding. Her gamble had paided off! Tris calmed down and began to consider what she was going to do with Rule.

Tris thought that even though she had an order of protection it was always best to have more than one layer of protection. Tris did not want the Senior Elder demon to have any knowledge of her involvement in this situation. After all, one did not get to be a Senior Elder and live as long as he had with out a few tricks up his sleeve and if he survived the situation some how, she did not want to become his target.

Tris laughted and thought that she could hide behind Rule. Tris could bind Rule with the contract by stating that as long as he told no one about her knowledge or involvement in this situation, Tris would put his name on the order of protection as well. Tris smiled, if the Senior Elder tried to kill Rule the order of protection could block any blow or allow him to receive the punishment and later be healed it all depended on how Tris wrote his participation into the contract.

Tris thought about it and decided that it would be better if Rule received the punishment and that way it would delay the Senior Elder's knowledge that he had been sold out and if the Senior Elder survived and saw that Rule had survived as well with that would come the instant belief that it was Rule who sold the Senior Elder out.

If Rule opened his mouth to implicate her, the order of protection would vanish and Rule would be unable to defend him self from the Senior Elder's attack. Tris smiled, even though there was a good possibility that the Senior Elder demon would end up on Lucifer's dinner table, until she knew the fate of the Senior Elder it was best to take no chances. The less he knew about her the better! Tris thought I will pay a visit to Rule tomorrow morning.

Lucifer found much in Tris' story of genuine interest. The fact that Uself was the Senior Elder involved, that the prey was an elemental and her mate seemed to have some interesting qualities too. Instead of anger at the plot to over throw him, Lucifer was actually relieved. Life in hell had become predictable and somewhat dull. Lucifer actually welcomed an attempt to over throw him . . . a good battle always got the blood pumping! Lucifer was not surprised that the Senior Elder was Uself.

Lucifer had been extremely angry when Uself had failed to bring down his assigned angel. Before the fall Lucifer had assigned each of his chosen angels a task to bring with them another angel of equal rank and strength. Uself had failed in this assignment. Lucifer had to make an example of him and his punishment was both long and extremely painful but even worse it was humiliating and embarrassing which Lucifer believed was worse than the pain.

If Uself had not had an angelic heritage he would not have survived. Uself still bore a grudge both against Lucifer and Gabriel, the angel that did not turn, for his pain and punishment. Lucifer smiled, "the elemental" Uself would think that someone like this would or could be the base of his power . . . it was a good assumption and it made perfectly good sense . . . too bad it was completely wrong!

Elementals were an extremely good power source, Lucifer had met one once when he was looking for the human who possessed his soul (or the soul that Lucifer intended to posses). Lucifer was extremely impressed by her but he did not have time to study her because she not only recognized him but she called him by name. With his power devolving and his time limited Lucifer thought that this was not a good time to pick a fight (especially since he was not entirely sure that he would win because he did not know enough about what an elemental was or her power source and even if he did win the battle . . . it would be at what cost to both his energy and time?).

Now Lucifer knew a great deal about elemental and the possibility of owning one sent his taste buds soaring. However, soon he left this thought for a more practical one. The capture of an elemental was still a long way from a sure bet but Uself on the other hand was practically on the dinner table! Lucifer estimated that if Uself was able to capture the elemental it would increase his personal power to around 55 to 60% of that of Lucifer'(Lucifer kept track of the personal power levels of all of his Senior Elders) This would provide Uself a nice power boast . . . enough power for a good battle but not enough to win the war!

The information which won Tris' case was that she answered some questions that Lucifer deeply needed to know but questions that he knew he could never ask. Tris had informed him in a round about way that Uself did not know the source of Lucifer's power or the level of his strength. Was he seeking that knowledge, "yes?" If so, was he looking in the right direction, "No?" Lucifer took a deep breath and felt safe for the first time, in a very long while, since these questions began to worry him. It was because Tris did not know the true value of the information she gave him and because what she thought was important to him had limited value at best.

Lucifer had questioned her thoroughly and she did not know or understand anything more than she had told him. Lucifer had learned to smell deception too many years ago to count, Lucifer took deep breaths during Tris' presentation and from beginning to end there was no deception in either the information she gave him or was she holding anything back about this issue.

She answered Lucifer's questions clearly and concisely and when she did not know the information he questioned her about, she would simply and honestly state that she did not know. So, Lucifer was generous toward her and he gave her, her life then six extra newly dammed souls, the order of protection and as a after though a bottle of blood wine from his personal stock. Lucifer included in the order of protection a personal note that praised Tris' loyalty and told Tris to feel free to contact him if she found out anything else of which she felt would be of value to him.

Lucifer thought, plan "A" if she is stupid enough to drink the wine she will be addicted to it and the only place she could get more was from him . . . this would turn her into his own personal information broker, she would no longer be an independent contractor he would own her. Plan "B" If she did not drink the wine and Tris learned any sensitive information, information that Lucifer did not want any one else to know . . . he felt sure that Tris, now being aware of his generous nature, would bring the information straight to him.

If the information was of a sensitive nature, especially information regarding his power source, he would first insure that she had not informed anyone else about this knowledge and then he would kill her. After all Lucifer felt sure that Tris knew the risk she took in contacting or interacting with him.

Chapter Twenty-Nine

Tris took the rest of the evening to think. Lucifer had given her a bonus of six extra souls and the bottle of blood wine. Both gifts were over the required ten soul payment that she expected. Tris was not a fool, she recognized that Lucifer had found or heard something in what she had said that was extremely important to him but she simply did not know what it was and she was grateful for her ignorance and for the protection it gave her.

If Tris had to guess the blood wine he sent would be the best she had ever tasted . . . it would also be addictive. Lucifer intended for her to keep coming to him with information and Tris had no doubt that the moment she found out something that Lucifer did not want anyone to know . . .her life would be over. If she drank the wine she would need to keep coming back to him over and over again each time receiving less and less for her information until it ended with her death. Tris was a long way from a fool, she opened the bottle and she took a deep sniff, just as she suspected she could smell the overtones of something she had never smelled before in her wine.

The broker Tris had learned her trade from, tris had bartered sexual favors for information, bartered sexual favors for information and since she had once been a truly beautiful woman and a greatly skilled courtesan; later a madam of her own establishment, they had come to an agreement for her training. Tris asked questions and once when he was in a relaxed state had told her how he became in slaved to Lucifer, he told Tris the information in bits and pieces until she finally had the whole picture.

He informed her to be thoughtful in her dealings with the great one especially if he was generous with her, regarding any information she brought him. Lucifer would never continue to pay for some one's services if he did not have too. He had told her how he proudly received the gift of the blood wine from Lucifer and how he became addicted to it after the first slip. Then finally he told her what he should have done with the wine . . . . information he learned later which would have saved him a life time of servitude. Tris laid quietly beside him and she though that the reason he had said so much was because he thought she was a sleep and he was verbally reliving his situation, however, Tris listened to his every word.

Tris took the bottle to her wine cellar and poured exactly one ounce into each keg of wine in her cellar until all the wine was gone. The point of this was to dilute the wine a thousand plus percent so that it would increase the over all quality of her current wine but at the same time dilute the addictive aspect out of the wine. Tris had gambled and won, she was smart enough to leave the table and not press her luck. What ever Lucifer wanted to find out he would have to do it with out her intervention, she had no intentions of ever broking any information with him again, the risk was simply too great.

Decisions, Decisions, Decisions! . . . Lucifer thought. Should he wait to see how things turned out for Uself in his attempt to capture the elemental soul . . . and since her defense systems had been activated it would made her capture just that much harder . . . If Uself failed, to capture his prey, he would belong to me anyway . . . or should I wait to see if he succeeded and if so, then kill Uself and take the elemental soul . . . or should I allow Uself to try to challenge me for the ruler ship of hell and then and only then allow Uself to find out during this battle with me that he never had a chance of defeating me. That he was not as strong as he thought he would be . . . or that the elemental was not my power source and that I am much, much stronger than he ever knew and use him to make an example out of to remind all of hell who rules here . . . Decisions! Lucifer decided to expand his information base and dispatch his own spies to track and trail Uself so that from now on, he will know Uself's every move.

Lucifer's Story

Lucifer was in one of his rare thoughtful moods, one where he started to see life from more than one perspective. Lucifer was extremely good at looking at the perspectives of others but this talent simply did not extend to him self. However, having spent so much time in the human mind, in his efforts to destroy them, Lucifer had to admit (if only to himself) that he had developed a grudging respect (along with equal parts of anger) for humans over the years.

They are so unique, each one similar yet vastly different he had learned that early when he tried to develop a handbook for capturing a human soul. Lucifer found that what worked extremely well on one human, did not work at all on another or worked only to a limited degree with another even if the humans had similar characteristic.

On some basic level, that Lucifer could not grasp, they were simply different each of them.

Humans possessed a range of talents and abilities that are so varied and as unique as the stars! Yet they are so strongly unaware of the obvious nature of their gifts! These ungrateful creatures possess the rarest and most unique of all gifts . . . a soul. A gift with unlimited potential and mind staggering possibilities in its vastness and what do they do with it . . . they limit their own possibilities!

As if the vastness of the gift is too much to accept as it is, so they need to limit and define it according to their will! Rather than accept it as it is and let it define them! The nature of man is very much like the growth of a child. That child carries the generic material of the parent and the freedom to do with his talents and abilities that which he chooses. At different stages of his development, he is actually a different person.

The parent loves, teaches and punishes him but in the end, the fate of each child is the reflection of and in his will. Then Lucifer thought of how he was limited to either hell or earth and again he thought, man like his father can travel in many dimensions, but man has chosen to limit himself to three.

Like a child choosing to play only in the sand box rather than explore the whole park all around them. The sand box has rules, four walls, consistency and the feel of the sand. The box provides protection or so the child tells himself. And all of this simply faith is because man can see where the sandbox begins and ends.

The parks however, exist even if the child ignores that fact. It does not mean that the child is free from the influences of the park; no, it simply means that the child is unaware of those influences and does not see or understand where those influences are guiding him, usually until it is too late. All because he thinks he is safe in his sandbox or safe in the world he has created for him self, when nothing could be further from the truth.

Lucifer's realm had become like the hidden influences in the park and he knew that he and his demons worked better when they did not have to fight the obstacles of belief or when no one believed that they were there! Lucifer though back to many, many eons ago since the day of the great fall, the day when one third of the creator's angels lost their grace, the day when hell was created.

A war began, a war between the inhabitance of hell and man. In its simplest rational the reason for the war and for the fall was that piece of god, which god gave to his child (man) but not to his angels (who thought of them selves as the creator's children too). After the fall, with out god's presence and the light of god's love the "third" found that they were slowly devolving.

Lucifer watched in horror as many of the third, not only became the opposite of what they once were, in that they were turning from angels to demons but once the transformation was complete, the demons became insane and attacked any one or every one. Chaos was starting to descend but it was Lucifer, who was looking for something else, when he stumbled upon or found the solution to the problem that hell currently faced.

Lucifer saw the outcome of his anger against man. Lucifer knew that age and strength played a role in how fast the angels changed since it was the newly created angels who disintegrate first and fastest. He could feel the process starting to change him but because he was among the oldest, he knew he had more time than most others. Lucifer did not see any way to alter his fate, so he said before my end, I will have a piece of god again even if I have to figure out a way to get it from a human!

So while the others were being consumed with fear and death Lucifer decided to focus the greatest part of his remaining energy on absorbing a soul. Lucifer studied his objective from all views and found that the soul was naturally protected, in that he could not simply reach in and take it. Lucifer knew this because he tried that initially! Pain shot through him at the touch of the soul and the firmer he gripped it the more intense the pain. The pain was so intense that he thought he was burning up from the inside out, Lucifer had to let go! This first attempt simply made Lucifer all the more committed to absorbing and owning a soul.

Lucifer was consumed with the thought of how to get a soul away from a human. Lucifer could see no way on his own, then out of desperation Lucifer thought, "I wonder if the man thing knows how to release the soul?" Lucifer knew he had only one option left and that one was a long shot! But before he died (or went mad as the case may be), he intended to do all he could to possess a soul.

So he did the one thing that he truly did not want to do, he would have to actually talk to and establish a relationship with the man thing and learn what the human knew about the possession of a soul and how to get him to release it. Once he had chosen a direction he pursued it with all of his energy. Especially since he had exalted all of his other options and no other option was open to him.

Lucifer started looking at what type of human to choose for this venture. Lucifer ruled out intelligent, strong and confident humans. He did not want to fight through the type of natural defense system or a defense system that such traits provided. Lucifer started developing a check list of traits that would suit his needs:

a. The human had to be stupid but with in the normal intelligence range.

b. The human needed to be full of ego, arrogance and pride which supported a belief system that felt he deserved better than his current circumstances. Whether the human was right or wrong in his belief did not matter, it was only important that he believed he deserved better.

c. Personal blindness, the stronger the better. Lucifer needed a human who lied to himself about his true character. This type of belief system would give Lucifer something to work with. Humans for the most part acted from their belief so, Lucifer was looking for one who lied to him self on a consistent bases and if he truly believed his own lies, it would be that much easier for him to believe Lucifer's.

d. Lucifer needed a small minded, weak, mean-spirited and cruel individual. Someone whose world of thought included only what they chose to believed. Someone easily lead but who will easily believe that he is the opposite of his true nature and that a large part of his problems is that others simply do not understand or appreciate him.

e. Lucifer also needed someone who had no friends, the last thing that Lucifer wanted was for some good friend to give him advice he trusted and knock Lucifer out of the running at the last minute!

Armed with the list of qualities he needed in a human, Lucifer started looking for just the right human. Lucifer found the spoiled son of a rich merchant who thought himself so much more superior to those around him. He was weak and lazy yet he blamed his faults on others. But the real selling point was that he had a natural cruel twist to his personality. He hurt those under him or those he considered weaker and he hated those which were his equal or above him in rank, especially those who saw him for what he truly was.

This human thought that others looked down on him, when in fact they simply saw him as he was and they wanted nothing to do with his negativity and cruelty. Lucifer smiled and said I've found my man. Malki, had no friends; he believed that the reason for this situation was that they were all jealous of him. Servants avoided him when ever possible because often he would mistreat them simply because he was board. His mother preferred to think of him as misunderstood and his father was disgusted with his lack of character and embarrassed by his cruel nature. His father simply stayed away from him as much as possible.

Lucifer watched and observed Malki as he figured out the best approach for interacting with him, then it hit him, Malki needed a friend! One almost his equal but not quite, Malki needed to feel superior in any relationship or friendship, which is why he had none. Lucifer introduced himself to Malki as the son of a merchant but one who was thought of in less regard than Malki's father since his family had just arrived in the province.

This approach set Lucifer up as an equal but not quite. Since he and his family were new to the province, this explained why he did not know Malki's reputation and why he himself had no friends.

Over the upcoming weeks Lucifer mirrored Malki's life back to him but always in a subservient position.

Malki had just met his first and only friend, and because he had never had one before, he did not look too closely at his new friend's character, actions or motives. Slowly little by little Lucifer started feeding Malki negativity. Increasing his ego and helping Malki to believe that he deserved even more than he had thought before. Over the weeks Lucifer feed his ego, arrogance and pride until it ran so deeply that even Lucifer often laughed at the little human's belief that he was god.

Lucifer made an intense and interesting discovery during this time. The more of his negativity he fed Malki, the sicker Malki became; the calmer and clearer Lucifer became. Lucifer examined this concept and found to his surprise that the more Malki **agreed** with him the more Lucifer gained access to Malki's soul. No, he still could not touch it but he could draw strength from it. Strength in equal but opposite amount to the negativity Lucifer fed him. The strength he drew was like medicine for his demonic illness, it did not eliminate the fact that he was turning into a demon but it slowed down the process; cleared his thinking and diminished most of the symptoms.

Lucifer scanned Malki physical and mental state, Lucifer had to limit the amount of negativity he fed him and the amount of strength he took from him, if not soon Malki would be too crazy to make an informed choice when Lucifer needed him too. Lucifer needed a binding contract (he had no intention of loosing his soul, because now he thought of Malki's soul as his own). No, he did not want his human to be too insane to know what he was agreeing to. Lucifer watched as Malki's soul tried to re-direct its energy toward helping Malki heal, Lucifer induced a slight fever in him then fed him the belief that he was too sick to be up and around.

Lucifer implanted the belief that Malki needed to go home and rest that he needed to take care of himself. As a good friend Lucifer took him home to give him time to recover somewhat, while Lucifer rethought his next move. Lucifer scanned himself, he saw that the illness (which is how he thought of his descent in to demon-hood) literally had been halted by the energy he drew from Malki. Lucifer needed that soul! If the energy that the soul produced was this powerful, then the actual possession of the soul could cure him. Lucifer examined the process by which he was able to absorb Malki's energy. Every time Malki agreed with some negativity that Lucifer was trying to convince him of, a flood of energy washed over Lucifer. Lucifer examined this process each time he had had access to the energy from Malik's soul. Malki had to **agree**! The moment, no the second he agreed to accept the negativity that Lucifer was trying to convince him of, a flood of energy washed over Lucifer. This was how Lucifer had gained access to the energy from Malki's soul! This is it! Lucifer thought with excitement . . . that which could not be taken, can be given away!

Lucifer thought about it further, it was the power of choice; no one could take that away from man. The soul, that which the creator had given to him belonged to man, man could do with it as he wills. Man could be talked into giving away his soul! After the emotional high, Lucifer felt a great low, after all how would you or could you talk anyone into giving away something which is a gift from the creator.

At that moment Lucifer felt domed to failure. Then a thought hit him, "does man even know he has a soul much less believe that the soul was a gift from the creator? . . . Does man know the value of a soul?" Lucifer considered this concept and thought that if man does not understand the value of the gift he is born with, then getting the soul away from him may not be as hard as Lucifer originally thought.

Days later (especially with out Lucifer feeding him negativity, which in Malki equaled illness) Malki was feeling much better. To celebrate, Lucifer offered to take him out and buy lunch and drinks as his treat. Lucifer started asking Malki questions, designed to learn what he knew about his soul. Lucifer was completely astonished to learn that Malki's knowledge was so limited it was the equal of nothing at all, Lucifer started to laugh he could not believe his luck! This being held the rarest of the rare . . . . a piece of the creator inside of him as part of his birth right, no less. Yet, like the oyster who never considered the pearl anything more than an irritant, these humans had no appreciation of the importance of this gift.

This was the deal sealer for Lucifer, that which you do not appreciate is that which you do not deserve to have (it is also that which you will bargain with because it has no value to you). Lucifer now focused his observations on exactly what it was that Malki did value or wanted. He wanted money, lots of money; because he thought money was power. He wanted respect or so he thought, again he felt that money could provide this for him. Lucifer laughed and thought what he really wants is to be feared. The fear of others would feed his ego and sense of importance and make him believe that he was powerful. It hit Lucifer like a bolt of lightening, all he needed to do was barter!

Give to the human the useless things that he valued so highly for the (priceless) thing that he did not value at all, his soul. Several days later the opportunity presented its self. Lucifer met Malki at the local drinking establishment, Malki was angry it seemed that his father had refused to increase his allowance simply because Malki refused to waste his time learning to run the family business.

Lucifer stepped in and stated that it would be his honor to buy drinks and lunch. Then over lunch Lucifer said, it is a shame that you father does not appreciate that the day in day out running of a business is for underlings and not for someone as important and gifted as his son. You my friend have rare talents which need to be nurtured and respected, you deserve only the best! Malki agreed and Lucifer felt the flood of soul energy wash over him. To bate the trap and to amuse himself further, Lucifer said let me tell you a story my friend to get your mind off of your problems.

The story was about a man who sold his soul for wealth, position and respect. At the end of the story the man said that it was the best deal he had ever made! Lucifer waited for the story to sink in and then he actually started a conversation about something else when Malki interrupted Lucifer and said that, "the man in the story was in deed extremely lucky! If I could find some one to make such an exchange with me I would take it in a heart beat." Lucifer smiled, the trap was set all that remained was time and opportunity.

Two weeks later, Malki had had an even stronger argument with his father. Malki went to talk to his father again about increasing his allowance. Malki got so angry because his father was making a mandatory demand, his father stated that if Malki did not learn the business, not only would he not get an increase in his allowance but his allowance would be cut! Malki in what he believed was righteous indignation, hit his father. His father ranged for the servants and had Malki removed from the house! His father told him not to come back until he was ready to apologize for his actions and assume his responsibilities.

Malki went to the address that Lucifer had given him seeking his friends help, advice, sympathy and support. The address that Lucifer gave Malki had a device like a buzzer that let him know when someone was knocking or trying to gain entry into his temporary address. Temporary, because Lucifer could initially only maintain human form for a limited amount of time, but he had noticed that that too had increased since he had been sipping energy from Malki.

Lucifer appeared at the door after the third knock, it took a minute to materialize a minimum staff. Lucifer answered the door and said that he was sorry for the delay but today his father had granted the staff the right to attend the local festival and service was somewhat slow.

Lucifer offered Malik wine, dinner and a place to sleep as well as a sympatric ear. Lucifer told him he had, as his friend, looked into the situation that they had discussed the other day and found out about the man who sold his soul for the wealth and the respect he deserved. It seemed it was as simple as signing a contract that upon your death you release your soul as payment for the wealth and privilege you would receive while living.

Chapter Thirty

Lucifer had gotten a copy of the contract for his friend, Malki who was currently drunk said, "give it here I'll sign it now!" Lucifer replied, as you friend I think you should make the decision with a clear head so I'm going to let you sleep the wine off and tomorrow after breakfast we will discuss the matter further and if this is still what you want, so be it!" Not only did Lucifer want Malki to have a clear head when he signed the contract, Lucifer knew he would be even more desperate in the cold light of day, knowing he had no other choice than to beg his father's forgiveness and crawl back home, that is if his father would let him.

Later, if the ownership of the soul was challenged, Lucifer could say he gave Malki every opportunity to make a different choice even to pointing out that, willing though Malki was, Lucifer did not let him sign the contract while drunk! Malki woke the next afternoon with a hangover but otherwise no worse. Lucifer provided lunch and something to ease the effects of too much wine and then Lucifer talked of other things while he waited for Malki to bring up the topic of the contract. Then Half way through lunch, Malki asked, did you say something about a contract last night? Lucifer seemed reluctant to discuss the issue, knowing it would increase Malki's interest.

Finally, Lucifer got up to go get the contract (he had the contract on him but going somewhere else to obtain it fed the concept that Lucifer was not sure about this action his friend was thinking about taking) Lucifer slowly came back into the room and sat at the table. He put the contract in Malki's hand, they began to discuss the pro's and con's of the contract and this they did for most of the day until finally, Malki felt he had the contract he deserved.

They had spent the day together; Lucifer had no intentions of letting Malki out of his sight until they had finished this business. It was after dinner when Malki stated that a contract, such as the one they had discussed, he would sign. Lucifer called a scribe forward who produced a contract which had everything in it they had discussed. Lucifer said to Malki, as your friend I really think that you should take this time, while the scribe is writing out the contract, to really think about what you are about to do. In fact as your friend, my advice is that you do not sign this contract. However, I know I will envy you if you do.

With that Lucifer left the room and went out into the garden, stating he needed some air to clear his mind. Shortly after Lucifer left to go into the garden, a scribe returned with both the contract and a mixture that Malki though was ink. While Maliki was sleeping his blood was drawn and mixed with the ink like substance to insure that the contract would be binding. Lucifer felt Malki's signature sing to him as the ink mixed with Malki's blood hit the parchment. Lucifer knew he could not claim ownership of his soul until Malki was dead or dieing. However, the span of a human life time was so brief, that the wait time for Lucifer seemed like a few weeks instead of years, the time he would have to wait hardly mattered.

The next day Malki's father died and all of his considerable wealth passed in equal shares to be divided between him and his mother. Malki went through his portion of his father's wealth with in a few short years. Then as if part of the plan; just as his money ran out, his mother died from a heart attack; she was dead before she hit the floor. His mother was a thrifty individual and she had not spent but a small amount of the funds left to her by her husband. Therefore she left most of her part of her husband's fortune to Malki. Three years after his mother's death, Malki found that he was dieing too!

Malki had the wasting sickness for which there was no known cure. It was an illness that seemed to eat you alive, from the inside out (Cancer). On Malki death bed Lucifer appeared, contract in hand to collect his soul. It was not until the moments, leading to Malki death, that the truth of his actions all became clear and he seemed to understand the intrinsic value of the soul he gave up and the nature of the individual who had talked him out of it. Malki took his last breath knowing he had condemned his soul to hell!

In the second after Malki's death Lucifer concluded his bargain. The soul fluttered in his hand. Lucifer could hardly contain himself. Before he knew it he had consumed the soul. Lucifer closed his eyes as the soul fought the total darkness with in Lucifer.

The feel and taste of the soul was like nothing Lucifer had ever experienced, for a moment it was as if he had touched the light of heaven again. His mind cleared and peace like that he took for granted when he lived as an angel in heaven descended. Lucifer felt more like himself than he had in a very long time. A few minutes later, Lucifer noticed that the enjoyment was fading. Lucifer did a personal scan and saw that the soul was dieing or leaving. It seemed that the light of the soul is interracially connected to the life of the human and the soul's intrinsic nature returns to the creator and all that is left is the soul matter, or the matter in which the soul is encased in, while inside a living human being. Those few seconds of paradise, was all he was to get for all his hard work. Lucifer screamed it was not fair; he had gotten the soul legitimately, now it seemed he was not going to be allowed to keep it!

Once Lucifer calmed down, he did a personal scan, the high was gone but the genetic material of the soul or the soul matter, was still a powerful counter to the demonic transformation that hell was causing on his DNA structure. It seemed that the human soul had given him minutes of an indescribable high, while the genetic material or soul matter slowed the demonic transformation considerably and increased his strength. There was one finally unexpected surprise, those few minutes before the soul left, was the most powerful drug in the universe and Lucifer knew that he had to have more, much, much more.

"Hell is empty and all the devils are here"
Wm. Shakespeare in the Tempest

Lucifer was about to turn hell into a soul re-claiming center. Lucifer knew that the addictive nature of the first five minutes of the soul (while it still contained the intrinsic god like qualities) could never be known. Both for his own safety (any weakness must be hid at all cost!) and in order to feed his addiction and need.

Lucifer scheduled a meeting with all of the occupants of hell. At this meeting he asked, "What cost would you pay to gain your freedom from this slow and maddening death of degeneration? The crowd shouted, "all you ask . . . Lucifer, Lucifer, Lucifer!

Lucifer held up his hand to quiet the crowd and then he spoke. "I have been spending my time trying to find a cure for this illness we are all afflicted with. I told no one of my activities because I did not want to raise any hopes until I was sure I had succeeded. From this day forward I require all of the occupants of hell to swear an allegiance to me. Acknowledging that I am the one and only ruler of this domain and none will challenge my authority on any level; all must agree to my terms.

Any one who breaks this rule (and any others that I create) also agrees that their life is forfeit and belongs to me! Once each of you give me your allegiance and loyalty . . . I will reward you with the knowledge you need to both survive and stop this de-acceleration of your cells. All of those who believe that this valuable knowledge is worth the price I have outlined, come forward and give me your loyalty, allegiance and respect and I will give you your life!"

The room was so quiet you could hear a pin drop, Lucifer was apprehensive yet he looked completely serene as if he was doing them the favor not the other way around. This coo took nerves of steal as Lucifer risked much to gain everything and the ownership of his world.

Soon a cheer when up from the crowd and they chanted . . . Lucifer, Lucifer, Lucifer. Lucifer sat on a thrown like chair as each demon gave their allegiance, loyalty and life to him. Lucifer felt unbelievably content, ruler of all he surveyed and then he felt a thought. "It was truly better to rule in hell than to serve in heaven!"

Lucifer now began to explain the solution to their situation and the other additional cost. Lucifer stated the first five minutes of the soul's death always belonged to me. The first reason for this statement was to insure that no one knew the power he absorbed during this process. The next reason was to keep the knowledge about his addiction from ever being known.

To insure that this knowledge was never found out Lucifer stated, "the first five minutes of the soul's death has a deadly virus for our kind, one that has no cure and will not only infect the demon who is exposed to it but others who come in contact with that demon. I am the only demon who knows how to counter act this virus. This is why any transgression of this law had only one punishment and that is a swift and painful death."

Lucifer's third reason (that the first five minutes of the soul was forbidden) was because he knew that any older demon that became addicted to the taste of a newly dammed soul would be a demon that would equal him in power and strength, then strive to challenge him for ruler ship of hell.

Lucifer believed in dealing with problems before they happened if possible. The second payment that Lucifer requested was five (5) percent of every captured soul's genetic material. Lucifer explained the benefits of the soul's genetic material and since none knew of the addictive nature of the first five minutes this seemed like little to ask. Since Lucifer was allowing them to keep 90% of what they caught it seemed as if they gained more than they lost, so none had a complaint or problem with the arrangement, which was exactly what Lucifer's intented.

Lucifer had pulled it off! His addiction would have an unlimited supply. The first five minutes of every dammed soul was his! Plus five percent of the genetic material or ten percent of each dammed soul, this was more than enough to keep Lucifer from any thing but an extremely slow transformation; More than enough to consistently increase his strength beyond all others and the transformation that would take place now would hardly be noticeable and look like nothing at all.

However, what seemed generous on the surface was greed underneath! Lucifer would make up in volume what he lost per individual soul and since none felt that he had dealt with them in any other way than fair, none would seek to question his generous offer for fear that he might go up on the price.

None had notice that the concept of "fair" coming from the ruler of hell, in and of its self was a suspicious concept. Now Lucifer would have an unlimited amount of soul genetic material which would also increase his strength over time making it almost impossible for him to be beaten and disposed of as the ruler of Hell.

This was what Lucifer was concerned about, had anyone discovered the secret of his power? If anyone was looking for that secret and if so were they looking in the right direction? This was why Lucifer was so generous with Tris because she answered these questions that he dared not ask. In a round about way Tris informed Lucifer that Uself and no other had any truthful knowledge about the real source of his power or any idea of where to look for his energy source.

This was the information that Tris brought to Lucifer that was of such great value, this and the fact that she had no knowledge of what the true value of what her information was worth to him. Tris was a smart demon, too smart to be left to her own devices. If she did find out something of real value to him, he wanted to insure that he was the first (and last) one to know. This is why he sent her the blood wine which was blended to his strength level but at the same time it would be addictive for her at her level of strength. Once she was addicted to the wine, he was the only means by which she could get it and that meant the instead of paying dearly for any knowledge that she acquired, all it would cost him was a bottle of wine which he had in abundance.

Rule had received a message telling him to be at Vane's house tonight at 8:00. Rule knew that something was going to happen soon but he hoped he was wrong. An hour later he hears a mental knock on the door and when Rule opened the door Tris was there. Rule was surprised first because he really did not think she could help and second because he did not think she would help but her presence at his door had to be a sign of good news!

Tris walked in and the first thing she said was let's take a walk I need some air. Being in the information business, Tris knew that demons spied on each other and Tris knew that the Senior Elder demon would have a listening devise planted in Vane home, but the Senior Elder may have considered Rule not worth the effort but to be on the safe side she again decided to speak with him some where other than his home.

Tris again invited him to her home for a glass of blood wine. Once in her home Tris felt better because she had her home swept for bugs once a week and she had an anti-bug device installed which monitored frequencies In her home and any frequency not a part of her approved system would automatically give off a silent alarm tuned to a frequency especially adjusted for Tris' hearing only.

Tris usually saved this treat, her blood wine, for herself alone. But after today she could afford to be generous. After all she had just made a fortune off of the information she got from him. Tris invited Rule into her living room and she poured two glasses of the wine. At first, neither of them spoke as they appreciated the unique feel and texture of the wine as well as the human agony it was laced with.

Then Rule spoke, I guess this means you have good news for me, Tris smiled and said, "You could say that." I have secured an order of protection. Rule was so surprised that he would have dropped his glass if he had not just sat it down minutes before. Tris handed him the document, she was the only one who could add anyone's name to it so she had no problem letting him see it and or hold it to confirm that it was authentic.

Rule was again impressed with Tris, she had not only had an audience with Lucifer but achieved her objective. Then Rule read the information that Tris had written on the form. The order of protection will extend to the demon Rule under these conditions: that he tells no one that the demon named Domintrist had any knowledge of or involvement in or with this situation. The second condition is that, if the demon Rule breaks this binding oath; the order of protection is immediately rescinded.

Rule's first response was profound relief. If she added his name to the order, not even a Senior Elder demon could harm him. It crossed rules mind that he should ask why it was so important to her to be unknown in this situation or what she had gotten out of this deal but frankly Rule did not care. He had been living with the threat of a death sentence for days a threat that was now up graded to fear with Vane's request to be at his home to night at eight. And now all it took to end his agony was for Tris to put his name on the order of protection.

Tris had been watching Rule's face as he read the order she could almost pin point the moment he was ready to agree to any terms she dictated, in order to have her put his name on the contract. Rule looked up and said, I agree to your terms. Tris said, we will celebrate our arrangement with another glass of wine. Shortly after that Rule left and Tris smiled and thought, they both got what they wanted out of this deal. However, yet again Rule did not think! Rule did not even ask her what she had gotten out of her meeting with Lucifer or if there was anything that he could have also received.

Since Tris wanted Rules name on the contract she would have given him as much as half of one of the souls she received from Lucifer but since his relief overwhelmed his ability to think; he did not ask what she received from Lucifer and she did not offer any information. For now both he and Tris were satisfied but Tris knew that Rule would think about this situation later. However, by then he would have lost his leverage for any additional payment because she already had the signed contract! Tris laughed and thought, "Rule truly is a fool and it is a wonder he has stayed alive this long!"

Justin and Katelyn would be in the forefront of the battle. Bree would monitor and feed Katelyn energy if and when needed, since they were compatible power sources. They both had back up energy sources in that a tea had been made from their plant and they each drank a cup each day. This allowed both Bree and Katelyn to see, enhance and unfold their powers as an elemental. They had both become far more powerful than even their mates knew.

At first it seemed that the plant was increasing their power exponentially but after the first two weeks this growth spurt slowed down. In reality the plant was not so much increasing their power as bringing them to their full strength, as an elemental. Now, that the power level had been reached the plant simply helped to maintained them. The second thing that the plant had accomplished was finding dormant power levels and levels of knowledge with in them and activating those levels which enhanced and increased their understanding about what it meant to be an elemental.

Just as Bree had learned to blend her powers with Ariel, it was even easier to do so with Katelyn. So now they had the power of two elementals at full strength and then some. Elementals that could at a moments notice combine their energy; the power in this situation was off the charts!

Jason could not be fed energy during the battle because it would be noticed by Uself and provide a clear indication that something was not right and it was essential that Uself was given no indication that he was not in complete control. Gabriel and Raphael had discussed and implemented a plan. They had each; every day enhanced Jason's energy levels. Raphael had built layer upon layer of energy into Jason's mind and Gabriel had did the same with his shields. Raphael and Gabriel had noticed one unique energy signal that only they would see buried deep in Jason's soul which was a gift from the creator.

The energy signal was time encoded, which meant it could only be opened at a time of great need. Finding this encoded energy signal informed Gabriel and Raphael more than anything else, of the seriousness of the upcoming battle and they re-doubled their efforts, paying attention to the smallest details, trying to do all in their power to insure that Jason would have every advantage they could give him.

Gabriel wanted to be the energy back up for his son, but he would be some where being held prisoner (because he would be pretending to be Bree) and no doubt once imprisoned his energy signal would be monitored and or blocked. Gabriel had to put the needs of his son first, Raphael spoke before Gabriel could ask and said, "after all you and Bree have done to help us keep Jason safe, it would be my honor to be your son's reinforcement in this battle; I hope you know that all that is in my power to do, will be done!"

They each knew they were fighting not only a battle to yet again contain evil but fighting for the health and safety of those they loved. They knew for the first time that this is what humans feel in the struggle of good and evil; they had a deeper appreciation and respect for the race that faced this battle every day on so many levels. Seeing this situation from the inside out, with those they loved on the line was so completely different from seeing it from the detached view of a none personal involvement which angels usually worked from.

Justin had been helping Katelyn hone her instinct as an elemental they had also developed some internal signals which would convey with a word needed information such as, "I need help or I'm fine don't worry."

They had worked out a series of ways to communicate assuming obvious methods of communication were blocked. They developed one special, intimate method of communication that no one but the two of them would know or recognize. They had made love, and Katelyn was sleeping in his arms. Justin was going over every detail of the plan looking for any loose ends. Katelyn had become his world; Justin intended to use every ounce of talent, skill, training and ability with in his power to keep her safe. Failure was not an option they would win or loose together because each was incomplete with out the other.

CHAPTER THIRTY-ONE

Jason had been told to be present tomorrow at Vane's home around 8:00 in the evening. Uself had said he had a few last minute details that he needed to put in place before the meeting. Jason figured that Uself intended to begin the battle tomorrow as soon as he kidnapped what he believed to be Justin's mother. This time tomorrow he would have her and be ready to attack. The meeting Uself referred to would in fact be his notice that the battle had begun and Uself would begin to issue instructions on what he wanted Jason to do.

Timing, it was all balance and timing; this trait was a throw back to Uself's days as an angel, this appreciation for balance and timing!

Uself had a score to settle with Gabriel. Gabriel had made his early life in hell extremely painful. It had taken many, many centuries before Uself could even began to work his way back into Lucifer's sight and many more for a chance at beginning to make up for his failure! This punishment was exceptionally bitter because Uself had once been part of Lucifer's inner circle.

Before the fall each member of Lucifer's inner circle had to earn that honor by convincing another angel over to Lucifer's point of view. Gabriel had been Uself's assignment. Gabriel had a lot of hidden resentment against man (that is why he was targeted) resentment that Uself fed at every opportunity.

At the last minute when Uself was all but sure that Gabriel was converted, Gabriel let go of enough of his resentment of man which allowed him to follow his faith and the creator. This meant Uself could not present

Gabriel's talents and abilities as a gift for his new master thus insuring his place in Lucifer's inner circle.

Uself never forgot or forgave Gabriel for changing his mind at the last minute (Gabriel had never chosen to join Uself but Uself had convinced him self that all was as he wanted it to be). During the first centuries of the torture Lucifer had put him through, Uself's pain turned to hatred. The thought of the pain that Justin death would cause Gabriel was now an emotional high for Uself, as he thought that revenge is sweet!

Uself had learned centuries ago that although Gabriel still seemed indifferent to his human consort, he was extremely fond of his son who was often at his side. Based on what he had seen in Jason's mind, Uself knew it to be true. Justin's movements were so much like Gabriel it was almost painful to watch.

As Uself watched Justin in battle, Uself had a flash back of him and Gabriel fighting side by side. Justin's movements expression and energy signatures was so much like Gabriel it was as if time had stopped and he was transported back to a time when he and Gabriel had been friends, brother's in arms.

At that moment, Uself hated Gabriel more than ever before. Uself went over his plans; this was another reason why he could not fail! To fail twice, once with the father and then with the son was unthinkable! He would not survive that failure! Uself had barely survived the lost of Gabriel, when hell was new and current rules and procedures were not yet in place. Now, by today's standards Uself would end up as Lucifer's dinner guest, not in a seat but on the table!

Katelyn knew that Justin intended to give up his life if necessary to save hers. He was her life, so this option made no sense to her. When they trained together Katelyn worked hard, pushing herself to the limits of her ability. She would do all in her power to keep him safe and she could not or would not be a liability for him on any level.

Katelyn took nothing for granted she knew he would fight until his last breath for her and Katelyn had determined to hold her own if for no other reason than to insure that he would not have to! They were in this together, however this situation ended that would not change. So she trained hard, not as if her life depended on it but as if his depended on her, trying to show him in actions what she could not find the words to say. In a strange and very hard to describe way, this though eliminated her fear and gave her a clear level of focused peace.

Gabriel was taking no chances, right after their last meeting with Ariel and Raphael, Gabriel moved Bree into his apartment. As an added precaution it was decided that Ariel would also stay with Bree in Gabriel's apartment. After all, at any given point in the battle, Uself might recognize Jason as Raphael's son and this might call for an alteration in his plans.

Bree had her plant and both Bree and Ariel were connected to the others so they would not be blind or inactive in this battle. Bree, Katelyn and Ariel had connected on several different levels. Each knew they had an important part in the upcoming battle and much depended on them all in different ways.

The women had found that they could connect their powers but the energy still responded differently as if flowed through each. Katelyn or Bree could allow Ariel to tap into the powers of an elemental, which would allow her to take that energy and shape barriers around her energy signal so that she could actually connect with and bend another being to her will.

Katelyn and Bree could tap into Areil's power and flow like air through another being and see their thought and intents. They learned some interesting things along the way, the learned that the more they were able to blend their strengths and talents the stronger they became individually.

Then when Jason tried to assess Uself by entering his mind, the ladies had learned a great deal from that experience and they had developed what they believed to be an effective counter that would allow them to enter any demon's mind with out harm.

The Birth Of Hell From The Creator's Point Of View

Before the fall of "the third" the creator had looked into the very essences of each of his angels. He knew which angels were most willing to believe Lucifer's lies and half truths and which angels would continue to follow there faith and maintain there grace. Built into the conception of hell, was a process that over time and after serious payments, even "the third" could and would be given an opportunity to become what they once were, what they were meant to be. Lucifer was the only exception to this rule. Lucifer had used the power of choice to re-create himself in his own image, leaving the creator completely out of his choices.

The soul is like water because water is never destroyed. It passes through many forms of life, lingering for a moment then passing own. The oceans turn water into mist and the mist is evaporated and absorbed by the clouds. The clouds get full and the water is sent back to the earth in the form of rain. Rain is absorbed by the earth and then by the food we plant in the earth. When we eat the food the water is absorbed by humans. Once we absorb enough water our bodies eliminates it as urine. This water then flows back into purification plants or back into the ocean. The ocean produces mist and the process starts all over again. It was this concept that inspired the purpose of hell.

The soul is a spark of the creator and like the creator it was meant to live forever. After the death of a human, the soul was intended to return to the creator to be purified, reshaped and strengthen from the knowledge and experience it gained while in human form. One soul will live many life times, gathering knowledge, wisdom and abilities until it had grown enough to evolve and take its place with in his father's presence.

When Lucifer figured out how to divert this process for his own survival, the dammed souls consumed by darkness do not die or at least not in every sense. The soul is enslaved and tortured with the knowledge that its very existence is food for negativity. The soul must watch, participate and sustain a living breathing cancer. A cancer which occurred when the third were banished from the love and nurturing light of the creator. It was this light which purified and sustained them.

The genetic material of the human soul provided a spark of divine light, a candle in the dark if you will, which was the closest a demon will ever get to the light of the creator's love again, in his current demonic form. The human soul provided enough light to keep the darkness from consuming the demon.

This was how the genetic material of the soul slowed the demon process of devolution, this process which would lead to the point of insanity or the point of no return which was death for the demons. The greater the number of dammed souls a demon owned the stronger and more dangerous the demon became. These dammed souls feel every hurt and pain that their energy, used by the demon, is responsible for causing others.

The soul's energy is drained away over a period of time until a metamorphosis occurs. The soul, with no infusion of positive energy over a long period of time, undergoes a transformation to an inanimate object and as such for a while it goes dormant. It is at this point that most demons should eliminate the soul.

The soul can no longer provide an energy signal fit for demon consumption. If the demon does not get rid of the soul while it is in the dormant stage the soul can become potentially dangerous to the demon, because once the soul leaves the dormant stage it reactivates and starts to feed off of the demon!

The soul will then accelerate the demon's descent into madness and self consumption, which will cause the demon to die and thus the soul, will free its self at the demon's expense. This is why the demon must strive at all times to both monitor all souls with in his possession; get rid of any soul which has reached the dormant state. The demon must strive to keep as large a number of dammed souls as possible to insure that his energy source does not diminish.

Unknown to the demons, once the soul is removed and discarded (or frees its self) then the soul is reclaimed by the creator. The soul is purified, reshaped by the knowledge and experience of living as a dammed soul. All of the knowledge, wisdom and insight that the soul has gained through being dammed is redirected into a positive usage.

A soul that has been dammed and reclaimed has gained the knowledge of several lifetimes and it is these souls that the old folks refer to as being "born wise." The pain and regret that the soul experienced as a dammed soul forms the instinct of that soul in a new life, an instinct that is so strong it not only gives out warnings but it will nag and worry the individual incessantly when it sees that person starting down a path that might lead to becoming a dammed soul again!

These souls now have a built in understanding that helps them avoid the traps and pit falls that might ensnare other souls.

Soul recruitment was now the business of hell. This was every demon's focus because each soul had a different shelf life. Some souls went dormant with in a mere fifty years! Some souls lasted centuries, at first there was simply no way to be sure how long a soul would last.

This was until some of the older demons started looking into this problem. By examining the traits that longer lasting souls had in common. This provoked a great debate in hell regarding soul recruitment skills because before now it was a haphazard process which lost as many souls as it caught.

It was now accepted knowledge that where ever possible you looked for certain traits in a soul. This did not mean that you turned down an easy catch but the focus was on quality and longevity. Demons started to tailor there seductions attempts to include such things as personality, temperament, ego and intelligence. Few demons were lucky enough to secure a Hitler (which was the equivalent of winning the lottery) but if the demon looked for distinctive core level traits in there prey, they would seldom go wrong.

For example, you matched skill to prey by looking for the type of human you have in the past had the greatest amount of success capturing and then you kept refining the process.

Some demons preferred men because they usually carried greater ego, limited personal insight and often believed themselves to be one thing when they truly and clearly were something else. Some demons preferred younger men because in addition to the above general male character traits, younger men tended to be inpatient, thoughtless, selfish and seldom thought about the consequences of their choices.

Some demons preferred middle age men because of the wealth of hidden insecurities they carried, fear of aging and a need to be looked up to. Some demons preferred older men because they were usually dealing with some type of sexual frustration, rigid mind set, or the belief that he is always right. As well as the limited ability to see anyone else's point of view especially those that disagreed with his.

This focus on the capture of souls provided a system of order in hell. Because of all of the above, demons rarely competed with each other over human souls the way humans competed over wealth, there was simply to many to choose from so why waist your energy in an unnecessary fight when you could be adding to your strength with the capture of a new soul!

Ninety percent of the demons in hell were the proud owners of at least a minimum of ten souls. The ten percent that did not own souls were demons which fell under several categories:

1. Those who failed to capture there prey.
2. Those who were already insane and on the verge of dieing.
3. Those who had committed a crime according to the rules of hell.

Therefore choosing, ensnaring and capturing souls took up most of your time and attention. This provided a means for demons to live in the same realm with limited negative contact and interaction or in fighting, because this took too much time away from getting food!

The power of choice had a second concept associated with it and that is punishment and payment. Every action, like every choice, has an equal and opposite reaction. It is not until you feel the effects of your actions (punishment) that true growth is possible. Hell was a soul reclaiming center but not entirely in the manor that Lucifer intended or envisioned.

Souls dammed through their choices and actions would spend time in hell being demons and capturing other souls or being food. At first this will seem as if this was all there is but over a period of time they will began to re-live every hurt, every negative action that they visited on others.

The dammed souls would feel these actions as if they were happening to them; then understanding, feeling and paying the interest payments which was a bi-product of there actions as well (payment). It takes a long while for the demons to get to this point in their evolution and even longer for them to walk through each choice and every interest payment of that choice and feel every pain or hurt that these choices caused. However, this time is necessary to insure that the soul truly learns and that this knowledge is cemented deep with in them.

Through this action is forged a core level, soul level aversion to the negative choices of the past. In the soul's next life time, from this core level knowledge an instinct if formed from the power of unmanageable pain that says to the heart "NO" not this path again!

No soul, like water, would ever truly be lost. All souls can be reclaimed but the path to redemption is as varied as the choices each individual makes to require redemption. This is why revenge was and is always a path of the uninformed or newer souls. They did not understand that to punish anyone you must become worse than the person you seek to punish. Because in doing so you are striving to dictate to the creator how you think this process should unfold.

All of this god allowed, for the sincere and intense love of his child.

Uself never lied to himself, he had learned a long time ago that although this practice may make you feel better about yourself, it always provided the foundation for blindness and that meant you over looked something that could get you killed. Uself had lived a long time as both an angel and demon he had seen others fall on this one concept alone, self delusion. Self delusion was a luxury he could not afford and survive. The truth was simple, Uself wanted to rule hell he wanted the power to kill Lucifer. Uself had nursed a grudge against Lucifer as well as Gabriel. Lucifer who had once been like a brother to Uself had turned his back on him for centuries treating him like a poor cousin who should be grateful for the leftovers on the table. Over the centuries Uself had re-gained his place at the table, now he wanted to own it but two things stood in his way: 1. Lucifer 2. The need of an incredible power source.

Uself felt the slow burn that he had felt for more years than he could count, that was the need to know the origin of Lucifer's power. Uself stated to re-think everything he knew, casting his memory back to the foundation of or creation of hell to see if he could pin point the moment when Lucifer's power began to grow. As Uself thought back he remembered he noticed that there were slow and subtle changes that he saw then before that he remembered that Lucifer had spent a great deal of time on the earth. Lucifer was obsessed with the idea of owning a soul and if Uself's memory was accurate (during that time they were all slowly devolving and there was a fussy haze around his memories of that time) Yet Uself felt certain her remembered Lucifer's obsession with owning a soul. Lucifer spent a great deal of time on the earth during that time; then a sort of quiet change came over him, Yes it was after this change that Lucifer introduced the concept of why demons needed human souls.

Did Lucifer learn more than he told any one else about regarding the nature of the soul? Or, was his power created before it was enhanced by the "every soul tribute?" It was widely thought that the source of Lucifer power was the tribute he demanded per each dammed human soul. But what, Uself thought, if the tribute had not created Lucifer's power? What if it had something to do with the first five minutes of the soul that Lucifer said contained a virus for there kind . . .. . .what if it was all a lie? What if the tribute simply enhanced Lucifer's power but his power started with the soul of an elemental?

Uself brought his thoughts back to the present, he had made his arrangements and he had sent a demon disguised as her son plus a contingent of demons as back up should something go wrong, to kidnap Gabriel's consort. He had to supply the energy for them to reach her dimensions because her home dimension was out side the energy range that most demons access or reach. Uself had sent a message to Jason, Vane and Rule for each of them to meet him at Vane's home at 8:00 that evening. Uself had a vague and uneasy feeling as if his every move was being watched but he dismissed the thought because he believed that he was just hyped up due to the upcoming battle. Uself looked at his watch it was after three o'clock they should have Gabriel consort and be on there way to the safe house.

Lucifer's spies were quick and accurate mainly because he would tolerate nothing less. With in a day they had confirmed Tris' story and added some interesting detail. They had watched and listened as Uself made arrangement to kidnap the consort of an angel and the mother of a light warrior. Uself believed the light warrior to be Gabriel's son and he was planning to kill both mother and son. Lucifer's spies had the gift of complete invisibility (bestowed on them by Lucifer so that they could be his eyes and ears in important situation) therefore they were there when Uself made arrangements for the kidnapping and set a time table for the remaining events to unfold. Lucifer was a master chess player and he saw at least three different ways that this situation could play out plus Lucifer had not discounted the creator's involvement in this situation which equals a fourth but unknown way that this situation could also play out. Lucifer wondered how many moves ahead in this game Uself had actually thought out?

Lucifer decided on a non-active role for the present. Often the best thing you could do to aid someone's downfall was "nothing" simply give them enough rope to hang themselves; besides Lucifer figured that someone held the loosing hand and if he had to guess who it was, his money was on Uself. Uself was going against a first angel, a light warrior, a elemental at full power(that was the blinding light that Tris had spoke about when Rule tried to enter the elementals mind) and Lucifer suspected, the creator would also be in this some how.

Yes, Lucifer's money was on the other side. Why not, if they win Uself becomes dinner and a clear example to all who would think to take his place. Why not sit back and let the other side do the work for him while he simply reaped the rewards! Lucifer laughed and thought, first I will drain the blood to make a superior blood wine then the meat will be roasted slowly and he could taste the crackle of the meat in his mouth as Uself's anger exploded in his flesh.

Chapter Thiry-Two

Bree (Gabriel) was getting bored he had been imitating Bree for three days now when he heard a mental knock, he said enter and Justin appeared. Gabriel was so glad to see him that he sent a burst of angelic communication to him but instead of a reply, Gabriel received a buzzing sound in return. Bree (Gabriel) had turned around to offer Justin some lunch so Justin did not see the expression on Bree (Gabriel) face. Immediately Gabriel knew that the individual who had entered Bree's home was not Justin (the buzzing sound was what returned after you sent a burst of angelic communication to any being unable to receive it).

Bree (Gabriel) smiled when she turned around and offered him some lemon aid. Justin (demon in disguise) smiled as he sipped the lemon aid and said, "Mom I have a surprise for you but I need you to come with me to see it with no questions asked." Bree (Gabriel) smiled sweetly and said, sit down and eat some lunch as Justin sat down Bree (Gabriel) said let me water my plants before we go it will only take a moment.

Bree (Gabriel) grabbed her watering can and headed to her special plant toward the end of the garden. Once there Bree (Gabriel) bent his head and sent the plant a message which stated, "please put a unseen block between us and the person at the table so that they can not pick up on the energy signal I am about to send out. With in moments the block was in place and Bree (Gabriel) sent the clear message to all . . .. "NOW."

Two hours later as Bree (Gabriel) sat in a cell somewhere in hell he thought it was a good thing that he recognized the demon that looked like Justin as soon he did, because as soon as they left the house a communication restraint was placed on Bree (Gabriel). Gabriel could have easily broken it but he suspected that with the communication restraint would also be a monitoring devise. Therefore the moment he broke through the communication restraint he would be telling Uself that not only did he have the wrong person but somehow they had figured out his plan.

So Bree (Gabriel) sat in the cell looking as afraid and worried as he could while he listened for any information or knowledge that might be helpful to them all.

Jason was getting ready to go to Vane's house, it was 7:30 and he was due there at 8:00. Jason was about to open his door when he felt a strange feather light wind which felt like someone blowing air on his skin then he saw the word "NOW" flash strongly across his mind.

Jason could not get the "NOW" signal that every one else got because they were afraid that some one might pick up the energy surge. It was agreed that Ariel and Bree would make him aware. Ariel tapped into the power of air through Bree and sent a flutter through his angelic shields which would end with the word "NOW" like a sign across his mind this way no one could hear the energy signal first because it was extremely low and second because it would be absorbed almost immediately by his angelic shields. Jason traced the energy signal to Bree and his mother and then smiled as he thought what a team these two powerful women made!

Raphael was completing a private audience with the creator where he asked for forgiveness for his lack of trust and faith which ended up with his child walking this path full of danger. Then he said, yet I have gained and learned so much from this error in judgment I am torn . . . I would not knowingly put my child in this danger but how can I regret the knowledge, friendship, growth, faith and love I have gained from this experience? I honestly do not know how to feel, the creator responded simply, "You should feel well loved."

Rapheal smiled as he left, he thought as usual the answer is so simple yet so profound! Raphael was about to visit Ariel and Bree when he heard the word "NOW."

Bree and Ariel had truly become friends, a bond born of desperation had yielded a clarity of purpose that required both women to reach beyond there comfort zone and open themselves up to another in ways that, just a few days before these events began, they could not have imagined doing. Yet here they were two women use to there solitude now comfortable in the presence of another. Neither Bree or Ariel had ever had a friend, each felt warmth and comfort in the thought of their new found friendship. They were in the middle of lunch trying to keep each other's worry at bay by finding general conversation to take there minds off of the situation they could not control when they both felt and heard the word "NOW."

Katelyn had finished both her physical and mental training for the day. She and Justin had worked out a routine and developed some interesting and unique training skills. Katelyn had not minded the wait for the attack; the longer things took to begin the more time she had to have to hone her new skills and techniques. Justin on the other hand wanted this over and Katelyn out of danger.

He was so proud of her, she trained harder and harder each day and each day he could see her moving from student to master. Her movement was fluid and on half of the occasions he noticed her instincts and actions moved as one with out her having to think her way through the movements. Justin had just slipped out of the shower and katelyn was on her way in when they each stood extremely still as they heard the word "**Now**" reverberate inside of them.

Vane was completely upset! Nothing, absolutely nothing had worked out the way he had envisioned it. The Senior Elder had no respect for or appreciation of the great gift Vane was laying at his feet; worse than that the Elder treated Vane more like an underling who was lucky that the master condescended to speak with him.

Vane thought, "It was my plan, my gift and with out my help you would know nothing of the elemental." Vane nursed his anger in private, no mater how anger he was he knew his situation could and just might get worse. Vane dare not express his anger to Jason after all it was clear that if asked Jason had no loyalty to Vane and Rule was less than useless. So Vane kept his anger barely inside taking care to allow it to boil over only in private.

Uself listened to Vane's thoughts and laughed at the little worms feelings of outrage. Then Uself thought good! His anger will add a crackle to the meat after roasting. Uself thought the angrier Vane became, the better the crunch!

All was in readiness and everything was going according to his plan. Uself thought that Jason and Rule should both be on there way to Vain's home because it was almost eight o'clock. Every one knew that to be late, was to be insulting. Uself did not expect to be insulted. Jason arrived five minutes early and Rule came in three minutes after Jason. Vane was sitting on the couch trying to look as if he had not lost total control in this situation or as if he knew what Uself had planned instead all he managed to look like was someone uncomfortable in his own skin.

Jason said nothing as he stood by the fire place watching the flames dance in the hearth. Rule slouched down in a chair with a uncertain look on his face yet when he thought that no one was watching him Rule seemed to exhibit a new found confidence like somehow who actually did know something that no one else knew.

Jason stored the information in his mind like a piece of a puzzle that you can not yet see the hold picture. The clock chimed eight o'clock and on the last chime Uself appeared. Jason felt he had been there all along watching to see what could or would be said in his absence. Uself cleared his throat and said, "Demons, shall we begin!"

Uself stated, "Jason you and I are going to access the prey together, only you will look like me and I will look like you. Uself's strategy was to use Jason as a decoy, for the following reasons: first to buy time to position him self to strike the light warrior hard and fast and with all of the power of a Senior Elder demon with the intent of getting in the most deadly attack as soon as possible (Uself wanted the battle to be over quickly).

Second, Uself knew that in battle if you took out the strongest warrior first, it would strike fear in the hearts of his weaker associates and they would be more apt to flee than to fight. This meant that the focus of the light warrior's attack would then be on Jason. Finally this would mean that Jason would be weaken from the attack and if all went well Uself could finish Jason off with out too much trouble (Uself had decided that it was in his best interest to have no witnesses to this affair and useful or not intelligent demons still made Uself uncomfortable).

Contrary to what Lucifer thought, Uself did not underestimate his opponent which is another reason why he did not want the battle to linger on and give them time to figure out his deception or smoke screen/mis-direction strategy in posing as Jason. If they did however figure this out the next move or plan "B" was to materialize Justin's mother; lie to the warrior to get him to give up and then kill both the warrior and his mother. As Uself did one more scan of his battle plan he thought plan "B" would take more time but in the end when both Gabriel's consort and son ended up dead it would be worth it, it would just take more time, time he was reluctant to use. Plan "C" would be in acted if things went seriously wrong because this plan included an escape plan.

The minute Uself said that they would switch places; Jason immediately knew he was to be sacrificed. Jason knew that he had only one option left and that was he would not fight. If Justin or Katelyn killed him quickly they would not have to waste there energy and time on a decoy. Then Uself would have to not only stand and fight but reveal his true self. Jason knew the path he walked was full of unseen pitfalls he had been prepared once before to give his life so that the greater good could be served. Now it seemed that he was being called upon again to put his life on the line. Jason gave Uself a vacant smile and said I'm ready when you are.

Uself told Vane and Rule,"do not to leave this spot and when I call you, you are to follow my instructions to the letter and materialize where and when I tell you and not one moment late, do I make my self clear." Uself continued to say, "If you are a second late, I will consider this action an insult and I do not take insults lightly." Both Vane and Rule nodded their heads in confirmation. Uself then changed both his appearance and Jason's right before they stepped into Katelyn's mind and disappeared.

Katelyn felt the intrusion the moment they entered and a second later so did Justin. It was the weekend and they had been sitting on the couch quietly talking, Justin had been holding Katelyn and the moment she went ridged Justin went on the alert. There were two of them, under normal conditions a warrior confronted with demons would simply attack however Justin projected an image of himself on the path that the two demons were traveling and said, "you are not welcome here, leave! Uself was starting to get uncomfortable because the warrior did not attack and neither did

Jason. Uself tried to move closer and Justin said, "Stand where you are do not take one step closer, you will not enter here!

Jason did not attack, in fact to Uself's horror Jason had simply sat down. Jason was extremely still when he heard the words of his great uncle spoken clearly in his mind, the words were: "Let all things be what they genuinely are, through the power of love, I transform you in to what you are so that all may see." After that a golden shower of light held the two demons completely immobilized and when it ended the demons had changed places with each other.

Justin was intrigued, Jason was relieved but Uself was enraged! It was turning out that this battle had many unforeseen elements to it and Uself hated surprises, Uself found himself trying to push his rage back, so that he could decide on his next move. Since Uself knew that he could no longer get close enough to the light warrior to use a surprise attack, he decided on another. Uself materialized Bree/Gabriel in front of him as he held a knife to her throat. Uself then stated that if Justin did not allow him access to the elemental by eliminating her defense systems he would kill his mother.

Justin saw the triumph in Uself's eyes as he waited for Justin to choose his mate or his mother. Justin, however, remained calm and stated: "How do I know that that is my mother after what we have both witnessed, how do I know that this is not simply another attempt at deception?

Uself hated to give any ground yet he knew that the warrior would need proof to believe him, so he told Bree/Gabriel as he lowered the knife a little, to convince her son of her identify with knowledge that only she would know. Bree/Gabriel lowered his head as if trying to think of something to convince Justin with when suddenly Uself was hit with a blinding blow which knocked him back to almost the entrance of Katelyn's mind.

Then Bree/Gabriel lifted his head, with his eyes shinning and said, as he transformed into his true self, "that would be difficult to do since I am not his mother." Uself wanted to scream at how his carefully laid out plans had turned to ashes. Gabriel was a first angel and Uself knew that he could not defeat him in a fair fight so now it was time to clean up this mess and kill of all of the witnesses and bring out hidden weapons.

Uself was sitting on the floor after Gabriel's blow, with his head down as if he was dazed but what he was really doing was calling forth the ancient negativity that he had infected Gabriel with a long time ago. Uself called and called and he heard no reply then when he looked up and saw that Gabriel was not being attacked from with in as Uself had requested of the ancient negativity, Gabriel replied, "It is gone!" I feel your attempts to activate something that is no longer a part of me and with that Gabriel sent a blast of angelic power into Uself. Uself deflected fifty percent of the blast but the rest hurt like hell.

Katelyn materialized behind Justin as the battle began (at first it was difficult to move inside her own consciousness but with practice it got a lot easier), her intent was to insure that nothing reached Justin from behind. Katelyn had initially sent angelic communication to the demon that looked like Jason and heard a buzzing sound in return. Katelyn communicated this information to Justin and he said that it could not be Jason. Justin switched plans and started to talk to the demons to give them time to figure out what to do about Jason but it seemed that that too had been taken out of Justin's hands when to golden shower of light transformed the two into them selves. Katelyn continued to remain vigilant watching for any type of danger to Justin and observing the battle.

Uself knew that not only was he was running out of options but some how they had figured out his plan (Uself screamed how)! It was time to put an end to this situation and escape as soon as possible. Uself bent his head again as if he was exalted from the last hit but what he was really doing was sending for Vane and Rule. Uself told Vane to materialize in front of him but what Vane did not know was that he too would be doing so looking like Uself. Uself then spotted the elemental that had materialized at her mate's back as she was simply watching the battle. Uself told Rule to materialize beside the elemental and transport her immediately to Vane's home in hell.

Vane materialized where he was told too and it took him only seconds to realize that he had materialized right in the middle of the battle. Vane then realized that he and Uself had changed appearances. Vane had Uself at his back telling him to fight and a seriously upset angel in front of him it was at that moment that Vane realized he was about to die. Uself screamed at him in his mind to fight, so Vane thought if I am going to die anyway at least I can do so fighting.

Vane headed toward Justin because he thought he had at least a chance of winning with Justin rather than absolutely no chance in a battle with an angel; Justin rushed forward to meet him. Katelyn's attention was on the battle that Justin was about to engage in, Justin was quick and got in a blow which cut off one of Vane's arms, Katelyn's attention was on Vane as he scream in pain which is why before she could turn around good to see what was touching her she felt her self being transported to hell while being held by a demon.

Justin was in full battle mode, next he took his light sword and stuck the demon straight through the heart and then beheaded him. Vain was laying there convulsing and breaking into pieces when Justin looked around and screamed, "Where is Katelyn!"

While Vane was being turned into a shade and all of the attention was on the battle, Uself slipped out of Katelyn's mind and retuned back to Vane's home where he had told Rule to bring the elemental. Uself reviewed his situation, Vane was dead and Rule would be bring the elemental to Vane's home any minute now then he would join Vane, Uself had left Jason in the battle zone and he was sure to be the next one killed. That meant that the only witness to Uself's involvement with the elemental was Rule and he had plans for Rule.

Katelyn was gone and so was the fourth demon, Justin's look of pure devastating loss cut through Gabriel like a knife. Gabriel noticed that Uself had used the demon that Justin had just killed to distract them, cover his retreat and take Katelyn. Then when Gabriel looked next in his son direction, he did so in time to see the fourth demon disappear with his son's mate. Justin had a look of such intense loss that Gabriel opened himself up to an concentrated prayer to seek guidance and help for his son.

Justin was trying to contain the black hole which had open up in his heart and seemed to be sucking every thing he was into it, when a blast of pure light shot through him countering and shrinking the black hole. The light contained a message, "Justin all is not lost, a door way to Katelyn is being constructed and it is almost ready. In seconds you will be flooded with a vast amount of energy open yourself up to it and be ready to move when all is in place."

Gabriel felt the touch of the creator and received the following message, "give your son all of the energy you can spare leaving enough for you to transport your self and to aid another." Gabriel smiled and thought a plan was in place. Even thought Gabriel had no idea what the plan was, his heart was lifted then when he looked again at Justin and saw shear determination in his expression. Gabriel knew that only the knowledge, that a direct message from the creator could have brought his son out of his blinding pain.

Chapter Thiry-Three

Jason continued to sit quietly as chaos unfolded around him until he heard a voice in his head that said, "You have had every opportunity with in the last few weeks to choose as your soul wills. At every opportunity you chose your faith, genuine faith a faith that at times you had no knowledge of how it would work out and yet at each step you choose me." I have one more task for you to perform and with its conclusion your time in hell is over. I require your faith again in what I am about to ask. Of everything you have been through this next task will require the most from you; are you willing to put your life at risk one more time?" Do you wish to know what I want from you before you answer? Jason smiled and said, "All I need to know is that you require this of me, all that I can give is yours."

The creator then replied, Katelyn has been taken to hell and in order for Justin to get to her a portal must be constructed. However, since the last time that a demon kidnapped a human and brought her to hell, Lucifer has put in some safe guards. This portal must be constructed of specific material, first it must be alive, second it must have the feel and smell of hell or hell will not allow it access in to its realm and finally because the two materials of which the portal must be constructed are mutually exclusive, because nothing alive can exist (for long) in hell, Lucifer is content in his belief that no such portal can be constructed.

Justin is going to need speed and stealth to get into hell and since I have given this realm to Lucifer, I will abide by the rules he has established. The portal therefore is the only way to get Justin in with out even Lucifer knowing and the only way out because all in Lucifer's realm answers to him and once he is aware of the portal Lucifer will try to close it. Jason listened with out questions, pleased that the creator had taken the time to explain even though Jason stood ready to do all that he asked with out explanation. The creator replied to Jason's thoughts, "and that is why I explained, because you did not need or require an explanation."

Here is the first thing that I want you to do. I need you to return to hell and fill these two containers one with earth and small rocks the other container with water from this realm. The scent of hell is fading on you as we speak but there is enough left, especially if you add your anger to the mix of your emotions (the anger will boast the scent of hell on you) it will make it easier for you access and pass into hell; return to the highest of the upper regions of hell as quickly as possible. While the creator was giving Jason his instructions he was also speaking with Justin.

Rule did as he was told, he grabbed the elemental and headed to Vane's home. At first he did not think he would make it because it seemed that he felt him self beginning to start to burn and then as quickly as it started it stopped. Katelyn felt a demon's touch and then she was traveling. The second the demon touched her katelyn's elemental senses were heating up to burn him into ashes but they were already in route and Katelyn resisted the urge to burn the worried little demon because she did not want to end up in some sub-region of hell with no knowledge of where she was or how to get out. Katelyn figured that she might be easier to find if she let this little drama play out.

With in minutes Katelyn was with in someone's home another demon was waiting for them. A moment later the worried little demon who was transporting her was blasted away. Katelyn had no love for demons but she did not want to see any one die in front of her. Katelyn kept her defenses at high alert but they looked like they were dialed down to a vague hum. Shortly after the death of the worried little demon the older demon reached for her and ran full force into her defense system which flared the moment he tried to make contact with her. This time Katelyn (Katelyn did not want to make the same mistake twice) had her defenses on automatic and when he reached for her he pulled back a stub; his hand had been burned to ashes.

Jason was back with the items that the creator had requested. The creator said, the construction of the portal was intended to be a riddle in that it must be constructed from material that is and is not of hell. You, Jason are the answer to the riddle. Jason understood, he was alive and he had spent the last few weeks in hell, it was his body that the creator needed to use to construct the portal into hell.

Jason felt no pain as his body expanded and changed, it was as if everything that made him Jason was all placed with in his mind and his mind was now the guardian of the portal. Jason knew he was in for a fight once Lucifer knew he existed but he intended to pore all of his energy into maintaining the portal and that included the energy he would need to sustain his life.

Bree, Ariel and Rapheal all received the same message at the same time, "a plan is in place for Justin and Jason. Justin needs each of you to give him all the energy you can spare. They each prepared to do so the moment that Gabriel gave them the signal of which was again "NOW." While the portal was forming and almost complete,
Justin walked over to Jason and touched his new form in wonder and gratitude and he said thank you for the help that only you could give. Justin felt a smile settle on his heart and he knew it was Jason's reply.

At that moment Gabriel sent the word "NOW" an incredible amount of energy poured into Justin. Justin became a sponge, he was absorbing energy at a rate and amount he would not have thought possible. As the energy flowed into him, he could feel each of the donors and each sent him a message of encouragement and support.

Justin marveled at the fact that a process that felt like it should have taken hours took in fact, less than a minute. Justin had just stepped in side of the portal when he heard Katelyn voice fill with concern about him and asking if he was alright. It felt like she was talking to herself and yet the information was communicated directly to him when she asked "is he alright, where is he?" Justin sent her a replied, "I'm on my way!"

Rule was in complete awe, one moment he was burning alive under flames so intense he could feel his body melting away from his bone as he started the process of becoming a shade and the next moment he was in his apartment in one piece, whole and pain gone. Then it hit him, Tris had put his name on the order of protection as they agreed! He could not be killed by the Senior Elder demon and he was not dammed. He had made it through this with out being dammed! Rule had been home for hours, which seemed like minutes to him because he was still trying to adjust to the fact that he was not a shade, when he heard a knock on the door. Rule went to open the door and a messenger from Lucifer stated that "the great one wanted to speak with him now." Rule thought as he followed the messenger to Lucifer's home, "I knew it was all too good to be true!"

As Rule walked behind the messenger he thought, "What have I done to bring myself to Lucifer's notice and what ever it is it could not be a good thing." It was difficult for Rule to come up with a defense, when he did not even know what crime he was being charged with. These were the thoughts that were going through Rules head when the messenger lead Rule in to Lucifer's study to wait for him.

Lucifer walked in and Rule fell to his knees, Lucifer told him to rise and offered him a seat and a glass of blood wine. Then while Rule was truly enjoying the wine and stating to relax, Lucifer said tell me everything that you know about this situation with Uself, up to and including tonight.

Rule lowered his glass of wine and told Lucifer everything that happened from the time he requested help from Vane up to ending up in his own apartment whole and intact a few hours earlier. For once in Rule's life as a demon, he told the information with as much honestly and clarity as he could. The last thing on Rule's mind was giving Lucifer any reason to be angry with him.

When Rule finished telling Lucifer everything that he knew or his part in the story, Lucifer told Rule that he wanted him to stay at one of his safe houses as his guest (of course all his needs would be taken care of) until his testimony against Uself was required.

Lucifer then stated with intently, that no one was to know that he was not dammed. Lucifer wanted Rule to leave from his home to go with a personal escort to the safe house. Lucifer stated that, "If Rule followed his instructions to the letter and at trial he was willing to open up to a memory review (this was something that the demon had to agree to willingly or the memories would be distorted). Upon the successful conclusion of these events, Lucifer would give Rule five souls and a bottle of the blood wine made from Uself's blood.

Rule agreed to all of Lucifer's conditions and terms and as he was being escorted to the safe house by one of Lucifer's personal guards he thought, "Revenge is sweet!" Lucifer watched the relieved little demon leave and leaned back in his chair to think. Uself was a Senior Elder demon, who thought that all the witnesses against him were or would soon be dead, of course he would demand his right to a trial.

Katelyn watched Uself as he turned his head toward the window trying to regain his composure. While he was looking out of the window Katelyn reviewed her position. Katelyn was surprised at the intensity of her power and at how natural it all felt. It was as if all of the restraints (inherited from generations of elementals) had dissolved and in its place a door way opened up and all the knowledge of what an elemental truly was and how those powers could be used poured into her. Filling her with subtle and intricate ways that her power could be used and how she could combine those powers with another.

Never in her life had Katelyn felt so complete and so in control. She was looking into the eyes of a very old demon yet she was not afraid! And if that were not enough she could fell the fear in him. Katelyn's mind questioned her powers and the answers poured in. Can he harm me, "NO, not unless you let your shields down." Can he break through my shields, "No, your shields are constructed of pure love and there is no stronger force in the universe."

With these answers Katelyn's thoughts turned to Justin and she asked, "is he alright, where is he?" These questions did not receive the instant reply as the other questions did. A few minutes passed and Katelyn felt a thought laced with incredible power that at first seemed as if it was going to slam through her when suddenly the power turned into a caress and she heard Justin's voice as he said, "I'm on my way!"

Katelyn's heart lifted and she could not contain her smile. It was at that moment that the Senior Elder demon turned around and all of his control slipped. The anger in his eyes told her he would kill her in a heart beat if he could. Katelyn continued to smile as she thought, "soon killing me is going to get a lot harder than you know!"

Uself thought he had his anger under control; unfortunately controlling his fear was harder. He had come up with a plan of trying to talk her into lowering her shields and then strike before she could even see him coming. Uself took one more deep calming breath and turned around. The first thought that entered his mind when he looked at her was rage, "How dare this insignificant human mock me with her laughter!" Uself took a chair and with all of his strength he smashed the chair against her shields, the chair disintegrated the moment it touched her shields.

Uself's rage was fueled by his desperation and his knowledge that his time was running out. He could feel Lucifer's attention focused on this location because of the intense energy she was generating. Uself's rage needed a victim and his life depended on eliminating her shields or at least weakening them to the point that he could break through for a swift kill.

Uself gathered his considerable power to send the most intense energy blast he had ever released; seconds before he released the blast, Uself felt another energy presence that materialized in front of her, a presence which seemed to be immediately absorbed through her shields. The additional energy source made Uself's efforts look like child's play as the energy bounced off of her shields and the blast was reflected back to Uself. Uself hit the wall and blacked out for a few minutes; when he came too, Lucifer was standing over him crackling with anger.

Lucifer was watching the show, he had connected with one of his spies and through their eyes and ears he saw and heard everything. Lucifer smiled as Uself thought he had killed off any remaining witness to this situation with Rule. Lucifer knew the moment that Tris had added Rule's name to the order of protection therefore Lucifer knew that Rule was at home and safe. Lucifer was contemplating when he should intervene in this little drama when he saw Uself reach for the elemental and pull back a stub. Lucifer could not decide which he found more entertaining, Uself's shock at her power or his lost of a limb or the fear he smelt on Uself as he tried to control his emotions and think about his next course of action. Then when caught up in his frustrations, Uself smashed a chair against her shields, Lucifer almost laughed out loud.

Lucifer sat back in his chair and he thought this is getting better and better. Lucifer read Uself next intent and watched to see if he would get through her shields. Then another player entered the game, Lucifer took a deep breath and smelt power. Power that settled in front of the elemental which was immediately absorbed by her shields in less than a second. Power that deflected Uself attack back to him. Power that materialized into the form of a man who reached for the woman and held her tight . . . Ah! Lucifer thought "her mate."

Justin reached Katelyn at the moment Uself was gathering energy to try to blast through Katelyn's shields. Although Justin knew that the energy would not get through her shields (he had helped her defense system to develop her shields out of pure love) he knew that they were as forged out of the strongest level of love, still the ideal of anyone attacking her brought out every protective instinct that Justin had. Justin moved in front of Katelyn a few moments before the blast was sent and Justin deflected the blast and sent the energy back to Uself.

Justin stepped back and Katelyn's shields absorbed him as he turned around and held her tight in his arms he whispered desperately in to her mind, "I thought I had lost you and I was ready to die too!" Justin then did a mental scan of Katelyn to reassure him self that she was alright and the second he finished the scan the doors to the room they were in splintered apart, then Justin and Katelyn looked directly into the eyes of Lucifer as flames were exploding in his eyes.

Like any realm hell had its rules and Uself had broken almost all of them. First he had sought to overthrow Lucifer, second he was both directly and indirectly responsible for two live humans entering hell! Breaking this rule truly angered Lucifer. One of his best feats had been to convince humans that hell does not exist. One of his favorite lines during seductions was, "have you ever met any one who has been to hell." Lucifer had learned quickly that the fewer humans who believed that he or hell existed the easier it was to talk them into damming their souls. Anything that could negatively impact on the collection of souls got Lucifer's attention. This was a major violation and a direct insult to Lucifer.

Lucifer was just about to make a grand entrance, with the question in his mind of what he should or could do with the two powerful humans in his domain. A demon had brought a human into hell once before and Lucifer had killed them both . . . some how Lucifer doubted that the solution would be that simple again.

Lucifer had materialized out side the door to Vane's home and a second later the door splintered into pieces and Lucifer was looking the two humans in the eye, disappointed that they showed no fear. Lucifer walked over to where Uself laid unconscious and Lucifer reached into his mind and willed him to consciousness. Ah . . . Lucifer thought, "This is much more like it." As Uself woke to Lucifer standing over him, then pure genuine fear shot through Uself's eyes.

The creator had been monitoring as these events unfolded. Timing is critical to success, the creator had to step in after all had chosen their paths and at the moment when those choices had run there course. It was at this point, when their direction was uncertain that then and only then could the pieces be formed into a new whole.

The creator reached his hand into the dark void that was engulfing Justin during the moments he believed that Katelyn was either dead or dieing and on a deep instinctual level the creator offered Justin a choice of blind faith and trust Justin replied, "I choose you." At that moment the darkness began to dissipate and direction and new purpose took its place.

The creator had felt Gabriel reaching for him, hurt on a level that he did not know he could feel as he watched his child suffer a pain that seemed to be trying to rip him apart and consume him. Gabriel faith was clean and clear as he asked simply for guidance and help in what ever form the creator choose to give. As the creator communicated his instructions to Gabriel, the pain Gabriel felt melted away and even though he did not know how or why, he knew much had already changed. When Gabriel looked again at his son, the change was confirmed!

Lucifer's mind was working on several levels, he had informed his spies to materialize and bind and gage Uself, then take him to the dungeon in Lucifer's home. However, as he was issuing these instructions Uself screamed, "I demand a trial as is my right as a Senior Elder!" Lucifer smiled and said, "As you wish." While Uself was being carted away Lucifer put a communication black out around the house. Since Lucifer was the only one who could order such a thing every demon knew that no amount of curiosity was worth trying to breach the black out because it literally translated into,"if you intrude you die."

Lucifer was a master of illusions and he knew that what a being perceived was his reality. If you can control that perception you dictate their reality. If no one knew what actually took place then the information he would give out to his spies would be the only information the inhabitants of hell would know and since every one would hear the same story, all would believe it to be true!

Lucifer's eyes died down as he contemplated this situation he had inherited from Uself. Lucifer realized that he may or may not be able to defeat the two being in front of him with force and Lucifer never willingly put him self in dead ended situations. No, Lucifer recognized that his best chance of success was deception.

Lucifer now wondered about who had constructed the portal, how they figured out the riddle and what type of actual material had been used. A portal was the only way now that a living being could enter hell and Obviously someone had figured out the riddle of construction and found a way to get the necessary elements for construction of the portal . . . pity, now he would have to come up with a new riddle and a means of construction that would be much hard to attain.

Hell was Lucifer's domain and that meant that every thing and every one answered to him. Any portal had to have something of or from hell with in its construction; otherwise hell would not recognize or connect with it. This meant that the portal answered to Lucifer. Lucifer sent a strong signal for the portal to close! Gabriel was monitoring Jason when he picked up his distress.

Gabriel connected with Jason and saw that he was literally under attack and Jason was fighting to stay open. Gabriel connected with Jason's angelic shields and activated them because Jason did not have the strength to do so. This action triggered the energy reserve stored with in Jason's shields and this reduced the demand to close from eighty percent to twenty percent. Gabriel also shared half of his remaining energy with Jason.

Both Jason and Gabriel knew that Jason would need another infusion of energy when Lucifer sent a stronger order to close once he noticed that the first order had not been obeyed. Gabriel sent a blast of angelic communication to Raphael, Ariel and Bree informing them of the situation and Jason's need for energy. With in moments Rapheal, Bree and Ariel materialized in the upper realm of hell where the creator had constructed the portal and where Gabriel and Jason now were. Rapheal helped an exhausted Gabriel by sharing energy with him while Bree and Ariel connected with Jason. Ariel and Bree waited to each take a turn at strengthening Jason when the next order for closure came from Lucifer.

Justin knew he was looking into the eyes of hell it's self, Lucifer. Any fear he may have had died quickly against the need to keep Katelyn safe (when he touched her mind he found that she had the same conviction about him and he had to fight to keep from smiling). Keeping Katelyn safe meant getting to that portal. Lucifer smiled as he read Justin's body language which indicated that Justin was going to try to get to the portal.

Lucifer was about to smile and state that the portal was closed when he did a brief sweep to insure that this was so, the smile died on his lips when he realized that some how the portal was still open. Justin reached out to locate the exact location of the portal when he felt that Jason was under attack, Lucifer sent an even stronger command for the portal to close, then at the same moment Justin also sent energy to the portal which reduced the energy strength that Lucifer had sent to about half.

However, that half still hit Jason like a sludge hammer as he felt the intense pressure on his mind to obey Lucifer's command. Jason was resisting with almost every ounce of energy he had to keep from giving into Lucifer's command when both Jason and Justin felt Ariel lift about ninety percent of the crushing weight off of Jason's mind. Raphael watched Ariel fight for there son, never in his existence had he been more surprised and proud of her and as he heard his son's relaxed breath. Raphael knew that from this moment on he would trust her with all of his heart and treat her with the respect of a partner an equal to him in every way!

Lucifer changed his appearance, he projected an illusion he seldom used, he became what he once was, an angel of the first order. Lucifer knew that humans had found his angelic form extremely handsome and that this image had the added advantage of projecting the illusion of trust.

Lucifer asked Justin a question, in a very old form of angelic speech, who was his father? Lucifer's intent was simple, elegant and deadly. He intended to ask as many questions as he could about the male and his family (simple). Then with each answer look for some hidden weakness, old hurts or grudges (elegant). After which, take that information and fashion a web tailor made to get the male to open the door to his soul and invite Lucifer in (deadly). Because when that occurred Lucifer would have them both. Getting though there outer defenses with force could have been difficult but once he as inside he would seize control of the male and through his connection with the female grab her equally as fast before she could see him coming.

Chapter Thirty-Four

Justin had not missed the calculating gleam in Lucifer's eyes after he had banished the other demons and then turned his attention toward them. Then when Lucifer changed both his appearance and manor toward them Justin's alert status went up even more. Justin knew he was watching the original master of deception and lies and then when Lucifer used the "old speak" part of Justin was drawn to it. Then when Lucifer asked for the name of his father, Justin saw little harm in reliving his curiosity and he was about to speak when Katelyn invaded his mind and snapped him out of the exceptionally strong but hidden compulsion woven into the simple question, this subtle but deadly attempt at seduction that Lucifer was weaving needed only Justin's reply for Lucifer to establish an entrance into Justin's mind!

Lucifer had felt the male about to respond to the small but extremely strong compulsion he had put in his request. He almost had the male when the female literally cut his connection to the male. Lucifer turned his head to look out of the window, portraying a casual stance as if waiting politely for an answer. But inside he was angry as hell, he had underestimated the female and he had lost his best shot at deception, a deception with the elements of simplicity and surprise on its side.

Bree had sent Justin ninety percent of her energy when she received the original request. However, she had asked for and received a leaf from her very special plant and the moment she finished sending the energy to Justin, Bree put the leaf in her mouth and chewed it twice before she passed out. Fifteen minutes later when she came to, she was at about sixty percent of her energy level and gaining strength quickly.

Later when they got Gabriel's second communication Bree was back to her full energy level. When she got to the level in upper hell where Jason and Gabriel were, she knew that before this was over she would need every bit of her energy and more. Bree monitored Jason and Ariel went to see what help he needed as Rapheal looked after Gabriel. Bree had an instinct that told her to let Ariel take the first turn at helping Jason and later she understood why.

Lucifer had underestimated the female, in fact because she stood so quietly behind the male he literally forgot to factor her intervention and the fact that she too had power into his plans. Lucifer turned from the window and looked at Katelyn and said, "Well played my dear, but I don't make the same mistake twice."

Katelyn was monitoring the subtle battle between Lucifer and Justin. Both seemed so focused on each other that it almost seemed that they forgot she was there, which was fine by her. Lucifer was speaking and Katlyn had just finished her scans, she had located the portal. She was about to tell Justin when she felt the hypnotic lure of Lucifer's words looking for a way in to Justin. Justin was just about to answer Lucifer's question when Katelyn's instincts screamed "NO!"

Katelyn reached into Justin's mind and prevented him from speaking then at the same time she snapped off the compulsion from Lucifer and willed Justin to see and understand what her instincts had picked up during the process and why she acted the way she did. Justin sent her love and warmth as he now built into their shields a filter to block all compulsions from Lucifer in the future.

Lucifer manufactured a chair and sat down and then he said, "Do either of you know what the Alamo or the Spartan three hundred had in common?" They were each out numbered with no re-enforcements coming in a timely manor and they had no way out of there current situation except for death. Tell me, do you see any similarities in there situation and your?

Justin knew that there was a great deal of truth in Lucifer's question. There was no possibility of reinforcements and if the portal did not stay open they had no means of escape from hell. Justin knew that with one method or another over a period of time Lucifer could wear down there energy and with that there defenses.

Justin knew that it was a genuine possibility that he might not survive this confrontation with Lucifer. Justin's best chance of success had been to get in and get out quickly, which had a high probability of success when they were faced only with Uself. But now that Lucifer had taken Uself's place and Lucifer also knew that their best probability of success was to do just that get in and get out, Lucifer intended to take his time and wear down there defenses.

Justin had ten percent of his energy focused on the exact location of the portal that Katelyn had shown him, Justin had this knowledge shielded from Lucifer because no matter what or if things went wrong it was his intent to hold on through sheer will power if necessary to insure that Katelyn got into that portal. Katelyn had been monitoring Justin's thoughts and she knew that he planned to give up his life for hers.

Katelyn knew she had to act, there was a little know talent that elementals possess, knowledge known only to those in the past of both great strength and wisdom, knowledge that did not intentionally get passed down to every elemental. This knowledge was dangerous especially to the elemental because it meant pouring her self her very essence into another's soul, literally giving away her will, her power and her strength to another.

This meant that the individual receiving this gift was the only one who could release her back into herself because he had her will! In the past, individuals who received the trust of an elemental on this level and experienced this increasable level of power found that they could not let go and that meant that the elemental was trapped and subservient to the will of another usually for the rest of her life. Therefore, unless she could trick him into releasing her, this would be her fate.

Lucifer thought, "I have them now!" All I need to do now is to decide which form of attack I will use to wear them down. Lucifer opened his right hand and a ball of energy appeared. Lucifer smiled and said, "This little fellow lives on energy and at first your shields will obliterate him but then he will regroup and reform to twice the size of his last one. Each time he is eliminated he will return quicker at double the size and strenght. This process will continue until it will take more and more of your combined energy to eliminate him, until you are weak enough for me to reach in and control you at will." With that, Lucifer blew the energy ball at Justin and Katelyn.

Katelyn saw in Justin's thought that this was exactly what he was expected Lucifer to do. Justin was forming a plan to make a run for the portal and throw Katelyn in to it while he fought to keep Lucifer's attention on him and not on either the portal or Katelyn. Justin figured that as Gabriel's son and a light warrior if Lucifer had to choose between either him or Katelyn that Justin would be the choice he would make and this would give Katelyn the necessary time to escape.

Justin was now thinking of a diversion to throw at Lucifer to buy more time while he got Katelyn to the portal when he heard Katelyn say: "we do this together or not at all, where one goes we both go." It was this action and the knowledge that she did not want to live with out him that made her decision easy and once it was made she felt genuine peace because she knew she was doing the right thing.

Katelyn stood directly behind Justin so that Lucifer would not see or notice her, her body began to become translucent and then she literally stepped into Justin's soul and from there she reached out and merged with the connection which were already established between them with in his mind, heart, sprit and body.

Suddenly Justin felt inscribable strength infuse every part of his being; strength which caused a metamorphous right in front of Lucifer's disbelieving eyes! The strength that Katelyn had poured into him had triggered his angelic DNA. Unknown to Justin he started to glow. In fact he was not just an angel but an angel of the first order, like Lucifer had once been.

Knowledge poured into Justin both from untapped areas of his angelic heritage and from Katelyn's old soul which housed the knowledge of her heritage. In the blink of an eye, Justin understood what had occurred and why he no long felt any possibility of failure. Now he had too many options and abilities at his disposal and as his mind calculated the possibilities of his situation, he knew with clear certainness that he could defeat Lucifer.

In fact, there was one detail of the knowledge that poured into him which explained exactly how this could be done. The knowledge explained the process step by step, which was that any demon had to obey any command, including that of ending there existence, if there birth name is spoken in a command surrounded by angelic light and sent to them with angelic communication.

Right before he received the knowledge of how to kill Lucifer he also received the knowledge of why he could not, Justin clearly understood, he knew Lucifer's purpose and why he had been created. Justin knew why eliminating him would destroy the balance of the universe. Lucifer had so many names but Lucifer was the name he chose for him self, it was not the name he was given at his conception. Lucifer also knew the power in a name and as long as he had so many names no one was sure which one was really his. As an extra precaution, Lucifer never ever used the name the creator gave him at his conception. This was a name that no one but Lucifer and the creator knew. Justin traced the knowledge line back in time until he knew Lucifer's birth name, the name the creator gave him at his conception.

Justin used a small (very small) part of his mind to monitor Lucifer as he thought of and rejected a variety of options regarding his next more in this situation. For every option that Lucifer developed Justin developed a counter move. The small part of Justin's mind which was monitoring Lucifer effortlessly also kept Lucifer from being able to monitor him in return.

Justin thought that as fascinating as this aspect of his mind was, it was nothing compared to what took place in the larger part of his brain. Justin watched in awe, as changes with in him unfold as he watched. His mind was like an intricate multi-layered lock and as pieces of the lock fell into place a wealth of knowledge showered over him revealing wave behind wave of knowledge and abilities. This process took place at the speed of light when he looked at it from the outside in. but when he merged with the knowledge he could slow it down adjust it as he choose and examine one or several pieces of it with intense care. Then with what seemed like a mental click, a complete picture was now in place.

Justin stood patiently, listening to Lucifer's thoughts monitoring his turmoil. Lucifer's ego and pride told him that the only being more powerful than him self was god; however Lucifer could not dismiss the evidence standing right before his eyes. It had been a long time since he saw that secondary glow of intense yellow light shining out from Justin's heart, that was the glow that radiated from the mark of a first angel it had been a very long time since he saw that mark but all of him recognized it and the power the individual in front of him wheedled.

Even as Lucifer thought, that maybe the being in front of him might not know the extent of the power at his command, which was a weakness to be exploited if he was right and if he was wrong he would not get a second chance. At that moment, Justin quietly said,"you are wrong I know how to use what I am."

Lucifer snapped his head up and stared at the being in front of him as he refused to acknowledge that anyone could see or hear his private thoughts if he did not so choose. Justin said again, equally as quiet, "you are wrong again." Pure anger poured through Lucifer's as his eyes turned blood red and became a living flame his body changed into that of a powerful demon in an effort to intimate or ever better strike fear in Justin. Justin did the unthinkable, he smiled.

A strong sense of self protection kicked in and overrode all other emotions as Lucifer returned to a diminished version of the angel he once was, an angel with out the shinning light of the creator's love glowing through him like Justin. Lucifer stated, I see Gabriel's mark on you yet your are not him? This time it was safe to answer, and Justin smiled again and said, "I am his son." Lucifer said, "Your father once loved me and I him." Justin looked deeper and saw a great deal of envy in Lucifer directed toward Gabriel.

Justin took a moment and noticed that the little energy balls had multiplied and they were trying to access more energy. With a thought Justin created a gust of wind and blew the little balls out of the door and then the splinted door reformed. Now it was Justin who had Lucifer and not the other way around. Lucifer could not get out of the door!

Lucifer was many things but he was not a fool! He saw his equal when he looked at Justin (he actually saw much, much more but his equal was the most he was willing to admit too). It had never been Lucifer's policy to enter into a battle with out a minimum of an eighty percent possibility of wining and Lucifer acknowledged that his odds were a long way away from eighty percent. It was now time to do damage control and try to figure a way out of this situation which allowed Lucifer to save face. However, more importantly the actual truth of this situation would be one of those experiences that he would keep to himself!

Lucifer was thinking of how to turn this situation to his advantage when a patch of ground appeared and then a chair appeared on that ground. Justin moved Lucifer from the chair he was sitting in to the new one and then bounded Lucifer in the chair. This was necessary to insure that both the chair and the ground answered to Justin and not Lucifer. Lucifer was livid, but the moments he calmed down and thought about this move he understood why Justin had acted in this manor. All things in hell answered to Lucifer therefore the ground and the chair he sat on could not be of hell and continue to bind him.

Lucifer asked, "How do you know that I will not send for my personal guards, you know that I could summon them with a thought?" Justin smiled again and said,"No you will not, the master of hell can not afford to allow any of those who answer to him, to see him bounded. Besides, we both know that they would only turn on you!"

Justin then said, "the restraints currently are not painful however if you send another command to close the portal I will insure that you feel an equal and opposite amount of pain." The thought of doing just that was an idea starting to form in Lucifer's brain and Justin had countered the thought before Lucifer had finished forming the thought.

Lucifer's mind sent command after command for the ground and chair to release him. It was inconceivable that anyone could come into his realm and bind him! And for the life of him Lucifer could not understand how, this being had created something in his realm that Lucifer could not control. So Lucifer asked how, what he was doing was possible. Justin spoke Lucifer's angelic birth name and than said, "As you know there is a great deal of power in a name."

For the first time in Lucifer's very long life he was completely surprised. No one should have had that knowledge! Also for the first time since the fall of the third, Lucifer actually felt fear! Lucifer knew beyond any doubt, that the being in front of him had the power to kill him with a thought. Lucifer assumed a submissive pose and asked, what will happen to the restraints once you leave? As you said, if my minions find me bound they will attack me. Justin replied, they will dissolve, because they are not part of your world. With that, Lucifer watched helplessly as Justin entered the portal and Lucifer thought, "were is the female?" Lucifer assumed that he had sent the female into the portal earlier and blocked him from seeing it.

Once Justin entered the portal and was one third of the way through the portal where Lucifer could not see Justin started to feel Jason's distress. Justin released Katelyn and with that he released a great deal of his strength, strength that held Lucifer bounded to both the ground and chair that Lucifer was sitting in, in place. Justin did not want to whole Katelyn in his soul a moment longer than was necessary plus the power that they created together made it as difficult for the portal on the inside as Lucifer would have made it on the outside. One minute later, after Justin released Katelyn the portal was attacked viciously from the outside where Jason was not only given a command to close but each minute he stayed open he would feel greater and greater pain.

Once the chair and restraints resolved, Lucifer got angry. No one came into his realm and caused him to feel insignificant. Name or no name, Lucifer sent his strongest command to the portal to close in the hopes that the being inside would be hurt or better yet killed in the process. Lucifer sent pain, waves and waves of pain with the command because he wanted everything and body associated with this outrage to feel his wraith!

Ariel called out a distress signal and Bree stepped in, Bree's instincts were right when they told her to hold off because all of her strength would be needed toward this end. She could almost feel Jason loosing the struggle as pain radiated through out him both mentally and physically.

Bree reached in and blocked the pain from Jason's mind and then stabilized the inner walls of the portal. A few minutes later Bree felt Katelyn's energy signal with in the portal and they combined their energy to become something greater that its two parts. Together they were able to block any additional pain, eliminate the effects of the pain Jason had already endured and block and eliminate the pressure to close the portal as they stabilized it.

Ariel insured that Jason's life energy remained stable and Raphael activated the energy that he had poured into Jason's mind to insure that he got through this with as little trauma as possible.
Justin was still a little weak from the separation but yet Katelyn felt no ill effects at all from the separation, in fact she felt well rested!

One minute Jason was in unbelievable pain on several levels physically and mentally. The next moment, peace! The pain and pressure were completely gone and he felt his mother voice telling him to rest and she would maintain his life energy. Moments later he felt his father's touch with the message of how proud he was of him after that, Jason let go and became unconscious, he could now do so because he was secure in the knowledge that after the creator, he was in the safest hands possible.

Chapter Thirty-Five

Lucifer had tasted fear for the first time in a very long time and it left him in a mood to kill! He sent another and final close order to the portal as strong as possible, complete with an order for the portal to be in concentrated, increasing pain for every moment it stayed open. He may not have been able to kill the being that had invaded his realm but Lucifer thought he could if possible strand them in an unknown region or world between earth and hell, a region that may require a life time or two to get out of.

Lucifer calmed down and then smiled, as he reviewed his current situation. Actually it was not all that bad, in fact with a few serious public relationship tricks he could spend the situation to his advantage because the only two other being who knew exactly what went on in this house were gone and this left Lucifer's version of the situation . . . "as the only version of the situation!" Lucifer smiled again as he thought, "perception is reality."

Katelyn felt Justin give the order to release her and suddenly she was back in her own body again. Justin kissed her fiercely and quickly and said,"thank you for the incredible gift of your trust and belief I will never forget your faith in me and in us." They started to run because they felt the portal under attack.

Katelyn placed her hand on the inner walls of the portal and every where she touched was like a soothing balm and then she felt Bree's energy signal and connected with her and together these three women (as Ariel fed energy into Jason's life support systems) did the impossible and the unbelievable. They protected Jason, helped to rescue Justin and defeated Lucifer attempts to close the portal all as their mates watched in stunned admirations as their women held it all together.

It seemed as if they had been running forever and Justin was loosing energy and trying to hide this knowledge from Katelyn, until Katelyn noticed the tired strain he was trying to hide. Katelyn immediately connected with the energy lines that they shared and sent to Justin the energy he needed, as she did a scan of his mental and physical condition.

It seems that her ancestors were exceptionally foresighted; once the elemental had been released they took the majority of the combined energy with them. This triggered an energy drain which they had built into the process of merging. This energy drain insured that the individual who released them would do so in a weaken state so that he could not force them back through blackmail or any other form of cohesion.

The drain of energy slowly but literally shut down the systems of the person the elemental merged with. If the elemental did not stop the energy drain the individual could die. It all depended on whether the elemental was blackmailed into the merge of if she did so of her on free will and later found herself captured. Once she talked her host into releasing her, this process would allow the elemental time to escape and insure that she was not recaptured.

Once released, it was the elementals choice as to whether the host lived or died because only the elemental could stop the drain and heal the host individual. This was the information of which Katelyn was informed when she asked the power with in her, "what is wrong with Justin!" With that knowledge came what and how to heal him and that is exactly what Katelyn did.

A few minutes later Justin and Katelyn stepped out of the portal. As they did so the portal began to re-shape and become an exhausted and unconscious Jason.

Lucifer had reconstructed the battle from the time Uself was carried away by his spies until (in his version) the human being were killed and of course they died begging for mercy that every one knows hell does not have and certainly was not given. Lucifer pretended to be to busy torturing the humans to notice that the communication black out shield was slowly fading and this permitted other to see what was occurring with in.

In a whirlwind of showmanship, Lucifer finally burned them alive (the simulated images of Justin and Katelyn) and scattered their ashes to the distant regions of the universe! As a warning to all who would enter his realm with out his consent. At the end of this seen Lucifer pretended to notice and be surprised by the applause as he finished with the humans. Lucifer smiled to him self as he thought, "perception is reality!"

Gabriel and Raphael had shared their energy and currently they were both maintaining the shield which kept Lucifer from knowing that they were all in one of the upper region of hell. They were also ready to step in and help their wives if the need occurred. One of them would maintain the shields and the other would provide any needed help. As they monitored the portal and the women, while maintained the shields they were witnessing a sight that neither angel would have ever thought possible and that is saying a lot for an angel!

Neither of the women either needed or asked for help from their consorts/husbands. Katelyn was healing Justin, Ariel was keeping Jason alive and Bree radiated the type of power and energy that even Gabriel would not have thought possible. Both angels could hardly believe the evidence of their own eyes!

Bree, Ariel and Katelyn then gathered everyone into a circle with each of the women positioned at a point of power with in the circle. Ariel was at nine o'clock, Katelyn was at three o'clock; Bree was at six o'clock in the circle. They stretch out their arms toward each other and then the women began to chant:

Wholeness requires each being to be at one with the elements of life and fate. To know one is to need the others, through out the life state. The earth creates and nurtures the body, air rises and falls with each breath and thought you intake. Water floods the sprit to teach control over our emotional state. Fire is the element that Tran-mutates every part into a new whole, that few can contemplate. "Such then are the rules of fate."

At first the women repeated the last rule of fate together and it seemed as if the circle then became self supporting. Like pieces coming together to form a whole; then when they repeated the last rule of fate, the second time. It seemed that with each line they spoke, power upon power began to build.

Gabriel, Justin and Raphael could actually see a circle of self sustaining energy flowing from each woman to the next!

As they continued to chant, the power that they generated provided its own protection and shields. Gabriel and Raphael no longer needed to shield their presence from hell.
After they repeat the final rule of fate for the third and final time, Bree said take all connected to and with in this circle to my home! The women provided the power to transport everyone to Bree's home in her home realm.

The creator watched the successful conclusion of the healing of two families. With each member getting what they needed to begin the process to becoming the best they could be. The creator then turned his thoughts to the rules of fate. These rules were intended to be thought confusing and contradictory. They were written in a manor that would require a great deal of work to figure out, all as a means of or in the hope of teaching simplicity.

The rules of fate were written in a manor which required the individual to drop all perceived notions and approach the rules with an open mind and a willingness to learn. To focus their attention not on the things that they already knew but to open themselves up to the possibilities of things they had never conceived of before.

I wrote on each individual's soul, at the moment of the thought of that soul's conception, a blueprint for ascension and growth. This knowledge is stored in a multi-layered vault with in the core of each individual soul. The universal laws are the keys which unlock this vault, level by level. With each level of the vault unlocked, a flood of information is sent to every part of the individual(mind, heart etc.) which allows him to look at old situations with new eyes, hear what people mean and not just what they say, broadens their perspective to include knowledge or information that was in the past was ignored. Each key or level reveals important information about the things you need to learn for your growth. Once you have learned what each level has to offer you, you are then lead to the next key or the next level!

The understanding and appreciation of simplicity is the final lesson which each individual needs to learn to find the keys to this multi-layered lock, with in which, the blue print for their individual fate is stored. These universal laws lead and prepare the individual through growth to gain the strength, will and ability to access and embrace the blue print or knowledge stored in the soul.

The universal laws have two main purposes:

1. To harness, control and focus the individual's own power and will and to allow the individual to become one with this power.
2. To help the person to become their best self and discover his own fate, which will then lead to his personal road for grace.

This is why simplicity is the last element necessary to begin this process of real growth. Simplicity leads your thinking out of thoughts of chaos and confusion to understanding and clarity. Now with this knowledge you are ready to see, use and appreciate these universal laws. Why? Because, life; the universal are simple, uncomplicated and fair. However, unevolved people, who always seek to get what they are not willing to give, are a mass of conflicting thoughts and confusion.

THE UNIVERSAL LAWS

1. Personal truthfulness: You can not change anything with in you, if you can not see it.
2. Fairness: this provides the rules and regulations which allow you to deal effectively and correctly with the truth you see.
3. Attention to detail: this law allows for an intricate understanding of human nature which keeps fairness and truth focused and always with in right action.
4. Do no harm: often when we are caught up in the chaos of human nature, we do not know what right action is? When you find yourself in such a situation simply look for the course of action which does no harm or the course of action which does the absolutely least amount of harm.
5. The power of choice: this is the understanding that choice is the power that shapes our world. Such a power deserves our deepest respect. Remember, when ever we use this power it should embody all of the four laws which came before.
6. The power of laughter: this power cleans and heals. It provides balance and renewal because it reminds us that joy is essential to health and life.
7. Understanding: one of the greatest aspects of this law is that it allows us to act with out regret. This law embodies all which have come before it, in that it advocates the importance of widening your perspective. The more open you are to knowledge, ideas and the motives of others the less likely you are to act without though which means fewer mistakes.
8. A living faith: this is the concept of knowing and working from what you believe: "what you believe is the parent thought of your choices. Your choices are the parent thoughts of your actions. Your actions

shape your world!" Our life becomes a daily reflection of our belief and faith, in which every choice is faith in action.

9. Humility: this is working from the concept, on a daily bases, that for every one thing that you know there are ten things that you do not know. Therefore excessive pride is the actions of fools. Through humility comes greatness because these two concepts are flip sides of the same coin.
10. Love, this is the strongest force in the universe and almost always completely misunderstood. Love is not just a power, it is a force which sweeps away all negativity in its path.

Epilogue

Today was the date for Uself's official trial and it seemed as if all of hell was in attendance. It was not every day that a Senior Elder Demon was brought up on charges and had to prove his innocence. And the fact that the trial was occurring meant that Lucifer had some pretty damming evidence against him.

Huge amount of bets were being laid on whether Uself could or would get out of this situation with his hide intact or as many in the crowd wondered, if Uself was found guilty, could they afford a glass of the wine which would be made from his blood. It was common practice that when a demon underwent a trial and lost his appeal (and his life) three bottles of blood wine was sold per glass to the general public. The glasses were small and the price was high and many in the crowd were wondering if they could afford a glass of such a rare treat!

Uself struck his most confident pose, when Lucifer's guards came to get him for his trial. Uself had to believe that all who knew anything about his participation; or interaction with this situation was dead or a shades. Shades had no standing in hell and as such could not be called to a court of law to provide testimony or as a witness. Other wise, Uself knew he did not have a prayer!

Uself kept going over in his mind the events which happened and how he planned to spin the information to his advantage. If what he said was not strictly true, it would be wrapped around as much truth as possible to make any lie he told that much harder to see, hear and more importantly smell. Uself kept thinking that as long as Vane, Rule and Jason were dead, he had a shot at avoiding that fate.

Uself was lead to the podium; the hall for the trial was packed there was not even standing room left. Lucifer held up a hand and the room got so quiet you could hear a pin drop, no one wanted to miss a word, as Lucifer began to speak.

Tris had paid dearly for a seat in the balcony and not just any seat but one that provided her an excellent view of the stage while she could adjust the curtains to obscure her presence from others in the crowd and on the podium. The outcome of these events would answer her curiosity about all of the players in this little drama and decide Tris' next move. That is, if the Senior Elder Demon was killed, Tris would simply go home and be grateful regarding her good luck in this matter. If he survived, Tris would take a very long vacation in some very obscure and difficult to find place.

Lucifer began to outline the rules and laws of hell that Uself had broken and with each charge he placed against Uself the crowd listened with rapped attention. Then Lucifer asked if Uself would agree to a memory review to refute the charges, Uself did not reply. Lucifer smiled as he completed his summary of events (like any good lawyer, Lucifer did not ask any question that he did not already know the answer to and he knew that Uself would not agree to the memory review). As Lucifer concluded, Uself was allowed to offer his rebuttal.

Uself was equally as eloquent as Lucifer. He told his version of the events with simplicity and with the conviction of a wrongfully accused innocent victim, expressing his horror of being accused of the terrible crimes he was supposed to have committed. Uself got so caught up in his version of the story that he started to believe his own lies. Therefore, in righteous indignation Uself stated at the end of his speech, "I defy Lucifer to produce any witness, just one . . .. . to offer any evidence against the honest version of events I have just stated!"

Uself went back to his chair and looked at Lucifer with distain and at the crowd with such innocence that none at this point, could guess how this trial would conclude. Uself had expected to see some uncertainty on Lucifer's face or anger, yes anger would be better! Anger would give a clear indication that even Lucifer knew that Uself had a good chance of winning his case. However, Lucifer did not seem bothered at all and this caused Uself to feel very uneasy with Lucifer's response.

It was a good thing that Uself had sat down, because if he had not, his legs would have fallen out from under him as he watched Lucifer call his bluff. Lucifer gave a signal and Rule walked onto the podium. Uself was in such shock that for a moment his mask of calm, cool, self assurance slipped and anyone who had been watching closely saw terror on Uself's face which he quickly tried to hid but with out a great deal of success.

Lucifer had asked Uself to open himself up to a memory review this was one genuine way to prove his innocence with out doubt, but it was also considered an insult to ask a demon to prove his statement. Which meant that Uself's ending statements of his speech was a direct insult to Lucifer (in return for Lucifer insulting him initially by asking him to open up to a memory review), in truth all Senior Elder Demons lied about practically everything which is why none would allow a memory review by opening up there thoughts to others.

To allow a memory review was the ultimate in innocence because these memories could not be changed or altered, they were the facts as they happened and as the individual lived them. Plus a memory review could not be forced, the demon must allow this knowledge to be seen of his own free will if not the images came out blurred and incoherent and everyone would know that the information was forced therefore it could not be accurate. When Rule reached the podium Lucifer asked him if he would allow a memory review, and Rule replied, "Yes." Uself thought, "I am now dead."

The crowd went wild and then silent again because they did not want to miss a word or scene of Rule's memories. Rule began with his attempts to get Vane to help his with his prey, to Uself stepping in to take over the operation, to the battle in the prey's mind, to Rule doing as he was told to do by bring the elemental to hell as Uself demanded and it ended with Uself's betrayal of Rule when he blasted him with enough fire to melt every bone in his body; showing Uself's attempts to eliminate the last remaining witnesses to Uself's involvement in this situation.

At the conclusion of the memory review the crowd went wild. Lucifer walked over to Uself and whispered in his ear, "not only did you fail to capture the elemental but you were stupid enough to leave a witnesses" and just so you know that you never had a chance of success, know this . . .. an elemental is not the source of my power" then Lucifer smiled and Uself's blood turned ice cold!

Lucifer was a master showman, while still on stage Lucifer waved his hand and two blood draining machines were instantly attached to Uself's arm. To heighten and strengthen the flavor of the blood (as well as put the icing on the cake) Lucifer materialized a chair and sat down next to Uself and began to feed him images of what Lucifer planned to do to him just bits and pieces at first. Lucifer stopped the images and began to speak, in a slow clear voice. First we will drain only six of the eight pints of blood in your veins. Three of the pints will go into a blood wine that will be sold at public auction and the other three are for me.

Next I will halt the normal process of producing a shade. Your body will not be cut up and fed into hell's general population . . .No! you will be served whole on my table. Next I will allow you to keep at least two pints of your blood because I like my meat roasted slowly and as the last of your blood drips slowly into the pan with the basting liquids it kicks the flavor of the meat over the edge!

Lucifer then allowed Uself to see an image of him tied feet and hands to a spit, Uself's eyes widen when he saw an image of himself with two flaming hot pokers stuck into him, one from behind and one through the mouth as two Kitchen demons turned the rotating spit with him on it slowly over a medium fire.

Now we come to the crème de la crème (or the best of the best) every fifteen minutes you will be basted with a lemon, oil and herb mixture. The oil will help to produce just the right crackle on the surface of the meat; it will also hold the lemon juice on your skin so that it can seep into the uncooked meat underneath which will both season the meat and keep it tender. You will burn from with in (as the acid of the lemon juice burns both the charred outer skin and soaks into the raw meat underneath) and you will burn from with out as you turn slowly over the roasting fire.

The result will be that I will have meat that is both tender, exceptionally well seasoned but still maintains a wonderful crackle with each bite! Finally, I will bind your shade so that it has to stay in the room, in a well lit corner, during dinner so that I and my guest can watch you wither in agony as you feel each and every bite on your roasted flesh. Lucifer knew exactly who those dinner guest would be, the five oldest of his Senior Elders, a group of which, Uself had once been a member. This was more than a dinner party it was a not so subtle warning of what happens to anyone who dares to challenge him, Lucifer was sending a clear message and none at the table would fail to hear it. Lucifer laughed as Uself screamed, and with each scream Uself's blood bubbled (transferring his fear, humiliation and anger into the blood) and the crowd went wild!

Lucifer got up and left Uself while he was still screaming, he walked over to Rule and informed him that not only was he going to receive five souls for his help in this matter but he would also inherent Vane's home (Since Vane was now a shade and all of his property now belonged to hell aka Lucifer). The final honor was that Rule was to receive the fist glass of the blood wine which was to be sold to the general public for free!

Tris watched the trial with complete attention, trying to see if her intervention would be noted in anyway. She was amazed as the order of protection completely prevented Rule from mentioning either her name or her involvement. Even the memory review was not allowed access to that information. Tris went home after the trial, she had spent enough on her seat(two whole souls) and she decided not to try to buy a glass of the really expensive blood wine being sold to the very rich at the cost of a whole soul and a half price for one small glass. Shortly after she got home a messenger arrived with a gift, a pint of the blood wine made from Uself and the card said, "Thanks for your help in this matter." "L."

Tris took a deep smell of the wine but it smelt clean of any addictive qualities. However, as an added insurance she still diluted it as carefully as she had the last gift of wine Lucifer gave her and sure enough the diluting revealed all of the hidden elements in the wine! The wine had a strong compulsion put in to it. Only this time the compulsion, which surrounded the addictive qualities were hidden and the smell was masked. Tris began to get seriously concerned about Lucifer's continued attempts to try to use her as she though, 'maybe I will take a long vacation after all."

Both Katelyn and Justin had quit there jobs and she had moved in to Justin's home with in the earth realm. Justin told Katelyn that as far as he was concern that she was his mate and that was a bond that was light years ahead of being married. However, if she wanted a traditional ceremony they could do that too. Katelyn thought about it for a while and realized that the only thing she needed or wanted was him.

Justin took a set of wedding rings out of his pocket and said, “I would then appreciate it if you would wear these especially when we are in the earth realm, I want every other male to know that you are taken. Katelyn laughed as she open the box and found a set of the most exquisitely beautiful rings she had ever seen. Katelyn was no expert on jewelry but the rings looked really expensive.

A few days later Katelyn took the rings to be appraised, with the intent of having them registered and insured. Katelyn was sitting down when the appraiser came back and informed her that the rings were worth one and a half million dollars! Katelyn sat for a few minutes in stunned silence and as soon as she was able she left and went straight home. Justin was home and Katelyn asked how in the world can you afford a set of rings which cost one and a half million dollars. Justin was fixing dinner and he turned around and smiled and said, “Yeah, I though I should have spent more but the jeweler informed me that in this situation less is more.”

Katelyn sat there with her mouth open trying to form words that did not seem to want to come out then finally she said, “Just how much money do you have?” Justin smiled and said, “We have a little over ten billion dollars.” Katelyn fainted, the shock was simply too much. Justin thought,”I will never understand women! She faced the master of hell with me and she never once blinked an eye and now she faints over money?”

Later Justin explained that from the equivalent of the human age of sixteen, part of his education and training required that the males of his race were taught to explore different methods of creating wealth and encouraged to find a method that was comfortable for them to work with. Therefore, by the time they were the equal of the human age of twenty-one most of the males of his race had several millions at their disposal. It is amazing the amount of good that money can do when no greed is attached to its usage. It is a tool like any other and often makes our job easier.

Jason, later on that evening, met up at Justin and Katelyn’s home on earth for dinner. They were discussing plans to have a home built in Justin’s home realm close to Bree. Katelyn was starting to address Bree as mom but it was taking a bit more time to get use to a father in law who was an angel!

Katelyn finally had a family, a real genuine family. A brother, Jason, who now teased her and told stories about Justin as a child. A mother, Bree, who looked at her with so much love that it warmed her every bit as strongly as her memories of her own parent's love. An Aunt, Ariel, who was shy, sweet, thoughtful and a wonderful listener. And, Katelyn had a husband who was her world.

Justin's great uncle, asked to be introduced to his newest family member. He was so sweet that Katelyn fell in love with him after their first visit. Later that evening when she was wrapped up in Justin's arms after they had just finished making love she thought, "This may not have been the family that she had always dreamed of (there was still so much to get use to) but in so many other ways it was so much, much better!

The Seven Rules Of Fate

Rule one

Can you seek, what you do not want to find . . ..even if it is all you need? To find all you are and so much more, first you must knock at death's door.

Second Rule

Water opens the emotions and floods the gate, with so many feelings it is difficult to relate. Water overwhelms and this is a different state, acceptance is required or immobility will be your fate.

Third Rule

The time of true mating is a test for the soul, few are chosen and even less beholds the blessings of such a state, because at each step more than death awaits."

Fourth Rule

Fire burns in different states, one may heal while another annihilate. Fire can purify all it holds like the phoenix of old rising from the ashes of its soul. A pure fire can burn both body and soul, which . . .. depends on the sprit you hold."

Fifth Rule

To let go of your strength when you need it most and walk in faith when there is no hope.

Six Rule

Can a master step into a student's place with humility, love and grace? Then yet again, learn what is needed in faith?

Seventh Rule

Wholeness requires each being to be at one with the elements of life and fate. To know one is to need the others, through out the life state. The earth creates and nurtures the body, air rises and falls with each breath and thought you intake. Water floods the sprit to teach control over our emotional state. Fire is the element that Tran-mutates every part into a new whole, that few can contemplate. "Such then are the rules of fate."

The Poems

If you choose to love me

Do not love me for a day
For this kind of love will never stay
Do not love me for what you see
For age will steal your love from me
Do not love me out of need
For this type of love always turns to some level of greed
Do not love me because I love you
This type of love is never true
Do not love me because you owe me such
This type of love always turns to hatred, anger and distrust
Love me because the love in you, request that you do
An offer of love freely chosen, like my gift to you
Love me because I spark a fire in your soul
Because without me your life would be cold
Love me with all you have to give
Free in the knowledge that no matter what
You would love me still
Love me until time slips away
With your last breath, on your last day
For this is love, real and true
The type of love I offer you.

Illusions

He said I was beautiful and none could compare
With my soulful eyes and long dark hair
My laughter, my lips and the sway of my hips
Made his imagination run wild, he loved my class and my style

I said not a word, as I listened and heard
All of the things that he wanted from me
Not once did he ask,
If I would agree to the task
Of no longer being me
And become only what he could see,
What he wanted me to be

It is so clear that what makes a woman dear
Is the beauty of her mind and her thoughts,
The sweetness of her sprit,
The warmth of her soul
These are the things that will never grow old!

Why did he not ask, about my character and my faults?
Why did these things never enter his thought?
Ahh . . . it seems that he was never talking to me
But only to the illusion
He wanted me to be!

You can live a life time in a moment

You can live a life time in a moment, so no matter come what may, Loving you completely is what happened here today. As the day fades into night and loving you feels right . . . for this hour, this moment, today.

I descend slowly into your arms and all the world seems calm. The passion in your eyes, is such a sweet surprise. You touch me in a place, where there's no time or space, I've loved you, forever . . . today.

You can live a life time in a moment, in an hour or a day.
Sometimes, things happen that take your breath away.
As we make love one last time and all of you is mine, for one precious moment in time.

So Much More

My heart cries out for so much more, than I have ever seen before. A love so real and rare, with genuineness and care. I don't want love that's here today and tomorrow gone away, I want a love that grows each day!

I want to know how you think and feel. What thoughts to you appeal?

To understand just why you cry, what makes you fear and why. To know your mind, your heart, your faults . . . My love, to share your thoughts.

Is what I ask for so unreal, a love that time can't steal? But instead let time revel, the love we have is real. If my life should end today, I would like to truly say that I have loved and been loved in a way, that warms my heart even as my breath slips away.

Short Story

FOR THE LOVE OF MY CHILD

Once a long time ago, in a time before recorded time a discussion took place between the creator and one of his first angel, Lucifer. Each was expressing opposite thoughts about the creator's newest creation, man.

Lucifer stated, "Man is weak and the least among your angels, applying little to thoughtless effort, could talk the man thing into abandoning your blue print or plan for it.

The Creator replied, "Man has with in him the foundation to be all that he wills . . . for choice is my gift to man. So here is where we disagree, you think that choice makes him weak, I think it makes him free."

Lucifer said,"So free, that a thought planted in his fear and nurtured though and by his blindness can destroy his faith!"

The creator smiled and stated, "You can not give a gift and direct its usage or its fate."

Lucifer replied, "How can you believe in man with such clear faith. You know the evolving levels of its soul, the malice and hate. You know better than us all, that this creature should have a limited fate. And, yet here you state . . . man's path can be great!"

The creator replied with a smile, "unlike an angel who would strive to hide any malice and fear deep in side, until it grows in the dark to an unbearable size. Man's malice and fear are there for all who choose to see. But, through experience a thought can be planted in the soul, surrounded with truth it can then take hold, of enough love to expand and grow the soul."

The discussion concluded and Lucifer did hide, all the anger, malice and jealousy he felt for man inside. As the creator had predicted it had grown in size. Lucifer now felt the need to destroy man in the creator's eyes.

The creator watched Lucifer leave, sadden by what he knew Lucifer believed. The seeds of hatred the creator saw when they first began . . . the creator knew that this first angel, would have trouble with the very idea of man.

As the creator pondered the situation he knew that some of his angels would accept man out of love for him, some would accept man because of the dictates of their faith and others would feel hurt and unable to relate . . .to the creator's desire to create a creature free to do as it wills and establish its own fate. This confused and chaotic creature, whom the creator states, can be great . . . many of his angels would hate.

What the angels did not understand, it that true love must be given freely and it can not simply be a part of your genetic plan. Angels were created with a built in love for the creator inside, to love the creator is essentially a part of being alive.

Man may choose to say, my will not thy will or "No!" I don't want to today. Things that an angel would never be allowed to say and remain in the creator's presence . . . for an angel would quickly be sent away!

Man, these arrogant little creatures with there ego and pride and that spark of the creator deep in side, which will allow them to rise through experience, choice and will . . . to their father's side.

Each human soul is like a diamond unique and rare and when the light of love hits it, it is beyond compare; it is pure and sweet like rain washed air. The love the creator seeks from man starts with a choice that only man can make. A choice, which is an outgrowth from man's soul; supported by the heart and given freely by his will.

An angel is god's creation and man is his child. This was the core of Lucifer's jealousy for man. For Lucifer was one of the few who truly did understand. This man creature had something he never would hold, man had a piece of god inside of him, some thing called a soul.

Lucifer could not contain his jealousy of the child he knew was one day fated to take his place. He tried to accept the creator's will but the thought was a bitter pill. Soon, Lucifer knew that he would have to act and remove this threat called man and afterward . . . surely god would understand. This man thing was unworthy of such a precious gift! Would not a first angel be more worthy? Lucifer struggled with this thought but he truly did not understand, why the creator did not prefer his angels to man.

And yet Lucifer's hatred too was part of the plan, how could man freely choose good if no other offer was at hand. Negativity was a necessary part of the plan. Lucifer's hatred which was all foreseen was allowed to flourish, comfortable in the belief that it was hidden and unseen. The creator watched as Lucifer plotted and schemed.

Lucifer would hate man much more if he knew what an important part he played in man's development and growth. Lucifer negativity now existed to serve man. Because, it is overcoming the obstacles that negativity confronts man with, which is god's plan for man. The creation will serve the child, although not the way it may think, the creation will punish the child when the child fails to think!

Finally, Lucifer could stand no more! Watching god pour out his love on "the man thing" that Lucifer abhorred. Quietly, Lucifer planted the seed of descent, using half-truths and lies . . . which were simply fear and need in disguise.

All to steal faith and belief from those who were born to truth and trust. Surely, Lucifer thought, "it would be far more difficult to change an angel's belief around and that having been done, man's fate was already won." For how could man rise under conditions where angels had fallen?

God watched as all took place. The development of evil was necessary although the process hurt him as it took place. It was like watching a cancer grow on a lovely face.

The creator knew that a third of his angels would loose their grace; he knew that Lucifer would lead them and try to take his place. All of this, the creator quietly allowed . . . All for the love of his child. Negativity is a necessary condition for choice and growth; if man is to evolve he must have both!

Lucifer raised his army and they stood at heaven's gate, demanding to be heard . . .conditions to relate, regarding "the man thing" debate. Lucifer stated "This man thing" should be put in its place! What right has an animal to aspire to grace? We, who have served faithfully, request and demand the right of a soul's grace, for we are much more worthy than man!

The creator responded, "You are my creation and I have given you that which I will, to question my actions shows there is much, you don't understand about me still." It is the role of an angel to walk in faith, to love with out question and maintain his grace. The questions you have raised have answers that are not yours to seek . . . "do you now presume, to tell god what to think!"

This story has been told in many times and in many different ways. Some describe the war as an epic battle of old; others who can not imagine such a war and felt unable to relate, so they would simply state . . . That a war took place.

The real war in heaven was the introduction of deceit and lies, the weapons that Lucifer used to persuade and compromise. The actual rebellion lasted only a fraction of thought. For that is how long it took for that rebellious one third, to be sent to the new realm that their actions brought.

Here they found themselves with out the light of the creator's love or hope of his forgiveness. Quiet and darkness was all around; then the silence broke, like thunderbolts . . . as angels started to scream, weep, wale and moan!

Lucifer was the first to push aside his hopeless despair. He realized that he had only moments to act, before the others had time to consider or relate to there current hopeless state and then blamed him for there fate. This fall from grace . . . Lucifer suddenly knew exactly what to do, who to blame and how to present it too.

Lucifer shouted for quiet, amidst the moans and wails. He floated above the crowd, surrounded with light, as he looked serene and proud. Lucifer then heard the hushed sounds, while silence began to prevail as he started to look around. To insure that all could hear what needs to be done, they would accept or he would fail, then Lucifer began his tale. Lucifer said with quiet hate, "Oh my brothers I have sad news to relate, our beloved creator is ill and therefore he can not see, that this man creature should never be."

It is our sworn duty from this day on, for each of us to pledge to help him find the way. We must from this day forward, do all that we can to prove to the creator that he should have no trust or love for man.

For we know the truth, this creature will turn against him and cause him great pain and we who truly love him will continue to remain, his faithful servants . . . our love for him unchanged!

Therefore, from this day forward I ask that you all make a sacred trust, to do all with in your power to reveal the true nature of this dust! And, let us never forget, that man is evil and as such, it is the man creature's fault that the creator has misunderstood our concerns and turned away from us, those who love him so much!

The speech was done and the crowd was won. Lucifer bereaved a sigh of relief, all seemed to find solace and comfort in his speech. They all seemed to look to him for a plan, to destroy the creature called man.

Lucifer was pleased, for he now had the recognition he secretly believed he deserved. And a platform on which to be heard, in fact he thought he saw adoration in a few eyes. Lucifer was enjoying himself so, when he thought, "How odd . . . is this what it's like to be god?"

After the banishment of Lucifer and the third, the creator and Gabriel were discussing all that had occurred . . . The birth of evil and the possibilities that such a creation would have on the world of man. Gabriel said, "You know how long it will take for man to understand, how much you have sacrificed for him to grow and expand. Will man ever know . . .that evil was the price you paid for him to grow, all because you love him so?"

And, yet before man can grow enough to find this thought, you know the pain you will fell when he cries that evil is all your fault. When man in his self-inflected pain, seeks someone else to point to and blame. When he screams and cries that you do not care, why else would you leave him in such misery and despair. Man will believe that he was left to do battle with evil with out halt, when evil is something you could have killed with a thought.

My heart weeps for you, this is such a burden for a parent to bare. Then tears ran down Gabriel's eyes, as his rich voice broke . . .God smiled and then spoke, "Everything is in place for my child to grow, the price it has cost me he will never truly know. My child now has to decide if he will choose evil or a thoughtful fate . . .fear and pride or all of the traits of me inside.

Children are never aware of the pain a parent feels when their actions are unfair, selfish and reveal what the child does not understand . . ..maturity demands discipline and discipline demands that the child must stand on his own. The final lesson the parent must teach, if the child is to one day be considered grown. Growth is a process of trial and error and often it looks as if the parent does not care. But, in fact, sometimes real love means to **not** be there.

Things are not always what they seem, like the empty space in the bowl. The real use of this tool is in what it can hold. I have placed with in him a blueprint for grace, complete with the traits and qualities of his father's estate. But he must seek to find the path of truth that I have written on his soul, somewhat like the empty space inside of the bowl.

For only through his mistakes can he see the path unfold. Now he has all the things he needs to command the fates: love, honor, strength, intelligence and grace. I'll tell you a secret old friend, . . . when I put my love for my child aside, even I have to laugh at his self-important stride . . . my proud, willful, arrogant, gifted, beautiful, spirited child.

THE UNIVERSAL LAWS

1. Personal truthfulness: You can not change anything with in you, f you can not see it.
2. 2Fairness: this provides the rules and regulations which allow you to deal effectively and correctly with the truth you see.
3. Attention to detail: this law allows for an intricate understanding of human nature which keeps fairness and truth focused and always with in right action.
4. Do no harm: often when we are caught up in the chaos of human nature, we do not know what is right action? When you find yourself in such a situation simply look for the course of action which does no harm.
5. The power of choice: this is the understanding that choice is the power that shapes our world. Such a power deserves our deepest respect. Remember, when ever we use this power it should embody all of the four laws which came before.
6. The power of laughter: this power cleans and heals. It provides balance and renewal because it reminds us that joy is essential to health.
7. Understanding: one of the greatest aspects of this law is that it allows us to act with out regret. This law embodies all which have come before it, in that it advocates the importance of widening your perspective. The more open you are to knowledge, ideas and the motives of others the less likely you are to act without though.
8. A living faith: this is the concept of knowing and working from what you believe: "what you believe is the parent though of your choices. Your choices are the parents of your actions. Your actions shape your world!" Our life becomes a daily reflection of our belief and faith, in which every choice is faith in action.
9. Humility: this is working from the concept, on a daily bases, that for every one thing that you know there are ten things that you do

not know. Therefore excessive pride is the actions of fools. Through humility comes greatness because these two concepts are flip sides of the same coin.

10. Love, this is the strongest force in the universe and almost always completely misunderstood. Love is not just a power, it is a force which sweeps away all in its path.